The Chameln are an ancient people of the continent of Hylor who live in a wide and beautiful land of lakes, grassland and forest. They are ruled by a double sovereignty, chosen always from two families, the Firn and the Zor. Aidris Firn, her father's heir, learns the traditional skills and duties of a princess. But powerful forces are threatening the rulers of the Chameln. The parents of Aidris are assassinated and her own life is in danger. When Esher Am Zor, the remaining ruler, dies, the warlike neighbouring state of Mel'Nir invades the Chameln lands and the princess must go swiftly into exile to avoid capture.

Aidris is practical and well-schooled. She does what she has to do to survive, though it means leaving friends and comforts behind. A secret journey through the forest and the need to fend for herself and an unexpected companion harden her determination. When, in the moment of greatest danger, a splendid champion appears, she still does not reveal her identity.

Through long years Aidris keeps her secret and leads the life of a cavalry soldier, a kedran, in the peaceful realm of Athron. She has strange adventures and hears strange tales; she experiences love and friendship. Aidris comes to terms with her own royal heritage and learns to work her own magic. All this is in preparation for the day her people throw off the yoke of Mel'Nir and come for her. And when this day does come she is able to face the difficult life of a queen, in war and peace.

This is the first book in a trilogy.

A PRINCESS
OF THE CHAMELN

A PRINCESS
OF THE CHAMELN

• Book One of The Rulers of Hylor Trilogy •

Cherry Wilder

London
UNWIN PAPERBACKS
Boston   Sydney

First published in Great Britain by Unwin Paperbacks 1986
This book is copyright under the Berne Convention. No reproduction
without permission. All rights reserved.

UNWIN ® PAPERBACKS
40 Museum Street, London WC1A 1LU, UK

Unwin Paperbacks
Park Lane, Hemel Hempstead, Herts HP2 4TE, UK

George Allen & Unwin Australia Pty Ltd
8 Napier Street, North Sydney, NSW 2060, Australia

Unwin Paperbacks with the
Port Nicholson Press
PO Box 11−838 Wellington, New Zealand

© Cherry Wilder, 1984, 1986

British Library Cataloguing in Publication Data

Wilder, Cherry
 A princess of Chameln.
I. Title
823 [F]   PR9639.3.W4/
ISBN 0−04−823295−5

Printed in Great Britain by
Guernsey Press Co. Ltd., Guernsey, Channel Islands

THE RULERS OF HYLOR

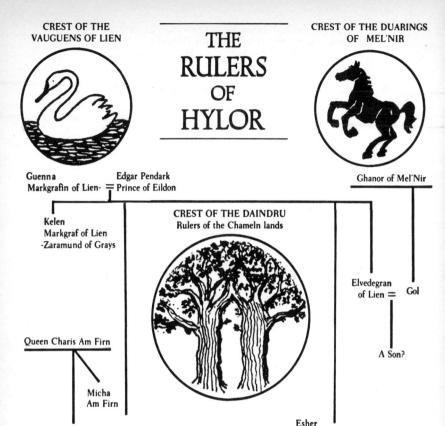

CREST OF THE VAUGUENS OF LIEN

CREST OF THE DUARINGS OF MEL'NIR

CREST OF THE DAINDRU
Rulers of the Chameln lands

Guenna
Markgrafin of Lien- = Edgar Pendark
Prince of Eildon

Ghanor of Mel'Nir

Kelen
Markgraf of Lien
-Zaramund of Grays

Elvedegran
of Lien = Gol

A Son?

Queen Charis Am Firn

Micha
Am Firn

Racha Am Firn-Hedris of Lien

Esher
Am Zor-Aravel of Lien

Aidris Am Firn

CREST OF THE MENVIRS OF ATHRON

Sharn Am Zor   Merilla   Carel

Duke of Varda-Imelda Golden Hair
(Imal Am Firn Younger sister of Queen Charis)

Vor Prince of Athron

Prince Flor   Prince Terril

THE RULERS
OF HYLOR

"**W**e of the Chameln, though our lands are shrunken now and threatened, we are those who have always been, the true children of the Goddess."

Nazran, the Chancellor, speaks to his young pupil, the Princess Aidris Am Firn, who will one day be co-ruler of the Chameln lands with her cousin, Prince Sharn Am Zor. Together they will form the Daindru, a curious double sovereignty.

The neighboring kingdoms of this northern continent, Hylor, each have a distinct and different landscape and history. The largest kingdom is Mel'Nir, home of the giant warriors who came as invaders through the eastern mountains. The Mark of Lien flourishes like a garden between its two rivers. In the northwest lies the peaceful kingdom of Athron, and over the western sea is Eildon, home of an older magic.

The rulers of these kingdoms struggle for power and their weapons include magic and intrigue as well as the sword. Aidris Am Firn, related to these rulers, is caught up in their struggles. Her story and the stories of other royal children will carry the reader into all the lands of Hylor.

A PRINCESS
OF THE CHAMELN

CHAPTER

I

WHEN SHE WAS TEN YEARS OLD THE CHAN-
cellor Nazran, from her father's court, gave Aidris a bow and
arrows. They practised together in the birch grove beside the
palace. Nazran was old, rather scholarly in appearance, with
no reek of horses or the countryside, but he handled the bow
very well, speeding the small arrows into the chosen tree.

She remembered his explanations of her life more clearly
than any she heard from Racha, her father, or Hedris, her
mother. When she rode out with her father and her uncle to
the Turmut, the meeting of the northern tribes, the wonder of
the time was underscored by Nazran's quiet voice:

"There are two rulers in the lands of the Chameln; they are
descended always from two ancient royal houses, Am Firn and
Am Zor. Together they form the Daindru, the double sovereignty, the two . . . it is a word from the Old Speech. The line
of each house goes back unbroken for more than a thousand
years. The blood of these houses is precious; it is linked to the
earliest inhabitants of this part of the world, this whole wide
continent of Hylor. We of the Chameln, though our lands are
shrunken now and threatened, we are those who have always
been, the true children of the Goddess.

"We are of two races, and this can be seen in our rulers, the
Daindru. The Firn are a short, sturdy, dark-complexioned, dark-
haired people, with broad faces, eyes brown or hazel or green,
colors of the forest. The Zor are a blond race, fair-skinned,
taller, more delicate, with eyes grey or blue, sky-colored. To be
sure, the rulers do not always show this coloring, but the true
features always return. You are your father's heir, Dan Racha

3

Sabeth Aidris Am Firn; you show the blood royal most perfectly, and your father's co-ruler, Dan Esher, your uncle by his marriage, has the young heir Dan Esher Sharn Kelen Am Zor, and he is similarly blessed. You will succeed your father, and he will succeed his; eventually you will rule together. You will each found families, and the Daindru will continue.

"The line of the Firn is at this moment hanging by a single thread, as they say. You are an only child; the next heir is your father's sister, Micha Am Firn, a childless widow since her husband Count Ledler died. We should not worry too much just yet.

"Your duty, your trust, is to serve the Chameln, to love the lands and the people, to be a light for them in darkness."

The three mounted figures came on slowly across a vast plain of silvery grass. A wind sprang up, ruffling the surface of the small lakes, unfurling the long tresses of human hair upon the tall "spirit trees." There was a forest of these long poles, stripped of bark and branches and decorated with paint, fabric, shells, animal pelts, claws and teeth, topped always with the tresses of hair.

A sound like the wind grew and grew; the plain was dark with people. They murmured at first, then sang, then shouted aloud, long rhythmical cries that echoed away into the tree groves and the distant mountains. Other riders broke out from the waiting crowd and circled about the three riders and the standard-bearers who came far behind them. The riders from the northern tribes were young and fearless, balancing upon their saddles, flinging themselves sideways, whooping aloud. They wore leather breeches and short cloaks, fantastically decorated in blue, green, dark yellow, purple-red. The colored streamers from their cloaks spun out about them; one sailed through the air, and Aidris caught it easily across her saddle.

She rode in leading strings; it was an ordeal even for her well-trained pony; he shuddered as the riders came by. Her father, on her left, smiled; she saw herself in his smile. On her right Esher Am Zor smiled too, blue-eyed, ruddy-faced in the cold. She saw that the red streamer across her saddle was made of papery dried flower heads, dyed red and threaded upon reeds.

They came to the Turmut camp, to the inner ring of birch

lodges, tall structures decorated with round motifs in the same colors as the cloaks of the riders. Aidris saw that the people, running between the lodges or waving and swaying with linked arms, were of the two races. Many were of the Firn: sturdy, short, broad-faced, dark; yet rising among them were the Zor, with pale hair, taller, with skin so clear, matte and white that it seemed to glow.

Her father and her uncle, the Daindru, were lifted from their saddles and set on a high platform. She was lifted even higher than the rest, she rode above the crowd and was set down, laughing, on a tall, rickety stool of undressed timber, between the two rulers. The cheers rang out for the Daindru and then briefly for "Dan Aidris," for her alone. She held up her hands acknowledging the cheers and balanced easily upon the rough stool.

Aidris recalled every detail of the three days of the Turmut; it was a supreme test of her composure, as it was for her poor dappled pony. She knew that she was passing the test. The approach, the presentation, the speeches of fealty, the danc- ing—all without fidgeting, crying, yawning, growing sullen. Then the relief and strangeness of her own lodge, strewn with reeds, the big bed covered with furs and fine leather.

She was attended by Tylit, her own young nursemaid, and by two highborn women of the northern tribes. One was very tall and old, the other broadly built, handsome, with black eyes and a massive braid of black hair, escaping in curls and tendrils from its embroidered bands. They handled her with brisk rev- erence, reefing off her fine clothes to replace them with others equally fine but strange. The water for washing was icy cold and scented with floating handfuls of wild flowers. They dressed her as a doll is dressed, and the tall chieftainess snapped her fingers: two young women, still dressed in the colored cloaks in which they had ridden out to welcome the Daindru, came through the lodge carrying a tribal treasure. It was a full-length mirror made of thin polished bronze, smoothed over a wooden frame. Its border was finely worked with figures of animals, trees, warriors with sword and spear, all in relief.

Aidris saw herself, in white buckskin breeches, red boots, a tunic quilted in blue, furred at the neck and sleeves. She saw her own solemn face: high cheekbones, short, crimped black hair, green eyes. Her mother called her "my little cat." The northern women, watching, thought her perfect, and she understood their judgement. She was Aidris, her father's child; she was of the Firn; it showed in every lineament. She realised, as the younger women moved a prop on the bronze mirror, that it was in fact a shield, a "ground shield," so called, that gave shelter to advancing foot soldiers.

There was a man's voice at the doorway; the black-eyed lady glanced around the lodge and gave permission to enter. None of the fuss, the rustling and simpering of her mother's ladies in the palace dressing rooms. Then in came a friend, someone she had always known and always liked. He was often at her father's court: Bajan Am Nuresh, Count Bajan. He was dressed in his blue cloak still . . . he had been another who welcomed the Daindru.

He bowed as she cried out:

"Bajan!"

They smiled at each other. He was nineteen years old; she was eleven. Aidris thought of him as a man, a grown-up; she was proud that he bothered with her, played games, helped with her lessons, took her riding. She was aware of a distinct pleasure in the ceremonial lodge; all the women were smiling. Bajan, a high chieftain of the Nureshen, was the son of the black-eyed lady who had helped Aidris to dress. Bajan had come to lead the princess to her place at the feast table.

The Turmut seemed much further back in her memory than the events that followed it by no more than three months. Early summer in the capital; Achamar was filled with green boughs, and the first fruit was in the orchards. The town was made of wood; she rode out with Nazran in the mornings, and they admired the bridges, the broad streets, the marketplaces, the tall houses. The two royal palaces were wonders of the world, enormous buildings, grounded upon buttressed logs, thick as the oaks of Ystamar, then spreading and soaring into spires and balconies and into domes roofed with ancient shingles, thin and fine as silver leaves.

Before and behind, on their morning rides, trotted the bodyguard of kedran, mounted upon small grey horses with darker manes and tails: the Chameln grey, a rare, tough breed. They followed the outer ring-road; a red pennant flew over the South Hall, a place for distinguished guests. Two warriors of Mel'Nir stood guard in the outer court. They were the largest men Aidris had ever seen, tall and broadly built with reddish hair and blunt features. They were so tall that they might have been face to face with the battlemaids of her bodyguard, mounted on their small horses.

"The giant warriors of Mel'Nir are incomers," explained Nazran. "They are not native to the lands of Hylor. They came from the southeast, over the mountain passes, not more than two hundred years past. You will find many maps and chronicles where the land of Mel'Nir is divided into the Southland, the High Plateau and the Dannermark: now these are all provinces of Mel'Nir. I have heard it said that they took, besides the land, the language and the religion of the places they conquered. This is not quite true; they spoke some variant of the common speech; only the Old Speech of the Chameln and the Chyrian Speech of Eildon and part of the Southland were completely foreign to them. As for religion, they have none, or a very simple one to do with streams and groves. They have some gifts of prophecy; their wisest men and women practise a healing magic.

"Their days of conquest are not past; they exact tribute from the Mark of Lien and from our own lands. Let us pray to the Goddess that they take no more than our goods, at least during your lifetime, child."

She stored up his words; they were a study guide for her battle with the scrolls. Her life was sheltered; the groves and high stockades of the palace grounds were all her territory. It was a treat when she went with her father and mother to the White Lodge on the shores of the Danmar, the inland sea. She remembered the pearl divers and the distant wooded shore that was part of the land of Mel'Nir.

She roamed the pebbled beaches with Racha and his four Torch Bearers, his honored friends, and learned their names like a chant: Bajan, Gilyan, Lingrit and Wetzerik. Tall Jana am Wetzerik was the kedran general; she taught Aidris to swim. Lingrit am Thuven, Nazran's son, was a silent young man who went to Lien as envoy. Only Gilyan was within hail when Racha came to need him, and then not close enough.

A great deal of the gossip and foolery of palace life passed right over Aidris's head. Her mother, Hedris, and her aunt

Aravel, wife of Esher, were two sisters from the ruling house of Lien. They had brought their own ladies-in-waiting, beautiful, arrogant persons who found all the uses of Achamar utterly barbarous.

Hedris of Lien was of middle height, a soft, shapely woman with masses of dark gold hair. She would sing to her only child and tell her tales of Lien, of magic, of journeys on the rivers and over the seas. The stories Aidris liked best were of four children, a brother and three sisters, who lived in a country house. Their father had died when they were very young: only the two eldest, Kelen and Hedris, could remember him. Their mother was heart and soul to them: quick-tempered, loving, full of play. She came riding back to them from the city as often as she could and brought marvellous presents. Aidris was eager for more stories about Guenna of Lien, her grandmother, but sometimes the telling stopped. Aidris remembered a cold, a distant look on her mother's face.

"Trust no one," said the queen. "You are of the Chameln. The House of Lien is no friend to you. Mel'Nir is a place of violence and death."

Then in a moment Hedris was smiling again, as the ladies returned. There came Aravel, the younger sister, a more striking beauty, leading the young prince, Sharn Am Zor, while a nursemaid saw to his baby sister. There was kissing and cooing; the five-year-old prince was bored and devilish, in spite of his golden curls. Aidris seized his hand and escaped to the garden. She caught a glance from her mother and understood: Hedris did not trust her waiting women, her own sister.

The memories were no longer a continuous stream, as they had once been. Everything was wiped out and returned hazily. Everything sloped away from the deed as if it stood on a high hill of time. She was walking between her parents, Racha, her father, on her left; Hedris, seven months pregnant, wore a flowing robe. They walked in the garden before the palace, a formal garden after the manner of Lien, planted as a gift from Racha to his queen. The round beds were bright with flowers, but the paths were too sandy and soft and the young trees could not be coaxed into a formal shape. The garden was a hybrid, a blending of Lien and Achamar. There were gardeners, some members of the court at a distance, and the guards at the lower gate.

Aidris saw nothing until her mother uttered a scream. Two young men in dark clothes flung themselves upon Racha Am Firn and his wife and child. Racha was struck to the heart; he fell, half-covering Aidris. At the same moment Hedris was flung backwards, the knife of the second assassin raking at her body. Aidris cried out, everyone was crying out; there was blood, bright blood on the sand of the pathway and a thick gasping sound in her ears.

As the first assassin freed his long, curved knife and, kneeling, came after Aidris, he gave a thick gasp himself and fell forward heavily. The kedran officer from the lower gate had run in, taken aim and felled him with an arrow. A pair of gardeners beat at the second man with rakes, beat him almost to death. People came. Someone drew the body of Dan Racha aside. Aidris, uninjured, was lifted and carried very fast into the shelter of the palace.

The noise and violence did not stop. There was a continual shouting, the cries of women, the tramp of feet. She was almost flung down in her bedroom with guards rushing to the balcony and crowded in the open doorway. Tylit, the young nursemaid, was terrified; she and Aidris sat shivering together on the end of a padded settle. The Lady Maren, wife of Nazran, came in and shut the door against the soldiers. She wrapped Aidris in furs and had Tylit boil water on the nursery stove. Aidris drank tea, sweetened with honey, asked no questions and leaned against Lady Maren, sleepy and limp.

Then there was a woman at the door, one of the palace midwives, hiding her blood-stained hands under a dark apron. Maren shook Aidris firmly and made her stand up.

"There is no help for it," she said. "You must do as I tell you, child. Dan Racha has gone; your mother was not spared; her child could not live. She has a few breaths of life remaining, then she' too will go to the halls of the Goddess. She has sent for you, to know that you are safe, and you must go to bid her farewell."

Still Aidris did not speak; she was led through broad, sunlit corridors to the dark bedroom. Hedris lay covered to the neck, her face whiter than the bed linen, her hair spread out. Her sister Aravel had been summoned; she knelt by the bed together with four ladies in waiting. When Aidris was led to stand beside her pillow, Hedris smiled.

9

"I have had a dream," she said in a clear voice. "I have seen our dear sister Elvédegran and her child."

"Her child?" asked Aravel, hoarsely.

"A male child," said Hedris, "and she placed on its breast this Swan of Lien that we all wear, sister. Surely, surely I will come to her. Let Aidris wear my amulet now . . ."

Aravel nodded to the youngest of the women, Riane, and she came trembling to the head of the bed, took the medallion of the silver swan from around the neck of the dying woman and slipped it over Aidris's head.

"Let me . . ." said Hedris in a fading voice. "Let me be alone with Aidris."

The women did not move at once, then Aravel rose up and stretched out her hands to the others.

"Come, we will go to the end of the room."

"Leave us!" said Hedris more sharply. "Sister . . . I charge you!"

"Come then!"

Aravel bowed her golden head and shepherded the women out of the chamber.

Hedris smiled thinly at her daughter; her eyes were wide, as if she strained to see through a mist.

"Kneel by me . . ." she said. "Have they gone?"

Aidris cleared her throat, coaxed out a reply.

"Quickly," said her mother. "There is something else. A treasure. A secret. Feel the bed frame . . . the carved snake, then the three figures of the Goddess, then the flower . . ."

Aidris did not look away from her mother's pale face.

"The flower?" she asked, as her searching fingers moved over the dark, polished wood.

"Press its center!" The voice was growing weaker.

A small hollow opened two finger breadths from the carved flower in a circle of leaves. Aidris drew out a long, fine chain of bronze; the jewel or medallion on the chain was hidden in a pouch of soft green leather. She closed the hiding place.

"Hide it well!" said Hedris. "It is all my legacy, all I have to give. Guard it. Tell no one that you have it."

"I promise."

Hedris lay exhausted; her voice had faded completely, but her lips still moved. Aidris crumpled the treasure in her hand and thrust it down into the pocket in her right boot. These were her favorite boots, red leather, from the northern tribes; the long pocket was meant to sheath a dagger. She drew out the scrap of leather for polishing that stayed in the sheath, stowed the treasure far down, then replaced the leather.

"Mother," said Hedris again. "Mother, protect my dear child. It was well done . . . do not blame yourself . . . he was kind and good."

She moved a hand out from under the bedclothes and reached blindly towards Aidris. Then there was a sound in her throat; her hand was still. Aidris saw that it was bandaged; her mother had clutched at the assassin's knife. She saw that the bed beneath its embroidered coverlets was soaked with blood. She screamed aloud, and the women tumbled into the room. Riane led her to the lighted doorway while the others knelt round the bed again, keening softly.

"Aidris . . ."

Aravel stood in the sunlit corridor and held out her arms; Aidris was guided to her aunt's embrace.

"Poor mouse! Poor minikin!"

The sweet voice rang out above her head; the strong delicate hands held her tight. Once Aravel laid a palm on her niece's tightly curling black hair then withdrew it hastily. Aidris looked up into her aunt's lovely face, pale but unmarked by tears; she saw a new vision of herself, undersized, ugly. For the first time she glimpsed a whole world, looming close at hand, where she was not loved and cherished.

Aravel's hands moved to the child's throat, fingered the silver swan on its chain and the fastenings of her tunic.

"What else did your mother give you?" she demanded softly.

Aidris could not answer; she shook her head. The strong hands tightened a little; a ring grazed her chin.

"Where is it?" said Aravel.

"The swan . . ." faltered Aidris. "She gave me only the swan. You saw . . ."

Aravel took her by the shoulders and shook fiercely.

"Where is it? Where have you hidden it?"

"Danu Aravel!"

Lady Maren stood in the corridor; she let fall a heavy bunch of keys which clanged dismally on the polished wooden floor. Her face was heavy and still; two bright circles of color burned in her cheeks. Her voice was threatening. Behind her, like a

11

bodyguard, stood three elderly servant women carrying white linen. Aidris ran or stumbled to clutch at her robe. Aravel threw up her arms. She began to cry and keen aloud, swaying away from the restraining hands of Riane and the guard captain from the Zor household.

Maren directed the women, then led Aidris away, walking so briskly that she almost had to run to keep up. Outside the palace walls a restless crowd grew and grew all through the night, raising the keen, but Aidris was not shown to them.

II

DAN ESHER AM ZOR RODE OUT TO HUNT IN THE Hain, the royal grove, by Lake Musna. The sole ruler of the Chameln and regent for the Firn rode at the head of a large cortege, and it seemed to Aidris, trotting behind on her new grey, that his melancholy grew less with every furlong. The city, the palaces, were far behind.

The nine-year-old prince, Dan Sharn, rode at her side, suffering, because he had not been well taught and neither had his pony. He allowed Aidris to reach out and steady the contrary little brute as they rode quickly, down and up again, through a wide, shallow ditch, full of leaf mould.

The season was high summer. They rode between fields of ripening grain then up a gentle slope, where the ranks of nobles and the outer ring of archers and hunters could spread out from the road. Thick grasses, untrodden, stirred into silver waves by the wind, covered the downward slope to the trees. A mighty head of cloud, a cloud palace, reared up in the endless summer blue, to the east, over the hidden lake. The wood was of oak, birch, elm, planted in ranks and aisles, but in places so old that Aidris felt the breath of the true forest, the urwald, in its deep shades.

The hunt reined in on the long crest of this grassy rise. Dan Esher and those who rode nearest to him must go down first. Below, at the entrance to that broad aisle, the Royal Ride, were the hunt servants, including Tilman Loeke, the hunt master, holding four deerhounds, as many hands high as Sharn's white pony. On the king's right hand rode the envoy from Mel'Nir, Baron Werris, no giant but a handsome, dark man with a peculiar carriage of his head, as if he spent his life talking to giants. On his left Dan Esher had placed a family visitor from Lien, Bergit of Hodd. She was a tall, tough, jolly woman, more than forty years old, widowed and well-connected . . . to the ruling house of Lien for instance. She was the cousin of Kelen, the Markgraf, and his surviving sister Aravel.

In the stableyard that morning she had reacted with a strange "Lienish" delicacy to the timid suggestion from Aidris that she ride astride. No, no it would never do, the sidesaddle it must be.

"All very well for you breeched gals from this wild place . . ." she panted at the mounting block, hitching her sturdy booted leg over the pommel and watching while Aidris arranged the billowing skirts of her habit.

Then she peered closer with shortsighted blue eyes and saw who it was acting as her groom.

"Oh is it you, Dan Aidris? Well, I'll tell you a thing . . . as a gal I rode astride, too. Secretly on the estate at Hodd, flying through the summer meadows. Now this does well enough. I'm used to it. Never missed a season in the hunting field."

The royal party began to descend the slope to the wood; halfway down grew a solitary young oak. Aidris saw the movement at the same time as the archers; she checked and reached for Sharn's rein. An elderly man in a dark cloak limped out from behind the tree, a woman and a child came to stand beside him. They all held up green sprays of leaves, the sign of a suppliant. They looked peaceful enough, but the suddenness of their appearance was uncanny: the tree did not seem wide enough to have hidden them. What kind of folk rose up so recklessly in the path of the royal hunt?

The archers swung out with a soft whoop, circled the tree even as Dan Esher and his guests drew rein. The ranks of nobles and huntsmen all fanned out and checked admirably. Bajan came up in a breath on the left hand of Aidris.

"Steady . . ."

"Bajan, who are those fools?" demanded Sharn Am Zor in a shrill voice.

He looked the very picture of a Zor princeling, a young boy of surpassing physical beauty, golden-haired, blue-eyed, well-made . . . a being so bright and perfect in his blue tunic and red cloak that he might have ridden out on his white palfrey from an illuminated scroll. Aidris knew two things: the poor wretch was abominably spoiled, and he had great spirit. He was fighting back tears from his trouble with the ill-mannered pony.

"A petitioner, Highness," said Bajan, watching keenly.

He murmured to Aidris; "The old man serves the Lame God! See his staff . . ."

Aidris felt a shadow pass between her and the sun. She urged her dear new grey, Telavel, forward so that she could hear the suppliants address Dan Esher. A band of white woven stuff was crisscrossed around the old man's staff and nailed into position with large thorns. Aidris had been stalking Inokoi, the Lame God, and his followers for years now. She had the same morbid interest in this cult as she had in the lands of Lien and of Mel'Nir.

The murderers of her parents had been named as followers of Inokoi; it was also said that they were set on to the deed by the powerful neighbors of the Chameln. She could not penetrate the mystery; even Nazran was reluctant to speak. Yet the deed had such a dreadful power, it cried out so loudly, she wondered how it could remain a mystery.

Could Dan Esher and Danu Aravel come and go however cautiously with the demanding realm of Mel'Nir or with the patronising friends and relations from Lien if they believed one word of the rumors? Could the followers of Inokoi love humility and seek truth without ridding themselves of this accusation? She stared at the old man addressing the king, at Dan Esher answering briefly, at the clouded face of Baron Werris and at Bergit of Hodd, impatient, anxious for her hunting.

"Justice," the old man said, "for the lake village of Musna, threatened by the enclosures of a new estate."

Then the child ran forward with a scroll for Dan Esher and returning gave Lady Bergit a spray of oak leaves. The woman, who wore a long drab cloak, seemed gaunt and plain; she looked out from under her straw hat with a half-smile. The old man had a blank, pale face; his eyes were in shadow. Now the child, who wore a close brown hood, suddenly ducked under the neck of Bajan's horse and thrust a spray of green leaves at Aidris.

"Dan Aidris," it piped, "see the truth!"

She took the spray and the child sprang back nimbly. Sharn

cried out, and she clutched his rein as the hunt moved on, stifling a cry herself. She had seen that it was not a child who had given her the spray but a child-sized creature with wrinkled hands and bright eyes under its hood.

Having seen this, she doubted every one of the suppliants. The plain woman was clearly a young man in a long cloak. The old man was not old and his cloak was two-sided, one rough, one richly embroidered. She could not look back, the going was too steep and she had to take care of the young prince. As they came down at last to level ground, she saw that the tall thunderhead had spread out, darkening the sky. She looked back and could see only the "old man" under the tree, staff uplifted, as if he called down a blessing or some other working upon the hunt as it passed him by.

"Bajan!" she called.

The young Count Am Nuresh looked at Aidris, head on one side. He never showed impatience with her, but she had learned to see a line grow between his black brows. All around them there was laughter, a jingle of bridle bells, as the hunt reformed; the young men were a brave sight, the young women, in the habits of Lien or in the tunic and breeches of the Chameln, were beautiful. She was fourteen years old, and Bajan was not her esquire.

"Those people frightened me," she said. "How did you see them?"

"The priest is right, Princess," said Bajan. "The lake village is threatened . . . by a Mel'Nir landlord. But there is no need to be afraid."

His bay stallion, dancing, seemed to betray his own eagerness to get away.

"Good hunting, Bajan!" she said.

"Aidris!" cried Sharn Am Zor, an edge of tears in his voice, "they're going!"

She turned and smiled at her cousin.

"Here," she said. "Cheer up!"

She handed him part of her spray of oak leaves.

"Now you are the Summer's King!"

They rode off side by side, galloping at the pace of Moon, the contrary white pony, down the royal ride after Dan Esher. The horns blew up at last: the silver horns of Lien and the curled wooden trumpets of the Chameln. It was a part of the royal hunt, perhaps the only part, that Aidris enjoyed. She liked to be in the wood, under the majestic trees, bouncing along on the thick turf with the quarry and the kill far distant.

Two kedran of her own household rode as their bodyguard; a band of even slower riders, almost hunt followers, came after them at a distance, in the ride, and on either side, in other paths, the bolder spirits crashed and shouted. The horns sounded: Old Loeke and the hunt-servants had done their work well. A stag, a fire-crest stag, sang the horns, and the king's party, far ahead, plunged after him.

Aidris and Sharn came through the first clearing and checked to let by a stream of riders cutting back into the ride. They found their way past the roundhouse of undressed logs decorated for the hunt. Maith, the younger of the two kedran, reined in her grey gelding with an oath.

"Taken a stone!" she called. "I'll catch up."

Eri Vesna, the older captain on Aidris's left, barely slackened her pace; she shouted something to the young officer and they rode on. Moon, the pony, was going well, it was not a time to check. The path narrowed, and they took a right-hand path at the heels of a brightly clad party; she recognised old Lord Hargren and his new wife on her skittish roan. Aidris thought that this play-hunting at a child's pace might be no more than a disagreeable duty for the kedran and their horses. The small greys could ride all day, untiring.

The horns called a view, a view, far off. The wood had become very dark; up ahead they saw only two blue riders. They rode at a tall thicket, an unexpected wall of green across the path; the blue riders had vanished from sight. They turned into another path of untrodden moss and grass; up ahead thick yellow sunlight slanted down between the young elm rows. The going was smooth, but Moon was beginning to lag. The horns sounded a confused call that none of them could read. They listened for the movement of the hunt, but heard nothing. The shafts of sunlight died and went out, one by one, as the storm cloud covered the wood; they had reined in, almost involuntarily, to watch the sight.

Vesna gave a sigh.

"Must get back into the ride, my dears," she said.

"We have lost them," said Sharn.

They rode on into the place where the sunlight had been and found no way out except a small leafy path, very dark. Aidris felt a twinge of anxiety; she was glad when Vesna took the narrow path at a good pace. They came into a round clearing with a stone drinking trough in the center. They listened again, but the wood was absolutely still. Even the sounds of insects, the whisper of the leaves, were hushed.

Telavel pricked her ears when a bird gave a loud two-note cry and was answered by another, further off. Vesna was looking about at the three paths leading out of the round.

"Let's give a hail!" she said.

They called with the wildness of children who had not much opportunity to shout aloud. The hallooing sank without an echo; there was a distinct and distant burst of shouting, far away, not an answer to their call. Then horns were blowing, and this time they read the sounds: nothing for the hunt, but three harsh notes, repeated. The alarm. The kedran call to arms. Vesna's grey mare reacted before she did, flying towards a certain path.

"Come! Follow!" cried Eri Vesna to the children.

There was a thick sound, dull as a knock on wood, and Vesna fell backwards from her horse. Aidris tugged at Telavel's rein, as if she half knew what had happened, and urged Sharn's pony towards the trees. Moon whinnied and pecked; Sharn slid backwards to the damp ground over her rump. Aidris leaped down, eyes still on Vesna, and pushed Sharn towards a sturdy oak. She saw at last, across the clearing, the arrow shaft in the kedran's throat. The poor grey mare, riderless, dashed along a different path.

"Get behind the tree!" said Aidris to Sharn.

His mouth was open to protest, but he obeyed, crawling across the grass.

Telavel trembled, but stood still. Then there came a sound that froze the blood, the shriek of a horse, surely Vesna's grey, hidden from sight. Even Telavel could not stand still; she reared up. Aidris let go the bridle, then boldly seized it again, turned the mare towards the third, the widest path. It was the path nearest them, the one she thought must lead out of the wood, to the lake shore. She slapped at the grey rump, and Telavel galloped away with the pony after her.

"Aidris . . ."

Sharn was halfway round the oak, his boot heel caught in a tough loop of grass. She went two paces, bent down to release him; an arrow thwacked into the tree trunk above her. She

17

stayed down and crawled. She pushed Sharn before her and he went as fast as a weasel. They crawled like two terrified animals into the thicket, deeper and deeper in. Then close together, in a space no bigger than a fox's lair, they paused, panting, smeared with earth, torn by the undergrowth, and listened.

The earth-smelling darkness was lightened, suddenly; then came the thunder. The storm broke over the wood. Rain came roaring down all around them; Aidris took Sharn's short cloak and spread it over their heads. The noise of the storm frightened her more than ever: it must drown out the sounds of their pursuers.

"I can fetch help," she whispered in Sharn's ear, "but you must promise never to tell."

"Tell what?"

"Promise never to tell!"

"I promise!"

Without hope she fumbled the bronze chain out of her boot pocket. She had sent every year to the northern tribes for new boots, with the long dagger sheath; they had been pleased to serve their princess. Now she drew off the cloth covering and the large oval stone, rimmed with silver, glowed like a blue-green eye in the darkness of their hiding place.

"Help us!" she said.

The stone cleared; it burned red at the edges; in the center was a streak of light, it was a candle flame. The candle stood in some kind of chamber; she could see the covering of a table, the tall pewter candlestick. There was a movement in the stone; the Lady was half visible behind the candle flame. Aidris had never seen her clearly. Sometimes she was not in the picture at all.

"See us," she said, teeth chattering. "See us. Help us. We are in the wood by Lake Musna."

There was no sound in the world of the stone; the flame wavered as the candlestick was wrenched aside, and for a few seconds she saw the Lady's face. It was distorted a little because it was so close, like Sharn's face, cheek to cheek with her own. The Lady was neither old nor young; she had a fine fair skin and strong, handsome features. She was, as Aidris appraised people, neither of the Firn nor of the Zor; her hair was brown-black, her eyes a deep blue with dark brows and lashes.

She was already gone; the stone showed a tree, another oak,

18

old and gnarled, and beyond it lake water. The scene widened a little and she beheld the grey horse and the white pony, Telavel and Moon, sheltering beneath the tree, cropping grass. The stone went back to its normal blue-green color; it was a stone, nothing more, a beryl from the mines of Mel'Nir, polished but unfaceted. Aidris put the chain over her head and felt the stone slip down, cold between her breasts.

She led Sharn to the left; they rose into a crouching position and threaded their way between young broken saplings. The rain had eased off, yet the wood was full of the sound of water pouring from the leaves, running away into the crevices of the ground. They heard for the first time running footsteps, a single voice, then the bird calls repeated, dreadfully close. Two notes, then again two.

Aidris found a small path, the track of some animal in the bracken. They ran along it and there before them was the great oak in its own clearing. Telavel and Moon cropped the grass, just as she had seen them, and not far away was the lake. The grey mare lifted her head and whinnied as Aidris and Sharn appeared. They ran across the little space and clasped the gnarled trunk of the oak.

They waited for the pursuit, but it did not come. No one else entered the clearing; it was as if the power of the oak sealed them off from the world. They saw and heard nothing but the peaceful life of the wood.

"What happened?" asked Sharn Am Zor.

"We were attacked," said Aidris. "Did you see any of them?"

"What should I have seen?"

She stared at him. The prince was sitting on the grass, his back against the tree, prizing an acorn from its cup. He was dirty and his clothes were torn, but she sensed his unconcern, his fearlessness. She took it for pure innocence, an innocence she had lost, three years past. She sat down beside him and ruffled his golden hair in loving exasperation.

"You saw Captain Vesna fall down?" she prompted.

"The old kedran?" he said. "Was she hurt?"

"She was shot with an arrow. Did you see anyone . . .?"

"I saw the blue riders. You saw them too." said Sharn.

"Yes, I saw them. But after that?"

"Maybe there was an archer . . . a . . . a small archer. In a different tree, not an oak, not one of our good oak trees. There were these blue fellows, who climbed trees, do you think, and shot at you and the old kedran. And her horse. I expect they shot her horse because it cried out. I think these were dark, bearded men, frowning. They shot from trees or behind trees . . ."

"Sharn!"

He smiled at her, pleased with his romancing.

"Sharn . . . what did you see? Tell the truth!"

He had seen the blue riders; he had seen Vesna fall from her horse; he had heard the distant alarm. He had seen a movement in a tree, nothing else, and then the arrow that had driven them into the thicket.

"I wonder what the alarm was all about?" he asked dreamily.

Aidris was suddenly impatient with his ignorance and his story-telling.

"I am afraid Dan Esher might have been attacked," she said bluntly.

The prince flushed with anger; he hit out in rage at Aidris.

"I'll tell my mother!" he shouted. "You said they might kill my father! You are a dirty black dwarf of the Firn! They will kill you, my mother says, and you have led me into danger. That arrow might have hit *me!*"

"It might indeed!" said Aidris coldly.

She stared at Aravel's child giving out his mother's hatred and unreason. She went away from him around the tree to where Telavel stood and bowed her head against the mare's dark mane. She felt the hard ache in her throat that took the place of tears. She had seldom wept since her parents' death. The child's outburst was not much worse than the everyday tensions of Achamar. She found no peace between her struggle with books, the angry silences of the Council Hall, and the soft insincerity of the dressing rooms.

When her mother's presence was withdrawn, the bored ladies of Lien turned towards Aravel and her distaste for the world of the Chameln. From one hour to the next Aidris was dressed in long robes and cossetted, then mocked, secretly or openly. Even Riane, her favorite, carried tales, betrayed the child's and the growing girl's confidence a hundred times.

"Aidris . . . I'm sorry . . ."

Sharn Am Zor plucked at her sleeve. He had lost all his

20

willfulness; he looked woebegone and frightened. She put an arm around him; Sharn was always forgiven, poor wretch.

"Where is everyone?" he whispered, "I thought I saw . . ."

"What?"

"A movement in the leaves . . ."

They peered round the oak, examined every part of the encircling green, every tree and bush.

"Are there . . ." said Sharn hoarsely, "Are there *little people* . . . you know, dwarfs and greddles . . ."

Aidris knew it at once for a childhood fear, like the fear she had once had of the dark.

"Of course there are," she said. "Nothing to be afraid of. There used to be greddles at the palaces in Achamar. The last of them was an old woman, I think her name was Ninchi. A greddle is like a dwarf, it is a kind of misbirth, a creature to be pitied because it cannot grow as others do. But there are the Tulgai. Have you not heard of them?"

"They—they're hairy . . ." said Sharn.

"They are a tribe of small hairy folk who roam the great border forests; their leader is the Balg. They are hunters, skilled in forest lore. They still use the Old Speech, and some say they know the speech of the birds and animals, but I think that is only a tale. The Tulgai are part of our own folk, and if we come amongst them, they would do us honor. Every year, Nazran says, they leave tribute for the Daindru at Vigrund, the border town."

"Well, I would not mind *them!*" said Sharn firmly.

The storm had passed; watery sunlight came through the oak leaves.

"The others will be searching for us," she said.

"We are safe in Ystamar, the valley of the oak trees," said Sharn.

"Hush," said Aidris, "it is a holy place. If you speak of it, you will not come to it."

The spell of the oak tree held them fast. They seemed to be outside of time, and it did not help Aidris's real anxiety.

"Mount up!" she said. "We must find our way."

"Back *through the wood?*" whispered Sharn.

"No," said Aidris. "No . . . we dare not. We will go to the lake people, to Musna, the lake village."

When they were mounted, there was room to walk the horses round in a ring, under the oak's spreading boughs. They made a game of avoiding pursuit—around, around again, as if Aidris might lead off back into the wood, then around a third time. . . .

"Now!" she cried.

They peeled off, Sharn leading, left the shelter of the oak and galloped between two birch trees, heading for the lake. There was a jagged sound, a rending of the air as if they had crashed back into the real world by riding through a glass wall. Moon, the pony, danced about on the broad path at the water's edge but Sharn forced her to the left, with Telavel at her heels. Aidris looked back and saw a blue rider, a figure in cloak and hood on a dark horse, blowing a silver hunting horn. The call was "Gone Away."

She bent low and urged Telavel up beside the white pony. Everything depended now on poor Moon and on Sharn's ability to stay in the saddle. They had no protection; the road led round the head of the lake, a stout causeway of wood and stone set in marshy ground. The village rose up before them; the ancient pile dwellings hung in air over the lake shallows. The barns and the Meeting Hall on higher ground were roofed with red shingles, still wet from the storm.

They rode on steadily; there was a sound in the air; Aidris did not need to look back. The call of the silver hunting horn had drawn out archers, to shoot them down as they rode. The danger was so great that it made her senses more acute. She saw the hump of a wooden bridge drawing near, saw an arrow strike into its right-hand rail. She shouted to the prince, urging him forward, and took in at the same time the marsh below the bridge covered with blurred clumps of white. She swung Telavel off the road at a soft place and rode into the marsh.

A hard hand thumped her shoulder and another shook her saddle. Sharn Am Zor was on the bridge, clinging desperately to his pony's neck, but lasting. Then the air was alive with angry sound and hurtling white bodies. A hundred swans flew up honking with fury as Telavel splashed among them. They brushed Aidris with their heavy bodies and huge webs; they screened the bridge and the marsh with their beating wings. Aidris rode on, feeling her breath come in strange gasps. She brought Telavel out onto the road again beyond the bridge, while the swans still wheeled and circled noisily.

Sharn was safe. He had ridden into the shelter of a tall thatched archway over the road on the outskirts of the village. Two men came from their boat, a woman in a red tunic came running along the jetty of the first house. Up ahead a small crowd of figures pressed down the causeway.

Aidris rode slowly under the archway. The sunlight was fading a little, something seemed to drag her downwards, she could hardly hold the rein. Sharn had dismounted. He stood propped against the trembling Moon, still hugging her neck.

"Aidris . . ."

He could only stare and stare at her.

"Child!" said the woman. "Dear merciful Goddess, who has done this? Get help here . . . take her down."

"She is Dan Aidris!" cried Sharn Am Zor. "We were attacked!"

Dimly, as she was lifted from her horse, Aidris saw half a dozen men and women rush onto the bridge shouting angrily. A child came by nursing a dead swan with an arrow through its breast. Among the persons who lifted her down she saw a young man with long flaxen hair and a pale face. He wore a spray of oak leaves in his straw hat. She twisted her head to look for the blue riders, but saw only the long arrow embedded in her own left shoulder.

She saw a candle flame and dreamed that she was in the world of the stone. The Lady of the stone was caring for her; the Lady had taken all her pain and care away. She had healed the world and made it whole again. The dream vanished with the whiff of fever herb and the feel of bed linen against her skin. She lay on her back propped up with many pillows; at least this meant that the arrow had been removed. Earlier she had been lying face downwards, forced into consciousness by pain.

"Drink, princess," said a man's voice.

She sipped a warm brackish draught from a metal cup held to her lips. The man was holding a candle because the place they were in was cavernous and dark. Yet she knew it was still day, in fact not much time had passed. She looked up to the beams overhead and knew that she was in the Meeting Hall of Musna Village.

"Your right hand," said the voice. "Move your right hand."

She obeyed, focussing on him at last.

"Now the left. Move the fingers of your left hand."

It felt like a dead thing, a block of wood strapped across her chest. She concentrated and the fingers moved. There was a numbness in her shoulder that masked a deep pain. The man laid a hand on her forehead.

"You are very strong, Dan Aidris," he said.

She saw that he was middle-aged and clean shaven, with a long, pale, blunt-featured, almost comical face. His thick yellowish grey hair was cut sharp and square at the level of his jaw bone; his eyes were dark and up-curving.

"I am Jalmar Raiz, Healer," he said.

"Am I . . . healed?" she whispered.

"Your wound should heal," he said.

"How is Sharn Am Zor?"

"Unharmed. You saved his life."

"The swans did it," she said.

"Quick thinking," said the healer.

She moved her head and found that they were quite alone at one end of the Meeting Hall. She had been doctored upon a table covered with featherbeds. The bloody instruments, even the arrow itself, lay upon a side table. At the far end of the hall sat a silent group of villagers, three or four older men and women.

"The elders . . ." he said quietly.

"I must thank them," she said. "I have not even thanked you, Master Raiz."

"Drink a little more," he said, holding the metal cup to her lips.

The warm broth gave her strength, made her less light-headed.

"The court?" she asked. "The hunting party?"

"They have been summoned. We expect them."

He took her wrist between his fingers and sat beside the makeshift bed on a stool, staring at her intently.

"You were pursued by four men," he said. "Two mounted, two on foot. Do you know who they were?"

"No—no—enemies . . . I don't know!"

She moved her head from side to side on the pillows, and he held up a long hand to still her restlessness.

"One of the runners was caught," he said. "The smith of

24

Musna, the strongest hurler in these parts, felled him with a bolt of wood."

"Is he . . . ?"

"Alive? Certainly. We are holding him."

She sighed and it hurt to sigh. The left side of her body was full of aches and stiffness.

"How will this go on?" asked Jalmar Raiz, with a trace of strong emotion. "You have too much to bear."

"I am strong. You said so yourself."

"It is too much for the mind and the spirit," he said. "You may never be whole again."

"What should I do?" she asked. "Tell me what I should do, Healer Raiz."

"Leave the court and the city," he said shortly. "Save yourself."

He stood up and reached for his staff, crisscrossed with white bands, held in place with thorns. He rapped with it on the floor, and they came from nowhere, from the shadows: a young man with flaxen hair and a child-sized creature with a small balding head and thick reptilian skin on its hands . . . a greddle.

"These are my two sons," said Jalmar Raiz, "Pinga and Raff."

Pinga, the greddle, busied himself clearing the instrument table. The smiling look that he gave Aidris forbade pity. She cried out, "You met the hunt! You gave a scroll to Dan Esher!"

"We seek justice for the village, Princess," said the healer.

He gave her a cool bow and bent to give instruction to the greddle, his deformed child. Aidris felt bereft and desperate now that the healer had withdrawn his attention. She turned her head and found the young man, Raff, sitting at her bedside. He had a likeness to his father, a rather long, smooth face, not at all handsome, and lacking Jalmar's firmness; his eyes were deep blue, fringed with sandy lashes. His expression was one of wistful sadness; when their eyes met, he turned up one corner of his wide mouth and the sadness was suddenly comical, a shared joke at the state of the world.

As Pinga carried the healer's equipment away, Jalmar Raiz was pacing down the hall to summon the village elders.

"Do you follow the Lame God?" asked Aidris.

"Healers often follow him," said the young man. "We came here from a college of healing on the borders of Lien, where my father gave a dissertation. It is a foundation of the Pilgrim Brothers of Inokoi."

Outside in the sunshine there was a sound of shouting, hoof-beats, hunting horns: the royal hunt. The village elders, ready to approach a wounded princess, stood irresolute at the end of the hall: the king himself was coming.

"Help me!" said Aidris.

She moved on the pillows, and the pain began to spread out from her wound. Her tunic had been unlaced and drawn down modestly on one side only so that one arm and shoulder were covered only in bandages.

"Take the stone on the bronze chain from the table there," she said. "It must be hidden. The silver swan can be replaced around my neck."

Raff moved quickly and expertly; he smoothed her pillows and drew up the embroidered coverlets. She told him the hiding place for the stone; her boots, freshly cleaned, stood at the bedside.

Her head was clear now, but she felt weak, and the pain was beginning to trouble her. She smiled at those elders who had come to greet her and thanked them. An old woman in a starched cap wept and kissed her hand.

"So young . . . so young to feel the world's pain!"

Sharn Am Zor ran into the Meeting Hall dragging his father, Dan Esher, by the hand. After them strode Dame Bergit, her habit spattered with mud and stag's blood, and Bajan Am Nuresh.

Esher was a man of the Zor, tall, well-built, with golden hair and eyes blue as the sky. His skin was rough and reddened by the outdoor life he preferred. Since the death of his co-ruler, Dan Racha, a puzzled sadness had grown upon him. He seldom smiled, although Aidris felt that he was a man meant to smile and to lead the simple life of a country lord or a tribal leader. Now at last she had a smile from him, for the preservation of his son, for her own safety, even for the death of a magnificent fire-crest stag.

Aidris told her tale as simply and as urgently as she could. She strained to catch and hold Dan Esher's attention. She pleaded for him to hunt down her attackers . . . to "ferret them out," not to let them "go to earth."

"Child!" trumpeted Bergit of Hodd. "You shouldn't bother your head with such things. Have you no woman to attend you, to stand by while you were doctored?"

"Uncle," cried Aidris desperately, "do not let this attack remain a mystery . . . I ask it in the name of my father!"

She had gone too far. Esher Am Zor mumbled and hawked, letting her hand fall. In his blue eyes, she saw a flash of disgust and impatience. He rallied quickly.

"We'll scour about . . . we'll find the vermin, be sure of it."

He gave his arm to Dame Bergit.

"Come cousin. We're bidden to table . . . I've dust in my throat. Aidris will do very well here . . ."

Further down the hall the villagers had set out food and drink on trestle tables. Sharn, overexcited, danced away down the long room, clowning and chattering. At last Aidris was alone with Bajan.

"I have offended Dan Esher," she said wearily.

"He will pardon you," said Bajan.

"Bajan, why was the alarm sounded in the wood?"

"Fire," he said. "One of the roundhouses on the Royal Ride threatened to go up in flames. The kedran troop barely put it out."

"Was the fire set deliberately?"

"It might have been."

"And my good captain, Eri Vesna?" asked Aidris.

"Her horse was found down a bank with a leg broken. Then, close by, her body was found. The kedran fetched me from the head of the hunt, with Jana Wetzerik and some others. We began to search for you and for Sharn."

"Bajan, have you seen the man they caught, the prisoner?"

"I have seen the pit under the barn where the villagers are keeping him," said Bajan.

"See that he lives!" she ordered. "See that he lives and tells what he knows. See that he is not tortured."

"Trust me!" said Bajan Am Nuresh.

He was on the stool beside her high resting place, watching her, not impersonally as the healer had done, but with a more cautious look.

"Princess," he said, "you are wounded; I think you are in pain. You *must not* take the pursuit upon yourself, questioning and casting about in this fashion. You are not the commander of an army. Leave it, I say. Leave it to *me,* if you will . . . I beg you . . ."

She lay back and let out her breath in a long, shuddering sigh.

"Tell the healer," she said. "I do have some pain . . ."

She watched him stride away down the hall; her ladies were never tired of saying he was the handsomest of men, but she had never been able to see it. She did admire the set of his shoulders; he had a new brown beard now that contrasted with his black brows and the hair of his head. She remembered how he used to come to the palace gardens, the big boy who let her ride on his back.

Aidris was engulfed by a wave of despair, of utter hopelessness. She was accursed, a heavy doom had been pronounced upon her: it was her royal blood. All the evil that had come upon her could be laid to its charge.

When Bajan rejoined the hunting party, feasting on roast swan and pickled eels down the hall, a relay of ladies descended upon Aidris. They brought cool cordials; she received them graciously. Jalmar Raiz, the Healer, sent one of the kedran with a draught, measured for her journey, but did not show himself.

Aidris rode home from the hunt on a farm cart, padded with hay and featherbeds and the embroidered dowry coverlets of the women of Musna, which they gave willingly to their wounded princess. For some of the way Sharn Am Zor rode in the cart with the white pony, Moon, hitched behind, but his father had him mount up as they approached Achamar in the twilight of the long day.

For Aidris the journey was very long, and the draught from Jalmar Raiz, which eased her pain, sent her into a thick, unpleasant sleep. Once she had a nightmare: she was pursued through a clawing thicket. She could not come out of it, but then she did and found Telavel lying in a ditch with a broken foreleg. She had a bright evil-looking knife and knew she must kill the beloved grey. Then, with a painful jolt of the cart, she woke up and saw Telavel close by, led by a kedran officer.

III

FROM THIS TIME FORWARD SHE WAS RULED BY FEAR
and mistrust, which Nazran and Maren, those closest to her,
could not reasonably dispel. The attack in the wood was hushed
up; it was given out, vaguely, as some kind of hunting accident.

"A kind of accident," said Nazran, "to which kings and other
rulers are prone. And certain commanders in battle. We may
not come to the truth of this. Old Tilman Loeke and his hunt
servants have combed the Hain and the countryside, but they
have found no trace of your miscreants. The blue, that hard
midnight color, is a color out of Mel'Nir; Baron Werris quarters
it on his banner. Yet who would presume the man so stupid as
to clothe assassins in his own colors! I have questioned the good
old Lord Hargren and his new-wed lady. They rode close to the
blue riders and remembered one man, red-bearded. We will
search for him and see what else Bajan brings us."

Aidris was conscious of the prisoner, her assassin, in the
dungeons of Achamar; she felt his presence like an ache in her
wounded shoulder.

She lived with her shrunken household in ten rooms of the
palace of the Firn. While her wound healed, she came and went
like some noble prisoner between her bedchamber, a large workroom, and later the exercise paddock beside the stableyard. Here,
in the workroom, made fine but stuffy with the best hangings,
she received her Aunt Aravel, who came reluctantly, ten days
after the hunt.

Heavy rain met the queen consort and her ladies as they
crossed the city. They burst in, scolding the servants, shaking
water from their light cloaks and from their headgear, leaving
their wooden pattens in a heap at the door. Aidris sat in a heavy,
thronelike chair, with cushions for her back. Her wound had
been drained and dressed by one of the city doctors who served
the Daindru. She had sent to Jalmar Raiz, summoned him to
Achamar, but she had received no reply.

Aidris remembered a time when it had been painful to look at Danu Aravel because of the resemblance she bore to her mother. Now she did not feel this pain. She knew of the likeness in features and in coloring between the living queen and the dead one, but the small shock of recognition for a remembered look or gesture had faded completely. Aravel was more than ever a beauty, the last swan of Lien, only a shade less supple now because she was tight-laced, following the birth of her third child, another prince.

Now she swept in and halted, while to right and left her four ladies, Grisel, Madalen, Brizengar and Hurta, sank down in their deepest curtsies. Aidris felt the company drawn up like two battlelines: behind her chair the Countess Maren and on either side, also sinking down in a welter of fine clothes, her two remaining ladies of Lien, Riane and Fariel, together with a newcomer, Nila, a round, dark, shy girl from the northern tribes.

The queen consort did not speak; her head was on one side in a listening attitude; her gaze wandered about the room, but she would not look Aidris in the face. It was her place to speak, but Aravel remained silent, moving her hands in vague smoothing gestures over her hair and her clothes. The sun had come out after the heavy shower of rain, and beams of light from the balcony caught the queen's rings so that they flashed fire and sent points of sunlight scurrying over the tapestried walls and the dark ceiling.

Aravel was silent for an uncomfortably long time, and Aidris caught the anxious eye of Grisel, the oldest of the queen's waiting women. She knew at this moment that her Aunt Aravel was mad. Her behavior was not merely cruel and strange to Aidris, but to all those who came close to her. More than that, everyone in the room, herself included, was involved in a conspiracy to hide the queen's madness from the world.

"The streets are dirty!" said Aravel in a loud voice. "They should be swept clean. Do you always sit in darkness?"

"I hope you are well, Danu Aravel," said Aidris. "Pray sit with us."

There was almost a scramble for the chairs and settles. The queen was led to a place beside Aidris, and they touched hands. Aravel wiped her fingers and sat rigid. The visiting waiting women broke into a chorus of good wishes for the health of the princess and the healing of her wound.

"Thank you," said Aidris, "thank you all."

She was suddenly overcome by tears, real tears, and pressed the flowing sleeves of her linen bed gown to her eyes. Lady Maren and her own women, who had scarcely seen her shed a tear, were shocked.

"Dear Goddess help us!" said Lady Maren, "She must be feverish . . . Aidris, dearest child. . . ."

Aidris had been stricken by nothing less than hope. If her Aunt Aravel was mad, she might become sane again. She might become kind and loving, the evil spell might be broken. While the women tried to comfort Aidris, Aravel sat watching, her face a mask, her eyes hard as gemstones. She spoke at last.

"Don't weep! It will spoil your beauty!"

Then she laughed, a ringing peal of cruel, childish laughter that raised not one echo from any of the women. Grisel said in a low voice, "The queen is not herself. . . ."

Aidris, with new found pity, reached out and took Aravel's hand.

"Dear Aunt," she said, "I am ever your friend."

The queen stared at her, nibbling a thread of her golden hair that had escaped from a braid, and seemed to come to a decision. She gestured to her ladies.

"The music!" she said. "Is there a cup of sweet apple wine for me?"

At once the four visiting waiting women went about the room glancing into alcoves, patting the billowing hangings to the wall. Then they set themselves up some distance from Aidris and the queen, and drew all the others, Lady Maren included, into this group. They had brought a pair of recorders, a miniature Lienish harp made of bone and a small drum. Nila joined in, strumming upon her tarika, a big five-stringed instrument.

The music was sweet, and under cover of it Aravel said hoarsely to her niece. "He has failed twice. He will try again. You will not survive a third attempt."

Hardly breathing Aidris asked, "Who is it?"

"Fool," said Aravel, smiling dreadfully. "Firn-mouse! Why should I bother with you? You are ignorant as well as ugly!"

"I saved the life of Sharn Am Zor," said Aidris.

31

"The prince will not be harmed. He has promised that. It is part of his plan."

"Tell me . . ."

"I know only one of his names and one of his faces. He is the scaly beast, the eater of souls, the night-flyer. He comes to the most secret places, to the bedchambers of women, low-born and high."

The queen's voice sank to a terrible whisper; and Aidris, sipping the wine to steady herself, felt her whole body turn to gooseflesh.

"The name you know . . ." she persisted.

"Rosmer of Eildon," breathed Aravel. "My father's scribe, my brother's chief minister. All, all has been his doing from the first to the last. He commands the powers of earth and air. Only our mother stood against him. She did her best to save us, even if it meant a lifetime spent in these barbarous Chameln lands. Then she was humbled and thrust aside. . . ."

"But surely Guenna, my grandmother, has retired to a holy place," said Aidris. "She lives among the Moon Sisters."

Aravel shook her head impatiently.

"She is out of the world. Blind, feeble. The sisters care for her. You never saw her, little toad; she never stood by your cradle. She was proud and beautiful as the morning, but *he* brought her down. Elvédegran, her youngest, our sweet sister, was sent into Mel'Nir. She died giving birth to a monster . . . a misbirth ripped from her body and destroyed by the minions of the Great King. That too was Rosmer's doing, I swear it!"

Danu Aravel lay back in her chair, her fingers clutched about the medallion of the silver swan that lay upon her breast.

"So you have heard all . . ."

Aidris was unable to speak. She had made a bid for love and sanity and found a madness more terrible because part of it might be the truth.

At last she said, "I will leave Achamar till I come of age. I will save myself."

"Do as you please," said Aravel. "And keep the scrying stone. I know you have it. It is a poor dead thing by this time. What did you see in it? Reflections of the forest trees?"

Aidris made no answer, but she felt a glow of encouragement, small as a candle flame. She had not expected Sharn to keep the secret, but in some way the stone had kept its own secret.

They sat side by side until the last song came slowly to an end, then Aravel rose up and took her leave.

Riane said when the noise and bustle of the departure had subsided, "The queen comes and goes as if she were pursued by demons!"

"A woman's sickness," said Lady Maren, forbidding comment or gossip. "The queen has strange fancies. She has not recovered from the birth of her child."

Aidris sat in the high-backed chair, pale and shivering. Maren drew up a fur rug to cover her and said under her breath, "Ten days and now this. What did that distracted woman say to you?"

Aidris shook her head and could not answer. She was put to bed before sundown. She lay in the half darkness of the bedchamber trying to shut out Aravel's words: ". . . the eater of souls, the night-flyer." Her string of rooms in the vast wooden building had been specially chosen for security. The long windows of her bedchamber opened on to a wide gallery above one of the inner courtyards, and the women of her bodyguard patrolled there, day and night. She could just see the young kedran on duty outlined in the twilight.

Lamps had been lit in the outer rooms. She dozed a little, and then Nazran stood at the doorway with a candle.

"Princess? Aidris? Are you awake?"

Drops of rain gleamed on his white head; his face was strong and brown, the skin round his dark eyes netted with wrinkles.

"Bajan Am Nuresh sends greeting," he said. "He has gone to the north. His lands are flooded. He made a report."

"I am awake!" She eased herself higher in the bed.

Nazran set down his candle on the press at the bedside; he sat in a chair, bending forward so that he could take her cold hands.

"The man who attacked you and Dan Sharn was a guard officer dismissed from the service of the Zor for theft. He was recruited in the city here by mercenaries out of Lien, Redbeard and two others. They carried gold. Two were trained archers."

"What was their plan?" whispered Aidris.

"Some evil working," he said, "some ceremony within the wood, in that clearing with the stone drinking trough. Sharn was to be wounded, lamed, and by an arrow of the Firn. You were to be killed. When you managed to come out of the wood, so the wretch claimed, the other assassins became desperate, shooting to kill lest you should reach Musna Village. They were afraid of some dark master. The leader, Redbeard, swore that you two escaped by magic. . . ."

"We did," said Aidris. "I have told you . . . the oak tree sheltered us."

"It may be," said Nazran, shaking his head. "What has your poor Aunt Aravel been saying to you?"

She told him as best she could, but the words were cold, they had lost their power.

"Is it true?" she asked. "Why would that old Councillor of Lien so set upon the house of the Firn, to do us ill?"

"There might be reasons."

"And has he so much power?"

"Has anyone?" asked Nazran drily. "Does the master of earth and air need to hire assassins? Dark magic is like fear, it grows and festers in our own minds. I have more trust in the magic of the earth itself, the benign powers of the Goddess . . . the magic of hidden Ystamar, the Vale of Oak Trees."

"Nazran," said Aidris, "what became of my Aunt Elvédegran in the court of Mel'Nir? No one will tell me."

"She died in childbirth," said Nazran. "There is no mystery here. She bore a deformed child to Prince Gol of Mel'Nir and it died or was put to sleep at birth. This may have been a kindness."

"She bore a son," said Aidris dreamily. "She held the child in her arms and placed on its breast a silver swan of Lien like this one I wear. . . ."

"Who told you that, child? Was it Aravel?"

"No," she said, "it was my mother. As she lay dying, she saw Elvédegran with the child and thought she must come to her sister in the Halls of the Goddess."

"In those bright halls," said Nazran sadly, "we are all made whole and sound. Take my blessing now, child, for what it is worth, and sleep."

"Send to Ledler Fortress, to my father's sister, Micha Am Firn," she said. "I will come to her when my wound is healed; I will go out of Achamar."

"After that you can come to Thuven Manor," he said. "We have often thought of it as a haven for you."

He made no argument at all, and Aidris knew that her plight must be serious.

34

The summer weather had broken. Oakmoon, the midsummer month, went out in showers, and Applemoon was no better. Throughout the grain basin of the Chameln lands, from Achamar south to the inland sea, the harvest came in with bone-breaking haste, and some of it was lost. The freakish weather continued with storms and whirlwinds, and in the north the smaller lakes spilled over with floodwater until the land became like the sea. Word came out of Lien, to the southwest, of terrible flooding in the land between the two rivers; there the harvest was entirely lost, and poor folk came over the border into the Chameln lands at Nesbath and camped along the highway.

It was in these days that Aidris first saw the giant warriors of Mel'Nir going about in some numbers in the city. They were peaceful enough; it was like the old riddle: "Where does the Great Grey Bear lie down to sleep? Anywhere he wants to." They were young men, not veterans, and they were the house-carls of the southern landlords. As autumn came, after the poor ending to the summer, Dan Esher called off the Dainmut, the council meeting, for fear of street fighting between groups of vassals.

On the day that she left the city there was still one debt to be paid. Baron Werris answered her summons and brought with him a certain Hem Rhanar, his countryman, proprietor of a newly gathered estate by Lake Musna. Rhanar was a middle-aged junker with a tawny beard; he had to stoop down to enter the workroom. Their business was simple: it had been arranged that Aidris would make him a gift of forty acres of best bottom land from one of her estates bordering his own, and he would give up all claim to the lake shore. The Village of Musna would be saved.

She received these two men of Mel'Nir with little formality; Riane sat at her embroidery frame listening to their palaver; Nazran stood in the shadows, letting his pupil conduct the interview. Rhanar reared up in the midst of the quiet room like a rock or a tree. His rumbling voice, his muscular shoulders, his enormous hands, were overpowering.

When she looked at him, Aidris thought of the High Plateau of Mel'Nir, where the wild horses rode free in their herds. She imagined the raw life on his estate: cold water, stone floors, loud voices, a life shared with horses and dogs. It was a life she had sometimes envied when the ladies of Lien pressed too closely

35

upon her. By contrast with Hem Rhanar, Werris, the Envoy, was a courtier.

She could see that Hem Rhanar found her a puzzling figure, half a child still, dressed in the Chameln style with a fine linen tunic over soft leather breeches and boots. There was a jocular note in his voice, which showed that he found it difficult to defer to any half-grown girl. He cast admiring glances at pretty Riane, a true woman in a flowing robe.

"Have you obtained your estate by purchase?" asked Aidris.

"No, Highness, not all," answered Rhanar, "for my mother was a lady of the Chameln. I inherited a manor from her brother."

Aidris smiled.

"Then you are of Chameln blood. I will make a new bargain with you. I will extend the gift of sixty acres if you will take it as a feoff from my hand and give me your allegiance."

Baron Werris was not amused; Nazran gave no sign of what he felt; Riane delicately smothered a yawn.

Rhanar slapped his thigh loudly and said, "Agreed! I will do it!"

Nazran hovered as she altered the deed and the map. She wrote well in the common or merchants' script, but not in runes or the straight-letter. Aidris rose up and drew from its silver sheath the short bronze sword, a treasure of the Firn. When Hem Rhanar knelt before her, his eyes were almost on a level with her own. He was enfeoffed of the land and swore himself her liegeman in respect of the land.

The audience was over. When she was left alone with Nazran, he said, "It was well done. Musna is saved."

He opened the tall wooden shutters onto the balcony and let in the fitful sunshine of an autumn day. Thornmoon, the month of sacrifice, was just beginning.

"Has it occurred to you that *this* might have been the plan?" he asked. "Jalmar the Healer was determined to save the village. Musna rendered an unexpected service to the Daindru."

"Jalmar Riaz hired the assassins? I cannot believe it!" said Aidris.

Nazran sighed and looked out into the streets of the city. The maples around the distant Zor palace were turning blood red and gold.

"Look there!" he said, his frown lifting.

Aidris came to stand beside him at the window, and he moved

the shutter so that she remained in shadow. He pointed into the street beyond the palace stockade, and there was a young man, a soldier in elaborate strip mail, mounted on a tall white stallion. He wore a shining helmet with a plume, and behind him rode a kedran, a battlemaid, with a banner showing a white tree. Their two horses were picking their way through drifts of red leaves and patches of mud.

"Ah, I can read those two," said Nazran with a chuckle. "A knight questor and his esquire, come out of Athron. That banner is for the Foresters."

"But what does the knight seek?" asked Aidris.

There was something ridiculous about the young man, his fine trappings, his plume, his banner.

"He is looking for adventure," said Nazran.

She rode out at nightfall through the northern gate of the city with a troop of nine kedran. Esher Am Zor came with the kedran of his own bodyguard to bid her farewell. Two of the Torch Bearers, her father's companions, were present: Gilyan and Wetzerik. She thought of the lights going out in the palace of the Firn; in all its hundred rooms, its galleries and corridors, only darkness and silence.

She travelled to Ledler Fortress on its high hill and stayed almost to the year's end with the quiet, dark widow woman, Micha Am Firn, her closest relative. Then, before the snow became too deep she rode westward with only two kedran, the officers Kira and Maith, to the distant manor of Thuven, near the border range, on the edge of the forst. Nazran and Maren were already there to welcome her. She remained at the manor house for more than two years, undisturbed.

CHAPTER
II

THE MANOR HOUSE HAD BEEN REBUILT OUT OF an old water fortress. A shallow lake spread out before it, and behind rose a man-made hill, low and grey. It was a barrow for the dead; no one knew who had made it, but the bones that came up to the surface of the long mound were small, almost child-sized. Aidris once found a small dagger made of polished bone, golden with age, twisted into the roots of the grass.

The house and the lake were enclosed in a ring of trees, poplar and birch; on the eastern side there was a windbreak of spruce and pine. Beyond these darker trees the plain swept away; the road east could be seen crossing the plain. She used to watch the traffic on the road, coming from distant Achamar and the towns that lay between. A smudge of dust became a solitary rider, a moving scrap of yellow among the wild flowers grew into a laden wagon with a bright hood. They came on, wagon and rider alike, and passed by on the road.

Looking westward from the manor house she could see the plain come into the shadow of the forest. Here, where plain and forest met, the deer came out to graze, and she saw or imagined hunters stalking the deer. Oak mingled loosely with dark firs here on level ground; there were pleasant glades and woodland pools. Then the forest closed its ranks. Massed dark trees covered the world farther than eye could see and clothed the knotty slopes of the border mountains. The road ran on out of sight, cutting through the forest to the town of Vigrund. Beyond the town by several leagues the road crossed through a mountain pass into the land of Athron.

Aidris learned to study alone while Nazran was absent in the capital. Lady Maren's household was very small; there were few visitors. When riders or vehicles struck out from the road towards the manor, there was always a moment of tension until the newcomers were recognised. When pedlars came in spring or autumn or the Pilgrim Brothers in any season, she did not show herself. If they caught her out in the open air, she kept her distance or rode Telavel up onto the barrow.

One evening in late summer, the Hazelmoon, after she had been at Thuven half a year, Lady Maren came to her in Nazran's study.

"You had better come down," she said.

Lady Maren half frowned, half smiled; as they walked onto the landing, she put her finger to her lips. Aidris peered through the railing and looked down into the hall. Two hunters stood below holding the carcase of a young white deer. They were both bearded men, well-proportioned and muscular, their hair dressed in shining curls and tresses; they wore deerskin tunics and sturdy boots. They were tiny men; they stood little more than waist high to Maith, the kedran on duty; they were hunters of the Tulgai.

Aidris walked slowly down the stairs, unable to keep from smiling, and the hunters smiled back at her, teeth flashing in their dark, snub-nosed faces. The older man, whose beard was streaked with white, spoke up.

"*A gift for the heir of the Firn!*" he said in the Old Speech.

They laid the deer on the flagstones of the hall, and stepping forward, they knelt down at her feet. Aidris felt a rare moment of pride and delight.

"*Rise up,*" she said. "*I thank you from my heart, brave hunters of the Tulgai.*"

They stood before her, blinking a little in the lighted hall.

"*My greeting to the Balg,*" she said. "*Let me send a gift to him in return for the white doe.*"

As they heaved up the deer again and headed for the kitchen, Aidris called after them, "*Did the birds tell you I was here?*"

The younger hunter smiled over his shoulder, shy and fierce.

"*We have heard . . .*" he said.

"What will they be given?" she asked Maren.

"Honey," she said. "Salt. A firkin of apple brandy as your gift to the Balg. They come in about once every two years."

At Thuven she began to sleep peacefully; her nightmares went away. She began to think of her fear as a childish thing she had outgrown. In spite of reading, riding, caring for the horses, apple picking, her life seemed pleasantly empty. She waited eagerly for Nazran and for the dispatches he sent. She treasured up the news from Achamar, from Lien and Mel'Nir, and the stories of Athron and its delights, which were common in this border country.

Bajan came in her sixteenth year and stayed for the year's end: for the Ashmoon, the month of changes, the five days of the Winter Feast, and the Tannenmoon, Old Man's month, the first month of the new year. It was a time of so much rejoicing that she became anxious. Could this be herself, Aidris Am Firn, who woke every morning, eager and unafraid, and looked from the window only to see if more snow had fallen?

She began to work her own magic. On the day that Bajan took his leave, the snows of a mild winter were still patchily covering the ground. She rode out with Bajan and his northern escort beyond the pines of the windbreak, far on to the plain. Parting he leaned from his horse and kissed her formally on both cheeks; they clasped gloved hands. She wheeled Telavel and galloped back again, then turned up the path to the top of the barrow. She did not look at the small cavalcade heading northward across the plain.

On the summit she dismounted and sat on one of the large boulders that crowned the barrow. She pulled her snow-colored cloak of lynx and fox, Bajan's gift, around her, right to her toes, and felt herself invisible. After digging a place in the half-frozen ground with the bone knife, she planted an acorn wrapped in warm earth from the seed boxes in the cellars. *"Let it grow,"* she said in her mind, firmly, reverently, using the Old Speech. *"Let it grow for my deliverance and for the good of the Chameln and their lands."*

She looked about for a sign, but there was nothing particular to be seen except the beauty of the winter day. Telavel, covered almost to her hocks in a quilted blanket, nibbled at a twist of cold grey grass. Aidris drew out the stone from under her cloak and warmed it in the palm of her hand, under her glove.

She thought of her long involvement with the stone. She had learned first of all to hide it skillfully, moving it from place to place so that it was never found. Then she had learned not to approach it too often, not to question or weep, not to expect messages or miracles.

She felt the stone warm on her hand and drew it out and looked into it. There were two tall red candles in gold candlesticks and sprays of evergreen. It looked like an altar for the Goddess at the Winter Festival. There was shadowy movement, the sleeve of a robe came into view, the whole scene blurred, breaking into sparkling points of light, then cleared again. Three objects lay between the candles; a hand, the Lady's hand, moved each one forward for her to see. A small bound book in the style of Lien, with purple-brown leather cover and a silver fastening; a dagger in a green sheath; a cluster of yellow stones on a long gold chain. The three objects were tapped, each one, with a forefinger, then the two hands opened in an offering gesture.

"Oh the book!" said Aidris, pointing. "I will choose the book!"

There was a gesture, hands together, of greeting and farewell; the picture faded. She was schooled by this time to feel no disappointment. It was like a game played on New Year's Eve, with coins and charms in the fruity-bread. She hoped the book meant "good fortune in the coming year."

II

A DAY AT THE END OF THE WILLOWMOON, THE month of planting, she was sky-larking in the stableyard with Maith and the grooms. Kira, the senior kedran, looked out of the topmost window of the manor house.

"Something to be seen!"

Aidris ran indoors, panting, wet from the water fight, and began to climb the kitchen stairs. She ran onto the second landing and into Nazran's study. As she stood at the window Kira came down from the attic and presently Maith and the Countess Maren came to stand behind them. A troop of cavalry were crossing the plain: thirty warriors of Mel'Nir mounted on their battle chargers.

"If they turn off the road?" said Aidris.

"Goddess help us!" said Lady Maren.

"No sense in taking chances," said Kira. "If they turn off the road, those draught horses will give us a few moments grace. Dan Aidris and Maith will go on foot through the orchard and into the near forest."

The mounted warriors moved like a ponderous war-engine; one could almost hear the beat of their hooves, the harness of men and animals jingling as they went along. They passed the point where they might have turned off towards the manor house and rode on until they were hidden by the trees.

"Something afoot!" said Maith. "Countess, shall we send into Vigrund town and try for news?"

"Tomorrow," said Lady Maren.

Aidris knew that this tomorrow meant "a day like today," another peaceful spring day at Thuven. She was restless and wished they might send for news at once, but she said nothing.

Tomorrow did not come. The next day she was awakened very early, before sunrise; Lady Maren stood there in her night-gown holding a candle.

"I have brought your milk posset," she said. "You must dress quickly and go down to the hall. Nazran is here. I have to tell you . . ."

"What? What has happened?"

"Dan Esher is dying . . . dead . . ."

"An attack?"

They were speaking in whispers. Lady Maren sat on the end of the bed and wiped her eyes.

"No," she said. "A wound-fever. Lockjaw. He took a small, deep wound in the foot from his own boar spear."

"Sharn Am Zor? My aunt Aravel?"

"Danu Aravel has taken the children and gone into Lien."

Nazran stood at the foot of the stairs; he looked older than ever, but full of vigor. His white hair stood up in peaks, the hand gripping his saddlebag was gnarled like an old tree root. He was driven by a frantic haste; he drew Aidris to the end of the long refectory table. She saw a shadowy group of followers at the end of the hall.

"Werris has claimed the double regency for yourself and Sharn Am Zor," he said. "There has been fighting in the city, in the north. Gilyan stood up as regent and Esher's Torch Bearer

Zabrandor... nothing served. There are a thousand warriors of Mel'Nir in Achamar, more have crossed the border. The Chameln lands are in the power of Ghanor, the so-called Great King."

She uttered a low cry and stifled it quickly.

"What must I do?"

"You must not come into the hands of Baron Werris," said Nazran. "You must go at once into Athron, to the house of Nenad Am Charn, the trading envoy in Varda."

"Yesterday we saw a troop of warriors."

"They have gone to close the border at Rodfell Pass. You must take another way, through the forest. I have brought a guide, from Vigrund, a man who is loyal to your house. You should leave within the hour."

She gave a sharp intake of breath, and he waved a hand with frantic impatience.

"Princess, they have that poor widow woman, Micha Am Firn, shut up in Ledler. They will find out this place soon enough."

"I am ready," she said.

Nazran led her down the length of the hall; it was just daylight.

"Here is your guide, Dan Aidris," said Nazran formally.

She had seen Nazran's two elderly esquires; the third man was much younger, well-built with a short brown beard. His face was familiar.

"It is Master Ric Loeke, the son of the master huntsman. He will bring you safely into Athron."

Ric Loeke strode forward, solemn-faced, and knelt before Aidris.

"Ever the faithful servant of your house, Princess!"

The formality was not so reassuring to her as it was to Nazran. It did not suit the man; she thought his face must have another expression, but could not picture what it might be. She gave him her thanks; he sprang up again, brisk and businesslike; she thought all might be well.

"It is a simple journey for anyone who rides well," said Ric Loeke. "We will come into Athron in eight days at the most."

Maren beckoned to her; she had a saddlebag and the new fur cloak.

"It is cold in the forest."

She drew Aidris aside and made a business of swathing her in the cloak.

"Take care, dearest child," she said in a low voice. "You are going into a strange household, in Varda. You are a young girl. Guard your chaste treasure, Aidris."

Aidris embraced the old woman fiercely.

"I will take care."

Ric Loeke came up with Nazran giving him instructions. He handed the guide one of the locked and sealed state pouches that were used for carrying jewels, coin and state papers. He handed a scrap of paper to Aidris.

"Contents of the pouch," he said. "The few jewels may be kept or sold, as you wish."

"Lord Nazran," said Ric Loeke, "I had promised to take other travellers into Athron by this way."

"Other travellers?" snapped Nazran.

"I am yours to command," said the guide, "but it would do no harm if these ladies came along. I know they are ready to ride at once. The widow of a fellow guide and her daughter. It would lend us some disguise, and it is more fitting that Dan Aidris travels with attendants."

Nazran had received a nod of assent from Lady Maren.

"Agreed!" he said. "But remember the oath of secrecy. We have put all our trust in you."

They went directly to the stableyard; Telavel stood ready. Aidris embraced the two kedran, Maith and Kira. The spring sun was rising over the forest; fresh green shone out among the dark conifers. Nazran came and stuffed a small package into her saddlebag.

"A New Year gift," he said. "It belonged to your mother. A servant brought it to me in Achamar."

She waved once and did not look back, but followed Ric Loeke's tall black gelding along the outskirts of the forest to the road.

He turned his head and said, "We'll go some way towards Vigrund then move into the South Ride. You had better wait while I go into the town."

He was unsmiling but not awkward.

"What will you say to the ladies?" she asked.

He shrugged and rode on. They crossed the road into the south ride, a wide grassy bay in the sea of forest trees. She hated to be left alone; when Ric Loeke had galloped away, she rode further in and stood behind a tumbledown brushwood shelter, in a place where she had a clear view of the road.

She did not have long to wait, although it was long enough to awaken her old fear, running over the back of her neck like a cold breeze from the depths of the forest. Loeke's black horse came pounding down the road with one companion, a woman in an enveloping green cloak beside him, mounted sidesaddle on a broad-rumped brown mare. Aidris came out of hiding expecting introductions, but Loeke spurred past her, shouting for her to follow. He whipped the horse of his companion, and the three of them went thundering down the South Ride. Then the guide turned off to the right, and they went more slowly but still at a good pace down a well-trodden path. He drew rein suddenly; the woman began to speak, but Loeke held up a hand for silence. They heard the sounds of the forest.

"Were you followed?" asked Aidris.

Loeke rode on without answering, and she repeated the question, thinking he had not heard. He gave her a single glance over his shoulder, frowning, then seemed to recollect himself.

"Horse troopers," he said. "Questioning travellers."

There was a burst of laughter at her side.

"You made the bird talk!" said a sweet voice.

Aidris looked and was amazed. The third member of the party was a young girl not much older than herself. She was pretty, more than pretty, a beautiful girl with loose red-gold curls escaping from her green hood, a beauty even by comparison with Hedris and Aravel and the ladies who had served them, Riane and Fariel and the rest. Her elaborate gown, her slender hands in their green gloves, all told a tale that Aidris thought had ended. This was unmistakeably another lady of Lien.

"Don't gape, little kedran," said the girl. "I know I look a fright."

Aidris looked away; she felt herself blushing. Loeke rode on, surly and unperturbed, and they followed. They had to follow, thought Aidris; he was their guide.

"You come out of Lien, I think," she said to the girl.

"From the capital of Lien, from Balufir," said the girl proudly.

"I have been presented at the court of the Markgraf Kelen, and I have walked in the rose gardens with his Markgrafin, Zaramund. You may call me Sabeth—"

"But that is . . . a royal name," said Aidris. She almost said, ". . . one of my names."

"Ask me no questions and I'll tell you no lies," said Sabeth smiling. "I was expecting a battlemaid, hard as wood. But you are not yet trained, I suppose. What shall I call you?"

"Aidris."

The name, she saw, had no associations for this strange girl.

"I was expecting to travel with a widow and her daughter," she said.

Sabeth cast a sidelong glance; her eyes were blue as cornflowers.

"My lady mother is unfit to travel," she said. "I must journey alone into the magic kingdom of Athron. There is a destiny waiting, I am sure. A place will be kept for me. Perhaps the Prince—Prince Terril, the elder Prince Flor is married—will catch sight of me one day, playing a stringed instrument, harp or lute, at an open casement. . . ."

"Sabeth," growled Ric Loeke, "stop your blethering."

Sabeth, checked in the midst of her romance, gave Aidris a quick, shy, knowing smile. They rode on in silence. The path was broad and level, carpeted with pine needles. The majestic trees rose on either side in thick, dark ranks, like giant warriors. The wind sang a constant song in the upper branches.

They made a brief halt at midday, then rode on steadily until sunset. The going was easy, but Aidris was tired; Sabeth drooped in her uncomfortable saddle, cramped and exhausted. When Aidris came to help her dismount, she waved her aside and waited for Ric Loeke. She slid into his arms with a tired, melting smile, and he carried her and set her down in the bracken. Their camping place had been used by many travelers; it had a clump of stones for a fireplace and a spring nearby. They had come up the side of a low bluff and could look down to a forest pool, fed by the spring.

Aidris went about helping Loeke to put up the two ingenious tents that he carried; she gathered kindling for the fire. When Sabeth revived, she set out the food, some from each of their saddlebags. The guide, dour and quiet as ever, grilled a trussed fowl from Aidris's store of provisions. He drank apple brandy, and it made him suddenly more cheerful. Sabeth peeled an apple with a little silver knife and fed pieces of it to Loeke with all kinds of teasing looks and pretty gestures.

She produced a tiny Lienish harp of bone and sang songs in a low, sweet voice. Aidris found herself a shade embarrassed by the performance, perhaps because all Sabeth's behavior was a performance. It seemed strange for this lovely creature to perform for the surly forest guide, even if she was his betrothed or his sweetheart. Whenever Loeke slouched off into the bushes, Sabeth left off singing and threw Aidris an exhausted grin. Then after a few more tots of brandy Loeke swore aloud and told her to stop that damned yowling, it was giving him a headache. Sabeth yawned prettily; Aidris crawled off to one of the tents. She lay on her bracken bed hearing the forest all about her and slept, too tired to puzzle over the ill-assorted pair.

In the dawn she heard riders pass through the camp, going west towards Vigrund. Ric Loeke greeted a fellow guide. She lay still, holding her breath, and came cautiously out of the tent when they had gone.

"A man and his wife," said Loeke, "coming home from their daughter's wedding in Athron."

They packed up quickly and rode on. Sabeth was fresh and fair, full of high spirits. Even Ric Loeke was more communicative. He pointed out signs of the Tulgai to Aidris; knotted grass at the foot of an oak, runes cut through a dead pine. As the path narrowed along the side of a ridge, the brown mare stumbled, Sabeth was nearly thrown. An hour later the mare was lame; Loeke got down, cursing under his breath, and took stones from the injured hoof.

"We need a smith. The shoe is half off," he said to Aidris. "I must go by Aldero, the forest village."

Deliberately, thinking things out, he changed the clumsy sidesaddle to his own horse and let Sabeth ride it. He put his own saddle on the mare and handed the sealed pouch to Aidris.

"Aldero is no place for valuables," he said.

He turned off, leading the mare tenderly down the ridge; the village was out of sight but they could see a thin trickle of smoke rising. The two girls rode on slowly towards a crossroad with an elm, where Loeke would come up from the village again. Sabeth, in high fettle, was giving Aidris some advice.

"You should grow your hair out and have it ironed straight," she said. "It gives a pleasing effect. You are what my mother calls a "pony girl." Green eyes are rare and attractive. You should wear a touch of green to bring out the color."

Aidris laughed aloud, and the laugh died in her throat. Telavel had heard the sound too; she pricked her ears and danced about. Riders coming behind them. She turned Telavel aside into the trees and called urgently to Sabeth.

"We must let them pass."

"The path is wide enough . . ."

"We must hide. Quickly!"

Elster, the well-mannered black gelding, obeyed, and they went further in.

"I don't see why . . ." whispered Sabeth.

"There is trouble in the Chameln lands," said Aidris. "You saw the troopers at Vigrund. And I have Master Loeke's gold pouch."

The riders came on, and she saw them with a stab of fear. Ten troopers of Mel'Nir, in painted strip mail, mounted on the monstrous horses bred to bear their weight. She heard at last the jingle of harness, the earth-shaking hoofbeats.

Sabeth shivered deliciously.

"Such big men," she whispered. "I have heard such tales . . . Some women are too small in the hips to bear their children. It happened to the Markgraf's youngest sister."

"Be quiet!" said Aidris.

She felt a wave of revulsion, remembering Aravel by her side, dropping poison. Up ahead the troopers drew to a clashing halt at the crossroads; now Sabeth was afraid.

"If they search?"

"We can outride them," said Aidris firmly. "We will go straight in among the trees. They cannot follow."

"We would be lost!"

There were shouted commands, then came a murmur of voices. Aidris urged Telavel gently through the trees and came just within earshot. The ten great horses stamped and snorted; she heard the rumbling voice of the officer, and a high quavering reply. The troopers were questioning an old woman. At first she wailed and pleaded for them to leave her alone, then came the end of a reply.

". . . Grafell Pass?"

The officer spoke again, and the old woman repeated the question.

"Travelers? Young maid? Shame on you, big bocks. There be no maids in Aldero!"

A ripple of laughter from the soldiers; the old woman cried out again:

"Am Firn? Am Firn? Here in the forest? Today or yesterday?"

The questioner prompted.

"Ah," she cried, "those ones? The black, the brown mare and the chameln grey? What about those ones?"

Aidris held her breath.

"Thank you," sang the old woman. "You're a king's son, my darling. Prince Pine will bless you, and Lady Rowan will deck your first-born's cradle. Those travelers are four hours ahead of you along this road to Grafell Pass. Straight on . . . turn downhill at the stone slide!"

There was a shout, and the whole troop took off at a gallop. Sabeth came up.

"They've gone!"

"She sent them away," said Aidris. "The old woman saved us. She had no love for the warriors of Mel'Nir."

She rode Telavel boldly out onto the road, and Sabeth followed, protesting. They came up to the crossroads with the tall elm, and there stood the old woman. Aidris had pictured her as small and bent, a Firnish old woman, but she was tall and grey-brown, like a tree in winter. As they came up, she stared and then laughed and gave a whistle. A thin black hound crept out of the bushes and came to heel.

"Look there!" sang the old woman. "Look there, dog dear— two beautiful princesses. Am Firn and Am Zor, the bright and the dark."

Aidris blushed; she looked at Sabeth, who only primped and laughed. She was used to compliments.

"What will *you* give me, children?" asked the old woman boldly. "Those incomers gave me bronze bits."

"Don't give her any more," said Sabeth. "She has turned her trick for today."

Aidris did not like this rudeness from Sabeth. She had intended to give the old woman money, but she had none in her pocket and dared not open the sealed pouch. She took a silver

49

ring, Nazran's gift, from the little finger of her left hand.

"My thanks . . ." she said. "What is your name good mother? Do you live in Aldero?"

The old woman took the ring, slipped it onto the tip of a bony finger. She smiled, and Aidris saw that her teeth were perfect still.

"I am Yekla," she said. "I am the horse doctor."

"You sent the troopers away to Grafells."

"They may not come safe home," said the old woman softly.

Aidris remembered the curse that had sounded like a blessing: a coffin of pine and a wreath of rowan.

"Give us a true blessing," she said, "and tell us which way to go."

"Your guide on the brown mare will know that," said Yekla. "The Carach trees will bless you when you come into Athron."

She strode off down the hill towards Aldero, followed by her lean hound, and turned back to cry out loudly, *"A virgin should not ride with a whore!"*

Aidris turned to Sabeth and saw her sitting very erect in the saddle, lips pressed together, like Sharn Am Zor when he tried to hold back tears. She hated the old woman's cruelty and felt ashamed of her own ignorance. She saw with pity that the cruel words were true. Sabeth was a fancy woman, one of the singing-girls of Balufir; anyone else would have seen it at once. She drew Telavel in close and bending over kissed Sabeth's pale, perfumed cheek.

"The old woman is mad!" she said. "She is teasing us."

Sabeth gave a wan smile. Ric Loeke was coming up the track from the village riding the brown mare. When he heard the story of the troopers, he became angry, his face dark as a thundercloud. Aidris caught a whiff of spirits on his breath, from the tavern at Aldero.

"The old witch did us a good turn," he said, "but now we must ride another way, by the Wulfental."

"Is it hard riding?" asked Sabeth. "Will it break my little bones?"

"We must go through some dark places to reach this pass," he said.

He took back the gold pouch but kept to Imba, the brown mare. He turned off on to a narrow track, and they followed; he led them on, unspeaking, deeper and deeper into the forest.

III

THEY WERE AMONG THE FOOTHILLS OF THE
mountains. The trees were dense and strange; a black beech
forest clothed the low hills. The valleys were dark as night, and
the trails they followed through the shaggy pines were like dank
tunnels. They came one nightfall up through the beech forest
to an open place on the crown of a hill. An old standing stone
rose up in the midst of a circle of hard, bleached grass, flattened
by wind and snow. Squat trees crouched at the edge of the
circle; the remains of a fire and some kind of shelter stood at
the foot of the dolmen. Loeke cursed and unexpectedly thumbed
his forehead in an old sign to ward off evil.

"The place has become a witch-hold," he said. "We must go
on further."

Sabeth moaned for sheer weariness and was echoed by a faint
bird cry. A small hawk flew up across the clearing and soared
away into the wind.

"It is a bleak place," said Aidris, "but what are the signs . . . ?"

"The stone is marked," said Loeke.

She saw black marks on the side of the stone nearest them
that might be runes.

"Please," she said. "Let me read those runes and speak a
prayer by the stone. We can pitch our camp here on the edge
of the trees. We are too tired to go further."

Ric Loeke stared at her a moment, considering, then nodded.
Telavel was restless; she did not care for the place. Aidris dismounted, then dug into her saddlebag and found the bronze
sword of the Firn. She did not buckle it on, but carried the
glittering scabbard as she approached the stone. It seemed to
be a long way off; she missed the shield of the trees.

The dolmen was of grey-white stone, twenty feet tall and
subtly shaped. It had grown into the earth. Colonies of lichen,
yellow, brown and white, patterned its surface. It had the grace
of a veiled woman brooding on the lonely hilltop. Large, angry
marks defaced the stone; there was a rune *om* and a rune *thorn*
and there were runes she did not know. She thought this must

51

be a strange speech with even the runes *om* and *thorn* having a different sound. The writing was done in a gritty brownish black paint or ink; she guessed it was a mixture of charcoal and blood.

"O Stone, O Goddess in the stone," she said, "I pray for deliverance, I pray that we may pass a safe night. I pray that rain will come to wash away the runes and purify this place. Grant my prayers in the name of the house of the Firn!"

She drew the sword and held it upright so that the runes on the blade were near the stone. Then, as she lowered the sword, she felt another person standing at her elbow and jumped, nervous as a shrewmouse. There was no one beside her. She walked to her right, sunwise, round the stone and came to an old tent frame and the ashes of a fire.

The evening wind was cool, here on the hilltop, but now she felt a thick, icy cold seeping up out of the ground. Among the ashes were bones and the blackened round of a small skull. A dead bird hung from a thread on the tent frame. She had come to a place where everything was crooked, where time and the natural world slid and shifted. Just out of earshot there were gusts of sound: shrieking, howling, cold voices, the hiss of arrows in flight and the beating of dark wings.

She turned, she was turned towards the stone, and it was black and shining, like a mirror of basalt. A man stood in the depths of the stone, half-turned towards her. He was pale faced, with flowing dark red hair, and his loose robe was blue, a midnight color, with snakes and vines writhing upon its hem. His arms were upraised; he turned slowly as if to make a circle, and in her mind a voice said: *"Sheath the sword. He will know you."*

Aidris gathered all her strength of will and sheathed the sword. Then she felt a stab of pain in her chest, a small bolt of lightning, and before the man in the stone had turned towards her, she fell backwards. She came out of the power of the stone and lay sprawling on the cold grass of the hilltop. The stone was grey and lichen-covered again, with an old campsite at its base. Yet she knew the stone for what it was: a watch post where that sorcerer looked out upon the world.

She felt the scrying stone, her own jewel, swinging cool against her skin; it had stabbed her with pain and driven her out of the circle of the sorcerer's power. She drew it out now, but it was without light; a few sparkles around its frame were all that remained. She scrambled up and ran back to the others.

"What is it?" cried Sabeth. "You look so pale. The witches have stolen your soul away!"

"Not yet," said Aidris. "You were right, Master Loeke, the standing stone is bewitched."

Ric Loeke cursed under his breath.

"Shall we go further?" he asked.

Aidris stared at the distant stone.

"No," she said. "We might as well stay here, in the lee of the stone."

They sat down, bone weary, and ate cold food. There was a spring across the clearing, but they watered the horses from their own water-skin. It was not a night for singing; Loeke stayed on watch, red-eyed, drinking his brandy.

"You're a brave lass," he said to Aidris.

She lay down to sleep in her tent and was glad when the moon, the great avatar of the Goddess, rose full and white over the hilltop. They broke camp early, just before dawn, and rode back the way they had come, then turned off on a new path into the next valley.

From this time, she believed, their journey was perilous. They were accursed, all three, and she could not tell whether this was the work of that watcher in the stone or whether it was their brief meeting with the accursed spot working on their own natures. They entered another damp, pine-filled valley, and all that day Ric Loeke paused to listen. He was silent as they rode, and when the girls talked in whispers, he called for silence. He said at last, "We're followed!"

Aidris could hear nothing but the noises of the forest: water trickling, the sough of the branches. Her old fear was awakened; when a bird flew up she started and made Telavel nervous. Sabeth had lost her cheerfulness; the long way was telling on her; her hands were blistered. She whispered to Aidris, "He's haunted. Don't you know why?"

Aidris shook her head.

"His applejack has run out."

It seemed no more than a joke, but Sabeth was perfectly serious. They camped again in a pleasant place, half out of a valley on a hillside, with a running stream where Loeke caught crawlers, delicious shell-backed creatures that lived under the stones.

"You call them freshwater crawlers," said Aidris at supper. "What are the other kind? From the sea?"

It turned out that she was the only one who had not seen the sea. Loeke, more surly and cross than ever, admitted that he had travelled once to Cayl and Port Cayl, south of Athron. Sabeth told one of her romances of a trip in a pleasure boat, down the Ringist, the smaller river that bordered Lien in the north as the Bal did in the south.

I will see the sea, thought Aidris, trying to imagine the boundless ocean, wider than the Danmar. I will go in exile to see the ocean.

Sabeth sang a chanty, a sailors' song, and would not sing certain verses because they were too gross.

"Oh, sing away," said Aidris, who hated her coyness. "I know the kedran songs and those from the stableyard."

"Those are songs of kedran love. . . ." said Sabeth.

"Are sailors so different?" asked Aidris.

Sabeth laughed aloud, and Loeke cursed them both into silence. He started up and prowled round the camp, listening again. For the first time Aidris fancied she did hear something: voices in the distance, a crackling of underbrush. She slept uneasily and woke once to hear Loeke and Sabeth quarrelling in the tent they shared. Next day the weather broke for the first time, and they pressed on through dripping branches that arched across the trail.

The eight days were past, this was the twelfth, and they seemed to be as far from the border as ever. They came to a place where the trail crossed a wider path and without warning ran straight up against another party of travellers. There was a small wagon like a pedlar's cart, with a fabulous beast painted upon the black side panels. Aidris took in three others besides the man driving the wagon: a middle-aged woman in a foot mantle, astride a sorrel pony; two mounted men in brown, full armed. One of these two was the leader; he challenged them boldly.

"Bound for the Wulfental?"

He had a scar that lifted the corner of his mouth and grey hair straggling from under his bronze helmet. Loeke gave a gruff assent, and the man rapped out more questions.

"Seen the Melniros? The big troopers? So far back?"

Then the man on the wagon passed a word to the woman who passed it in turn to the leader. Aidris felt her whole body grow cold. The man on the wagon was bearded, he wore a soft hat with a dagged tail and a pheasant's feather, but she knew him. It was Jalmar Raiz, the Healer. She wondered if his two sons were crouched inside the wagon, if he would suddenly denounce her.

"I'm Hulth, woodcutter," said the leader. "These are my people and I know them."

Ric Loeke answered in his gruff way.

"We've nothing to hide. I'm Loeke, forest guide out of Vigrund."

He nudged Sabeth to speak up.

"I am a daughter of the house of Delbin," she said loftily, from the depths of her green hood. "Mistress Delbin of Lien, travelling to Varda."

"Kedran Venn, travelling to Varda," said Aidris, who had worked out her false name long before.

Her voice sounded strained and unnatural. The bearded man gave no sign; she began to have doubts, to think she must be mistaken.

"The Melniros have driven out the Chameln rulers," said Hulth suddenly. "They comb the forest for a certain royal lady . . . a good price on her head."

Aidris tightened her grip on Telavel's rein, ready to make a run for it. Ric Loeke was solid as a rock.

"Let 'em fight their own battles," he said. "You and I, friend woodcutter, do the best we can. Can you spare me a bit to drink?"

Hulth turned down his mouth, but Loeke persisted.

"Just for myself," he said. "Surely your 'woodcutting,' down in the Adze, has yielded a few good logs!"

Aidris understood. Hulth and his party were not woodcutters at all but illicit miners. The Adze, a wedge of territory, bordering on Lien, had silver and precious stones in its hills. Grumbling, Hulth went to the back of the wagon; Loeke passed over some coin and two leather flasks to be filled.

She kept her eyes down. Then when they were ready to ride off, she found the second horseman at her side, tall and muscular, his face swathed below his helmet. His eyes were a sad dark blue; it was Raff Raiz.

"Go well, kedran!" His voice was muffled.

She was past before there was time to smile. She felt a pang of regret and wished that he was her travelling companion. She turned and waved, and he waved back as the other cavalcade began to move on.

When they were out of earshot, Sabeth burst out indignantly, "Scar-faced brute, asking questions. And that fat woman in the foot mantle is no better than she should be. Serves them all with more than pease porridge."

Ric Loeke, after a pull at his new-filled flask, told her to hold her tongue.

They came through a very long valley with the trail winding slowly upward. The camping place was like their very first because it was not far from a lake. The forest had changed: this glade was darker, even more beautiful, with young pointed spruce and gum pines tightly pressed in a circle. The lake was a mountain tarn, still and blue-black. At its rim Aidris found moss springing with star-shaped greenish flowers and runes of the Tulgai in white bird-lime on a black stone.

"This is Tulna Lake," said Ric Loeke, "the home water of the Tulgai. You may see them sailing in bark boats no bigger than cradles."

They were all in high spirits; dangers seemed to have been passed. She helped Sabeth cook up a stew of corned lamb and onions, more than they had eaten for several days. The fire blazed up, and Loeke, more cheerful, gave each girl a few sips of the new liquor. They sang songs together for the first time.

"Listen to that!" said Loeke. "Wind getting up. We'll have more rain tonight."

The wind played a new sound in the tops of the trees, but down below by the fire it was cosy as a round room. The smoke and sparks whirled upward, and overhead Aidris thought she could just make out the night sky and the stars.

Sabeth, her cheeks rosy from the fire, combed out her hair and spread it over her shoulders like a bright mantle. She confided to Aidris, "I'm glad you came along. It would have been tedious..."

"Your mother could not travel."

"She is not my mother," said Sabeth, still confiding. "Oh,

she is called Mother Lorse or Widow Lorse, and I called her that too. We have been together for four years, and she has taught me a good deal. But I am an orphan . . . my real parents were somewhat finer."

She gave Aidris a sharp look.

"I know what you are thinking!" she said. "That old wish-dream of being a noble foundling. Every girl wishes to be a princess."

Aidris could only stare in astonishment.

"Who would wish *that?*"

Sabeth stroked back her fiery mantle of hair.

"Anyone would want fine clothes and jewels," she said. "Palaces and country houses to live in, noble companions, servants to command!"

Aidris could not answer; she felt an emptiness, as if part of her soul *had* been stolen away. She went off to check the horses as she did every night, and when she returned, Sabeth had already gone to her tent. Ric Loeke had lost his customary scowl, the lines had gone out of his face.

"Sit down again," he said. "Drink one more sup. You are a brave lass, Dan Aidris, and bore yourself well today, with those diggers."

She sat down again, pleased to hear him so genial.

"Have we far to go?" she asked. "Is this the Wulfental?"

"Not far, not far," he said. "I know the way, never fear. Know the forest like the palm of my hand. My old man would have had me for another huntsman, another royal huntsman, for the Zor."

She saw that he was drunk and had an urge to speak. She had seen many people who were tipsy or drunk, usually at feasts or banquets. They frightened her a little because they were "out of themselves." She remembered, suddenly, that long ago, when she was very small, she had burst into tears when someone, a tall man, swept her into his arms and danced about with her. Then her mother came and told her to hush, not to be a silly goose.

"A damned bad hunter . . ." rambled Ric Loeke, giving her a smile. "I would not be bound to him, Princess. A fool with horses, a fool with dogs, blind to a spoor and clumsy with his weapons, poor devil. He led my old man a rare dance in that bit of a Hain."

She realised he was talking about Esher Am Zor and was embarrassed, for the dead king and for Loeke, who might regret what he had said.

"My uncle loved to hunt," she said, trying not to sound stiff. "It is a pity he was no hand at it."

"You ride well," said Loeke. "A princess . . . a little kedran maid of the Firn. A brave little lass. Come to be queen one day and the mother of royal children."

"I hope so."

She knew he was too familiar; he smiled and stared, with burning dark eyes. When his attention wandered for a moment, she gave a goodnight and went to her tent, glad to get away.

As she was on the verge of sleep, all her fears held at bay, Ric Loeke crawled into her tent. He sprawled heavily across her body, and she was wide awake in a panic. Yet she could not believe he knew what he was doing; he had gone to the wrong tent. She struggled and pushed, not wanting to hurt him or to cry out too loudly. She whispered in furious embarrassment, calling him "Master Loeke," telling him to go, go to the other tent. He held her tightly, thrust a knee between her legs, ran wet lips over her face. "Princess . . . a little virgin maid . . . a sweet vessel . . ."

She became mad and terrified. She fought wildly, scratching, struggling in despair as she felt his strength. He panted, laughed a little; she was screaming aloud. Then he swung away, changing his grip, and she went out under the side of the small tent. She knelt on all fours, gasping, then ran towards the fire. Loeke came blundering out of the front of the tent. He caught her ankles, flinging her to the ground so hard that she was winded. Then he hauled her long underdrawers over her stockinged feet, past her knees.

She tried to double up but he was on her again; she struck his eyes, his mouth; he held her shoulders against the ground. Her breath was still uncertain but she managed to cry out, louder and louder, until he hit her in the face. She felt a stone in her left hand and as he fumbled at his own breeches she beat at his temple, twisting and turning her lower body to forbid his entry.

Sabeth was there, dragging at Loeke and crying out. She fastened on one of his arms and clung like a burr, finally wrenching him away. Aidris crawled, stumbled and ran off behind her own tent into the darkness. She was bruised and scratched and her ribs ached; she was dying of disgust and shame. She thought of the sword in her tent; she thought of driving it between her ribs. Yet she was a virgin still.

Voices from the camp increased her self-disgust; she had left Sabeth alone, coping with the monster. She hitched up her tattered drawers, smeared her tears away and went round the tent, ready to plunge in after her sword.

Ric Loeke sat on the ground, and Sabeth was giving him a drink from her own silver cup. She saw Aidris and gestured behind Loeke's back: *keep out of sight.* Sabeth's face in the fire-light was hard, softening only when she turned back towards Loeke, crooning, soothing his bleeding face with a kerchief.

Aidris crawled into the tent again, shaking with pain and weariness. She sat in the bracken-smelling darkness and wished for death.

After a long time, Sabeth came into the tent.

"He's off," she said. "Sound asleep in the other tent."

Aidris began to weep. Sabeth flung back a flap of the tent to see her better.

"Come," she said, "come then . . ."

She had the kerchief wrung out in water, and she unfolded Aidris like a child and wiped her face and her body.

"Did he . . .?" she asked, almost matter-of-fact.

"No," said Aidris.

Then the mystery of the thing overcame her and she clung to Sabeth, crying and questioning. Why would he? Why? She had done nothing. She had not been lewd or forward or over-friendly. He had given no warning. Why would he treat her so when he had sworn to bring her safely to Athron and knew her for . . . a maid.

"Hush," said Sabeth. "You did nothing. No one blames you, no one will ever know of it."

"But why?"

"The new spirit was very strong. Loeke was drunk. It takes some men that way."

Aidris was conscious of many things that she could not say, which had some bearing on the mystery. Why would Loeke neglect his beautiful companion, his leman, and come to her? There could only be one reason: her royal blood. He was two-minded: a virgin princess was to be protected or to be used

59

brutally, as if her royalty was a goad or a temptation.

Sabeth brought her silver cup with water and spirit and ordered her to drink.

"It has medicine in it. Mother Lorse gave me a sleeping powder—I fed it to Loeke. You must have some too; you must sleep sound."

Aidris lay down under her fur cloak still shuddering, still weary of her life.

"I will stay here," said Sabeth. "I wish we were come into Athron."

She lay down on the bracken under her own green cloak. They both heard light rain come down and the wind in the high tops of the trees.

Aidris woke in broad daylight with Sabeth shaking her. She gave a cry as she remembered what had happened; Sabeth was pale-faced.

"Loeke has gone. He is not in the tent."

Aidris swung up and looked out; Elster, the black gelding, was still tethered with the other horses.

"He must be round about," she said. "Has he gone to the lake to wash?"

"I looked down the path," said Sabeth, "but he is not to be seen. Then as I came back into camp I thought I saw something among the trees..."

"What was it?"

Aidris reached for the sword, which lay unsheathed.

"A fairy," said Sabeth, her face crumpling with tears. "A little dark thing. I am so afraid."

"Oh, it is one of the Tulgai," said Aidris. "They are nothing to fear, truly. I will go to the lake and wash. Make up the fire... Loeke will come back."

Aidris took fresh clothes and took her sword. She went down the path wrapped in her cloak. She was sore and stiff and dared not think of what had passed. She did not wish to see Ric Loeke again and wondered how they could travel together after what he had done. She went along the lake shore a little beyond the place where the path ended and washed as thoroughly as she could in the icy water of the tarn. She climbed shivering into her leather breeches and her tunic.

It had rained heavily in the night; now the sky was clear,

but there was a stiff wind blowing. It whipped up small black billows on the lake and tore among the pines by the shore. Aidris had one instant of foreboding, like the tolling of a bell. As she turned back towards the camp, she saw a dark trough in the leaves beside the path . . . on her way down it had been hidden by a sapling. She stepped warily across the damp ground: a pit had opened. It was a hunting-fall of the Tulgai, cunningly roofed with leaves and boughs. She looked in and knew what she would find.

Ric Loeke lay at the bottom of the pit, his face deep in muddy water. Aidris looked up and saw Sabeth at the top of the path, peering fearfully.

"Come here!" she called.

She leaped down into the pit, heaving at the stiffened limbs, lifting up the damp head. Sabeth looked down and gave a glad cry.

"He is dead," said Aidris. "He fell into the trap and could not get up again."

Loeke's eyes were glazed, a froth of bubbles oozed from his nostrils. He was cold, and his arms and legs were stiffening against the sides of the pit. Aidris climbed out and sat in the leaves. She felt a black wave of nausea and guilt; she had wished the man dead, and now he lay at her feet. She wondered then if this was all some evil working pursuing her, as it had done all her life.

Sabeth had gone down into the pit. Now she dragged herself out and fell into a passion of weeping. Aidris put her arms around her, but she would not be comforted.

"Was he your sweetheart?" asked Aidris helplessly.

"*He was our guide!*" cried Sabeth. "We are lost. He is dead, and we are lost in the forest!"

Then Aidris felt a deep loss, a real regret for this useless death. Ric Loeke had known the forest; he had guided them well, as he had guided other travellers. Now there was no one to mourn for him; he was gone in a breath, in a few gulps of fiery spirit, one drunken night among many. They would come out of the forest, she felt certain of it, but he would never wake.

She helped Sabeth back to the camp. The fire had come up again, and they ate a little dried fruit and drank water. Aidris watered the horses and gave them some oats; she packed her own saddlebags and folded her tent as best she could, then went into the other tent and brought out Loeke's saddlebags and the sealed pouch and took them to Sabeth, by the fire.

Sabeth was more composed; she gave Aidris a very sharp look.

"The money," she said. "His treasure."

"What did he tell you about this journey?" asked Aidris.

It was one of the moments when she was ready to tell all. She had almost trusted Sabeth or expected her to guess the truth a hundred times.

"He was bringing a treasure into Athron," said Sabeth with a queer light in her eyes.

"And about myself?"

"Why, that you are going to some Varda merchant's house to be trained as a kedran."

Aidris was more deeply puzzled than ever. Loeke had kept his oath; he had told nothing to Sabeth. Perhaps he disregarded her as a mere singing-girl, or distrusted her. Perhaps he had talked, and Sabeth had simply not grasped the truth.

"The treasure in the pouch belongs to my house," said Aidris. "It is my keep, in Varda. I am forced to go there because of the warriors of Mel'Nir; our family is loyal to the rulers of the Chameln."

Whatever she thought of this, Aidris could see that Sabeth only half-believed the information about Loeke's treasure.

"Who can deny us the money?" she asked. "Did your people pay him to guide you?"

"I expect so," said Aidris. "What was the sum?"

"Fifty silver dumps," said Sabeth promptly. "Five gold gulden or four gold royals from Lien."

"Did you pay so much?"

"Mother Lorse was his friend," said Sabeth. "A friend to all the forest guides. I travelled free and bore him company."

"Where are you going?"

"To a lady's house in Varda," said Sabeth very precisely, "to be her waiting-woman."

"Break the seal," said Aidris, "and you will find in the treasure pouch gold and at least two strings of pearl beads and a golden apple on a chain."

Sabeth went to work, breaking the seal, which showed the double oak trees of the Daindru, without examining it. She poured out gold and silver onto their table stone and held up pearls, three strings, and the apple on its chain.

"It *is* yours then," she said with a pout.

Aidris packed the money away. She took a string of the pearls and slipped them over Sabeth's head.

"Yours," she said. "And we will share the gold."

Sabeth fingered the bubbled, milky pearls in wonder.

"They are freshwater pearls," she said, "from the Danner-mere. A string like this is worth a lot. I thought you meant mother-of-pearl beads, as they sell in Balufir. Your house is richer than I thought."

"Hush," said Aidris. "I am going into exile."

She turned reluctantly to Ric Loeke's saddlebags.

"Master Loeke had kin in Achamar, that I know," she said, "but did he have friends in Vigrund?"

"His fellow forest guides," said Sabeth. "He lived in their guild house."

"I will take out all the food and any maps," said Aidris. "The rest should go back to the guild house, with his horse."

"How?" exclaimed Sabeth angrily. "You are mad. We are lost. We will be robbed and murdered. We will never find our way."

Aidris set her teeth and picked over Loeke's excellently neat and ordered possessions. She took out the maps and a letter, sealed with a butterfly in pink wax; Sabeth snatched it away, but not before Aidris had read the address in a fat sprawling merchant's script full of curlicues: At the sign of the dove, Fountain Court, Varda.

"It is from Mother Lorse to the lady of the house, the household, where I am going." she said.

There were no ornaments, no mementoes, only the well-kept equipment of a guide. She was a carrion crow picking out a dead man's eyes. She found a purse of gold and added five gulden to it. Perhaps Nazran had already paid for her journey . . . she did not know. All had hung on Ric Loeke, and he was gone.

"I can get help," said Aidris, "but you must be brave."

"What do you mean?" asked Sabeth.

"You must wait here, alone, with the horses. I will go round the lake, on foot, and find the fairy-folk, the Tulgai."

"No!" said Sabeth. "No, I must come with you. Why will you leave me? I cannot *guard* the horses. Please, please don't leave me here alone in this place, with the dead so close . . ."

"You don't understand," said Aidris. "The Tulgai are a very shy and secret people. Even I cannot be sure of finding them, although I speak their language. But I must ask them to help us. It is our only hope."

It was a bleak prospect, yet she could think of nothing else to do. They crept about the camp and packed up all their belongings. Sabeth had not even a tent to shelter in if it rained. She looked so woebegone, shivering by the miserable fire. The green cloak was too thin and had rents in it from the journey. Aidris took her new fur cloak, Bajan's gift, from where it lay on her saddlebag and put it around Sabeth's shoulders.

"You will be cold, later . . ." whispered Sabeth.

Aidris took up Ric Loeke's short riding cloak of dressed russet leather. It fitted well enough; she had already buckled on her sword.

"I will hurry," she said. "Keep up the fire."

CHAPTER
III

BEFORE SABETH COULD ANSWER, AIDRIS RAN OFF down the path. She dared not think of their helplessness. She turned aside to go round the head of Lake Tulna; the pointed spruce grew right down to the water's edge. There were no shallows, only a bed of sharp stones, shelving into icy depths. Aidris pushed into the trees, fought through their ranks and was driven out by bundles of thorns set between the trees. She crawled and scrambled around the barricade of trees on the very edge of the water.

Beyond lay a wide clearing where the forest had been thinned. The trees grew in clumps among the forest grasses, and there were thickets of berries: blackberry, blueberry, cranberry, beside a path. She was certain that this was the land of the Tulgai; there was an enclosure of undressed logs beside the path, but it was empty.

"Where are you, brave warriors?" she called.

There was no answer, not even a rustle in the trees ahead. She hurried on down the path and came to a second rustic enclosure where six milch deer were grazing, with their fawns.

"Warriors of the Tulgai—I need your help!" she cried again.

There was a flurry of movement in a tree, a burst of sound: bird-calls echoing over the quiet lake. She passed the second enclosure and saw ahead a grove of trees curiously shaped. Before she could call again, Aidris was surrounded. A ring of Tulgai warriors, swart and strong, appeared in a breath. Their long curled manes of hair glistened; they advanced with very long metal-tipped spears held shoulder high by two men.

"Stranger! Keep out!" cried a voice in the common speech. It was a gnarled old woman with a milk pail.

"I need the help of the Tulgai," said Aidris keeping to the Old Speech and holding her ground.

A warrior laughed, and with his companion brought his spear very close.

"You are a longshanks woman!" he shouted.

Aidris felt a thrill of righteous anger; she struck the spear aside.

"Receive me in peace then!"

"Why should we?" shouted the little man. *"You must fear us in this place. You have invaded our sanctuary."*

He gestured, and the ring of warriors began to grimace and to jump up and down. It was ridiculous and frightening.

"Stop!" cried Aidris.

She drew her sword and flourished it. A beam of watery sunlight caught the blade, and it flashed fire.

"Do you read these runes? I am Aidris, Heir of the Firn!"

The movement stopped in mid-bounce; the Tulgai reacted, always, with a swiftness that was unnerving for a *kizho*, a longshanks. The hideous grins were frozen on their faces for a split second, then wiped away or transformed into timid smiles. The leader who had taunted her ran up to Aidris, glanced at the sword and stared into her eyes.

"Forgive me!"

He fell on his knees, but she quickly raised him up.

"Forgiven," she said. *"No ceremony."*

She held up the sword to the ring of warriors and said, *"Dear warriors of the Tulgai, I come in an evil hour, travelling into exile.*

I will have no rejoicing, only help for my journey. I will sheath the sword until a happier day when I return."

She returned the sword to its sheath, and a ripple of sound, a sorrowful murmur, was drawn from those watching.

"What shall I call you?" she asked the leader.

He was a youngish man, about thirty years old, so far as she could judge, with hair of rusty black confined by a bone clasp then falling in long curls to his boot heels. He had a broad, handsome brow and light hazel eyes.

"Akaranok!" he said. *"First Watcher."*

"Good Akaranok—have you heard that a dead man lies by the lake shore, just beyond your barricade?"

"No such thing reported, Dan Aidris," he said. *"Who is this man?"*

"Alas, it is Ric Loeke, a forest guide, who was leading another lady and myself into Athron."

"Princess, how did he die?"

"By accident. In the night or early morning he stumbled into a pitfall. He had drink taken and could not come out of the trench again. He lay in water and drowned."

The telling made her sick; she swayed on her feet and shut her eyes. There was a burst of concerned chatter. Many hands fastened upon her gently; she found herself urged forward and settled upon a pile of logs up against the fence of the deer pen. The old woman with the milk pail and another, sturdy and young, with red cheeks and hair fantastically braided, were tending her. They held a cup with fresh water to her lips and crushed a leaf of lemon balm for her to sniff, against faintness.

"Akaranok?" she asked.

"Here, Princess."

He stood before her again, their eyes on a level.

"You know what help I need. The poor man must be buried, his horse and gear returned to the guild-house at Vigrund town. Then I need a guide to bring me and my friend through the Wulfental Pass into Athron."

"We will do all of this...all that we can," he said.

"My poor companion, the lady Sabeth, sits alone in our camp, near the lake. Our horses and baggage are unguarded..."

"We will set a watch at once!"

"Akaranok," she said. *"Sabeth knows nothing of the forest or of your people. Do not frighten her, I pray."*

He gave one of his ferocious Tulgai smiles.

"Not a leaf will stir..."

"Then, let me go to the Balg, if he will receive me."

"He waits...he waits..."

Akaranok gestured, and there was a bustling high and low, bursts of bird-calling, strange drum music and the music of Tulgai voices. She stood up, thanking the little women, and there was a carrying seat for her. A dozen warriors had made a frame with their spears. She sat on this platform, and they lifted her shoulder high.

"Feather light!" cried one. *"Light as a true Tulgai!"*

So she was borne through the sunlit woods past the tilled strips, the flowering apple trees, the low, reeking smokehouses of this most secret people. They came to the shaped trees, and Aidris saw that the tops of the trees, which were sturdy mountain beech, grew through a wide canopy of basketwork and thatch. Their trunks were the living pillars of the hall of the Balg, and between the pillars were walls of short dressed logs, polished and engraved with runes, in bright colors.

There were similar buildings clustered around the hall, and the earth was trodden bare and smooth between them. She was set down on a deeply trodden path. The forest trees, the dark conifers, ringed the settlement closely, so that there was not much light. It was as if the Tulgai lived here always under cover, in a huge tent.

The place teemed with people, but they were hardly to be seen. Dark faces looked down from the very tops of the trees; there were rustlings all over the roof of the great hall. A bush at her side suddenly became overladen and spilled out before her six or seven creatures...little children, the littlest children, plump, brown, half-naked, with their hair scraped up into bunches on the tops of their heads. She half-screamed, half-laughed, and one, bolder than the rest, scrambled up her cloak and sat on her shoulder.

She took the climber between her hands and held it before her face. It stared at her with huge brown eyes. As it was opening its mouth to roar, she gave it a kiss on the cheek and set it down in the bush again.

There were guards before the hall, but Akaranok would not step aside for them; he was determined to lead Aidris into the Balg's presence himself. They came into a corridor lined with painted bark where it was impossible for Aidris to stand upright. Ahead there was a greenish light; they came out into wide airy spaces. The roof overhead had panels of the thatch lifted off or rolled back so that sunlight came in through the leaves.

The hall had been made beautiful for spring. It was like a glade, with the tree-trunk pillars painted white, fur rugs upon the earthen floor of a surprising yellow-green, and a fountain playing in the center, from a gilded tree stump. Behind this fountain rose a wooden screen carved with slender young trees, their branches interlaced.

Akaranok was received at the screen by an old man in a green robe. His beard was snow white and carefully divided into two long forks that fell past his knees. He bowed to Aidris, then took her hands tenderly and stared up into her face.

"Dear child..." he said in a deep cracked voice. *"I have seen none of your house since I brought tribute once to Charis, your father's mother. I am called Rognor; I am the Balg's Runemaster. I cast the runesticks yesterday for the Balg's lake journey, and there it seemed to say: Death brings an honored guest..."*

"It is very plain, good Runemaster," said Aidris. *"My forest guide is dead, by accident, and I have come to you for help."*

Akaranok was impatient. He whispered to Rognor, peered round the screen.

"Is this a feast day for the Balg?" asked Aidris. *"Have I intruded upon some festival?"*

"You were awaited," said the Rune-master. *"The royal household hoped for a sign. Now they can embark. It is that day of the year when the Balg sails across the Tulna water."*

He took up his painted staff and struck a long wooden drum that lay by the screen; it gave off a sweet, hollow note. He led the way into the presence of his master, Tagnaran, the Balg of the Tulgai.

The ruler sat upon a carved wooden throne, set not on a platform but on a small hill, roughly stepped in places and covered with pelts. Clusters of servants waited around the base of the hillock, and Aidris saw that they were prepared for the Balg's feast. They carried baskets of food, garlands of leaves, even long netted fish-poles and hanks of rope.

Aidris had it fixed in her mind that the Balg was old and fat. A description of some earlier Balg glimpsed by a chronicler had given her the image of a spreading white-bearded King Toad, somewhat taller than his subjects. It had never occurred to her that the Balg might be a young man.

Tagnaran had short up-curling hair of coppery red, a royal color not found among his subjects; even his skin was red-brown. His smooth face, with wide-set yellow-brown eyes, had the startled beauty of a forest creature. He wore a short tunic of creamy linen and laced high sandals; on his head was a circlet of bronze set with jade and pearls. He was at least four feet in height, much taller than Akaranok or Rognor, but of a height with those who shared his hillock, an older man and two women.

At his side, wearing a pearl crown and a short dress of iridescent feathers, was an exquisite young girl, springtime itself. Her hair, feathery and short, was red-gold, Sabeth's color. When Aidris entered, she hid her face behind a feather fan and gave her hand to the second woman, dressed in a tunic of spotted fur, who sprawled below the throne. The second man stood behind the throne and sipped from a drinking horn, his auburn mane falling into his eyes, his gaze hard and penetrating.

Akaranok ran forward at once and prostrated himself at the base of the hillock. Tagnaran came slowly from his throne, raised up his officer and spoke urgently with him. They looked several times at Aidris, where she stood or towered, and Rognor at last touched her arm. She went forward and knelt before the Balg.

"Royal Tagnaran," she said, "I am sorry to disturb the peace of the Tulgai."

He raised her up, keeping his place on the hill so that he remained taller than Aidris. His hand was strong, with pointed nails and finger rings of silver and gold.

"You are in flight!" said Tagnaran in a high voice.

"I must go into Athron," said Aidris, puzzled by the sharpness of his tone.

"You have lost all," said the Balg. "You have no land, no throne, no hall, no sanctuary."

Aidris shook her head.

"No, cousin," she said. "I have none of these things."

"You have been ill-served then, ill-advised," said Tagnaran. "You are half a child, wandering in the forest, begging for help."

"This is my native land," said Aidris, "even if I never come to rule over it. I am a traveller. I am not without means. I have asked for a guide to the Wulfental Pass. Will you give me one?"

"*Stay here!*" said the Balg abruptly. "*You are Heir of the Firn. We pay tribute to the Daindru. Let this be our tribute. You will stay here in the sanctuary.*"

"*No!*" said Aidris. "*Pardon me, Tagnaran, but I cannot do it. I have a companion waiting. Besides I would endanger the Tulgai . . . the giant warriors of Mel'Nir are searching for me.*"

"*Oh, we are used to giants!*" The Balg laughed. "*Stay with us, Aidris Am Firn.*"

"*Alas, I cannot, for my honor. Pardon me again for disturbing your feast day.*"

Tagnaran stared at her for a long time with a hard, imperious look. He was more than ever like a creature of the forest, but made fierce, ungentle, a stag no longer at bay, a lynx ready to pounce. Aidris knew with a thrill of fear that she could be kept against her will. She lowered her gaze deliberately and murmured, "*Royal Tagnaran—I would be poor indeed if I offered you no gift.*"

She brought out the hastily assembled package from the pocket of her borrowed cloak and offered it on her open palms. The Balg picked it up himself and, turning, carried it to the two ladies of his court. The lovely feather-clad maiden, his consort, had it unwrapped quickly and made birdlike sounds of delight. Aidris saw the Balg's slow, indulgent smile. She knew that she had been saved by two new silk scarves from Sabeth's pack and the golden apple of the Firn on its long gold chain.

"*We stay too long,*" said Tagnaran. "*Our days are ordered, cousin Aidris. We must cross the lake.*"

He waved a hand; there was a burst of music, and the court began to move towards wide double doors across the hall between tree pillars. He came to the foot of the hillock and said briskly, "*Akaranok will guide you. He may choose his own helpers. As far as the Lylan River, hard by the Wulfental.*"

Then he strode lightly from the hall in the midst of his people, giving his arm to the bird princess. Aidris stood with Akaranok and Rognor until the hall was almost empty. The Runemaster touched her arm.

"*We must see them set sail.*"

So they came out onto wide grassy lawns sloping down to the lakeside. The Balg and his family were embarked in a gilded shallop, its painted sails already taking the wind. Aidris felt a sudden regret, a longing, as the pretty boat began to move away from the shore. A shoal of smaller craft streamed out to follow: the fishing boats of the Tulgai, no bigger than cradles.

She was led out of the sanctuary by a narrow winding path that led up a hillside, avoiding the barrier by the lake. Akaranok pointed the way, and she ran downhill, found herself on the outskirts of the camping place. It sprang up before her, dark, cold, rank-smelling as the ashes of the fire, full of images from the world of men. Sabeth, rushing from behind a tree at her call, seemed tall as a bear. Her face was pale and tear-stained.

"Oh, have you found them?"

Her voice wavered into silence as Akaranok marched out into the midst of the glade. She put out a hand, wondering, and the little man kissed it gallantly.

"We are saved," said Aidris. "They must show themselves. Don't be frightened."

Akaranok gave a bird-call, and the place was teeming with warriors. The horses began to plunge and fret.

"Loeke?" whispered Sabeth. "Will they . . .?"

"He will be tended to. We must send back Elster and his pack."

"Mother Lorse will worry when his horse is brought in!"

"Write her a few lines," said Aidris. "I have a writing case. I will send a note of his death to the guild house and say that his last travellers are going on into Athron. But say no word of the Tulgai . . ."

They were on their way again before noon. Only Akaranok rode with them, perched before Aidris upon Telavel's neck. Three of his chosen companions went along Tulgai fashion, swinging through the tree branches, high above the ground. Even by Aidris and Sabeth, who knew they were accompanied, this escort was hardly to be seen. Now and then at the turn of a path they came into view or gave a sharp bird-note to which Akaranok responded.

The paths that were chosen led steeply upward through trees that were always dark and in some places oddly flattened and twisted by the wind. At last Aidris had some hint of the end of the journey. Through a cleft or rock slide, she caught a glimpse of naked slopes, drifts of unmelted snow and, at last, the summits of the mountains.

Their camping places, also chosen by the Tulgai, were small and secret. Often they had no fire, and wherever a fire must be lit, Aidris and Sabeth must do it. They bent over little mounds of twigs and leaves with Ric Loeke's tinderbox, coaxing out a thread of smoke. The Tulgai brought in a small haunch of fresh meat, about as much as the girls could contrive to stew up or cook clumsily on a spit. When Aidris asked about the rest of the deer, Akaranok laughed and told them it would hang in the trees until the warriors collected it on the way home.

So they came at last, one morning, to the lip of a high gorge. Far below, in the depths of the grey ravine, was a flash of silver—the river Lylan. It had been explained that this was as far as their guides could take them.

"The Lylan is the river of souls," Akaranok had told Aidris, at night by a smoky fire. *"It is our boundary in this life and the next. We will bring you to the Litch Bridge, also called the Bridge of Wraiths, Dan Aidris, and there we must leave you."*

Now, as they stood on the cliff above the river, the tradition was harder to grasp. They could see over the river. There was a mountain meadow, bright with rare plants, enzian and snow violets, and a perfect round tarn. The road to the Wulfental wound past this place, and the jagged peaks that enclosed the pass itself could be seen. There was a low building in the meadow, a loghouse; smoke curled up from a hut on the shore of the tarn.

"Dear Goddess!" cried Sabeth, "that *is* some kind of paradise. They have a bathhouse!"

"Who lives in the meadow?" asked Aidris.

"The brown men," said Akaranok.

"I have heard of this place," she said to Sabeth. "It is a hospice for travellers, built by the Pilgrim Brothers of Inokoi."

She was afraid again. She could see the road leading up to the hospice on the other side of the gorge, an easier road than they had taken. It would not be difficult to close the Wulfental or to watch travellers who came and went over the pass. She showed Ric Loeke's map to Akaranok, and he was able to mark out another way, a secret way they might take, once the hospice was past.

"There is the longshanks road," he said, "but if you go on a little and turn up left, past a finger rock, there is a trail . . ."

"Wait!" said Aidris. "How do you know this if no Tulgai, no living Tulgai, has ever crossed the river?"

He said patiently, "Princess, it is the way of the deer and the horned sheep."

"And they told you about it?"

Akaranok grinned, lowering his thick eyelashes.

"It can be seen from the tops of the trees," he admitted. "Only a Tulgai can follow it. We can see the place where the animals come through the Wolf Pass in spring or autumn, then leap over the Lylan gorge, higher up."

She was reassured. Sabeth, dying for the comforts of the hospice, could not understand the delay. They went down the bank of the gorge, and there was the Litch Bridge, of firm, worldly planking, with a good railing.

"What can I give you and your companions?" she said to Akaranok. "We owe you more than we can ever repay. You know our possessions. Will you have gold? Will you have cloth?"

The four Tulgai divided up Ric Loeke's smaller cooking vessels, his folding canteen of cutlery, two more scarves from Sabeth, a "housewife" with needles and thread that Lady Maren had packed for Aidris. Aidris and Sabeth rode onto the bridge and crossed, not looking down. Aidris turned back and waved and thought she heard a last bird call, but saw nothing, only the fir trees.

They rode down into the meadow, and it was even wider and more beautiful than it had appeared from across the river. They got down and let the horses, still saddled and laden, crop the green grass. There was a smoking chimney at the log house. They strolled closer, and a figure ran around the corner of the building: a young man in the brown homespun robe of the Brothers. He came on, running up the path, and stopped short a few yards from them, in a curious attitude, as if he might take flight. His robe was kilted up into a leather vest, showing his bare, bony legs. His neck, his wrists, protruding from the brown robe, were all bird thin; his face was hollow-cheeked, the eyes sunken in bony sockets—the skull visible beneath the skin.

"Stop!" he called. "Stop! Where is your guide?"

"I am the guide," said Aidris. "May we visit your hospice, Brother?"

"No!" he shouted. "No—keep off! Lead your horses!"

Aidris walked on; the young man stood still, trembling, then backed a few steps, then forced himself to stand still again. When she was about two yards distant, Aidris said, "What is the matter? May we use the bathhouse? We have come a long way; this lady is faint and weary."

The young man would not raise his eyes.

"No guide . . ." he mumbled.

"We can pay," said Sabeth, smiling winningly. "We can make an offering, dear Brother."

The young man lifted his head and stared at her with an expression of fear and loathing.

"You should not call me brother," he said in a nervous croak. "I am Dirk, one of the callants, the learners."

"Can we go to the bathhouse?" asked Aidris.

"It's ready," he said. "No one is there."

"Will you attend to our horses?" she asked.

He nodded. She had a piece of silver ready, but when she held it out to the callant, he backed away. She ran and took the reins of the horses, gorging themselves on the lush grass, and brought them to the path with some difficulty. Sabeth came to help; they removed their saddlebags. The young man stood with his eyes cast down. Before Aidris could hand over the horses, she was relieved to see a second "brown man," middle-aged and bearded, walking smartly down the path towards them.

"Well, Dirk?" he said. "Are you punished enough?"

The callant cringed and began to weep, wringing his thin hands.

"Good Brother," said Aidris, "can our horses be stabled?"

The Brother's gaze flicked coldly over herself and Sabeth and the two restless horses.

"What do they tell you, Dirk?" he asked.

"The b-breeched one is guide," whispered Dirk. "They wanted to go to the bathhouse. They offered m-money."

"Very good," said the Brother. "You may go and purify yourself."

The callant knelt down and kissed the brother's dusty clogs, then ran off, his legs flying out. The brother watched him with a faint, tender smile, then turned at last to Aidris and Sabeth.

"Now," he said, "where's the money? Silver? Very good. I'll take the horses—are they both mares? Ugh—it can't be helped. Get along then, the pair of you, we're expecting a large party, and the bathhouse will have to be purified. When you've washed, come to the north end of the hospice."

"Brother," asked Sabeth, "why are you so rude? What was the matter with that young man, the callant?"

"Ah," said the brother. "Rude? Yes. We don't deal willingly with brooders and breeders, with the half-made. The callant has come out of reclusion. He has been away from the world. You don't understand me, I know. Go wash yourselves."

"I understand," said Aidris, "but I'm not sure that your mothers would!"

"A proper creature of your sort *lacks* understanding!" snapped the Brother.

"How can the brothers be healers if they do not deal with women?" asked Aidris.

"Oh, some do," he replied cheerfully. "They have a gift for humility—they wallow in the world's filth. The north end, remember?"

He turned towards the hospice; another callant came to help with the horses. Aidris and Sabeth trailed across the grass toward the bathhouse.

"As bad as the Balufir beaks," grumbled Sabeth. "Don't deal with women . . ."

Aidris laughed.

"Don't you start talking in riddles. Balufir beaks?"

"The city magistrates," said Sabeth. "Oh, everyone knows it. The laws are hard on women."

"We are still in the Chameln lands," said Aidris. "There are no such laws here, and I think there are none in Athron."

She thought with dull anger of the followers of Inokoi. She had hoped always that they might redeem themselves when she met them face to face; they might be innocent and good. She had had a picture in her mind of kind, bustling, pleasant men, male counterparts of the Moon Sisters, with here and there a shaman, thin and wise, like the holy men of the northern tribes. These others, woman-haters, might do anything: they might strike down a pregnant woman and kill her child in the womb.

While Sabeth bathed, Aidris stood guard; she remembered the brother's words about a large party approaching. Must not these be men, soldiers perhaps, if he took them so calmly? The nearness of the pass was no comfort; to come so far only to be captured would be unbearable. She fretted, propped against the wall of the bathhouse in the spring sunshine, then slid down the wall until she was sitting on the grass. She dozed a little, and then Sabeth was back again, dressed in one of the three gowns she had brought along. They took up so much of her care and interest that they peopled her saddlebag like old friends.

"That is your best blue!" said Aidris.

"Only the surcoat," said Sabeth. "I will keep the petticoat and chemise until I arrive in Athron. Quickly . . . go in while the water is hot. I built up the fire. Remember to wash your linen first and hang it to dry on their hot racks."

Aidris went in and took her fine hot bath with more enthusiasm. The Brothers ran an excellent bathhouse. She washed her underclothes and regretted all over again that they *were* linen, stitched by the virgins of the northern tribes. Sabeth wore cotton-lawn from the plantations of Mel'Nir, and it washed and dried better and more quickly than the finest linen. It was considered a common cheap cloth, unfit for a princess of the Chameln.

She dressed in her second best tunic of grey doeskin panelled with wine-red velvet of Lien. Her breeches were of a heavier leather, her best boots were of oxhide from the High Plateau of Mel'Nir. She dressed dutifully, remembering how Lady Maren had instructed her on the tying of points, the set of a collar, the use of jewelry, according to protocol. She repacked her saddlebag and found, far down, the package Nazran had given her, the New Year's gift. She felt a thrill of surprise and delight. I will open it when I come into Athron, she thought.

"Dear Goddess, aren't we fine!" said Sabeth. "The colors suit you. That velvet alone must have cost the earth. Do Chameln women always wear trousers?"

"No," said Aidris. "Older women, and men too, may choose to wear a loose robe."

They lingered by the bathhouse in the sunshine, then took up their baggage again and went to the north end of the hospice. Breakfast smells assailed them; they found an open door and a brother sweeping a small room. They could look through a busy kitchen into a much larger room with trestle tables. The brother, a round-faced dark man, did not speak at all, but his manners were gentle. He bowed, ushered them to an eating place in the small room, fetched a tray of food. He waved away an offer of payment.

Aidris heard farmyard noises from beside the hospice; Sabeth was picking eagerly at the splendid breakfast. They began to eat hot bread, honey, boiled eggs, fruit-porridge, fried ham, apple curd; there was milk to drink, and rosehip tea.

"It is like a farm holiday," said Sabeth, wiping her fingers daintily. "I remember once the sisters took us to a farm in Hodd for the summer."

"It tastes of Athron," said Aidris. "The bread is different and the ham."

She saw that there were other diners in the large room, a family party; presently two women in mourning hoods of black and dark green came into their small room and were given breakfast.

"This is the place for women travelling alone, I think," she said to Sabeth.

She heaved up her saddlebag, left Sabeth sipping tea, and went to the stableyard. She stepped round the corner of a barn, and the world turned over. The yard was alive with troopers of Mel'Nir, stabling their horses. She stepped back instantly, then peered out and found that their two mares, Telavel and Imba, were stabled at the end of the long row of loose boxes, so close that she could see into their stalls. A stableboy, possibly a callant, was just then feeding Telavel some tidbit.

The world turned over again and wavered. An officer, marked out by crossed sashes, strolled up and began examining the two mares. Another man of middle height walked beside him. They seemed to be of equal rank; the second man was not a soldier; he wore some kind of blue hunting dress, with a short cloak, wide breeches and smart high-heeled boots. He had a sharp-featured, smiling face and a fine, shaped red beard. She saw him run a hand over Telavel's muzzle, then give her a friendly pat. He conferred with the tall officer, who had laid hold of the stableboy to question him. They started off towards her, she was right in their path, but the stableboy and a brother, feeding hens over a wall, came after them and redirected them. To the south end.

Then they were out of sight and the yard almost empty of troopers. She darted to the stall and set about saddling Telavel.

The stableboy came out of the shadows to goggle at her.

"Help me!" she said.

He *was* a callant, she saw it now, a tow-haired young man in a robe. He began to saddle Imba, turning to stare at Aidris all the while.

He began to speak, "They will search. The red one is called Hurne. They spoke of a bounty. They talked of . . . two women, ladies. . . . Highness, they will find . . ."

He knew her; he was the last to know her, the last servant of the Firn in the Chameln lands.

"Please," said Aidris, "say no names. Help me. Go at once to the smaller dining room and fetch my companion in the blue dress. Come through the barn if you need to."

She knew he might be breaking his rules to do this. He sketched a bow and ran off. She finished saddling both horses and looked at all the ways out of the yard, then mounted up, took Imba's rein and stepped out with Telavel straight across the yard, the way she had come. The brother, busy at the fowl yard, gave a shout, but she went on along the wall of the barn. She met Sabeth and the stableboy running, dragging her saddlebag. Sabeth, pale and frightened, scrambled up with the callant's help. Aidris threw the boy a gold piece.

"Till I come again!" she said. "Your name, friend?"

"Tibbit!" he said, bobbing. "Go well, ladies. Inokoi guide you and bring you to safety."

They turned the horses almost at the door of the smaller dining room and rode smartly down the grassy strip between the lake and the farmyard of the hospice. Cowshed, orchard, they were at a canter now, and they came into the shadow of the trees. They had been seen: there was shouting, and the pursuit was being mounted. There came a sound that had haunted her dreams: the long sweet blast of the silver hunting horn.

They rode on blindly: the forest, so open at first, with many ways leading to the road or to the Wulfental, closed in like a maze. They went up and down and found paths that ended in an impassable thicket or a deep ditch.

Sabeth cried out, "Oh, Goddess help us—that red devil! What is he doing in the Chameln land?"

Aidris reined in, panting.

"The red-bearded man? The one they call Hurne?"

"I have heard him called harsher things," said Sabeth. "He comes from Balufir. He is one of the city's Harriers, one of the worst of them."

"A Harrier? A kind of hunter?"

"They are a special troop of the city watch. They go about in secret. Not many know their names or their faces."

"But *you* know him . . ."

"Mother Lorse had a friend . . . a gentleman . . . who had some trouble."

The path they were on was very steep and it ran, so Aidris hoped, towards the road. They came through places where the trees thinned out until they were riding across the bare mountainside. There was the crash of a distant pursuit; they came out on to the roadside above the hospice. They could hear riders coming from below on the road and one rider following through the wood. But Aidris saw that for this moment their luck held good, the road was clear . . . it wound around a bluff going upward.

"Cross!" she said.

They whisked across and went into the trees on the other side, forcing their way in. There was a thunder of hooves, and four mounted troopers went by on the road. Aidris went in deeper still; she got down and led Telavel over the snow-roughened rocky ground, through felled timber, finding a way where Imba, the brown mare, could follow. They descended at last onto a broad path cut into the mountainside, that she knew must cross the road below the hospice.

She mounted up again, and they went on at a better pace; it filled her with despair to move away from the pass. They picked their way around the base of a fresh stone-slide. Above them loomed a grey bluff with a clump of hard yellow snow packed on its northern side. Beside the path, through a brake of stunted beech trees, was another mountain meadow, a stony round of green, with a little rushing stream.

There they rested at last, getting down to sit on a fallen tree while the poor horses rested. There was no sound but the rushing water; odd gusts of wind came down from the mountains. The day was very fine and clear. When Aidris walked to the banks of the stream, she could see the dark sweep of the forest-clad mountain wall stretching away northward almost to Rodfell Pass above Vigrund.

"We must stay here," she said. "At night we will try to go over the Wulfental."

Above them a bird screamed, an eagle, riding upon some column of air. A single rider was on the road, very close. In panic Sabeth sprang up, took Imba's bridle and led the mare into the trees at the lower edge of the clearing. Aidris went after her, leading Telavel into this small, dark clump of firs, all the cover they had. This was the end, she thought, they would be taken. She drew out her sword from the saddlebag and buckled it on with clumsy cold fingers. It was dark in their hiding place; they could not see out into the clearing.

A horse called, and Telavel answered. There was a movement close at hand; a man's voice cried out, "Who's there?"

Sabeth drew a long shuddering breath ending in a sob.

"I will go out," said Aidris wearily. "I am the one they are looking for."

"No!" pleaded Sabeth. "Do not leave me!"

"Come!" ordered the unseen horseman. "Come out of there!"

Aidris drew her sword and stepped between the trees. She saw a tall, glittering figure, horse and rider clothed all in light, the White Warrior himself, servant of the Goddess, come to carry her across the frost-fields to another world. She shielded her face to see better leaning against a tree. A young knight, mailed in black and silver, mounted upon a bay charger, stood in the clearing. He wore a plumed helmet and carried the banner of a white tree.

"Why . . . it is a young maid . . ." he said in a wondering voice.

They stared, not knowing how to address each other.

"Good sir knight . . ." said Aidris, "we are pursued . . . we thought . . ."

"*I* thought of brigands!" said the knight. "You are not alone, young mistress?"

A beam of sunlight caught his face as the beautiful bay side-stepped on the rocky ground. Sabeth came out of the trees and, taking a few faltering steps, clutched at the tree where Aidris stood.

"Lady . . ." said the young knight.

Sabeth stared back at him; she reached out a hand.

"Will you help us?" said Aidris.

She spoke softly, as if she might break a spell, for Sabeth and the young knight could only gaze at each other, spellbound.

80

"You were pursued," said the knight, "on the road to the Wulfental."

"We were trying to come into Athron," said Sabeth.

Then the knight set the haft of his heavy lance upon the ground and used it to vault from his saddle. He strode towards them and knelt down, lance in hand, its green pennant streaming out.

"I have been brought here," he said. "I have been led to this place only to serve you!"

Sabeth could only reach out a hand again, and the knight took it, but Aidris could see he was not bold enough to press it to his lips. She spoke up again.

"What may we call you, sir?"

"Why, I am Gerr of Kerrick," he said. "Of Kerrick Hall, by Garth, in Athron."

"This lady is Mistress Delbin," said Aidris, "and I am Kedran Venn."

"Put up your sword, brave kedran," said Gerr of Kerrick. "I am here. Your mistress . . . Mistress Delbin . . . is safe now."

"I hope so," said Aidris. "Did you come from the hospice? What was doing there?"

"As I rode past, there were troopers of Mel'Nir on the road to the pass and some going on foot into the forest near the hospice, beyond the lake."

"Alas," said Sabeth, "how will we come over the pass?"

"We must wait," said the knight. "Come, lady, sit down. I will make a place for you by this fallen tree."

He strode about, taking a blanket from his own saddlebag and settling it on the ground. Their two horses had come out of the trees, and he approached Imba, the patient brown mare, and took the cloak of lynx and fox, which lay across Sabeth's saddle.

"A lovely cloak . . ." he said.

"It came from the northern tribes," said Aidris.

The knight set it gently around Sabeth's shoulders. He had taken off his helm and looked even younger. His hair was a rich brown, and he was tanned by the sun; his eyes were grey-blue. He had fine straight features, almost too straight. When he grew older, thought Aidris, he would look like one of the warriors carved in wood on the panels of the Council Hall in Achamar. He sat on the fallen tree, and Sabeth sat on the ground;

they made a handsome pair, a knight and a fair lady from some tapestry.

Aidris saw into the heart of the matter right then, at that moment, but no word had been said and she would put nothing into words herself. She was held back by a certain shyness and by fear, a sly, wretched fear that said, deep down: It is better that no one knows . . . She could only guess at what their rescuer believed. She walked up to the path and stood on watch behind a tree. No one came by; there was no sound of a chase.

So for the rest of the long day they remained in that green round with their rescuer, Gerr of Kerrick. They sat together peacefully or walked to the path or further down the banks of the rushing stream. During that day Aidris sometimes forgot her care; she was, for a moment, carefree. She would check, hearing Sabeth's laugh or Gerr's eager voice and think: This is a dream of how life might be.

They lit no fire; they ate bread and apples from Gerr's store of provisions and the last of the dried fruit from Ric Loeke's pack. In the twilight Gerr spoke up formally.

"Kedran Aidris has spoken of travelling into exile. Where will you go, my lady?"

"Oh, do not call me such a name," said Sabeth in a low voice.

"I will do nothing to displease you," he said, smiling. "All that has been, all the dangers of your journey, these things will never be spoken of again. Only come with me in Athron to my home, Kerrick Hall. Let my father and mother welcome you and give you help in this sad time. My mother would receive you, Mistress Delbin, as one of her ladies; and you, good kedran, could enlist with our captain, Megan Brock, who has all our kerns and kedrans under her charge."

Sabeth gave Aidris a quick pleading look. All her artifice had gone; she had sung no songs for Gerr of Kerrick.

"You are very kind," said Aidris, "but let us answer you when we have come into Athron."

He smiled, boyish and shy, but full of confidence.

"Oh you will see what a fine place it is. Athron is a magic kingdom, and Kerrick Hall is the very heart of Athron!"

He had spoken of his home very often during the day, and Aidris thought of it already as a marvellous place, awaiting them. Its trees and warm stone walls and broad parklands reminded her of some tales half-remembered, a place in a dream.

"Now you must sleep a little under the stars," said the knight cheerfully. "I will move nearer the pathway. When the moon sets, we will try for that secret path that the Tulgai showed to Kedran Aidris."

When the knight was out of earshot, Sabeth buried her face in her hands and wept bitterly. Her whole body was wracked with a fearful sobbing.

"Why?" whispered Aidris. "Why do you weep *now?*"

"My life . . . my wretched life . . ." sobbed Sabeth. "I am accursed. None of it was my fault."

She would not be comforted. Her tears dried up at last, and she stared at Aidris in the growing darkness.

"It was my dream, always," she said, "that a true knight, a prince, would find me and rescue me. Oh he is so fine and good! Could we do as he says? Could we go to Kerrick Hall, forget all that has been, forget our former lives?"

Aidris looked at Sabeth and thought of the long way they had come. She wondered, not for the first time, if it was possible to know another person. She thought of Nazran's own quick judgements and his criticisms: what kings and queens of old he had plucked from the scrolls and held up saying: "She was a good judge of character." "He chose his advisers very wisely." It was a royal trait, and she, Aidris, should have it or cultivate it.

No one that she knew, neither Nazran nor Maren nor Bajan, none of the ladies of Lien, would have granted Sabeth, the beautiful singing-girl, more than a scrap of pity. All their judgement would center on that part of life where they knew or thought they knew all and she, Aidris, knew nothing. Yet she trusted Sabeth.

She knew what it was to be afraid, dreadfully afraid, as Sabeth was afraid of the forest, and still to endure. She owed a debt to her companion for that perfect kindness and understanding Sabeth had shown in that dark hour when she was half-dead of shame. *"No one blames you. No one will ever know."* She knew what it was to be or to feel accursed.

"Yes!" said Aidris. "We could go there. We will put all our lives behind us to this hour. You are Mistress Delbin, and I am Kedran Venn. Gerr has promised as much . . . no questions will be asked. You are a lady in distress, just what such a young knight dreams of, and now he has found you."

"You must like him . . . love him too," said Sabeth. "Is he not the finest man you ever saw?"

"I do like him," said Aidris, smiling. "and I never saw a more handsome knight."

"What will *you* do?" asked Sabeth. "Will you find a husband? Will you seek . . . kedran love?"

"Why," said Aidris, surprised, "I am betrothed. I have always known the man I will marry."

She could not recall that she had ever been told of her betrothal. It was simply part of her life.

"Betrothed!" said Sabeth in exasperation. "You have never spoken his name! Is he old? Is he hideous? Do you not love him? Is he rich? What is he . . . a soldier?"

"A landowner," said Aidris. "He is nine years older than I am. My mother's ladies always said he was very handsome. He is my friend . . . I . . . I trust him. I don't like to think of him now, when I am going so far away."

"Have no fear," said Sabeth. "He will not forget. He will find you again."

They lay down "under the stars" for a few hours sleep, bundled in cloaks and blankets against the chill air of the mountains. Aidris found that she could sleep; she fell at once into a strange dream. She walked in a city, rather like Achamar but in her dream she knew this was Varda, that she had come into Athron. The people in the street wore queer clothes, dagged and scalloped, in half-tones, grey-green, misty violet, soft pink. She asked the way to the trading envoy's house and found that the people could neither hear nor see her. She was invisible, and her voice had faded to a whisper. She walked on in the dream, not much alarmed, and woke up, wide awake on the instant, in the clearing on the way to the Wulfental.

She let Sabeth sleep a little longer. When she had splashed her face at the stream and given the horses the very last of the oats, she went to find their rescuer. Gerr was on watch near the pathway; his charger, Firedrake, waited, all newly caparisoned for their journey.

"Good!" said the knight when Aidris came up, through the cool, undark spring night. "We must make some preparations."

He had a hood in his own colors, white and green, for her to wear, in order to pass as his esquire. He suggested a change of horses: Sabeth to ride "the palfrey," as he called Telavel, and Aidris to take Imba, the brown mare. He sensed her unwillingness and said, "You said your horses were perhaps known by the troopers. We can cover the brown mare in Firedrake's other mantle and the palfrey in a blanket. The change of mounts does add a touch of disguise too . . . perhaps the troopers expect a kedran upon a pony and a lady upon a brown mare . . ."

"Telavel is not a pony or a palfrey," said Aidris, "she is a Chameln grey. I will change willingly, but I thought, with Telavel, I might more easily lead the way through that sheep-path. Still, I will try it with Imba. She is a good mare and has come all the way from Vigrund."

"You are very sure of yourself, Kedran Venn," said the knight laughing. "I am sure there is no better escort in the world."

Aidris felt a thread of impatience with Gerr of Kerrick.

"What do you know of the trouble in Chameln lands?" she asked.

"You are invaded by Mel'Nir," he said promptly. "Already, in Athron, there are a few who have travelled into exile."

"And do you know anything of our history, our rulers, our customs?"

"Not much," he admitted cheerfully. "I was coming to find out more, good Kedran, but destiny served me otherwise. Do you not have two rulers?"

"Yes, two," she said, "from two families."

It was difficult to speak of it, but she made an effort to probe further.

"Good Sir Gerr," she said formally, "can you answer me one question, with absolute truth, as you would answer in the Halls of the Goddess?"

"Of course . . ."

He was all seriousness.

"Did you hear, today, from the troopers, the name or rank of any person they were seeking?"

"Truly," said Gerr of Kerrick. "I did not."

"What if I said to you that I am the one, the object of their search?"

"To be sure," he said, a ripple of laughter growing in his voice. "But does that mean the Lady Sabeth is *your* escort?"

He could not help it; he laughed aloud. Aidris felt that the task was hopeless; she even had a twinge of wounded vanity. To the knight she could never look more than a kedran. At least he did not seem to have heard too much.

"We might have met by chance," she said, "and travelled together."

"Brave kedran," said Gerr of Kerrick, "I can be loyal as the truest heart and I can be secret as that heart's core. Let us have no more of this. Trust me. Let us wake the Lady Sabeth and try for the pass."

They came out onto the road below the hospice within the hour. The gibbous moon had set; they were in the midst of Birchmoon, the young girls' month, and if Aidris could remember rightly the day was Mid-week. All the dressing up of horses and riders had made the three of them more hilarious than anything else. They straightened their faces and came out on to the quiet, dark, empty road winding upward. A dim light burned at the entry to the stableyard of the hospice. They kept to the sandy edges of the road, which was a good broad expanse of packed earth, spread with gravel in places where the way was too soft in winter.

The loghouse of the brothers was unlit and silent; then came the challenge from the stableyard.

"Who goes there!"

He came under the archway, a solitary, sleepy young giant.

"We are returning to Athron, trooper!" said Gerr of Kerrick haughtily. "Do you read this banner?"

Aidris was afraid still; her heart hammered in her chest. She was afraid of a chase, afraid of a fight. She saw the young trooper pierced with a lance and a hundred warriors pouring out of the hospice. She was afraid all her flimsy disguises, with names and half answered questions, would be destroyed in a moment.

"A Forester," said the trooper. "And these are your companions, out of Athron?"

"My esquire and a member of my house," said Gerr. "What is all this? Are we at the border that you question honest travellers this way?"

"Pass along, sir knight," said the trooper. "You're not yet at the border."

They passed by, not daring to quicken their pace. A hen began cackling as they passed the farmyard, and Sabeth had to stifle a fit of laughter. They came to the place where Aidris and Sabeth had crossed the road to safety and turned the corner, heading for the pass. There, further on, was the finger rock on their left, and beyond it the path or network of paths taken by the deer and the horned sheep.

Aidris took the lead and urged Imba into the trees. The going was steep but straightforward, then the path became very narrow, against a cliff. She got down and led the mare. It was not dark; they were not shadowed by the trees, and the path itself was of light stone and clay. They went up and up and came to a place where the path divided, one way leading steeply down to the south, where the deer went to leap over the ravine of the Lylan, the other leading upward still, towards the Wulfental. She mounted up again and pushed through scrubby bushes, then checked at last and let Sabeth and the knight draw level.

They were well within the long dark ravine that formed the pass, high up on a bluff with a good but steep path running down at their feet.

"Look back!" whispered Gerr.

Aidris could see the glow of a fire in the pass, the way they had come. She watched and listened; horses stamped; a man hawked and coughed. The troopers of Mel'Nir had closed the pass at its narrowest point, but they had not reckoned with the sheep path.

"We must go down," said Gerr, "and ride like the whirlwind to those distant lights."

The lights were more faint than the stars, the red star of the Hunter at the horizon and the star of the Queen higher in the heavens.

"What are those lights?" asked Sabeth.

"A watch-post of Athron," he replied.

"Will we be questioned?" asked Aidris.

"I am known there," said Gerr of Kerrick. "Courage, my ladies. One more ride and all dangers are passed."

He urged Firedrake forward and led them down into the ravine. Aidris let Sabeth go down next, thinking of poor Telavel, encumbered with a ridiculous blanket and a sidesaddle. She followed with the brown mare, broad-beamed but certainly sure-footed.

They came down into the Wulfental, and the place itself was enough to make Aidris ride very fast. She felt again that evil, icy cold that had seeped out of the ground at the witch-hold, far away in the foothills. They rode quickly: trot, canter, then Firedrake galloped away with the two mares following. There was a wild hail behind them; they were pursued by the horses and riders of Mel'Nir.

It was no contest from the first. Firedrake went faster and Telavel, even with the unaccustomed harness, flew up along-side. Aidris, trailing, dug her heels into Imba, who responded with an unexpected burst of speed. They rode like the whirlwind through the dark maw of the Wulfental, and the lights grew and grew.

The watch-post had a low square building of grey stone and rosy brick and the lights shone through its windows. They clattered into a cobbled yard, and looking back, Aidris saw three troopers come up and draw rein, hidden in shadow. She wondered if there was another who waited, Hurne the Harrier, on his dark horse.

The yard was alight with torches and loud with drawling Athron voices.

"Who rides so late?"

A big man, struggling with a helmet, rose up beside her, taking her rein.

"Gerr Kerrick of Kerrick Hall," cried their knight proudly, "riding escort to a cousin of my house. That is my esquire you have there."

"Why are those danged Melniros wearing out hoof-iron," grumbled the big man. "Captain Rolf at your service, Sir Gerr."

He strode out of the yard and shouted back down the pass in a voice of thunder:

"Here are three Athron folk come home. You've nothing to seek, troopers."

The mounted men were silent. The captain bowed to Sabeth.

"Please to step down, your worships," he said. "Take an early bite with us in our common room . . . it is near day."

"I think we can do that," said the knight cheerfully.

He smiled at his companions.

"It is a pleasanter way when the sun has risen."

As they trailed into the common room, a young man at arms spoke to the captain, and Rolf, revealed in the warm light as bushy-bearded and stout, said again, "Danged Melniros. Nothing but trouble here at the pass since they came. We have a

88

man here under guard...tried to cross earlier this evening, but I did not like the looks of his safe-conduct."

"What sort of a man?" asked the knight.

They were in a comfortable well-worn place with old hangings on the thick winter-fast walls and broad settles.

"Who knows?" said Rolf. "Red-bearded. Thought he might cross with gold."

Aidris said, "Sir Gerr?"

When the knight turned to her she whispered to him, "I think I know this man."

"Let my kedran get a look at him," said Gerr in his lordly fashion.

He turned and helped Sabeth to a place. Aidris went after the captain, trying to still the beating of her heart, and they came to a door with a grating.

"Must everyone have a safe-conduct?" she asked.

"Bless you no," said the captain. "We let poor folk state a reason or name a friend or sponsor in Athron. This fellow overreached himself. His paper was signed by a dead man, old Elam Goss, Councillor of Prince Flor, but dead these six moons. We might still have let him through, but he tried to give us gold."

He held up the torch to the wide grating, and they saw a man sitting on a bunk, staring at them sharply. It was Redbeard, trim and fierce as he had been that morning in the stableyard, yet she knew that his luck had deserted him.

"I know him," she said. "His name is Hurne. He is some kind of hired bravo out of Lien. He's an evil man who hunts down exiles for the Melniros, for gold, for a bounty. He should not cross into a peaceful realm such as Athron."

"By dang, we'll send him back, then," said Rolf, grinning. "Thanks good esquire. Come have a bite..."

The way led out of the pass from the watch-post, bathed in the blue light of early morning. To the south, they saw the mountains with a tall, snow-capped peak, Mount Coom, rising close at hand. To the north, the mountain wall was just touched with light, the forest and the last snow fields beginning to glow rose and gold. Gerr of Kerrick led them over a last rise, through a swirl of mist. Sabeth cried out, and Aidris echoed her cry.

Spread out below them was the land of Athron, its green fields, hedgerows, neat villages red-roofed; its streams and groves and lush meadowland, all newly green for the spring. It was as if a burst of song came up to them, borne on the morning wind. The knight led Sabeth down the path, his plume lightly tossed, his banner flying out.

Aidris looked back the way they had come. She looked into the rising sun, sent out her spirit, in longing, over all the lands of the Chameln, then turned away and rode down into the magic kingdom.

CHAPTER
IV

GAVIN, THE WAKER, FOUND HER BED EMPTY, met Aidris coming back from the stable.

"Early up!" He grinned. "Here's the runt of the litter. Mucked out your little jade? Good. You have an hour or more before first breakfast and saddle-up. Where are you off to, Venn? Running? Shining your gear? Saying your prayers?"

"I'll be about," she said, passing off the question.

The waker was a limping, sallow man, one of Lady Aumerl's lame ducks. He was a busybody, who carried tales and spread gossip. She walked between the barracks and the barn and came upon the low house of sand-colored stone, which cast a graceful shadow over the path. Its pointed gables and fretted balconies still gave her that pleasant shock: "I have come to another country..." She rose early to have time for herself; there was a festival, and the kedran would get no rest.

Aidris came past the new north wing of Kerrick Hall and cut through the north court. She came suddenly, as one did in Athron, into an enchanted place. The courtyard was piled with spring flowers: snowdrops, mooncups, bluebells, shepherd's bounty, yellow bonnets and tall sword lilies, planted in boxes or standing in tubs of water. Four women in green aprons were weaving a huge garland of living flowers that stretched almost from end to end of the courtyard. They sang as they worked and sang instructions to their young assistants, a boy and girl who ran about from one to the other with more binding, more flowers, more armfuls of greenery.

> "Dearest love, bring me a fairing,
> Silken sash or silver chain..."

sang the women.

Aidris ducked under a wagon and pushed through the sweet vines that hung from it.

"Here with the twine... the red weed, a little more... more mooncups and some o' that lovers' bane..." sang the women.

She went through the kitchen gardens and a corner of the orchard. No one saw or marked her. It was early, she was invisible, a young kedran passing by in the colors of the house. The ballad the women sang had a plaintive melody; it was a tale of unrequited love. She found herself finishing the verse as she climbed the hill behind the house.

> "Flowers of Birchmoon to deck my bride bed
> Sang the Fair Maid of Stayn."

It was a hill she climbed, not a barrow, but Kerrick Hall did have a hint of Thuven Manor, that other safe house. She remembered the first time she had set eyes on the place, after the ride through Athron, in the springtime of the year. Now it was Birchmoon again. Coming up to the grove of trees that crowned the hilltop she murmured another verse of the song.

> "Long she waits in wind and weather,
> Ere her love comes home again,
> For another wears his token,
> Not the Fair Maid of Stayn."

It was a song of Athron, simple and bittersweet, without a hint of wildness. The trees on the hill were alder, whitethorn and holly. There was a small, hedged graveyard for the families of Gerr and of Kerrick: Lady Aumerl's parents lay there, and two of her stillborn children. A little way off, in its own white-painted railing, grew a single Carach tree, the magic tree of Athron.

It was beautifully shaped, with a smooth white trunk and palmate leaves of green and silver. The Carach always seemed to be on the point of defying nature: it was in full leaf before the snow had left the ground, and its leaves did not fall until the first snows came again. The leaves, when they did fall, were gathered up and treasured for magical purposes. Wishes and pledges were written upon Carach leaves; a Carach leaf in among the down of a featherbed ensured sound sleep; crushed Carach leaves were a charm against melancholy, woodworm, false promises and colic in horses.

Aidris squinted up at the tree and found it, like all its fellows, a little too self-conscious. This day she must work her own magic. It was the last day of Birchmoon; she had been in Athron a year and twelve days. Her birthday had come round again; last year, so soon after her arrival, she had almost forgotten the day. This year, a long and painful time having passed, she was eighteen. She had come of age; she was Queen of the Chameln, and Regent for Sharn Am Zor. Upon this day, in far-off Achamar, her proclamations, written out fair on vellum and parchment, would be nailed about the city, under the eye of the ruling power. The northern tribes would cry out her name and raise new spirit trees in her honor.

She sat on a wooden bench by the yew hedge of the graveyard and could only summon up a quick blessing for her land and her people. She had no magic left in her. She sat drowsily in the light of the new-risen sun and drew out her book. She kept it still in its cloth wrapper. She remembered opening it for the first time at an inn on the outskirts of Varda called the Owl and Kettle. Her New Year's gift, a bound book in the style of Lien, with a cover of purple-brown leather and silver fastenings, just as she had chosen it from the world of the scrying stone. Two worlds suddenly impinged upon each other, without warning, in the quiet bedroom of the inn.

She unlocked the book, that first time, as she did now, with its small silver key, and read its title page: *Hazard's Harvest: A book of delights, conceits and strange tales for the lady's bower, the fireside and the nursery.*

She had never seen the book before, but there stamped upon

the cover was the Swan of Lien, the badge of her mother's house. She turned the pages quickly, hoping for a message, then more slowly, examining the capitals, illuminations and pictures of this exquisite book. Sabeth came back from the window embrasure where she had been gazing out at their new world.

"Your present!" she said. "What . . . only a book?"

"I might have had a dagger," said Aidris, "or a yellow jewel. But I chose the book."

She imagined some scene at the fireside, in a lady's bower or even in the nursery, where the Lady, warm and real, offered her these gifts. Yet she had been alone on the barrow in the winter's cold, peering into the world of the stone.

"Let me see!" said Sabeth. "It *is* a fine book."

Then the strangeness of the gift began to reveal itself, for Sabeth could not open the book. The key held fast; she could not turn it. They decided that it had stuck in the tiny lock; Aidris took the book again, and the key turned for her at once. She opened it up and showed some of the delights and conceits.

When Sabeth had turned away to the window again, she noticed that a first page of the book had been tucked away under the leather slipcover. She prized it out carefully, and there was her message. A single name, bold and fresh, in straight-letter, with the serifs of the letters laced into a pattern. A name that explained and added to the mystery. *Guenna.* So she whisked the page back to hide this name, and she knew at last who lived in the world of the scrying stone. She felt warmed and comforted, as if she had indeed been sitting with this lady at her fireside.

Later that day she had gone alone into Varda, walking invisible through the cheerful streets. Sabeth had primmed up her mouth when Aidris asked if she had any message to send. She had, she declared, torn up the letter from Mother Lorse and was not expected in Varda.

The Trading Envoy, Nenad Am Charn, had a tall stone house, wonderfully foreign like all the houses she gaped at. The ground floor was an elaborate shop for goods from the Chameln lands. When a young Vardan came to wait on her by a table of beadwork she sent her sword in its scabbard to the master of the house. He came out, a round Firnish man, and kissed her hand, his black eyes darting about with apprehension.

"Come . . . Come Highness . . ." he whispered.

He led her into a storeroom beside the shop and fell on his knees.

"Ah, Dan Aidris! I had word, roundabout, from Lingrit Am Thuven, the Envoy in Lien. Nothing has come through the mountains . . ."

"I have come, good Envoy," she said, smiling and raising him up.

They sat knee to knee on two bales of cloth, heads together like conspirators.

"My house is yours," he said. "I will give it out that you are my sister's child. The Varda princes are flirting with the might of Mel'Nir. I must be very correct; I am watched. I have goods in this house that could be claimed by the usurpers in Achamar . . . you understand me?"

"How will you live?" asked Aidris. "You have no more goods coming from the Chameln lands, and you cannot trade except by treating with the Melniros."

"Princess," he said, "my loyalty to the Daindru is unswerving, but I cannot lie to you. I will delay and parley with everyone, the princes, the agents of Mel'Nir . . . then in a year or half a year, I *will* treat with Regent Werris and the usurpers. It is not so much that I need the trade to live . . . I could do well enough by trading elsewhere . . . but we must have an open border to the Chameln lands and a flow of news and goods. Better that I should remain envoy than that some bravo of Mel'Nir should take the post."

He looked at her seriously.

"You are right," she said, "but you must admit that it is dangerous for me to remain in your house."

Nenad Am Charn nodded, lips compressed.

"I have had some misfortune on my journey," she said, "but I have found help and protection."

She told of Ric Loeke's death, of help from the Tulgai and from Gerr of Kerrick. The invitation to Kerrick Hall impressed the envoy and pleased him, but he could not shrug off his responsibility.

"You are very young, Dan Aidris, to go about alone."

"Athron is a safe place," she said. "I know I will be well cared for at Kerrick Hall. Besides I have my travelling companion, Mistress Delbin."

"I will write a letter of introduction, using your new name, to Huw of Kerrick," said the Envoy.

"Put in Mistress Delbin too," she said, "for she will go with me."

Nenad turned away to a cluttered desk and wrote neither more nor less than was required:

To the noble Lord Huw of Kerrick, at Kerrick Hall, from Nenad Am Charn, Trading Envoy of the Chameln lands, at the sign of the double oak, Tower High Street, Varda.

I recommend to your care and hospitality Kedran Venn and Mistress Delbin, two ladies from my own country, seeking refuge from war and civil strife. May the Goddess send us in time that peace that ever abides in the land of Athron.

Then Aidris yielded to a vulgar curiosity.

"Good Envoy," she said, "do you know who lives at the sign of the dove, in Fountain Court?"

Nenad Am Charn flushed a little.

"I know," he said, "but in heaven's name, Princess, *you* should not!"

"Tell me!" she ordered.

"A certain Count Porell and his Countess live there," he said. "Most disreputable people. It is a house of assignation, if you understand me, for the young gentlemen of the court. How do you come to know of such a place, Highness?"

She had the answer ready.

"Ric Loeke, our poor guide, had those words written on a paper in his pack. I wondered if he might have friends or family in that place!"

"Tush!" said Nenad. "He had not, depend upon it. You have done all that you could and more."

So she went back to the Owl and Kettle and set out on that first magic journey across Athron, with Sabeth, looking beautiful as springtime, and Gerr of Kerrick, their true knight and rescuer. They came to Kerrick Hall and were received with warmth by Lord Huw Kerrick and his lady, Aumerl. Sabeth went to the great house as a waiting woman and Aidris to the barracks as a kedran; and now a whole year had passed.

A bird flew up, and she came to herself on the hill; for her birthday she drew out the scrying stone. Her relationship with the Lady had changed subtly; now she was to be seen at once, smiling, in the world of the stone. On the table or altar lay a bunch of oak leaves in honor of the day. The Lady set down a thin-shaped circlet of gold beside the leaves... a crown or coronet.

"Oh, will I come to this estate?" sighed Aidris.

The Lady nodded, seemed to counsel patience. Then she smiled again, and the stone was filled with a sparkling mist, which cleared suddenly. Aidris beheld a garden with clipped trees, neat paths and rose bushes... a garden in Lien? Three children sat beside a round pond watching the gold fishes. The eldest boy, well-grown for thirteen, was Sharn Am Zor. His sister Rilla, brown-haired, was eight years old and not a beauty; she was strapped into an elaborate Lienish gown and held the leading strings of the four year old Prince Carel, who had golden curls and was as devilish as his brother had been. Aidris watched them intently; she knew this was all her birthday, all her presents and festivities.

The bird shrilled again, just as the stone clouded, and she hastily tucked it away inside her tunic.

"Good morrow, Kedran Venn!"

He had come over the hill, through the grove, a dark, loosely built young man. He was not so handsome as his younger brother but in certain moods she liked Niall of Kerrick's face better; he would never come to look like a wooden warrior.

"Have you been collecting herbs and simples, Master Kerrick?" she asked.

The pouch slung over his shoulder was full. He smiled vaguely and sat beside her on the bench.

"How does the Carach this morning?" he asked. "Has no one come to ask its blessing for Erran Eve, our day of dancing?"

"It is early still," she said.

"May I see your book?" he asked.

She handed it to him, and he leafed through the tales and songs and riddles that she knew pretty well by heart.

"It is a magnificent book," he said. "Was it a gift?"

He shut it now and ran a finger over the silver swan on the cover.

"A royal gift..." he added.

"That is a badge of Lien, where the book was made," she said innocently.

"Do you know that some magicians can tell the origin of any object that comes into their hands?" he asked again.

Niall was teasing, as he often did, and she smiled, unruffled.

"Can you do that, Master Kerrick?"

He shook his head. She took the book back, locked it and slipped it into its cloth covering.

"The festivals divide our year," he said, "and help to stave off boredom a little. Erran Eve and Midsummer and Carach Troth and the Lamp Lighting and the Holynights and who knows what other days in between. Athron is prosperous and full of magic. My father is to blame for that . . . he brought back the Carach twenty-five years ago. It was his destiny, some would say. Kedran Venn . . . do you know what the driving force is in this land of ours?"

"I have some thoughts about it," she said, "but I would like you to tell me."

"It is the fact that Athron was once very poor. The memory of that dreadful time is fixed into the minds of the old and passed on to the young, who can't believe it, having known only prosperity and magic and hope. There are farmers, the parents of your fellow kedran, who hoard food, skimp and scrape in their households, eat meat once a week and kill their aged horses for glue and tallow rather than set them out to pasture. The towns are full of misers, muttering spells to increase their gold."

"Well I have seen another side of Athron life," she said, "and I would say the driving force is indeed your golden prosperity, but that it leads to recklessness, setting all at hazard. This is the place for games, risks, fortune telling and taking not much heed for the morrow because each day, each month, each year is as secure as the one before."

They looked at each other and laughed aloud. Presently she rose up from the bench and went off to pay her respects to the Carach tree. She slipped under the white railing and knelt on the short, soft grass. Above her she felt the leaves stirring like silver hands raised in blessing.

"Oak maiden—"

The voice was rough and smooth at once, rather like the purring of a huge cat. It made her shudder, not unpleasantly.

"Oak maiden," murmured the Carach tree, *"are you still here?"*

"You see me, Carach. Will you give me another blessing?"

"Take it then, Aidris Am Firn."

"Carach, when will I see my native land again?"

There was no answer; a wind shook all the leaves and then was gone. Aidris drew back from the tree and said formally, *"I bid you farewell, Carach."*

She turned to find Niall leaning upon the railing.

"What speech is that?" he asked.

"Why, it is the Old Speech," said Aidris.

"I have never heard it spoken," he said. "Who else knows it?"

"The Carach tree." She smiled.

"Ah, so the Carach speaks to you . . ."

There was a sound of singing; three young women were ascending the hill and a young page with a lute strumming rather listlessly as he climbed after them. The waiting women wore kirtles in the style of Athron, more simply cut and shorter than the trailing and floating garments of Lien.

> "Do not weep, O dearest Mother,
> Soon an end to all my pain,
> Do not blame my faithless lover,
> Sang the Fair Maid of Stayn."

The dark-haired Genufa and blonde Amèdine were no more than foils to the loveliness of Sabeth. In a year she had grown in beauty, if only because she no longer took so much heed of it. Her modesty and gentleness were as much a part of her as her singing voice, her gift for fine needlework. She raised a hand and waved to Aidris.

"Our swan maiden," said Niall softly, "flown to the warmth of Athron."

"Hush!" said Aidris. "I would hear the song."

> "O do you mourn for lord or leman,
> For kedran bold in battle slain?
> Nay, 'tis for one who died of waiting,
> Called the Fair Maid of Stayn."

"Truly it is a foolish old song," said Niall of Kerrick. "Would any die of waiting, Kedran Venn?"

"Nay, you mistake the theme, Master Kerrick," she said. "The Fair Maid, surely, died of love."

She ran down the hill and met the women. Genufa and Amèdine greeted her, all smiles, and Sabeth gave her a quick embrace.

"We will ride to the dancing floor," she said. "Will your company ride escort?"

"Why, Aidris Venn," said Amèdine, "Have you been taking instruction from yonder scholar?"

On the hilltop Niall Kerrick bowed to them, hitched the strap of his herb satchel and strode off into the trees.

"Ladies," whined Moss, the page, "are you going to the Carach? I want my breakfast . . ."

He played a chord all out of tune and fumbled with the pegs of his instrument. The three girls jollied him along, and Aidris ran back down the hill to the barracks.

She came into the muster hall in time and took her place for first breakfast. She sat beside Ortwen Cash, the big country girl who rode with her in Grey Company. There were fifteen Kedran, three companies, in this early muster, and ten men-at-arms.

"Where you been?" wheezed Ortwen softly.

"Up the hill."

"Who you see there?"

She reeled off the names, and Ortwen frowned, crumbling bread.

"Always ballocking around with the house folk. Han't you been taught your place yet?"

"You'll protect me, sweetheart," said Aidris, digging her in the ribs.

Ortwen went off into a guffaw of laughter, checked when Lawlor, their sergeant, raised her head. Ortwen had protected Aidris more than once during the past year. She had been bullied, set upon, accused of giving herself airs. She defended herself, but refused to fight in the "single combats," anything from finger-wrestling to staff play, that were popular in quarters. She knew enough of kedran ways not to pimp to an officer. She lost her temper only once when a burr was set under Telavel's saddle and left a sore. She flew at the arch bully, a hard-muscled girl from the west coast called Hanni, and fought so recklessly that the pair of them were hauled bleeding out of the stableyard, to the sick bay first and then the coop.

Aidris was ashamed to have fought in this childish way, even for Telavel's sore place. Any way she looked at it, behind bars for instance, with a loose tooth and swelling eye, it was a tactical error. She was the shortest and lightest of all the kedran. She was also Aidris Am Firn, and she had not endured attack and pursuit to break her arm or her head in the stableyard at Kerrick Hall. Ortwen made her give it out that she would not fight or take part in "single combat" because of a vow made to her family. It was a notion the kedran understood; they were full of promises, vows, magical compacts.

Towards the end of breakfast, as was usual on a feast day, Megan Brock, the captain, came in attended by her two lieutenants, to give the order of the escort. She was a tall, grizzled woman of fifty with a long, livid scar on her left cheek. Aidris remembered the first time she stood in the stableyard, unsaddling Telavel.

A man-at-arms had shouted out some jeering words on the order of "What d'ye call that . . . a pony or a wee grey dog?" A voice, resonant as brass, rang through the yard.

"What's with you all, bloody clodhoppers? Have you never seen a Chameln grey?"

Then the captain had looked Aidris herself up and down. Her blue eyes were bright and cold. They pierced every disguise, they saw into the lazy good-for-nothing soul of every kern and kedran on the Goddess's good earth. Aidris felt that she was known at once.

"Venn? *Kedran* Venn?"

"I have called myself kedran on the way into Athron," said Aidris, "but I have done no more than a few months training."

"Weapons?"

"The bow. A little sword play."

"Drill?"

"Mounted drill. A little."

"What news of my old comrade Jana Am Wetzerik?"

"She is the general now."

"Where did you do this bit of training, Venn?"

"With the palace guard . . ."

It was a slip. Megan Brock did not ask, "Which palace?"

"Let me guess." She smiled. "The palace of the Firn."

"Yes, Captain."

She felt the captain's eye upon her ever afterwards. When drill and dressage and the management of her gear became difficult, she heard the brazen shout of *"Venn!"* in her dreams. She was accused of being a favorite, one of Brock's pet lambs. For more than half a year she felt driven, put upon, singled out unpleasantly.

There were differences between herself and the other kedran that she could not hide and had never thought about. She was put in with ensigns, the cadet-officers, for "benchwork," because she could read, write and cypher. She was put on the lists for scribe duty with the two overworked scribe sergeants when it transpired that she could write straight-letter. She managed to hide the fact that she knew runes. She learned quickly not to answer more than once or twice when Megan Brock held a class on soldiering, on warriors of old time.

The kedran of Kerrick Hall were mostly farmers' daughters working for their dowries; they signed on for a four-year term, then went home. A few stayed for eight or even ten years and became ensigns or sergeants. There were no more than a dozen "true kedran" in ten companies, and they were veterans, mercenaries, from Cayl or Eildon or the Chyrian coast in the west of Mel'Nir. The five companies of men-at-arms were more equally divided: half of them were veterans, half farm boys or the sons of smaller landholders. There was no fighting to be done; this was not Mel'Nir, where turbulent warlords challenged the power of the Great King. It was not even the Chameln lands, where tribal disputes sometimes flared, where brigands lurked in the mountains, and where, of late, the rulers had needed protection.

The captain read off the escort order; the kedran and men-at-arms sighed a little; Aidris listened to the din of spoons and platters. She was in Athron, in the muster hall, in her company; she was safe, she was invisible. She was lost and far from her native land. So it would go forever: the round of the seasons and their festivals, turning slowly as the earth turned. Erran Eve, with dancing; bonfires at Midsummer; singing for Carachmoon; torchlights at harvest. She would grow grey as Megan Brock here in the service of Lord Huw Kerrick. She would die here, and they might find her sword at the bottom of her clothes press and wonder what talisman she had been hiding.

"Doan look so glum," murmured Ortwen. "We're leading off. You'll ride with your precious house folk all day long. It's a soft duty. We'll eat well and have a chance to tread the dance floor."

Riding to the dancing floor, Grey Company,—three dappled, one flea-bitten and one Chameln grey—crossed a wide meadow to the banks of the Flume. At a word from Lady Aumerl, ranks were quickly broken, and the ladies and gentlemen mingled with the kedran. Aidris, at the head of the troop, on lovely Telavel, two to three hands smaller than the other greys, found herself riding between two tall horses. A wind ruffled the grasses of the river meadow, and she was shaken by memory. She looked to her left and saw Lord Huw Kerrick, that still, dark-eyed man who had brought the Carach tree back to Athron.

"Will you go questing, Kedran Venn?" He smiled. "Your grey steps out so boldly!"

"Not I, my lord," she answered. "I am not one to look for adventure!"

There was a laugh from Lady Aumerl, on her right, riding astride in a high-backed saddle, as was the custom for Athron women. She was full-figured now, but handsome, with dark brows and firm red cheeks. It was not hard to think of these two as young lovers, riding on the many quests they were supposed to have undertaken.

"I think you hold questing for mere foolishness, Kedran Venn," she said.

"Ah, my lady," said Aidris, "I am not so churlish. I have much reason to be grateful that Sir Gerr went questing into the Chameln lands."

"I rode this way on a quest once," said Lord Huw, "and the one who rode at my side raced off, from about this old alder stump, just ahead, clear to the bridge, yonder."

"Race again!" said Lady Aumerl, "but let the kedran take my place. I will set ten florins and a firkin of wine for Grey Company on this sweet Chameln greyhound."

"What, against my Fireberry?" cried Lord Huw.

So the wager was made, because Gerr of Kerrick, riding behind with Sabeth, heard it all and Sergeant Lawlor winked at Aidris. Fireberry, full sister to Firedrake, was fast enough; Telavel was unproven to all but a few. Aidris felt herself more or less in the spirit of the thing; bets were laid, and the sergeant acted as starter.

Then Aidris whispered to Telavel, feeling a sudden desire to win the race, as Fireberry drew away. The grey set back her dark ears, and they were gone, over the soft, magical turf of

Athron. She thought of the silver grass of the plain, endless, and the locks of hair, high on the spirit trees. Then she was at the bridge; she heard a cheer from Grey Company as Fireberry came up behind her.

"A greyhound?" cried Lord Huw. "That little mare is the wind itself! Is she only a sprinter? How does she go over distances?"

"The Chameln greys are meant to be stayers," said Aidris. "They are bred for the plains."

They got down and walked their horses to the dance floor as the rest of the party came up. She was hailed as the winner and given ten florins for a race well run; she thought of her birthday. Then with Grey Company, she went to where their horses were tethered and stood watching the dance with Ortwen. Now that the party from Kerrick Hall had arrived, more and more country folk streamed across the bridge over the Flume to stand by the dancing floor.

It was a maze marked out on the ground with fences of dried grass and fresh wildflowers, knee-high to the dancers. In the center was a high mound of earth covered with white blossom; it put Aidris in mind of a grave. She shuddered when five village men in green, with bells on their ankles, threaded the maze to the sound of tabor and bagpipe, then circled the mound until a pretty girl, decked with red ribbons, rose up from out of the flowers.

"What villages are those across the river?" she asked Ortwen.

"Lower down is Greenbank," said Ortwen, "what used to be Lower Stayn. Stayn is just across the bridge. Right there, looking over the fence . . . that's the Fair Maid."

Aidris laughed aloud. A black and white cow crowned with flowers stared moodily across the river.

"Now see . . ." said Ortwen. "Here's another dance for the day."

A young man threaded the maze in a white cloak, and when he came to the center, he turned his cloak and showed that it was all streaked with bright red. He lay down upon the mound of flowers; the dancer was Gerr of Kerrick.

Aidris gave a shocked whisper, "Is he meant to be dead?"

"Not for long," said Ortwen cheerfully. "See—the ladies will try to wake him."

Three waiting women from the Hall and three village maidens

threaded the maze from different directions. They came to the center and bent down in turn to kiss the sleeper.

"No prizes for guessing his favorite," said Ortwen. "My troth, what a harvest that sir knight made when he found you and her both in the mountain passes."

Sure enough, when Sabeth kissed the sleeping lord of the dance, he woke straightaway. The music of pipe, tabor, dulcimer and flute rang out bravely as they threaded the maze together.

"That will be a match!" said Ortwen. "Depend upon it."

"I hope so," said Aidris.

But the ceremony was unsettling. She remembered how the northern tribes forbade the wearing of certain mourning bands, even in play. A pretended death would have shocked them unutterably. And she knew that the risen lord of the dance was a figure from the dark past of the Goddess's reign, in many ages since the making of the world. The young king or his chosen slave was murdered; blood was spilled indeed, for a sacrifice. In Athron they even played at magic.

So she came into Lindenmoon—in the Chameln land it was Elmmoon—in her eighteenth year and let the round of the seasons take her. It was as if part of her mind was sleeping, as if one Aidris pined and waited in some secret place while the other went about as a kedran. She found herself asking, as the other kedran did, "What year was that?" When did we ride to Benna with the wheat, to Parnin as the lord's escort? When did Hanni become ensign? When did poor Bertilde get herself into trouble with Sergeant Sterk and marry out of the troop? When did little Venn come down with measles, cow-pox and mumps, things every Athron child had before its tenth year?

During the days of the winter feast the barracks were emptied of all but a few kedran veterans. The younger kedran and men-at-arms went to their home towns and villages; the older men were married and did not live in quarters but in cottages on the estate. Lord Huw freely invited those remaining to live in the Hall until after New Year, but the older women went up only for a couple of nights' feasting, then stayed in the barracks, celebrating in their own way.

"Go along, lass," said Sergeant Lawlor to Aidris. "You have

a sweet friend up in the house. You doan want to stay here boozing with the old companions."

The sergeant was one of the ugliest women she had ever seen, Aidris decided upon first view, with long arms, a thick neck, eyes like black beads set in a face of crumpled brown leather . . . a walking reminder of that piece of homely wisdom that said a kedran was one that none would take to wife. Yet in a year or two or three she found herself astonished when a new recruit whispered, "My Goddess, yon Lawlor's face would turn the milk sour . . ."

"What would you have," snapped Aidris Venn, the kedran, "a kind and patient officer or a pretty one?"

Every year then she looked forward to her days in the Hall; Nenad Am Charn sent a big New Year's gift box of delicacies and presents from the Chameln lands for herself and Sabeth. One winter's night she met the young messenger from Varda lurking about in the passageway by the Hall kitchen, having delivered the box. He gave her a packet of letters.

She ran shivering up a little winding "secret" stair and took a candle into a window bay near the bright south bower where the fire was lit and the musicians played songs for the season. She sat hunched against the cold, mullioned windowpanes, broke the seal and saw Nazran's handwriting. He wrote without signature or superscription; it was a long dispatch rather than a letter:

> Werris makes no pretence of holding the north, he has not the forces to do it, his envoys and commissioners are mocked and harried and put to flight by the loyal tribes. It is a matter of Achamar and the south and the west. If the so-called Great King is hard-pressed by his own unruly subject lords, and if the garrisons and the households of the southern landholders are reduced in the Chameln lands, then there is real hope for our enterprise of arms. The spark will fall upon dry grass and the countryside will be ablaze from end to end, calling for the return of its true rulers and an end to the domination of Mel'Nir.

There was more in a similar vein, every line burning with hope. Aidris could almost hear the rattle of preparation, the storing of arms, the work of blacksmiths in the night. Then the screed continued:

Yet I must tell you of what is painfully rumored hereabout, of Werris's plan and of those others who are rumored to support this most treacherous shift. The Daindru shall be broken and Sharn Am Zor will rule alone. Kelen of Lien and his advisors will stand by this foul act in exchange for bounties, especially the gift of a slice of rich mining land in or near the Adz. I cannot learn with certainty what Danu Aravel feels in this matter, whether her judgement and wits are clouded or whether she bends to her brother's will. The prince himself was ever of good understanding, most forward and, as I have heard, tenacious of his rights. Do you, therefore, write to him most plainly, and our faithful envoy will see that it comes directly into his hand. Give some proof that Dan Sharn will recognise so that he will know who it is that writes to him, for it is often said that the Heir of the Firn is dead and will not come again. Do not be so bold, however, as to reveal any hint of your present refuge, lest the letter miscarry.

The letter had been written over a period of weeks, the inks and pens different, the script often cramped as if the light were not good or the hand that held the pen crippled. The old man's spirit flared out again in the final words.

The news is good. The call may come soon, so I charge you to be ready. Yet if we fail at this attempt, I swear that our spirit will never fail. All will be done again, though it take all our lives and all our strength. Be patient and be uplifted by the unending love and loyalty of those who serve you and your house.

The excitement she felt was almost stifling; she wanted to run and shout. *"The call may come soon..."* There was another fold of paper with Nazran's letter and a hard object, a coin perhaps, behind the rough thumbprint seal. She opened the paper and found a gold ring embedded in the wax, a simple gold ring with a turquoise. Once again the letter had no beginning and no end, it was no more than a few lines scrawled hastily with an ill-trimmed pen.

> Take this ring in token of my love and duty. We were true friends, I think, almost before you could speak or I could write, and I pray that this bond, tested and proved by an absence of long years, will grow into a more enduring love.

The signature was bold: Bajan Am Nuresh. Aidris leant her cheek against the windowpanes and fitted the ring first to one finger, then another and found that she could wear it best on the middle finger of her right hand. She was seized with terror and yearning. The northern tribes would rise up, the Chameln lands fly to arms, he would fall in the battle, and she would never come to him again. Almost she wished Nazran's plans and schemes away.

She heard footsteps and folded the letters quickly. The curtains parted before the window bay, and Sabeth came in, bright-faced.

"Thank heaven, it is you. Put out the candle!"

They sat in the dark and heard a rush of steps going past with a tinkling of bells and the voices of the other waiting women calling, "Sabeth! Sabeth!" Then there was a sound of heavier steps and a long whoop of "Where away? Lady! Lady!"

"Oh I was surprised and put utterly to shame," whispered Sabeth. "I had not a moment to set my hair to rights..."

"I have had news..." said Aidris.

Her voice was solemn, she could not control it; she could not help feeling impatient with whatever game it was they were playing. Sabeth, visible a little now in the snowy radiance from the window, turned towards her.

"Is that why you hide yourself away? Oh, I hope it is nothing bad to spoil the day!"

"It may be good news," said Aidris.

She longed to tell everything, to show her gold ring, to gasp out all her plans, but as before the words stuck in her throat.

"I may be able to go home again," she said.

"Goddess be praised," said Sabeth.

She was still preoccupied but she reached out and pressed Aidris's hand.

"Did Gerr or Niall speak to you?" she asked, "or Lord Huw...?"

"What about?" asked Aidris, mystified.

They heard the noise of bells and cries repeated, far away in the long gallery.

"About me, of course," said Sabeth, with a laugh that was almost a sob.

"Lady Aumerl said something." Aidris tried to concentrate. "Yes... she asked after your parents, and I said that they were dead. She asked if you were free to make contracts, if you were of age. I answered, yes, of course."

"Nothing about lands or goods?" asked Sabeth.

"Not a word."

"The dowry," said Sabeth. "I have thought about it even if he, dear soul, has not. Oh, here they come again!"

"What is it?"

"Oh you silly goose!" cried Sabeth in exasperation. "It is my bride-calling! It is my betrothal! Gerr has asked for my hand!"

At last Aidris understood.

"Well, I thought Lady Aumerl must mean something of that sort," she said, "but I knew nothing of this racing and chasing. As for the dowry I can promise you a little..."

"You have been so good," said Sabeth. "I know your family in Chameln Achamar are well-found. I wondered about that little store of gold we divided..."

"You may have it all and another string of the pearls, but when I come home again, we can do better. There is a place I know, called Zerrah, a little manor on the road from Achamar. It is not as large as Kerrick, but..."

"Is that where you live?" asked Sabeth, listening as the steps of her pursuers came closer.

"I slept there once," said Aidris. "On my way into exile."

Then Gerr pulled aside the curtain and gave a cry of triumph. "A bride! A bride!"

He saw Aidris in the corner of the window bay and said, "Now, Kedran, you have served this lady long enough and can safely give her up to me!"

"He will serve her better!" cried one of the young men.

Then the women, Genufa, Amèdine and the rest, cried out for shame, and Gerr led the rosy-faced Sabeth into the south bower to the sound of bells.

Aidris was about to follow the procession when Niall of Kerrick appeared round the billowing curtain. She could not tell if he had been part of the bride-calling.

"My brother is very jealous of his new betrothed," he said. "I hope his words did not offend you, Kedran Venn."

Aidris shook her head.

"I wish them very happy," she said. "It was a love match from the first."

"It is a tale from one of those knightly chronicles that Gerr and the Lady Sabeth read together," said Niall. "The dark forest, the frowning mountains peopled with goblin creatures and every kind of wayward spirit, then suddenly the loveliest of ladies, attended only by one faithful kedran . . ."

Aidris laughed and shuddered. "Do not mistake our peril, Master Niall! Your brother saved us from the giant warriors of Mel'Nir, not from elves and goblins. If he sets a kind of glamor over the meeting, it is surely because he comes from Athron, this magic kingdom."

"I had thought perhaps he was enchanted," said Niall. "That he saw only what he was meant to see . . ."

"No, you are wrong again," said Aidris. "He saw only what he *would* see . . ."

"Tell me what he should have seen," said Niall softly.

"You are teasing," she said. "Do you know that your brother swore a solemn oath, more than one, to Sabeth and to me? I do not like to speak of the time before I came into exile. Yet I will say one thing, just to tease you in return. I served no one. I was no one's faithful servant until I came to Kerrick Hall and joined your father's kedran troop."

Niall pondered this a moment and then began to smile.

"Are you telling me that the Lady Sabeth was *your* servant . . . ?"

"No, not that either," said Aidris, wearily.

She sprang up, took her candle and lit it again from a standing rack of candles in the corner of the landing. She settled into the window bay again.

"If you will pardon me," she said, "I have had letters."

Niall looked at her, frowning deeply, then let the curtain fall.

She reread the letters all through the feast days and when

she returned to quarters after the New Year she took a sheet of fine paper from Lien from her own writing case and composed her letter to Sharn Am Zor.

> *To the most excellent Prince, Dan Esher Sharn Kelen Am Zor, Heir of the Zor in the Chameln lands, Keeper of the gates of Achamar, Lord of the Wells, Lord of Chernak, Winn and Farsn, Markgraf of Vedan, Viscount of Hodd—*
> Dearest Cousin,
> I pray that you are well and greet you for the New Year, hoping that this next twelvemoon will bring us together in our rightful places. What these places are we have been well taught, since we were born. I am the Heir of the Firn, I am of age and therefore sole ruler of the Chameln lands and Regent for yourself, the Heir of the Zor. When you come of age, we will rule together, we will be the Daindru, which has ruled in Achamar for more than a thousand years. I have sworn that this ancient bond will not fail through any act of mine. I will hold to my right as long as I live and I beseech you to do the same.
> There are those who, claiming to be of better understanding, because of your youth, or claiming you owe them some duty, will urge you to break the Daindru, to rule alone or with some usurping Regent in my stead. Hold to your right and mine, dearest cousin, and resist these treacherous counsels.
> That you will know that I live and that this letter comes indeed from my hand alone, I will recall to you the Great Oak where we sheltered, and how we spoke there of the Tulgai and I said that they would do us honor if we came amongst them. And I will recall how we overturned a stone urn with a rosebush in the garden of the palace of the Zor at Achamar and ran off and were never charged with the deed.
> So by these memories of troubled times and of happier ones you will know that I am your Regent and above all your most loving cousin.
>
> Aidris Am Firn

The letter was sealed and wrapped and sealed again and addressed to Nenad Am Charn. It was carried to the trading envoy by the kedran officer of New Moon Company, who rode black horses and escorted the quarter's tribute to the princes in Varda.

She did not expect a reply to this letter, and indeed she had none. She read and reread the long screed from Nazran and the shorter letter from Bajan until the inks faded and the paper became soft, crumbling along its folds. No call came and no other news, either good or bad, reached her out of the Chameln lands. She looked weeping into the scrying stone, and the Lady looked back at her with a sorrowing face and shook her head when Aidris showed the letters. A trail of ivy was laid upon the table within the stone, and she knew its message: patience. So her hope, which shone so brightly, was slowly dimmed. She still looked at her letters from time to time and at the New Year, but they were no more than talismans, a memory of that one hopeful season.

II

IN THE SPRING OF HER TWENTY-FIRST YEAR, AID-ris rode with Grey Company and White Company and New Moon Company to Benna, on the border of Cayl, in the south. The kedran brought Gerr of Kerrick and Sabeth, his betrothed, together with their bridal party, to the Hospice of the Moon Sisters. They were married in a sacred ceremony by Mother Frey, head of the house, who was more than ninety years old. Then the blessed pair went on over the pass with a smaller escort, riding to Port Cayl, where they would take ship to Eildon for their wedding journey, many moons of pure honey.

Sabeth, all arrayed in white and green and mounted upon a new bay mare, a gift from Lord Huw and Lady Aumerl, was lovely as the spring morning. Gerr of Kerrick rode in full pan-oply, a knight questor of the order of the Foresters of Athron. Aidris felt a thread of disappointment when she was not asked to ride in the special escort. She had not seen Sabeth face to face for many days, with the wedding preparations, and could only hope that her gift of silks, sent by Nenad Am Charn, had come safely to her hand. She thought of Port Cayl up ahead and sighed.

"Never mind," said Ortwen. "That is the way with gentlefolk and nobles. Hoity-toity the lot of them. You should have had a place in the escort, everyone knows that."

Aidris was surprised.

"It is nothing," she said. "I don't feel slighted. And I know that gentlefolk and nobles cannot all be called proud."

She watched the knight and lady ride in over the pass in bright sunshine and thought of the border forest, the dark ways, the last wild ride through the Wulfental. She felt a real wave of happiness for Sabeth and her true knight. She realised that she was herself absolutely unafraid, she had been for years now, free of fear in Athron.

Lord Huw came up on Fireberry; he gave her a strange look.

"Be of good cheer, Kedran Venn," he said. "It is no time for sad thoughts."

"No indeed, my lord," she said, "but I have envied the party a little because they ride to Port Cayl."

"Port Cayl!" he exclaimed. "What's there to interest you? It is a rough place."

"I have never seen the sea," said Aidris.

Lord Huw was shocked.

"By Carach," he cried, "we must remedy that! You have a long furlough coming up, do you not? Then you must go to Spelt, a manor farm of ours on the western strand of Athron. You will get all the sea you want and more, and your sweet grey can race along the sands like the wild white horses of the salt marsh called the Shallir, the sea spirits."

"How fine that would be!"

"Hold me to this promise, Kedran," he said. "This year will be a busy one, and I need reminders. In autumn, when our lovers return, we have the visit of the two princes . . ."

When he had ridden off, Aidris turned back to Ortwen.

"You see?" She smiled. "Lord Huw is not proud but kind."

"True enough." Ortwen grinned. "But it doan follow. He is not of noble birth, our good Lord Huw, but a plain man of Athron, who went for a sailor once, before he came to this high estate."

So the spring wore into summer, and the great wheel of the year turned slowly. Kerrick Hall made ready to receive its royal guests: Flor of Varda would ride out from the city with his consort, the Princess Josenna, and a retinue as bright and bold as he could muster in the land of Athron. He would meet, just beyond the village of Garth, with the scion of an elder house and a land of ancient heritage: Prince Ross of Eildon. In the train of this prince would ride Gerr of Kerrick and his lady, returned from their wedding journey, and Kerrick Hall would give hospitality to the two princes, to the old magic and the new, for the whole of the Maplemoon, the month of plenty.

For the kedran this was certain to be a weary and unsettling time. A month on parade, long nights on watch and busy mornings when the rest of the world slept until noon; the prospect of having to remain sober when others did not. Aidris had to admit to a certain curiosity about her royal cousins, although she did not expect to come very close to them. To prove their magical inheritance, as far as she was concerned, the princes would have to do what she feared most, pierce her disguise at once.

She was quite clear about the connection to Flor of Varda. Forty years or so ago, before the Carach returned, his grandfather, Duke Ferant, had carried off her great-aunt, Imal Am Firn, a lady two places from the throne. Aidris felt a faint envy for the pangs of this ballad heroine who loved her poor duke "more than horse or hound," stole certain jewels of the Firn for her dowry and galloped off over the Grafell Pass "when the moon was dark." Yet Imal must have been an unusual Princess of the Firn, or else the ballads lied. She had gone into Athron legend as Imelda Golden Hair, tall and straight as the birch, modest and seemly, though of savage blood.

The connection to Prince Ross was more difficult for her to work out; there were at least three royal lines in Eildon, all richly entwined and intermarried. Her grandfather, Edgar of Eildon—that young father who died so soon that that only his own elder children had any memory of him—came from one house, Prince Ross from another, the aged Priest-King, Angisfor, from a third. She believed the name Ross had been borne by several magicians, warriors and poets in succeeding generations.

Eildon had a more distant and shadowy connection to the Chameln lands but she liked it better, as a legend, than the story of Imelda Golden Hair. Once, long ago, a prince and princess of Eildon had braved the seas and the long journey through the forests of the Southland, unconquered by Mel'Nir, to marry with the Daindru of their time. These were the Tamirdru, the Sea Oak Twins, dark Eilda, who wed the King of the Firn, and bright Tamir, her brother who was consort of the Queen of the Zor. Even the makeshift names of these two—Eilda or Maid of Eildon and Tamir or Sea Oak—seemed to make them more authentic. It was so long ago, Aidris reasoned, that their real names had been lost.

She went about her duties with a good grace and shared the excitements of the other kedran and the house servants as the time drew near. She had schooled herself to make no plans, to forget, from day to day, that she had ever had any other life but this; she would willingly have quelled her own dreams. Yet she was unable to do this, and every few nights she was tumbled into some childish drama of recognition and rescue, bound up with the coming of the princes. They loomed up in her dreams, she spoke familiarly with them, begged an army or an armory of magic. Prince Ross took her by the hand, and she flew with him through the air, high over the land of Athron and over the mountain peaks and came to Achamar. There below two figures waited, and when she flew down she saw that they were her father and mother, grown older, just as they might have done. She woke in tears and prayed to dream no more.

Then at last it was autumn; the maples burned blood-red across the downs and in the copses of Athron. The princes, those dream figures, those puppets, on whom so much expectation centred, as if they were wish-dolls hung on the Carach trees, were coming indeed. On the very morning of their coming, Aidris came without warning into a strange place. She had an adventure.

CHAPTER
V

THE MUSTER HALL WAS FULL: ON THIS DAY everyone had an early breakfast. Everyone was notably well turned out; the place reeked of soft soap and linseed oil. Aidris had spent hours on her boots; the man-at-arms across the table cursed and dabbed when he spattered honey-curd on his tunic. Grey company was one of five that had prime escort duty, due at the crossroads at two hours before noon by the garden dial, the barracks bell and Master Niall's clock in the tower of the north wing.

Towards the end of breakfast, Megan Brock came in wearing strip mail and the new officers' surcoat, her two lieutenants just as fine. She flicked a cool eye over the whole troop and bade them good morning but did not walk to her place.

"I need a pair of swift riders," she said. "No stripes or special placing..."

Aidris kept her eyes on her plate, but she had a feeling in the pit of her stomach as if she knew where the dice would fall.

"Venn! And you too, Cash; your dapple is newly shod."

Ortwen murmured wearily, "What in the name of hot horse-apples..."

They sprang out from their benches and saluted.

"Come outside," said Captain Brock. "I'll tell you the tale."

In the stableyard she squinted up at the clear sky and said, "First botch of the day, my dears, and it won't be the last. The watch at Garth Mill have gone over the hill some way. We get no signal."

On the conical cap of the silo by the barn there was a signal tree with colored flags; two kedran watched from the hoist

115

platform. News of the approaching cavalcades would be sent from the mill, two miles away, when they received signals from the crossroads.

"That is Sergeant Wray at the old mill, Captain," said Ortwen.

"And the young kern, Simmen," said Megan Brock. "Steady enough, both of them. Can't think what has gone wrong. We have time in hand, but not much. Ride to the old mill, send up the green flag "On duty," find out what is with those two rascals. Venn, you must press on to the crossroads and see that all is well, tell them about the hitch."

Telavel and the dapple-grey gelding Robin, Ortwen's pride and joy, were groomed and plaited to a fare-thee-well, both in fine fettle. Now they would lose their gloss long before the ceremonial ride. Both girls mounted up, grumbling, and flung off out of the yard, down the stately avenue of linden trees. The watch at the gate parted as they came through and took the road to Garth.

"You think the sergeant is drunk?" shouted Aidris.

"Naw . . . not he!" Ortwen called back.

They rode very fast on the perfect, newly cobbled road. The very hedges had been barbered for the royal visitors; the fields and trees were a picture. They drew rein at another watch-post, a kedran company on this near side of the village, doing nothing but watch the road to see that no hay wagon was taken out, no flock of geese toddled over the road at the wrong moment. In Athron, thought Aidris, they had no need to guard against anything else. The village pump and the houses were decorated with flowers and autumn leaves. A boy on a ladder was polishing the sign of the Bull Inn.

The company on watch had put their horses to graze on the banks of the Tanbrook. The sergeant and her ensign leaned on the bridge rail.

"What now?" asked Sergeant Clough.

She was a black-avised, wiry veteran who liked a quiet life.

"Captain's greeting," said Aidris, "and have you seen or heard anything of the watch at the old mill?"

"Wray and Simmen?" rasped the Sergeant. "Not a whisker!"

Everyone craned and peered in the direction of the mill, just visible upstream behind the poplar trees. Ortwen and Aidris

116

rode on. They came first to the handsome new mill of sand-colored stone, built in a curve of the Tanbrook. The wheel was still at this hour, and the sky reflected in the millpond.

Aidris paused at the wide bridge and said, "Shall we raise the miller?"

Ortwen shook her head.

"If old Wray *is* lying there drunk, best we tend to him . . . gives the troop a bad name."

So they rode on past more slowly and came to a narrow footbridge over the rushing stream, in the shadow of the old mill.

It was set back from the stream on a little rise, and it was a windmill, an enormous building, taller than the poplar trees. With its gaunt tower and broken sails above the bulging lower storey of buttressed grey stone, it looked like the hulk of a giant ship stranded in the meadows. They could see, high up, the signal frame, empty of flags.

"Did they bring horses?" asked Ortwen.

Aidris did not know. The men-at-arms were not a calvary troop like the kedran. They did not own horses, but Kerrick Hall ran a string of "house nags" for their use. The reason for Ortwen's question was plain enough: hoofprints in the soft earth by the footbridge. Yet no horses were to be seen tethered by the mill or grazing in its meadow. Ortwen got down and led Robin a little way along the banks of the stream, looking towards the next bridge.

Aidris gazed up at the frowning old mill and felt a twinge of her own particular unrest.

"The sergeant and young Simmen might have been attacked . . . set upon!" she said.

"Why for?" growled Ortwen, just as uneasy.

"This mill is the only watch-post that covers both roads," said Aidris. "Some others might want to know when the princes were coming."

"What? To do them ill?" said Ortwen. "Truly, I can't believe it. You've been too long in the Chameln lands among the wild folk. Will you go in and stir up those lazy beggars, or will I?"

Aidris might have walked Telavel over the footbridge, but she thought twice. She got down, walked across and pressed into the cool grass of the river meadow, tangled with buttercups.

She called, "Holla the old mill! Sergeant Wray! Are you there?"

No voice replied, but there came from the mill a desolate sound, a clattering of old timber stirred by the wind. Aidris felt how very cold she was, standing in shadow in the damp grass. Something moved inside the mill; a window, high up, went light, then dark again. She cried out, louder than before:

"Sergeant Wray! Kern Simmen! Come out... Captain's orders!"

There was a faint vibration, a rumbling, just within her hearing; the mill's huge broken sails moved a notch, no more. She saw the rank grasses growing at the base of the mill bend slowly down as if a wave of air were sweeping towards her over the meadow. She turned and ran through the clinging grass and tumbled onto the bridge again. Ortwen met her halfway, pale-faced; they fell against each other.

"Dear Goddess!" breathed Ortwen, "Are you..."

"The place is bewitched," said Aidris.

"You were *gone!*" said Ortwen. "You were vanished away like a scrap of morning mist. I thought I was losing my wits."

"Have you heard of such a thing before?"

"Never! The magic here is kind as the Carach trees. But I don't like this..."

"It could be some evil working," said Aidris.

She looked about quickly and seized upon an old peeled willow wand that lay in the grass beside the bridge.

"Here," she said, "some child's fishing pole. Throw it!"

When Ortwen looked puzzled, she explained.

"Throw it as far as you can into the meadow, to the place where I was standing."

"How do I know where *that* was?" cried Ortwen.

She took up a stance, made a run into the middle of the bridge and flung the rod like a javelin. It flew in a fine high curve, began to descend, then bent oddly, wavered before their eyes like a stick plunged into water. It was gone. They could see the mill and the meadow, shadowed but unruffled, but the willow wand had vanished.

"Yet it is *there,*" said Aidris. "I believe it is there, sticking in the grass, only we cannot see it."

"By dang," said Ortwen, "you are worse than Niall Kerrick with his kite-flying and stargazing. What shall we *do?* Run back to Brock, the old badger, and tell her the place is bewitched?"

"I'm going to raise the miller," said Aidris. "This may be some ancient witch-hold."

She ran back down the road, with Ortwen after her. A young lad was watching them from the bridge of the new mill.

"Are you the miller's son?" she asked.

He nodded, gulped.

"I'm Dickon Mora. This is Mora's Mill."

"Do you own the old mill yonder?"

"It stands on our land," said the boy uneasily. "What's with the place?"

"We think it is bewitched," she said.

The boy stared even harder, but he took it in quickly.

"I'll fetch Gran!"

He came back with a stout old woman wiping her hands on her apron. She fixed Aidris and Ortwen with a very knowing gaze; her eyes were a clear brown, like brook water. She heard the tale of the mill and the two men-at-arms.

"I knew the old mill was set up for a watch tower," she said slowly. "Were your two fellas there after nightfall?"

"Did you see them go by?" asked Ortwen. "Riding, maybe?"

"Horses went by in the night!" the boy Dickon piped up.

"Good mother," said Aidris, "what ails the old mill after nightfall?"

The old woman sighed.

"The old mill had a fetch," she said, "long ago before the Carach returned. More than twenty years ago, when Garth was a poor and needy place and Kerrick Hall the home of a poor knight, Dhalin Gerr."

"Was it your mill, Mother Mora?" asked Ortwen. "Did you work it?"

"Goddess forbid!" she replied. "It was a ruin even then. Garth had no mill, and folk hardly believed in the fetch because our magic had not returned."

"Would it do harm, this fetch?" asked Aidris. "We must lay it and soon."

"Easy said, Kedran," the old woman answered slyly, "but they do say . . ."

She turned to the gaping lad and said abruptly, "Dickon, get in and see if I turned the damper on the stove."

119

When the boy had gone she said, "A virgin would do it better than most."

She looked the pair of them up and down for no more than a few pulse beats and then said, "You two are maids. Walk in boldly. I'll give you a pinch of protection."

Ortwen grinned in embarrassment and shuffled her boots on the path. Aidris saw that she was afraid.

"I will go," said Aidris. "I wear a powerful amulet."

The old woman looked at her more keenly than ever and felt under her apron for a pocket, hanging from her belt along with keys and scissors. She drew out a little twist of cloth.

"Put that up your sleeve, child," she said, "there . . . next the skin. That's right."

They walked back to the footbridge, all three, and the boy Dickon came out of the mill kitchen again and followed them. Nothing had changed; the morning sun had not penetrated the shadows about the looming mill. The grey and the dapple-grey, Telavel and Robin, cropped grass beside the footbridge. Ortwen shuddered.

"Venn," she said, "you can't go in there . . ."

"I will," said Aidris. "I have been in worse places. Wait here and watch and fetch the captain if I do not return by the time the sun is over the third poplar tree. Fetch the captain and Niall of Kerrick, he knows about such things."

"Take a weapon," said Ortwen, "a staff!"

"No!" said Mother Mora. "Go in peace. Don't eat or drink anything while you're there. Bring nothing away with you . . . except the two fellas, that is."

Aidris went to the center of the bridge and drew out her grandmother's scrying stone. It had a sparkle of life round the frame.

"Keep me safe from harm," she said. "See where I go."

She let the blue stone hang down on the front of her tunic and strode boldly over the bridge into the meadow again. She could see the marks in the tangled grass where she had walked the first time. She walked on, and there was the willow wand that Ortwen had thrown. She plucked it up out of the soft ground and called aloud, as she had done before, "Sergeant Wray! Kern Simmen! Come out!"

Then there was that same windy clatter inside the mill, and the sails moved a notch, no more. Aidris looked back over her shoulder and found that the bridge had gone. There was only a shimmering veil in the air, like the sun dazzling on dewdrops. She thought, I am in another world, like the world of the scrying stone.

She took a few more steps towards the mill and saw the rank grasses flattened, the wind-wave rolling towards her over the grass. She braced herself, spreading her arms wide, and when the wave broke over her it was warm, a wave of warm air that stung and prickled. It drew up her hair into points and struck sparks from her belt buckle.

"Let me pass!" she cried. "I come in peace!"

There was a familiar sound, but in that place it made her jump. A horse nickered and came trotting eagerly round the side of the mill. She saw at once that it was no wraith, no nightmare, but a dainty live roan, a thoroughbred of the Athron stock, which had come from the high plateau of Mel'Nir.

"Wheesht," she said gently. "Come up then . . ."

She held out a hand and the tame, lovely creature came to her, tossing her mane.

"Who brought *you* here?" whispered Aidris.

She brought out of her pocket a piece of carrot that she had been saving for Telavel. She thought of the old woman's words about eating and drinking in a magic place. Did it apply to horses? This one had surely been eating the grass. It was a little lonely and nervous, waiting for its mistress or master, but neither bewitched nor wildly afraid. The mare's bridle was of patterned leather, elaborately scalloped; the saddle and girth were picked out with gold.

"What can you tell me?" she said to the mare. "Who left you here and went into the mill?"

Aidris looked at the doorway of the mill nearest her, a gaping black hole with grass growing over the threshold. She stroked the roan mare's warm neck one last time, turned away and laid her hand on the scrying stone.

"I will go in!" she said.

She pushed through the tall stalks of fennel and nightshade and crossed the threshold. She saw nothing at first; the place smelled dry, hot and old. Then as her sight cleared, she saw the ancient structure towering up all around her, an immense empty shell with only broken beams and a gaping pit at her feet to show where the machinery of the mill had once stood. There was a stairway that clung to the wall and rooms or the remains of rooms, with the flooring ripped away. Sunlight came in through gaps and chinks in the timberwork.

Aidris found she was stifling; there was a sudden reek of boiled hide and bones, a whiff of the knacker's yard. She became aware of a movement in the pit at her feet; it was full of liquid, a sea of hot foulness, boiling up. She tried to call the sergeant again, and her voice was stifled in her chest. She ran left to the stairway, the ground slippery under her feet. The first few steps were of stone. She looked back and saw a black tide bubble up out of the pit and follow her on the stairs. She could look down into a thick, oozy blackness, very hot, with green-skinned bubbles that rose and burst slowly, giving off a vile stink.

She climbed on the wooden stairs now, and for a moment her perception altered, she was high on the other wall of the mill, she was a spider in its web, an owl in one of the old owl nests, watching a kedran in a white and green tunic climb the zigzag stair that clung to the mill wall. Still the kedran climbed, and she, Aidris, felt a very cold and unearthly fear. She felt the presence of the fetch, the thing that lived in the old mill. It was like a seed beginning to grow, a flame springing up in the ashes of a fire. While she was divided from her own body, the fetch might come between, and she would remain cast out, a lost thing, howling upon the wind.

She made a great effort and was on the stairs again crying out loudly, "Sergeant Wray!"

The mill took her voice and broke it into a score of echoes; she came to the first landing of the stair. She could look down now and see that the pit was dry and full of weeds, with a lighter patch, perhaps an old sack, off in a corner. The mill creaked and groaned through all its timbers. There was a tumbling and thundering, the sound of voices shouting, the grinding of stone on stone, all the sounds of the mill in its heyday. Then, as these sounds faded, she caught a faint, groaning cry from above, in the dome of the mill where the flooring was almost intact.

Once again something brushed at her mind as if trying to be known.

"Fetch," she said aloud, "spirit, let me bring them out. Give them back. You cannot harm me!"

A terrible screaming cry rang out at her very elbow, and she

122

pressed back against the wall. Then she went on, step by step, past the second landing. She could look across to a hoist platform on the opposite wall, and it seemed that a man stood or hung there, she could make out his pale face and dark clothes. Still she went on and the last flight of steps was very dark, leading up to the room in the dome, which was filled with light.

Then the darkness gathered itself together into a heap, a shapeless clump of black in which there burned two points of light. The fetch reared up before her on the stair, but she mastered her fear because she had sensed its nature. It was less than human; it was a poor half-made thing.

"Let me pass!" she ordered.

She made a light movement with the peeled willow wand, which she still carried. The black shape bowed down, flowing away over the side of the stairs into nothingness. She ran up the last few steps into the dome of the mill.

There were three small windows letting in the light, and under the central one was a grey-haired, heavyset man collapsed like a sack of meal, his head bloody. Sergeant Wray. She ran to him, chafed his cold hands. He opened his eyes and gave her a dazed look.

"Sergeant!"

"Kedran?" he whispered.

"Come," she said. "We must go out!"

He raised slow hands to his aching head, licked dry lips.

"Schnapps . . . in m'poke . . ."

She felt in his pouch and there was a leather bottle. She gave him a taste, no more, then damped his kerchief and wiped his face.

"Holy Mother of us all," he whispered, "this is a fearful place. Venn is it? Venn, how came you here?"

"Can you walk?" she asked. "We must go out."

"The other fellow," he said. "Yonder. Some young fool from the city . . ."

She saw that a youngish man lay in shadow under the window on her right, the western window. She went across to him, avoiding a gaping hole in the floor. He was richly dressed, about thirty years old, with fine, pinched features and long, curled, perfumed silky hair, chestnut-brown, falling over his face. She lifted up a jeweled badge, a stag's head, that hung round his neck, and saw among his rings a signet with the same device and another with the monogram T. M. Terril Menvir, Prince Terril of Varda, younger brother of Prince Flor, who was expected that day: a cousin then, but not of the kind who rescued *her* in dreams. She did not understand his presence in the old mill; she slapped his royal face with a certain good will.

"Highness!"

His eyes were dark, they made him almost handsome; he smiled at her dreamily, then came wide awake.

"Highness, we must go out. The place is bewitched."

"Worked too well," he murmured. "Worked like a charm."

Prince Terril began to laugh, then choked.

"The place is deadly," he said. "How came you here, green-eyes? Who are you?"

"Kedran Venn of Kerrick Hall," she said. "We must go out!"

"It . . . it will not let us!"

"It is quiet now," she said.

"You are a witch, Kedran!"

He snatched at the blue scrying-stone, then drew back his hand as if it had burned his fingers.

"I may be," said Aidris grimly. "What were you doing in the mill, Highness?"

"Oh it was a stupid trick, nothing more. Did Fantjoy send you in, my man?"

"No," she said, "we missed the signal flag at the hall. Come . . ."

"Look out of the window, Venn," he said. "Look out of all the windows!"

He laughed unsteadily. She stood up to help him to his feet and looked out of the western window. She saw, in place of the bright countryside and the bridge where the kedran company were posted, a desolate place that she hardly knew. Yet there *was* a bridge. The season was autumn still. Garth was a shrunken brown village. There among a few bright autumn trees was a plain old house of sand-colored stone with no avenue, no barracks, none of the larger outbuildings. Four riders came over the bridge: an old man, a dark man and a woman with tawny hair. The fourth man was familiar, he had a look of Niall of Kerrick. Their horses were strange; the old man had a tall roan, the others rode shaggy, spotted coastal ponies.

Aidris tore herself away from the strange scene and helped Prince Terril to his feet. He staggered a little and then stood pressed against the wall.

"We were . . . three . . ." he murmured.

Aidris felt her heart miss a beat.

"Sergeant," she said, *"where is Simmen?"*

Then Sergeant Wray gave a cry of pain.

"O Goddess!" he said, gasping. "O Simmen, boy . . . I remember . . ."

He had clambered up onto his hands and knees, and now he crawled towards the hole in the flooring. Aidris went forward and so did the prince. They looked far down into the pit, and Aidris could see the young soldier lying spread-eagled, on his back.

"He ran mad," sobbed Wray. "I was half-stunned, I could not hold him. He ran mad . . . he went through . . ."

"What happened?" demanded Aidris. "Prince, what magic have you worked in this place?"

"A simple spell of binding," said Terril. "Fantjoy had it from some damned mountebank. Worked passing well in Varda, in the gardens."

Aidris was still mystified.

"What was your plan?"

Prince Terril frowned and shook back his lovelocks.

"A jape," he said. "A trick to be played on my brother Flor and that smooth-faced model of a prince, Ross of Eildon. It was a good plan. This mill overlooks the crossroads. We cast our circle from here, at moonrise, naming the concurrence of the victims . . . then zim-zala-bim, the princes meet when the sun is high and vanish from sight. They are held in the charmed circle until we release them, together with whatever is closest to them in the way of toadies, horses, whores . . ."

"You burst in upon us!" cried Sergeant Wray. "Prince or whatever you may be . . . you have done this thing, brought down this curse. We were up here, minding our business, sweating it out a little in this spooky place with a few uncanny sounds. Then in comes this fine young gentleman making passes, muttering spells. We were all overwhelmed: dark shapes, terrible noises, a rushing wind. I was flung against the wall; the very boards and timbers of the place rose up and fought with us. Then poor young Simmen. . . ."

Aidris bent down to comfort him and eased him back to the wall under the southern window. She looked out and saw the bright autumn day, the banners at the crossroads, men and women at the roadside, where the procession would pass. Something in the way these watchers behaved nagged at her. She could not see the sun. Once again she forced herself to look away.

"The charm rebounded on the mill," she said. "I do not understand the full working. You chose a bad spot for your jape, Prince Terril. The mill is bewitched; it has a fetch; your clumsy magic waked it into life. You are vanished away and held here inside a charmed circle. Do you have the word of power to release the spell?"

"Why, of course," said the prince eagerly.

"Hush!" said Aidris. "Do not speak it on any account until we are free. Do you have it written?"

"Here somewhere," said Terril, fumbling in his velvet sleeve. "It is only in runes though . . . I have learned off the sound."

"I can read it," said Aidris, taking the scrap of parchment from his hand.

"A witch indeed," said Terril with a wan smile, fixing her with his dark eyes. "A green-eyed witch maiden, among the kedran of Kerrick Hall . . ."

He turned to Sergeant Wray.

"Sergeant," he said, "I will pay for this foolishness all my life long, I think. I will also pay my debt to the young kern's family. If we come out, please try to forgive me."

"Well said, at least," growled the Sergeant. "But Venn, how *do* we come out?"

"I have tamed the fetch," said Aidris. "You must follow me."

"But Simmen?" he whispered. "He is gone for sure. How will we bring *him* out?"

"Wait!" she ordered.

She went to the dark place where the stairs went down and struck the topmost stair with her willow wand. There was a furry movement of the darkness where the fetch waited. She felt a thrill of power because it would do her bidding; she understood the temptation of the fetch.

She went down two steps and said in a low voice, "Bring out the soldier's body from the pit. Lay him outside the mill."

There was a horrid whimpering in the darkness, a damp, soft sound. She knew the fetch begged for reward, its only reward, release from the mill, freedom.

"Very well," she said. "You may come out with us, but you

must do my bidding exactly. If you do not, the power from this stone will find you out and destroy you or wall you up forever in some dark place!"

There was a change in the old mill; the air was soft and pleasant with a smell of meadow flowers. A thread of melody, a little song, lived in the old timbers. The fetch was docile, but she did not trust it completely. She went quickly up into the dome of the mill again, and as she passed by the eastern window, she was caught and held by the strangest scene of all.

She saw a windy autumn day, the sky full of mares' tails. A party of riders were setting out on the road to Varda. Their clothes were rich but somber; she thought some were armed. In the midst of the riders was a figure in white upon a white horse. It was too far away for her to tell if this mysterious rider was a young man or a woman. For a moment she thought of Sharn Am Zor, but she doubted if he would ever learn to sit a prancing steed so well. As she watched, the white rider waved a hand, slowly and purposefully, then the whole company was out of sight behind the hedges of the Varda road.

"Come then," she said to the two men, "we will go out. Take my hand, Sergeant, and you, Highness, take the sergeant's hand. Be careful on the stair."

They followed her like sleepwalkers; the mill was sweet and quiet. At one turn of the stair, they heard weeping; and at another, there was a globe of light that danced about over their heads. They went down and down, and Aidris led the way out of the dark door. The sun was covered by a thin film of cloud, and they could see the boundaries of the spell, the charmed circle that lay around the mill, like a mist. The prince's horse stood some way off, and now it was afraid, trembling; it gave its master a nervous greeting when he appeared. The cause of its fear lay close by the door: the dead body of the young kern, Simmen, pale and unmarked. Aidris guessed that his neck was broken.

"Bring the mare, Highness," said Aidris firmly. "She must carry out poor Simmen."

The prince moved cautiously through the grass and led the mare closer, then he held her head while Sergeant Wray lifted up his young comrade and laid him across the rich saddle. There came again that windy clattering from inside the mill, which struck fear into all of them. Aidris took the sergeant's hand

127

again, and then came the prince, leading his horse. They took the same track that Aidris had made in the dew-wet grass, now warm and dry underfoot. As she walked along, Aidris became aware of a little track that grew in the grass at her side, as if some animal walked beside her across the meadow.

So they came at last to the bridge, and Aidris walked on boldly into the mist itself, feeling the firm boards under her feet. She stared ahead and saw shapes form in the mist: men and women standing stock still, like figures in a dream. For a moment she was afraid, but then she saw that these were watchers of flesh and blood, waiting for their return. For a few paces she saw them as uncanny, dwellers in another world, and yet she knew most of them. Niall of Kerrick, Ortwen, Mother Mora and the miller himself, and Dickon, the young lad. Megan Brock stood there with an officer in strange livery, and a fair-bearded man, fancily dressed, whom she took for Fantjoy, the prince's servant. There were children come to gape, and Gavin, the lame waker, from the barracks.

Aidris came out of the mist completely and stood aside at the entry to the narrow bridge to let the sergeant, the prince and the mare with its burden go past her. The watchers came forward as if a spell was broken and gathered round the sergeant and the prince.

Aidris glanced down at the grass by the bridge and said quickly, "Go to Niall of Kerrick in the brown and yellow robe. Serve him faithfully. In his service is your freedom."

There was no sign that she had been heard; she might have been muttering to the air. People were coming towards her. She flung up a hand and spoke the word of unbinding given her by Prince Terril. A wild wind sprang up, whirling about the mill, catching at the hair and clothes of those watching, bending the poplar trees. Hats flew off, geese ran honking along the river bank, dogs barked, the horses plunged and reared. Then the wind was gone, as suddenly as it had arisen, and with a harsh grating sound like a long sigh, part of the old mill fell away as they watched, a wall crumbled and fell in, raising a cloud of dust.

"Venn," said Megan Brock, "did you do that?"

"No, Captain," said Aidris, "not entirely."

The kedran captain smiled at last, watching Aidris very keenly.

"It was well done," she said. "You brought out Wray and the

prince. We have heard something of the business from that damned courtier, what's his name, Fantjoy."

"It was too late for poor Kern Simmen," said Aidris.

She saw that the sergeant and a company of men-at-arms were preparing to take their young comrade's body back to the hall.

"Captain," she said. "I am uneasy about the whole tale. Where was this Fantjoy all night long?"

"Knocked silly behind the mill," said Megan Brock. "Or so he says. This spell or charm flung him some way when it was set down, and he came to himself after you had gone to the rescue. What are you saying, Venn?"

"The whole working was directed against the visitors, the two princes at the crossroads," said Aidris. "Oh, I am sure Terril meant it as a prank, no more; but if the charm had been set at the crossroads, the working might have been much worse than here. It was pure chance that the old mill had a fetch and the charm rebounded."

"I am not up in magic," said the captain, "but I accept your judgement. You must write a full report."

"I still don't know the time of day," said Aidris.

"Past four o'clock," said the captain. "There was no other hitch, Goddess be praised. Grey Company lacked two horses, but the whole thing went off . . . like a charm. The princes came safely to the hall. This little sideshow has been hushed up. You and Cash are excused from duty until the morning."

She saluted, cocking an eye at the prince and his servant who now approached.

"This is my witch-maiden," said Terril. "You see, Fantjoy . . . Kerrick Hall is full of surprises."

Fantjoy was subdued and weary, all his curls wilting. He had obviously been badly frightened. He snatched up Aidris's hand nevertheless, and she saw Ortwen grinning as he kissed it.

"Ch-charmed," he stammered. "You saved my master, Kedran Venn."

"You have put me in your debt," said Prince Terril. "Ask something, my dear. What will you have?"

"Nothing at this time, Highness," said Aidris steadily. "Perhaps when I ride home, one of these years, I will need something."

"Ride home?"

"The kedran surely comes from the Ch-chameln lands," put in Fantjoy softly.

"That explains a lot," said the prince airily. "They are all witches there!"

She escaped from the pair of them and came to Niall of Kerrick. The whole crowd of watchers had dispersed and were walking or riding away, some to the hall.

"You must tell me the tale one day," said Niall.

"It was a bad business," said Aidris. "They play at magic in Athron, Master Kerrick."

"I know it," he said, "but you have done bravely. Perhaps some good will come of this sorry jest. Look . . . I have found a friend!"

There at his side, tongue lolling, trotted a curly black dog, not as large as a lurcher but bigger than a terrier. Niall bent down and ruffled its poll.

"A stray," he said. "I'll call him Crib, I think, for an old dog I had once as a boy."

"It is a good name," said Aidris. "Here, Crib!"

The dog seemed to know its name already. It danced about, and she patted it and gazed into its yellow-brown eyes.

"I am sure it will serve you faithfully," she said.

Niall seemed about to speak again, but then he lowered his eyes and walked off in silence with the black dog gambolling at his heels. Aidris was left alone with Ortwen and their two horses.

"I'm wrung out," said Ortwen, "and Goddess knows how you must feel."

"It has been a long day," said Aidris, "but longer for you than for me. In there the time passed more quickly."

"Trouble," grumbled Ortwen, as they led the horses along the road. "You draw it to yourself, Venn, like honey draws the bees and wasps. Now it's more than house folk, it's a prince. And that sweet-smelling hand-kisser, F-f-fantjoy."

"Don't nag," said Aidris. "At least we're off duty and can sleep or go watch the dancing."

As they passed the mill, Mother Mora stood on its bridge. Aidris returned the little cloth-wrapped charm that she had carried up her sleeve. She thought of the mill and shuddered.

"What is in the charm, good mother? Can you tell me?"

"Carach leaves," said the old woman, "powdered fine and mixed with . . . certain other things. Our good Athron magic. You have laid the fetch. You have the power and the spirit for such things."

"I did not seek this power," said Aidris.

"It is a gift," said Mother Mora. "Give thanks for it."

Aidris mounted up, feeling a pleasant sense of the end of the adventure. She rode back with Ortwen through the cool evening, and when they came up the avenue to the hall, the lamps were already lit and they could hear the musicians tuning up for the night's festivities.

"The honeymooners came safe home?" she asked, "Lady Sabeth and Sir Gerr?"

"They rode in at the right hand of Prince Ross, so I am told," said Ortwen. "There was an awkwardness because the place should have gone to that poor plain thing, Princess Josenna, wife of Flor."

"Is she plain then?" said Aidris. "I'm sorry for her."

"She is bad-tempered and jealous of her rights."

"The world expects too much of a princess."

The courtyard before the main entry was lit with golden lanterns. There were kedran from the hall on duty and a company from Varda. Aidris saw for the first time men and women wearing the emblems of the Falconers of Eildon, one of the oldest of the knightly orders. Lady Aumerl, resplendent in her gown of green, came out onto the steps and stood taking the evening air with three guests.

"Who are those three?" asked Aidris, clutching at Ortwen's rein.

She saw that one was an old man, tall and silver-haired, and one a woman with tawny hair and the third a dark man.

"Psst!" whispered Ortwen, although they were a long way off in a patch of shadow.

"Those are the messengers. Uncanny, all three of them and full of old, dark Eildon magic. They serve the Falconers; some say they can fly about as falcons themselves. They come back every few years to Kerrick Hall . . . it is a wonder you have not seen them before."

"Why do they come back?" asked Aidris.

"To do honor to our Lord and Lady," said Ortwen. "They

helped our good Lord Huw bring back the Carach tree years ago when Athron was in its doleful dumps, a poor and wretched land."

"They *are* uncanny," said Aidris. "I have had enough of magic for one day."

She felt as if she stood upon the edge of a dancing floor or an arena for martial games. She had only to ride into the golden light of the courtyard and show herself to these messengers, and then, perhaps, her secret would be known. She would come out of the darkness, be invisible no longer. Yet she shrank back; the time was not ripe. She rode off to the bustle of the stableyard, and there was old Gavin, grinning with excitement. He gave them a wink and offered to groom their horses.

"You've had a hard day, my girls!"

"That's a kind offer," said Ortwen. "Come Aidris, you're all worn out with your witchcraft."

"We'll bring you some pickings, Master Waker," said Aidris.

That night and other nights she thought of the messengers as she had first set eyes on them, through the western window of the mill. She had seen them ride from Garth with young Huw Kerrick, on an autumn day in the past. She had seen the present too, from the southern window. But the future? She could still make nothing of the dark troop moving towards Varda, with the rider on the white horse.

The long month of the royal visit dragged out for the kedran and men-at-arms. There was too much to do at some times and too little at others. It was spit and polish all day and every day; it was rich food left over from banquets and not enough time to eat it. It was drooping in the saddle, swallowing a yawn; it was the crowded stableyard, where those who had yielded to temptation and become drunk were always under the pump trying to sober up. It was a guardhouse embarrassingly full of the escort troops from Varda and Eildon, who boozed and fought like folk on a fairground, blaming it on the Kerrick wine and beer.

The barracks rang with royal gossip, which Aidris found hateful and trivial. Prince Terril was also a guest at the hall, and whether his jape came out or not he was not on good terms with his brother and sister-in-law. Aidris could not deny that she looked with keen interest at all the royal personages. Flor was a solid, good-humored man who looked exactly what he was:

a Prince of Athron. He was prosperous yet not over-refined, dignified but not cultivated. Princess Josenna, daughter of an old Athron lord, was indeed plain and fretful; she was pregnant, having borne two daughters and miscarried twice.

Aidris puzzled over those lands where a woman could inherit only in default of a male heir. In the Chameln lands it was otherwise and in Eildon, but the arrangements of the ruling houses were as strange as all the ways of Eildon. The aged Priest-King Angisfor still lived in his mystical retreat, and his children and grandchildren ruled the land.

Ross of Eildon was more sparing of his presence than the Varda princes; he lived in the south wing of Kerrick Hall and kept his own people closely about him. Yet Aidris had seen him riding in procession or passing from one room to another in the evening with musicians and flamboys. He seemed to her a being so strange that he might have come from a land of legend, from Ystamar or from the kingdom under the waves. He was of great physical beauty, tall and straight, golden-haired and nobly bearded. Aidris felt sure that he never raised his voice, never moved quickly. His aura was so strong for her that she wondered how anyone could come into his presence without being aware of it. The air about him burned, gold or pearl-colored. She remembered her childish fancy, riding to meet the northern tribes: how the fair-skinned people of the Zor had shining faces. But their radiance had to do with health and the open air.

Once, during a turn off duty, she tried to find her way to Sabeth, to greet her after so long and to ask about Eildon. A new waiting women took in her name to the chambers where the young couple were lodged. She waited in the corridor, with strange courtiers and servants passing, for a long time, and then Moss appeared, the former page, now grown into Gerr of Kerrick's manservant. He had the grace to look embarrassed.

"Oh, Venn," he said. "We thought it might be you."

"I sent in my name," she said, foreseeing all and not prepared to let him down lightly.

"Therza couldn't understand your accent," he said, "but she gave a description. Not many kedran come hanging about in the hall without any duty."

"Moss, what is the matter? Is the Lady Sabeth resting? Was my name brought to her?"

"When the royal visit is over," he said, "Sir Gerr and Lady

Sabeth will have their days for petitions as Lord Huw and Lady Aumerl do now."

"I did not come as a petitioner but as a friend," she said.

"Venn, go along. It is the way of the world. Her estate has changed."

"Do you remember if a gift of silk arrived from Varda?"

"From the envoy, you mean? Yes, Nanad Am Charn sent a gift. The Lady Sabeth is a high-born exile from the Chameln lands, after all."

"The gift was from me and my family," she said, "and Nenad Am Charn would have seen to it that the gift was so delivered."

She turned away, but Moss came after her.

"Venn, please . . . be a good fellow," he said with a hint of his old whining tone. "There's a chance, a good chance, that they will be given something by the Prince of Eildon. I mean an estate, a title. They have to be discreet."

"Tell the Lady Sabeth I was disappointed," she said.

She went down the stairs feeling more puzzled than anything else. Could Sabeth have had her head turned so completely? She found herself thinking of things so petty and ignoble that she was ashamed. She wondered about the winter cloak of lynx and fox, Bajan's gift, which hung in Sabeth's wardrobe still because Aidris had no room for it in her small press in the barracks. She felt envious of Prince Ross because he had stolen away one of her wish-dreams. *He* would raise Sabeth and Gerr to a high estate. She sighed at her own foolishness: here she was a grown woman, a kedran of four years service, still indulging in the fantasies of a royal child.

She was cast down a little and seemed to drag herself through the toils of extra duty. Then, as the long moon came to an end, there was Fantjoy, curled and perfumed, at the barracks with an invitation, a royal summons, in fact, for Kedran Venn. He had already ch-checked with Captain Brock.

"Be damned, Venn," said Ortwen. "You must go! You cannot feign sick."

"I *am* sick."

"You're healthy as a horse. You can wear your best New Year tunic. . . ."

Her Chameln finery was admired by the kedran, who hated to wear skirts. She allowed herself to be coaxed into her good white, the fine doeskin breeches and the long tunic trimmed with beadwork, fresh as they were on the day the Lady Maren laid them in her saddlebag for the flight into Athron. But she waited until the last possible moment, and then slipped in through the kitchens.

The cavernous rooms were full of steam; the cooks and scullions ran and shouted and pummelled each other, purple with effort. There seemed to be twenty formal dinners being prepared besides a dozen cauldrons of simpler fare. She did not have far to go: a large plain room on this ground floor with doors to the north courtyard. It was named Hot Commons—it was so near the kitchen that food brought in had no time to get cold—and it had been chosen for the Varda Benefit.

The visitors from the city repaid hospitality and good service with a feast. There, milling in the corridor in their best clothes, were servants of high rank, soldiers and officers, waiting-women. The doors were flung open, and Prince Flor's major-domo began checking invitations and bawling out the names of the guests.

A hush fell over the company as they went in. As Aidris came up to the door behind a stately old woman in black silk, who turned out to be the mother of the head gardener, she saw that Hot Commons had been transformed. The plain room had been swathed and panelled in russet and gold cloth; gilded stags' heads for the house of Menvir supported swags of maple, golden ash and dark pine. Copper candle-racks blazed overhead, and an early fire had been lit.

Rushes had been spread among the short trestles, trophies of the chase hung upon the walls; and to complete the illusion of a hunting lodge, Prince Flor and Princess Josenna sat with their closest followers in a rustic bower beside the fireplace. The Varda musicians had begun to play. The major-domo, after his deafening roar of "Kedran Venn," gave her a sly, approving smile, and a little page led her to a certain table under a canopy of green netting.

"Venn!" cried Genufa, the dark-haired waiting woman, glowing like a jewel.

"At last a familiar face," she whispered. "Truly, Aidris, there is something afoot. I feel like a masker in a pageant who has not been given her place in the parade."

"Something afoot?"

"Look about you . . ."

Their table with its gilded pinecones and peacock feathers

was filling up now with eight, nine, a dozen young women. Aidris had already looked about for Fantjoy or Prince Terril, but they were nowhere to be seen.

"Holy Tree," drawled a red-haired beauty in the accents of Eildon, "are we to be the willow-sisters then, parted from the company of men to weep for the cares of the world?"

"Take some wine," said a kedran with a falcon on her tunic, "you'll weep sooner."

The first courses of the banquet were streaming into Hot Commons with hautboys, torches and gusts of savory fragrance. A number of the greatest delicacies—the roast swan with its golden crown, a great pasty of larks and pigeons, an aspic in the shape of a green rose—came to the girls' table.

"Alas," said the lady on Aidris's right hand, "I believe, dear sisters, that we are being fattened up."

Aidris ate brook trout—swan having unfortunate associations for her—and studied this lady. She knew that she had seen her before, but only a hint of the time and place remained. Sunlight after rain, horses, a feeling of sharp nostalgia. Was it autumn weather?

"You have that beautiful beaded tunic from the Chameln lands," said the lady, picking daintily at a pigeon leg.

"From my homeland," said Aidris, smiling.

The lady was somewhat older than herself and dressed in the style of Athron. She had a fall of dark brown hair and a skin lightly tanned as if from riding.

"Oh what a happy chance," cired the lady. Aidris had seen that the name upon her rustic place marker was Mistress Quade. "We were there upon our travels. I must present you to my dear liege. That is, if your partner will permit it."

"My partner?"

"What?" Mistress Quade smiled. "Do you not know, then, who will partner you? Look about you: we are birds in a cage waiting to be set free!"

Across the crescent shaped table a blonde maiden cried out, "There will be dancing in the removes!"

"Good Mistress Quade," said Aidris, still unable to place the lady, "how fares the Chameln land? How long since you returned?"

"More than three years," said Mistress Quade, rinsing her

fingers, "How quickly the time goes. We were there before and after the Protector came to power."

"Do you mean Werris?" asked Aidris as lightly as she could. "I would call him some other names."

"Oh forgive me," said Mistress Quade. "You are a loyalist, of course."

They were interrupted by a group of musicians and the major-domo who came to their table with a basket of favors. The other guests cheered and whistled as a serenade was played and packages cunningly wrapped in leaves or woven straw were given out.

Aidris found that her favor was a silver owl's head with green eyes; Genufa had a pomander of silver-gilt; Mistress Quade a little mirror in a bronze case. When Aidris looked into it, she saw a stranger with wide green eyes and red lips, a flush in her pale cheeks, dark hair that curled more softly in the air of Athron: a girl, she was pleased to admit, who did not look out of place at this table with the rest of the cage-birds.

"What news was there of the Daindru when you were in the Chameln lands?" she asked Mistress Quade.

"Ah my dear," she said, "you have heard the rumors. A history of blood. The kings both murdered, and their children imprisoned. We travelled first to Achamar, that lovely city at the end of the world, then crossed into Lien, through the Adderneck Pass, by Nesbath, at the head of the inland sea. We spent more than a year in Lien. We were not long in Balufir, it was not suited to our mood at the time; but we did see a Tournament of Song, as it was called, in an old fortress on the Ringist. We made a leisurely voyage to Eildon and its islands, and then our way led through the Chyrian lands of Mel'Nir. We climbed the High Plateau—I will never forget it—and searched for the Ruined City, the one that wanders in the mist."

Mistress Quade's voice trembled, she set down her goblet of wine.

"Did you find it?" prompted Aidris gently.

"No!" exclaimed Mistress Quade. "No, it eluded us. It was a very adventurous time for us both. We returned a different way. We crossed Lien in the west and travelled through the Adz and came into the Chameln lands not long after Werris had secured the passes. You were asking about the poor children—they were searching for one of them, the Princess of the Firn, at this time. We had come through the forest looking for the goblin folk. We were tired but kept up our spirits. We came to Addero, a tiny place. . . ."

"Aldero," said Aidris, taking a gulp of wine herself. "Aldero, the forest village."

"And then to Vigrund, a charming town, with a good inn. The place was full of the giant soldiers, there was no hope of getting over the Rodfell Pass, it was shut tight. We went back to the east, stayed in Zerrah . . . do you know Zerrah? . . . for a long time, three more moons, simply resting."

"And the children?"

"Yes, it is a horrid story. There will be pretenders to the thrones, I am sure of it. The royal children had not been seen in Achamar for years. The hue and cry at the border came to nothing. The young lad was drowned crossing the Danmar, that is certain. And the girl . . . I cannot recall if she was older or younger . . ."

"Older," said Aidris, "several years older."

"We heard it from the new head of the garrison at Zerrah Manor. The Princess was murdered at Thuven, a wretched old country house on the way to Vigrund. We rode home that way, having obtained our safe-conduct. We saw the very place where she is supposed to be buried, a barrow, an old grave-hill behind the ruins of the house. And the most touching thing of all was that some loyalist had planted an oak on her grave . . . it was already flourishing, almost a sapling."

"Thuven Manor House is destroyed then?"

"Burnt and razed. A place accursed. It made us shudder. The old man, mad I do not doubt, and with a wife as wicked as himself . . . Old Nazran was shut up in Ledler Fortress."

"Nazran Am Thuven is not a murderer!"

"My dear, you are young. You do not know evil and misfortune . . ."

Mistress Quade pressed Aidris's hand, and her dark eyes were full of tears. Aidris breathed deeply; she felt divided from herself as she had done in the old mill. She might soar up to the brass candle holders in the ceiling of Hot Commons and look down upon the table of girls, bright-faced and dressed in fine clothes, and see herself among them. The lying, foolish tale she had just heard touched her deeply, made her afraid and angry, and at the same time it did not touch her at all. It was a party jest, to be forgotten by morning. Yet Nazran and his lady were imprisoned and Thuven had been destroyed, that at least she believed.

She gave a start as hunting horns rang out. The doors to the north court flew open, and in came a company of young men in green and red hunting dress, all with plumed hats and gilded masks that entirely concealed their faces. They whooped and danced up and down the long room, teasing the diners, snatching tidbits from the platters, turning somersaults and scattering green marzipan "coins" stamped with a stag's head. A cry went up as they came down the room again:

"The birds! The birds under the net!"

The musicians struck up "Blackbird and Thrush," played as a jig, and the huntsmen descended noisily upon the table of the birds. There was a great deal of shrieking and rustling as they claimed their partners. Aidris, at the back of the table in a quiet place, heard Mistress Quade murmur "You *are* a dark horse, Kedran Venn..." as she was led off by a tall masker. Then she herself was claimed by a nimble gentleman with chestnut curls under his huntsman's hat.

"Green-eyes..." said Prince Terril.

She took his hand, and they led off the dance. Terril was a strong and supple partner, and she understood a practical reason for his choosing her: she was the right height for him. They leaped and spun and tried difficult figures. The music played and played and carried them away with it. She saw that Fantjoy partnered Genufa, and the young men who visited Kerrick on feast days had chosen the visiting ladies from Eildon and Varda. She noticed that by the time the musicians played "Cock Pheasant in a Bush" Mistress Quade and her partner had turned aside and settled to rest.

"Good Huntsman," she asked, "who is Mistress Quade's partner? Can you tell me?"

"What, has that beanpole caught your eye, little witch?"

"Of course not." She laughed. "But I have seen the lady before, and I believe it was in my homeland."

"Come, we will walk back to them," said the Prince. "You dance marvellously well, do you know that?"

"Only as well as my partner!"

They walked the length of the hall, and Aidris saw that the

tall man, Mistress Quade's partner, had taken off his mask. She knew him at once. Sunlight after rain, drifts of maple leaves, blood red in the streets of Achamar. Nazran laughed sadly and arranged the wooden shutter so that she remained in shadow. There in the street was a young Knight Forester upon a white horse, accompanied by a kedran... the first knight questor that she had ever beheld.

"Poor devil!" said Prince Terril unexpectedly. "They have a somewhat tragic history, those two."

"Should I hear it before we meet them?" she asked.

"We should not spoil the pleasure of the time," said Terril. "They cannot marry, that is the heart of it. A matter of inheritance."

So they came to the netted bower of the birds again, and she was presented to Sir Jared Wild of Wildrode.

Mistress Quade curtsied to the prince and said in a particular voice to Sir Jared, "The kedran comes from the Chameln lands..."

"Sir knight," said Aidris, "I am certain that I saw you riding once in the streets of Achamar, upon a white charger."

"That was long ago, I think," said Sir Jared.

He was very handsome in the manner of the Zor, with thick fair hair, cut in a round knight's crop, and pale skin. She contrasted him with that other handsome knight, Gerr of Kerrick, and thought of them riding side by side. Sir Jared lacked his right eye, he wore an eye-patch of white leather; a disfiguring scar held down the corner of his mouth on the right side. His speech was halting; his right hand twitched upon the table top. Aidris wondered what adventure he and his kedran had found upon the High Plateau of Mel'Nir, searching for the ruined city.

"I will always owe the Knights of the Foresters a special duty," she said, "for it was Gerr of Kerrick who helped me to come out of the Chameln lands into Athron."

"We met Gerr, did we not," said Sir Jared. "We met him by Vigrund, when the border was first closed."

"Yes," said Mistress Quade, soothing. "Yes, you are right."

The next courses of the banquet were being ushered into the chamber, and it was the sign for more foolery, for all the maskers must now be accommodated at the table of the young women. Aidris was glad to find herself between the Prince and Fantjoy, who ate neatly and drank moderately. The splendors of the Varda Benefit continued to unfold: jugglers, sword-dancers, favors and candies for all the guests. Before the next remove, when the dancing became general, the Princess Josenna had excused herself and sailed off with her women, leaving Prince Flor with his boon companions.

The lights burned lower; it was close to midnight. Prince Terril led Aidris out again into the rank of the dancers. As they came to the open doors, he danced her out into the north court where a sprinkling of other couples danced or sought the shadows. The night air was delicious. The prince took off his mask, and they strolled in the north walk, a cool covered way under the balcony of the long gallery. Terril tightened his arm about her waist, drew her aside between two pillars and kissed her.

She had not been kissed in this way in her life before, but it seemed a thing that could be learned quickly. They kissed again and sank down on a convenient bench built into the pillars. Terril's breath upon her cheek came less gently, but just as she became afraid, remembering Loeke, the forest guide, his reek and roughness, the Prince drew back, smiling, his fine dark eyes fixed upon her.

"Green-eyes," he whispered, "what a spell you have put over me . . ."

She could not look at him, but bent her head upon his shoulder.

"Sweetheart," said the Prince, "listen well to what I say, do not answer at once. I need you . . . come to Varda with me, be my kedran, my rune-mistress, what you will. Exile is long. I think I know your state. You are of decent birth, the daughter of some Chameln lord. You are not a child, but, by your kissing, still a maid . . ."

She wondered how to let him down lightly. She found herself reckoning with dreadful clarity that whether she went home or spent her whole life in exile this might be the pleasantest offer she would receive; a proposal that was dishonorable, certainly, but not unthinkable.

"Prince," she said, "you are indeed such a man as I might love, but I cannot do it. For one thing, I am betrothed."

"Ah, who is betrothed?" he whispered. "The kedran or the lord's daughter?"

"In Varda, I swear to you, I might be in danger and bring

141

danger upon others," she said. "Besides, I have been well treated in this place, in Kerrick."

He stared at her, lifted a hand to smooth the hair from her forehead. Torchlight from the courtyard showed his face, sad but not petulant. His own care, his life as a prince of Athron and a younger brother, showed in his face. She felt a moment of real tenderness for Terril of Menvir.

"The years are long," he said gently. "There is always a place for you. You did me a service, and I still have a favor to grant you."

"I will remember."

"I will tell you something," said Terril, "and you must believe it, for love and friendship. You have a friend who is no friend, who would be glad if you left the hall and came to Varda in my service."

She said nothing, did not say the name that first came to mind, and heard him with a kind of relief.

"I mean Gerr of Kerrick!"

"But why?"

He smiled, an intriguer's smile that she had seen often in the courts of Achamar, and it made her feel foolish, a child again.

"He is jealous of all those close to his new wife," said the Prince. "He will break all her former ties and guide her by himself."

She could only shake her head sadly, thinking of the long way through the forest, all the perils she had passed, with Sabeth, and how Gerr had saved them both.

"I count them both as my friends," she said.

There was a particular cheerful whistle from the darkness, and inside Hot Commons the musicians began to play "The Golden Stag," a kind of anthem for the house of Menvir.

"Drat!" said Prince Terril. "It is time for the toasts, and Fantjoy is calling me. Let us go in . . ."

"I will stay here," she said.

They kissed again, quickly and lightly. He was gone. She sat lone, breathing deeply, feeling that the world was full of leave-taking, of lying tales and false friends. She felt sick and stifled at the thought of the banquet room and so stole into the north court and crossed before the lighted doors of Hot Commons. A few huntsmen were reeling and laughing in the middle of the court. She came to an outside stair and climbed swiftly to the balcony overhead.

The long gallery, in the manner of Eildon, linked the new north and south wings of the Hall, but in Athron's mild climate, a balcony was also possible. Aidris liked it as well as any place in that fine house. It was long and broad and still, with blue fir trees that smelled of the Chameln lands and the winter festival. She looked up to the hill and wished she might speak to the Carach tree. She might have taken out her scrying stone, but it was tucked away in her locked press in the barracks.

She walked to the second tree and perched upon its stone urn, leaning on the balustrade. There were lights burning in the upper rooms of the hall where the "house folk" and their guests were still watching or feasting more decorously than those below at the Varda Benefit. She thought of Sabeth and Gerr, and wished she might come to them as a friend, as she had done in past winters. Where would she go in the New Year if they did not welcome her in the hall? She fell into a long waking dream in which she quit Kerrick Hall and went home to her own land, all alone except for Telavel. She slipped through the Grafell Pass or the Wulfental and went into the forest and accepted whatever doom she found. Perhaps to come to the northern tribes, to Bajan, wherever he was hiding himself. Perhaps to be captured and pent up by the Melniros in Ledler Fortress, where Nazran might still be alive. Perhaps to die in the forest, alone, but in her own country.

A door opened far away at the southern end of the balcony; she vaguely saw three, four dark figures come out. She remained still, in her shadow; soft voices drifted through the night air. She realised that the language was strange to her. It was not any variant of the common speech, the drawl of Eildon or the richer burr of Athron, and it was not the Old Speech. There was only one other tongue that it might be, and she could guess at only one group of persons who might speak it familiarly. This must be Chyrian, the old speech of Eildon; and those speaking it must be those mysterious messengers who served Prince Ross.

Her first thought was to escape by running down the stair again and hiding herself in the crowded banquet. She moved lightly to the shadow of another tree and heard a change in the tone of the voices. She had been seen. There was a soft hail, a woman's voice calling "Who is there?" Aidris was a long way from them; she stepped out boldly from behind the tree and began to walk briskly to the stairway. There was a command in Chyrian, and then they descended upon her, all three, their long cloaks billowing.

"Stay! We command you!"

She saw them over her shoulder quite clearly in the autumn night: the woman, the old man, the dark man. There was a quick gust of wind, a sound of bird wings high in the air above her head, and she saw only two figures. The dark man was ahead of her, blocking her way to the stair.

"Come, lady," he said gently, "the Prince would speak with you."

Aidris saw that a tall figure stood waiting. She lifted her head and walked towards Ross of Eildon. The messengers drew back and came slowly in her wake. She walked directly into his light. His strangeness did not diminish as she came closer. He was as tall as a warrior of Mel'Nir, yet without the hulking presence of the young giants. His face was very smooth and pale; his eyes were a luminous grey. She thought of the eyes of the huntsmen gleaming through their gilded masks.

"What do you call yourself, child?"

The voice was muted, soothing.

"Kedran Venn, Highness."

"You are the Heir of the Firn. What are your given names?"

"Racha Sabeth Aidris Am Firn. But I am called Aidris."

"You have hidden yourself very thoroughly. Yet you walk about in the night dressed in fine Chameln raiment..."

"I have been attending the Varda Benefit."

They smiled at each other.

"I begin to understand," said Prince Ross. "You were the kedran who came over the mountains with young Kerrick and his Golden-Hair. She is your waiting woman. Why did they not bring you to me in Eildon?"

Aidris could only smile and shake her head. Old magic, it seemed, was no protection against prejudice.

"Sir Gerr and Lady Sabeth are the friends of Kedran Venn," she said. "They know nothing of my state. I have told no one. I would remain unknown."

She turned her head towards the messengers. He summoned them with hardly a gesture; they flowed silently along the balcony, creatures of Eildon, strange as the prince himself.

"Dravyd," said Prince Ross, indicating the old man, "Nieva and Gil. The messengers of the Falconers. Servants of the houses of Eildon and of their kindred throughout the lands of Hylor."

Her servants then, or at least loyal to her house. The old man was thin and tall as a shaman, the woman, Nieva, held in her silvery hands a small stringed instrument, the dark man, Gil, looked at her with bright bird's eyes. She inclined her head and they bowed, smiling.

"Come, Aidris Am Firn," said the prince. "We will sit together."

She laid her hand in his cool hand, and he led her across the long gallery into a rich and pleasant chamber where a fire burned low. The messengers did not follow, there were no other servants. They sat in two cavernous chairs by the fireside, and Prince Ross poured wine into glass beakers set in silver holders.

"You are tired of waiting," he said; "but it is because of your youth. Exile must be borne."

"I will bear it!"

"You have chosen a comfortable place—Athron. I was exiled once upon a rock in the ocean, hardly an island."

"When?" she asked. "For how long?"

"Six years," he replied, "seven . . . I have forgotten. Ages past. I look strange to you, child, because I mask my years with spells."

He stretched out a hand upon the velvet cover of the table between them; the hand, well-fleshed and strong, wavered before her eyes. It became a gaunt, knotted hand, incredibly old, the rings hanging loose upon the fingers and the skin flecked brown and white. The transformation passed quickly, the prince's hand was well-formed again; the aged hand might have been the illusion, not the one she saw now.

"Your houses of the Daindru are bayed about with enemies," he said. "I cannot do much. In fact, I will not. But a touch upon the web can help. What will you ask of me?"

She thought, sipping the wine.

"My cousin, Sharn Am Zor, is in Lien," she said. "His mother Aravel is mad, his uncle Kelen is no friend to the Chameln lands. Sharn needs guidance and protection. There is an old councillor there at the court of Lien, one Rosmer, whose evil workings have pursued us. Do you know of him? He came out of Eildon."

"Prince Sharn can find a friend," said Ross of Eildon. "You think of him before yourself. Have you become too self-effacing in this Carach-shaded spot?"

"Rosmer . . . ?" she persisted.

"He will run his course!" said the prince with a touch of heat. "He is not unassailable."

"You know him then?"

"Let it be, child, let it be," said Prince Ross with a sad tremor in his voice. "I know him. I should know him. He is my bastard son."

They sat in silence, and when she dared to look at the prince again, he gave her a long smile.

"Choose for yourself," he said.

She bent forward, staring into the dying fire and considering.

"The messengers," she said. "They must fly into the Chameln lands and bring comfort to the people. They must tell it far and wide: the Heir of the Firn and the Heir of the Zor are not dead; they will come again, and the Daindru will be restored. And the messengers must visit Ledler Fortress and bring greeting and succor, even rescue, if this is within their power, to Nazran Am Thuven and his wife, the Lady Maren, who lie there imprisoned."

She said, as an afterthought, "If they still live."

"You choose very modestly. Is that all?"

"I would send a ring to my betrothed, Bajan Am Nuresh."

She was cold and sad. It was painful to be known after so long and to send these few poor tokens.

"It will all be done, so far as it lies within the power of the messengers," he said, "and word will be brought to you."

"No!" she said. "I must remain . . . invisible, here at Kerrick. I will wait until my own people come to bring me home again."

She began to tug from her hand a silver ring with a yellow stone, the only one she wore beside Bajan's gold band with the turquoise stones. It was a gift from Lady Maren; she remembered how she had given a similar one, Nazran's gift, to the old woman, the horse doctor, by Aldero, the forest village.

"Wait," said Prince Ross.

He spoke in Chyrian, and the woman, Nieva came in at once. At the prince's word she brought a leather box from a press and went away again like smoke and left them alone. Prince Ross opened the box, and the firelight blazed on the jewels, jewels of Eildon with heavy settings of dark gold, with rubies, sapphires, sea pearls, cairngorms and garnets.

She thought of the jewels of the Firn and of the Zor, treasures that she had never cared for or coveted, the ancient square crowns of gold and bronze lit with huge yellow diamonds and round emeralds, the lake-pearls, beryls, zargons, sardonyx and turquoise, the opals, jade, and lazulite woven into garments, all her birthright of jewels fallen into the hands of Werris and the rulers of Mel'Nir.

"Choose for yourself and for your betrothed," said the Prince.

"Only for him," said Aidris, tenderly. "These are jewels too fine for a kedran."

She stared into the box and found a ring with a band of oak leaves worked in silver set with a black pearl. It fitted her thumb and would be large enough for Bajan.

"You are gifted," said Prince Ross. "You choose well. That is the ring of Tamir, the Sea Oak Prince, and has a strong link to the Chameln lands."

"Will you spare me such a treasure?" asked Aidris.

"It is yours," said the Prince. "It will be sent into the Chameln lands to Bajan Am Nuresh before the new moon. I will charge the messengers."

The fire burned blue and green. She wondered if time had altered as it had done in the old mill, if she would leave the fireside and find that the whole night had gone. They walked out again onto the balcony and she was glad to see that it was still dark. They were alone; down in the courtyard a few determined revellers still reeled and sang.

"Go well, Aidris Am Firn," said Prince Ross.

He raised his hands and gave her a blessing in Chyrian.

She ran down the stairs again and came back to Hot Commons. It was the scrag end of the banquet; guests lay about, the tables were disordered, the princes had gone and so had the musicians. She gathered up cold capons, fruit and an unopened stone bottle of good wine and carried them back to the barracks in a cellarer's basket. She put this offering by the pallet where Ortwen snored away and woke in the morning to find that the Varda Benefit was already a legend, a byword for drunken horseplay, rich food, lost maidenheads and every kind of scandalous behavior.

The long Maplemoon was done and the princes were gone

indeed, and the whole of Kerrick looked like a banquet chamber when the feast was over. The wheel of the year turned; by the time of the Lamp Lighting the visit was fading into memory. The kedran went about their duties. Telavel took a stone that festered and had to be poulticed by Sergeant Fell, the old horse-doctor. Aidris would have taken another mount but Megan Brock sent her into the stores to help with the winter reckoning. She had more free time and sat on the hill and told and retold the story of her meeting with Prince Ross to the scrying stone. The Lady spoke, once or twice, her voice wonderfully clear and distant.

One morning Moss, Gerr's manservant, met her as if by chance at the door of the muster hall and told her she might care to step up to the hall again. She bade him go to the nearest dunghill and roll in it. Yet that same day, Gerr himself burst into the stores, his face white about the lips.

"Venn ... you must come! She is sick!"

She felt the color draining from her own face and flung down her inventory book and went with him, without asking leave.

"What is it?"

They were passing through the north court and up to the balcony; the newly married pair lodged in the south wing.

"You will see," he mumbled. "Venn, I ..."

"Hush," she said. "I was rude to your man, to Moss ... I did not know."

Then they came to a bedchamber. Sabeth lay in the huge bridebed, her red-gold hair spread out upon the pillows, her face whiter than the bed linen. Lady Aumerl stood at the foot of the bed, and there was the midwife from Garth, a tall woman in a green cloak, for the service of the Goddess. The waiting-woman, Therza, wept in a corner, and Genufa held a tray of cordials. Aidris hardly saw them. She felt a hard, rending pain in her chest. She ran and knelt by the side of the bed and took Sabeth's cold hand.

"Are you there?" Sabeth searched her face with a wide wandering gaze. "The forest is dark. It will be lost. It will be lost."

"I am here. We have come out of the forest. We are in Athron. Gerr is here, your husband."

"Yes ... my true knight ... Oh Aidris, help me, you are so brave, you went to the witch stone...."

Sabeth breathed deeply and shut her eyes. The midwife, whispering with Lady Aumerl, came and knelt beside Aidris.

"The child was past praying for," she said. "It is miscarried. We must hope and fight for her life. She answers to you, her friend. Her color is better. You must stay beside her, and the young knight, too."

"Mother," said Aidris, "we must use a healing magic. Something stronger than Carach leaves. Is there not a thing called cloak-of-sleep?"

"Wheesht!" The midwife rolled her eyes. "You are well versed. I wonder if these hall folk would allow it, Kedran."

"Send all away but myself and Sir Gerr. I can find out the charm if you bring me a bleached cloth, newly blessed."

"Find out the charm?"

"From my scrying stone."

"Ah, you are Mother Mora's little witch from the old mill."

Then she saw nothing else but Sabeth's pale face; the room was becoming dark. Everyone had been drawn away by the midwife who sat at the door having handed in a bleached cloth. Across the wide bed knelt Gerr of Kerrick.

"Sir Knight," said Aidris, "we will do magic, and you must help me. The midwife agrees. It is for her life."

He could only nod. Sabeth stirred a little and moaned. Aidris turned aside and looked into the scrying stone.

"You see what is played out here," she said urgently. "Cloak-of-sleep . . . it is in a tale in the book."

On the table in the stone there lay a doll, a poppet, woman-shaped with a fall of golden hair. The doll was wrapped this way and that in a kerchief and the passes were made over its body. She watched, concentrating with all her might, then turned back and stripped off the bedclothes. She expected the bed to be soaked with blood, as such a bed had once been, but there was not so much. She ran out the cloth and Gerr, teeth set, helped her lay it over and around Sabeth in her stained night-gown. Then she took the scrying stone that blazed blue and made the passes up and down the limbs. She shook Sabeth awake so that she might gaze into the light of the stone; she pressed it to her forehead.

Sabeth uttered one sighing word: "Gerr," then she was deeply entranced. Her limbs moved, her body in the bleached cloth seemed about to float up off the bridebed. Gerr made a wild sound, like a sob.

"It is the charm taking hold," said Aidris softly. "See how she sleeps. . . ."

Sabeth's head had turned gently to one side and lay among her golden hair. Aidris bent over and moved the locks away, then drew up a single coverlet. They sat for a long time simply watching her charmed sleep.

"We need not watch so closely," said Aidris. "Come, Sir Gerr . . ."

She found dark, sweetened wine in a flagon on the mantelpiece. She poured two beakers of it and brought one to him where he stood uncertain in the middle of the chamber, unable to take his eyes from Sabeth.

"Please," she said, "keep up your strength and your spirits."

He sat hunched over in a chair by the fire, and she took a chair opposite. Presently he looked up at her, his eyes hard and bright.

"You serve her well," he said. "You are some kind of witch or healing woman. Venn, we must speak. You must trust me. What is your real name?"

She saw dimly where he was going, and she was angry and afraid, not only for herself.

"I cannot tell you," she said, very low. "I have told no one. You swore an oath . . ."

"Do you remember?" he said eagerly. "Do you remember what was said that day on the road to the hospice, by the Wulfental?"

"I think I do . . ."

"You will say perhaps that I lied to you, but I did not, I did not. I simply used the form of your question. Venn, I know all . . . I have known from the first. Why, I know more than my dear lady seems to know. Have you put a spell on her to cloud her wits?"

"Stop!"

She put her hands over her ears like a child. She saw his face darken.

"I cannot speak of that time," she said quickly, "and we must not quarrel. It will disturb the working of the healing spell upon Sabeth. Please, let us be quiet."

It was a flat lie, a way of putting him off. He settled moodily in his chair, and she did the same, curled away from the fire, watching Sabeth as she slept. She thought of Gerr and his long courtship, of the closeness she knew must exist between married persons. Yet all this long while Gerr had clung to a false belief. Pehaps he had hinted and questioned and explained away Sabeth's innocence.

They sat in silence for some time, and then Gerr called her name and smiled.

"Forgive me, Venn," he said. "I see that you are bound to play this out to the end. We need your magic. Let us be friends."

"You will always be my true friends," she said earnestly. "Pray you, believe it!"

He went on in a dreaming voice to confirm her worst suspicions.

"Prince Ross must know the truth. He called her Golden-Hair, like the Chameln lady who made that unfortunate marriage with the upstart house of Menvir. We received many signs of his favor and indulgence. I might say we have expectations: a title or a manor. He is a generous . . . kinsman."

She could not look at him. There was no way out of the thicket. It was all her fault. She went to Sabeth's bedside again. The midwife came in and looked at Sabeth and sent Moss to them with a supper tray. They sat up all night, speaking little, dozing in their chairs and building up the fire against the first chill of winter that seeped in from the long gallery.

At last Aidris slept deeply for an hour or two and woke in the thin, grey light of morning. Gerr had measured his length on the settle before the fire and still slept heavily. His face, relaxed in sleep, was fine and young and straight-featured. Perhaps dreams of royal ambition filled his sleep. She knew, suddenly, that Prince Ross would disappoint Gerr and Sabeth; they would get nothing from him.

She went to the bedside, and Sabeth stirred in her constricting cloth and opened her eyes.

"Ah," she breathed, "you *are* here! He let you come to me at last. I thought it was part of my dream."

"Are you comfortable? Is there any pain?"

"Not any more."

She stared at Aidris, and her blue eyes brimmed with tears.

"The child was lost. It was not even half-formed. I was so

151

full of joy, thinking of his child..."

"Hush. You are young. The midwife said that you will surely bear more children."

Aidris poured a sweet cordial and let Sabeth drink from the lipped cup.

"I have had a strange dream," said Sabeth. "I wonder what it means."

"Tell me..."

"I think it was in the Chameln lands," said Sabeth in a faint echo of her old "story-telling" voice from the campfire. "I saw three riders upon grey horses. I think they were kedran. They came through a light snowfall and turned down into a deep valley. A small manor house, not much more than a farmhouse, stood in the bottom of this valley; and as the riders came down into the valley, I knew in my dream that the place was called Zerrah. There were lights in the house, and servants came out with torches. They knelt down in the courtyard."

"There is such a place," said Aidris softly. "We spoke of Zerrah on the night of your bride-calling."

"I had forgotten," said Sabeth. "The dream changed and became happier. We were all in this place, Zerrah—Gerr and I and you were there too, and some others that I loved. It was summer. The valley was full of wild heather."

"It is a hopeful dream," said Aidris.

Sabeth drifted into sleep again, and Aidris sat wondering about the dream. It was plain that Zerrah, which she had always thought of as a pleasant spot but not so dear to her as Thuven, was a chosen place. It even explained Gerr's wild talk about the oath that he had not broken in the mountains. She thought of Zerrah and of those others who had stayed there: Sir Jared Wild and his kedran, Mistress Quade. She forced herself to go back to that moment when she, when Aidris, not even a true kedran, demanded of the young knight: *Did you hear, today, from the troopers, the name or rank of any persons they were seeking?* And he, not lying, but using the form of her question, replied that he had not. In fact he knew very well who was sought: he had heard it from Sir Jared or from others at Vigrund. He had expected a princess of the Chameln.

She had held back then, and now she must still be silent. She wondered if there was prophecy in Sabeth's dream as well as a scene from the past. She had come once to Zerrah by night with her two kedran; perhaps she and Sabeth and Gerr would all be happy in that place together, in the future.

The grey morning began to grow into a grey day; the midwife came and tended to Sabeth and was pleased to find her so well. Her fever had gone; her sleep had given her strength. The sadness because of the child that had been lost was echoed in the stillness and greyness of the autumn weather turning at last to winter. Aidris left the midwife to watch and stole away back to barracks before Gerr of Kerrick was awake.

CHAPTER
VI

IN FOUR YEARS AS A KEDRAN AIDRIS HAD BEEN no further from Kerrick Hall than Benna in the southwest; but in her fifth year, she travelled clear across Athron and back again. The New Year came in with freakish warm weather; then in the Willowmoon, snow and wind. There was a gift of horses from the Kerrick stables to be delivered, some way off, and the journey was put off several times. Then at the last possible moment, Grey Company took the duty and set off for Wildrode Keep, in the far northeast, beyond the Ettling Hills. The two colts and two fillies were a splendid gift: one pair were thoroughbred of the Athron stock; the others were of the new Kerrick breed, taller and stronger, the colt red-roan, the filly bay, sired by the great stallion Fireking. Sir Jared Wild of Wildrode was to be married in the first days of the Birchmoon to the young daughter of a neighboring lord.

The going was easy in spite of the wet and the unseasonable cold, and the hills were passed almost before Aidris knew they had been climbed. The party stayed at an inn near the sacred spring where the river Flume had its beginning, and all the kedran made wishes at the spring. Aidris, looking towards the mountains that rose a handspan above the horizon in the north-east, knew her wish, and it happened she knew Ortwen's too. A new suitor had appeared at New Year in Cashcroft, and Ortwen, heir to all her father's acres, thought she would take this handsome fellow and stop soldiering.

They came to the old black-browed, mouldering keep in good time; but here in the border country, the order and the quiet magic of Athron did not seem to have so firm a hold. Their lodgings were poor, the local kedran and men-at-arms all curst and sad. It was, as Sergeant Lawlor said, more like a wake than a wedding. Aidris singled out the quartermaster, who was more approachable than his companions, and spoke to him of a person who had been in her mind during the journey.

"Where is Mistress Quade?"

They were in a little snuggery beside the stores with a few younger kedran and kerns clustered round a brazier against the cold. Master Roon grinned at her mildly.

"Friend of yours, Kedran Venn?"

"Yes," she said. "We met lately at Kerrick."

"Poor Jess Quade has her bower at the top of this tower we're now in. She will be glad to see a friend."

"Master Roon," said Aidris, "what is her estate?"

"Quade was the steward of the keep," said the quartermaster. "Young Jess was brought up as book-sister to the young lords, Garl and Jared; she was older than they were by four, five years."

"Was Jared the younger brother? Not the heir?"

"Not at first. Our young lord, Garl, died on his wedding day. That is one reason you find us a little cast down and fearful before *this* wedding."

"And Mistress Quade was the kedran serving Sir Jared . . ."

"Just so. They went on many a quest. They might have married. Then Sir Jared became the heir, and from their last quest together, Jess Quade brought him home wounded. At least she bore him no bastards."

The bluntness and cruelty of it surprised her. She climbed the stair of the dark tower they were in and came to a room beneath the battlement, with only a faint glow of light under its door. Her knocking brought no answer, but the door was not latched. She went in and found Mistress Quade, pale and handsome, in a gown of crimson velvet, seated in a great chair before the fire.

"Kedran?" Her voice was faint and cold.

"Aidris Venn of Kerrick Hall."

"Oh my friend . . ."

It was a cry of pain. She tried to rise but fell back in the chair half-fainting. Aidris went to her; there was no water in the room, the jug was dry and dusty. She lit a candle.

"Forgive me," said Mistress Quade. "I do not know how long I have been sitting here. I had not imagined I would be so weak and foolish when the time came."

"Dear Mistress Quade, you must eat and drink. Let me call the servants."

"They will not serve me," she said. "I should go to the buttery myself. It is close by."

"I will go."

Aidris went out, wondering how to wangle food and drink in a strange household, but at the buttery hatch servants were coming and going with laden platters. She helped herself to wine, bread, butter, broken meat and cheese, mumbled to an old woman that it was "Quartermaster's orders for the Kerrick visitors" and carried her booty up to the tower again.

"Forsaken," said Mistress Quade. "I made him do it. There was no other way."

She ate and drank, slowly at first, then with more appetite.

"What will you do?" asked Aidris.

"I am not the first woman whose lover married elsewhere," she replied. "I could wait a little and then busy myself with his life, their lives again. He would even take me to his bed again. Or I might keep some rag of honor and be elder sister to the married pair, teacher to their children. The bride is sweet and sensible; she will do her best to care for him."

"You could leave the keep."

"Where would I wander? I have no spirit to take up arms again."

"The world is wide," said Aidris.

"Not for a woman alone, without means," said Mistress Quade. "Would I go to Lien where they flay women as whores? To the Chameln lands or Mel'Nir? To Eildon?"

"Go to Varda," said Aidris. "Prince Terril knows your story. He owes me a favor, and this will be it . . . to find a place for you. I will write a request to him."

"A favor, dear Aidris?" asked Mistress Quade slyly.

"Not for anything you might imagine," said Aidris, just as sly.

"The Prince was very taken with you, anyone could see that. Did he make you some offer?"

"To be his rune-mistress."

"How quaintly phrased. And you refused?"

"He is still my friend," said Aidris, "but there were reasons why I would not do it."

"Oh, child," said Mistress Quade, "you almost give me hope to try again. Turn down a prince . . . there is something princely in the gesture. But what would he find for me?"

"A place as teacher or steward or scribe. Perhaps . . . a husband."

"Even that," said Mistress Quade sadly. "But it would have to be an old man. I am barren. I could nurse and care for an old man as I have cared for . . . my liege."

"Mistress Quade . . ."

"My given name is Jessamy . . ."

"Jessamy," said Aidris, "how came the knight to such a pass? I saw you both, once, from a window in Achamar. I thought it strange that any persons should ride abroad seeking adventure. There had been too much change and violence in my life."

"I have heard that you know something of magic," said Jessamy Quade, looking away from Aidris, "so you will believe me if I tell you that the Wilds of Wildrode are accursed. A bane has fallen over the family, and on this ancient keep. I think it even pursued us on our last quest."

"I have heard of such things but not believed them very much," said Aidris. "Yet I know what it is to be pursued by misfortune."

"The history of Sir Jared's line for more than fifty years is one of accident, disease and death. His mother lost ten children. His elder brother Garl, a fine man on whom so many hopes were centered, died after a fall from his horse, on his wedding day, five years past. His father, Old Sir Garl, was found dead in his chamber, mysteriously burned. With the lands it has been the same: even the kind magic of the Carach trees could not heal this corner of Athron. Some have said, pardon me, that we are too close to the wild Chameln lands and the mountains, but I believe it is a curse.

"We swore, Jared and I, to escape this dreadful thing. We

went off questing and did well and suffered no harm. Then Jared became the heir of Wildrode. We went off on one last quest. We travelled, as I told you, through all the lands of Hylor, and I must say we thought of ourselves more as travellers than as questors. We used no violence, did not seek quarrels. Then we came at last to the High Plateau of Mel'Nir.

"We searched in that enchanted place, that wilderness of mists and rocks and grass tussock, for the Ruined City whose Chyrian name is Tulach-na-Shee. I have told you and all our questioners that we did not find it, but now I am not so sure. Certainly we found no ruins; but one day we came through a mist and were in a place that was green and flourishing. It was beyond a small, dried-up riverbed no more than a league from the village of Aird on the plateau, travelling to the east.

"In this green place there was a spring near a stone cell, like a chapel to the Goddess, and beyond it, among the tall spreading black pines that grow on the plateau, we saw a grey stone gateway. It was finely wrought with statues of beasts, and through the gateway we could see a tall house, a mansion.

"We drank at the spring and watered the horses and then turned to approach the gateway. A young man stood before us. No giant warrior, no brigand, but a slender youth in a russet tunic. We began to walk across the grass to greet him when he called to us to halt. He spoke in a strange way, lifting up his voice and calling to us as if we were far away or as if he could not see us plainly.

"'Are you dark or light who come to us?' he called. I remember the words. I remember everything he said. We took it for no more than a queer greeting, on the order of 'Do you come in peace?'

"Sir Jared called back and said his name: 'Wild of Wildrode, come out of Athron.'

"Then the young man said: 'Stay back! You are not yet summoned! You must follow the way to the end!'

"We made nothing of it, but the words sank into my mind. I spoke up myself then and said, 'Good Sir' or 'Good young sir . . . may we not approach the great house?'

"But the youth flung up his hand before his face and cried, 'Go back! Go back!'

"We stood stockstill, and he gave a whistle, putting his fingers to his lips, like a village boy. They came from nowhere, he summoned them up: two gigantic hounds, like Eildon mastiffs but far more terrible. They were of a color between black and grey, their eyes glowed red. I had only a moment of terror, and then they flung themselves upon us. We were struck to the ground; I saw my dear liege overwhelmed, and I fell down and my head must have struck a stone for I knew no more. I lost my senses.

"When I came to myself, I was surrounded by a thick, cold mist. I cried out and began to crawl to the spot where I had last seen Jared. There he still lay, horribly stained with blood. I found the pulse in his throat; he was alive. His face had been mauled and one eye deeply scratched at the corner, but the wounds were not as bad as they seemed at first. I still had a leather bottle at my belt with brandywine out of Lien, so I was able to tend to him a little. The mist was slowly clearing; it was night on the High Plateau, the stars blazing overhead.

"We were in a bare, dry waste, without grass or chapel or gateway; it had all vanished away. I almost screamed with fright when I saw an animal shape nearby, but it was my horse, my own good Ilsand, and not far away was Sir Jared's charger, Snow Cloud, a white wraith in the night. They were unharmed, our accoutrement was untouched, the knight's lance lay where it had fallen from his hand. I took blankets and wrapped us both and sat trembling until the night was over. In the light of dawn, streaming over the plateau, I saw the strangest thing of all. Not far away there was a little heap of stones that might have been the coping of the stone basin about the spring of water, the only sign that anything had ever stood in that lonely place."

Aidris listened to the tale and was caught up by it. The quick, almost blunt way that Jessamy Quade used in telling it, convinced her more than flowery speech or traditional flourishes. She saw too how deeply the tale affected the lady herself, as if she lived it all again. Now she drew a shuddering breath and finished the story.

"There was nothing for us to do but staunch our wounds . . . my legs were scratched and torn but not deeply . . . and go on our way. The worst of it was that Sir Jared had no memory of the encounter at all. It had all been . . . taken from him. I told him all that had taken place, and we have puzzled over it from that day to this but found no true answer to some of the things that were said and done.

"Dear Aidris, I swear to you I have told no other person of this strange meeting, and I believe Sir Jared has not either. We felt shame and fear. It might seem a reason to smile now, but there was something shameful about an attack by two dogs, even if they were like the Hounds of the Dark Huntress herself. We have sometimes lied and told of brigands, but mostly we have said nothing at all."

"Could you ride away?" asked Aidris. "Sir Jared at least seems to have been gravely injured."

"Not at first. We rallied our spirits and made haste through the Adz and into the border forest as far as Vigrund. We were prepared to make light of this dreadful adventure and rode through the forest and searched for the goblin folk quite cheerfully. But we were both growing sick, a sickness of body and spirit. By the time we reached Vigrund and rested at the inn, Sir Jared had a fever; I was terrified lest it prove to be wound-fever, lockjaw, or the raging sickness from a mad dog. When we spoke to Gerr of Kerrick, still keeping up some pretence that we were merely fatigued, he urged us to go by the Wulfental Pass into Athron.

"Instead we dragged ourselves across the plain to Zerrah, where we had lodged once before, at the manor house. At Zerrah before there had been only a friendly steward who kept the manor for the Daindru. Now we found a garrison, led by a captain of Mel'Nir, but he was kind and let us stay there and had us nursed back to health. Sir Jared's wounds festered, he lost the sight of his right eye; I was nearly as bad. It was a vile sickness, which would not leave its hold; it wracked our joints and does so sometimes to this day. Sir Jared tires easily and is halting in his speech."

"And you see some link between that meeting on the High Plateau and a curse laid on the house of Wildrode?"

"I do. I think of what was said by the magic being we saw there. As if Wild of Wildrode was a name well-known, as if some old spell first drew us to the place and then caused Sir Jared to be cast out, driven away, because the curse was not yet worked out. Even the sickness was part of this family misfortune."

"Was there ever in the family a history of some wrong done to a person with magic powers who might have placed the curse?"

"None that I know of. But the story goes that the bane set in during the lifetime of old Sir Dirck, Jared's grandsire, a violent man, in the days when Athron was poor and full of misery. He buried three wives and died mad, chained to the wall of his chamber lest he do himself a mischief."

Jessamy Quade stared about the chamber, as if the telling of these old dark tales brought no relief but rather increased her unrest.

"You must leave all this," said Aidris. "Let us think rather of your new life. Let me write to Prince Terril."

"My dear," said Mistress Quade, "you have given me new spirit. I am glad I have told this tale and hope I have not burdened you with it. Guard it well. I know that I can never repay your kindness in coming to me today."

"Do you recall the story you told me at the Varda Benefit . . . concerning the royal children of the Chameln lands?" said Aidris as casually as she could.

"Another accursed race!"

"Not so!" said Aidris. "For I have heard out of Achamar that both of these persons still live."

"I cannot think this is possible. The captain I told you of was not a brute or a fool."

"Maybe not," said Aidris, "but he was a man of Mel'Nir. It was in his interest to believe such lying tales."

"How can we know the truth?"

"I know Nazran Am Thuven very well. He was a friend of my family. I know that he would never have harmed the Heir of the Firn or the Heir of the Zor. I pray you, do not repeat this tale you told to me."

"If you wish it," said Jessamy Quade with a smile. "I will be quiet."

She rose up in her trailing red velvet gown and walked to one of the slit windows of the tower. Aidris followed and stood by her side. She saw the mountains, towering close by, only a few miles away across the fields and the downs.

"How fine to see the mountains!"

"The hour is late," said Mistress Quade. "Come to me tomorrow, and I will have pen and paper ready. I must prepare for my journey."

As she went down from the tower on its dark, winding stair, Aidris took out her scrying stone. It had no light in it at all, it was a cold grey-blue. She looked around at the blackened stone walls of Wildrode Keep and felt it for the first time as a place accursed.

Next morning Sir Jared Wild was married in the Great Hall of Wildrode. The sun was shining and a concourse of young maidens from the Wildrode lands and the neighboring manors carried spring flowers. His bride was the lady Corlin Ault, youngest child of Lord Bran of Aulthill. The visiting kedran, looking down on the bright scene from a gallery near the musicians, saw that she was a fair-haired girl, slender, smiling as became a bride. Sir Jared, in his knight's surcoat, looked handsome, carefree, unmarked, just as Aidris remembered him from the streets of Achamar where he had ridden among the autumn leaves with his true kedran by his side.

After a ceremony among the maidens, of flowers offered to the Goddess, the marriage was performed by the bride's uncle, Sir Kenit Ault, a travelling justice out of Varda. The trumpets blew, the guests sat down to feast, nothing marred the happy time. Who could not believe that the darkness had lifted from this corner of Athron?

Yet before evening Aidris had spoken again with Quartermaster Roon and heard what only a few retainers knew. In the night Mistress Quade had dressed herself in her old kedran tunic with the emblem of the Foresters and had climbed up to the battlements of her tower and had cast herself down to her death. She had been found at dawn and her body carried secretly away and buried no one knew where and no word brought to Sir Jared to disturb him on that day.

Jessamy Quade had left no words of farewell but a few packets with jewels for those members of the household who had been her friends in happier days. One packet, which the quartermaster now pressed into her hand, was labelled for Kedran Venn of Kerrick Hall. Inside Aidris found an enamel brooch with a pattern of white jessamine flowers and a piece of thin, shaped grey stone, a mere chip of stone. She knew at once where the stone had been found. Now she was one of the very few persons who had heard the tale of strange adventure on the High Plateau of Mel'Nir. She was not sorry when Sergeant Lawlor took the troop away early and set out for Kerrick.

They rode another way this time, and the highroad carried them a little to the north into the lands of Lord Bran of Aulthill. The spring weather had made the countryside a lush soft green; they came into a village called Hatch and might have ridden right through the place without stopping. As they came gently into the square, however, they heard some kind of commotion in the distance, and two or three villagers ran up and hailed Grey Company.

"Pray you help us, good Sergeant," panted a fat man. "They are killing each other on the fairground!"

"Who then?" asked Sergeant Lawlor, raising a hand for the troop to stop.

"The tumblers and the kemlings, the hill-folk," put in a young woman. "They are tearing the ground to pieces and fouling the duckpond!"

Then the crowd that had gathered all begged the kedran to stop the fight.

"We are travelling to Kerrick," said Sergeant Lawlor. "Where are your own watch or your lord's kedran?"

"At the wedding by Wildrode!" was the reply.

The sergeant gave a signal, and Grey Company trotted out of the square in the direction of the riot. The fairground lay at the bottom of a gentle slope, and a fierce fight was laid out before them like the diagram of a battle. Twenty brightly clad tumblers were locked in combat with a clump of dark, shaggy folk clad in hides and beaded headbands.

"All right," said Lawlor, with a weary gleam in her eye. "Part them. Use your lances as staves, d'ye hear? Herd those hill-folk back to their tents."

She flung up her hand, gave the order, and Grey Company, in perfect order, with a walk, a trot, a canter, charged down the hill. Aidris had no time to feel elated or afraid. She was surprised at the way all the kedran shouted, herself included, as they descended on the fighters. Another tumbler went into the duckpond, a young kemling was nearly ridden down, but the effect of five mounted warriors, however untried, was over-whelming. The fight stopped, the shaggy ones were herded to the right, and the tumblers to the left. The fat man, who was the town reeve, came running down the hill.

"What now?" asked Sergeant Lawlor. "Why were they fighting, good Reeve? Can we work out the dispute?"

"The kemlings don't have much of the common speech," said the Reeve. "I think the tumblers have wronged them some way."

"Goddess, what do they speak then, the bears' language?" said Lawlor impatiently.

Aidris, who had heard the shouting, let Telavel move a few paces forward. She gave a salute.

"Sergeant," she said, "it is the Old Speech. Shall I talk to them?"

"Venn . . ." said the Sergeant, considering. They all stared at the hill-folk licking their wounds before a cluster of rude tents.

"Venn," said the Sergeant, "they are all yours."

Aidris gave her lance to Ortwen, got down from Telavel and led her across the soft, muddled ground towards the hill-folk. They were indeed hers. She perceived that *kemling* was a version of the word *Chameln,* just as Kerrick was another word for Carach. Yet these were the roughest, most primitive folk she had ever seen: by comparison the northern tribes or even the Tulgai were very tame and civilised.

She stood a little way off and called, *"Who is your leader?"*

The murmur of their speech was hushed; he came forward, a middle-aged man, gap-toothed, almost as broad as he was high. His face was black with anger and streaked with blood and sweat.

"Ark, Chieftain of the Children of the White Wolf!"

Aidris bowed her head but held her ground.

"Good Ark," she said, *"tell me what is played out here, and I will see that you have justice."*

"Justice," he rasped. *"Bleeding Athron, justice! What is a decent Chameln maid doing among these robbers?"*

She fixed him steadily with her gaze, looking straight into his black eyes as if he were a wolf or a mountain cat that must be tamed.

"I am in exile," she said softly.

He dropped his eyes.

"All right," he said. *"Come into the tent, lady. You will understand our plight."*

"Let someone hold my horse," said Aidris.

A young girl was pushed out of the crowd, and she took

Telavel's bridle and spoke soothing words to her. The crowd opened up, and Aidris walked behind Ark, the Chieftain, into the largest tent. It was dark but very orderly, and it smelled powerfully of pine and mountain and the Chameln lands. Ark sat down on a rough settle covered with hides and gestured to another. A younger man and a middle-aged woman had followed them into the tent; they fetched bone cups filled with a spirit that smelled and tasted like sour milk.

"*They have despoiled our treasure,*" said Ark shortly. "*A dancer named Enk or Ennerik came to have his future read and behaved lewdly and stole a fetish. We asked for it back. One thing led to another.*"

"*I saw it done,*" said the woman. "*This was a practiced thief. He thought our treasure could not see, being entranced, but I was there watching.*"

"Your treasure?" asked Aidris.

"The Blessed Maid," said Ark. "The Spirit Child."

"And the fetish?"

"*A crystal,*" said the woman. "*Her smaller scrying stone called the Wolf's Eye. The larger, called Garm's Fist, is set into the table top.*"

"And he behaved...lewdly?"

"*He bent forward and stroked her hair and her arm,*" said the woman. "*She is a holy person and should not be touched familiarly.*"

"May I see the Blessed Maid?" asked Aidris.

"Come then," said Ark.

They went out of the tent again and approached a smaller, colored tent set apart from the others. Aidris was aware of the kedran, the reeve and his people, even the tumblers watching them. Inside the colored tent there was a blaze of sunshine; the back flaps were rolled up and two older women had been helping the Blessed Maid to wash her hair. They were brushing it out to dry, a fine silky light-brown mass, longer than the hair of the bride at Wildrode.

She was about twenty years old and pale skinned, more of the Zor than her Firnish companions. Her eyes were grey of two shades, a dark rim round the light pupil; she was thin, bird-boned, not quite in her right wits.

"Blessed Ilda," said Ark, "*this kedran will help us find the Wolf's Eye.*"

The Blessed Maid looked at Aidris, lowered long sooty lashes to her pale cheeks and smiled.

"She cannot even find her way home to the two oak trees..." she said in a sweet voice.

"Oh, I will in time," said Aidris. *"Perhaps the Blessed Ilda can tell me when that will be?"*

"Soon enough." said the maid. *"Give me your own scrying stone, little queen, little oak maid, it is stronger than the Wolf's Eye."*

"No," said Aidris, "I will bring your stone back again."

"She talks in these riddles," murmured Ark, *"but her gift is great."*

"It is indeed," said Aidris. "Good Ark, come with me to the village reeve and my sergeant and the leader of the tumblers. We will find out this Enk or Ennerik."

He thought it over, glowering; looked to the Blessed Maid who nodded.

"As you will," he said.

As they went out of the tent the Maid cried out, *"Do not lose your heart!"*

Aidris found a place for them both to stand and called to Sergeant Lawlor and the reeve. When they came, she made introductions, always presenting the others to Ark, as the chief. He responded with dignity.

"We need the leader of the tumblers," she told the Reeve.

He ran back to the tumblers and sorted out a tall old woman and a younger man. They were well dressed in a kind of striped motley, red and yellow. Aidris felt the ground lurch under her feet. She thought: how tall, how well-grown he is now. His hair was a very smooth long cap, pure gold in the sunlight, his eyes were the dark remembered blue.

"Kedran Venn..." said Raff Raiz.

"Master Raiz." She felt herself blushing.

The old woman, Mother Storry, folded her arms and glared at Ark, the chief.

"We've been attacked and put upon..."

"Wait, I pray," said Aidris. "This will be easily settled, good mother. Is there a tumbler called Enk or Ennerik?"

"Henrik the Fire-Eater," said Raff Raiz. "What is it this time?"

"A large crystal from the fortune-teller's tent," said Aidris.

"Who says so?" demanded Mother Storry. "Why should we believe that poor crazed witch-girl from the mountains?"

"He was seen," said Aidris, "by the chief's wife. Would they leave their Blessed Maid unattended? Your Henrik is a fool as well as a thief. I believe these people."

"You would, wouldn't you!" said Mother Storry. "You are their kin, for all that you are a kedran."

"Let it go," said Raff Raiz, "let it go Storry, my dear. I'll warrant Henrik has the crystal."

He turned and shouted suddenly. There was a scuffle. Ortwen and Nedda, the two kedran nearest the pond, moved their horses and seized a man, literally by the hair of his head.

"Wait!" said Sergeant Lawlor.

"Little bastard," said Mother Storry, "to bring this trouble upon us. I'll give him fire to eat."

They waited while Lawlor and the ensign, Hanni, dealt with the unhappy Henrik, who squealed now and rolled on the grass. Presently Lawlor came striding back carrying a leather pouch.

"Phew..." was all she said.

"Where did he have it?" asked the reeve.

"In his codpiece," said the sergeant.

"Might have been worse," said Mother Storry.

She held out an open palm; Lawlor emptied the pouch. The crystal blazed in the sunlight, and Ark gave a satisfied grunt. Mother Storry, with an ironical curtsey, handed the stone back to Ark, who bowed with a similar irony.

"Surly old devil," said Mother Storry.

"Sluttish old witch!" said Ark.

"The stone is returned with thanks on both sides," said Aidris in one language after the other.

"Thank the Goddess that's over," said the reeve. "Mother Storry, I'll trouble you to clear the duckpond before your people leave."

She walked back with Ark to the Children of the White Wolf. He held up his hand with the stone, and they gave a ragged cheer.

"Where do you live?" she asked. *"Is there a secret pass over the mountain?"*

"We live in the distant north, where it is called the Roof of the World," said Ark. *"We come by small trails down here into Athron to sell our hides. We make a bit of silver here on the fairgrounds*

166

with wrestling and fortune-telling. Sometimes we have a dancing bear."

"Do you pay tribute to the Daindru?"

"Not lately." He grinned.

"They will come again," said Aidris. *"Ask the Blessed Maid."*

He thanked her solemnly, and they clasped hands.

"Oh, take my love to the Chameln lands," she said. *"I long for the time when I will go there."*

She took Telavel from the young girl and gave her a few coins for holding the mare. As she walked away, she hardly dared to raise her eyes; she knew Raff Raiz stood waiting for her. The kedran troop were already mounted up; they had only a few moments together. He held her stirrup.

"Where is your father?" she asked.

"About in the world." He smiled. "I am not with him this season."

"You are a kedran now," he said again. "At Kerrick Hall?"

"In Oakmoon I go on leave," she said. "To Spelt Manor Farm on the west coast. To see the ocean."

"I know the place," he said. "It is near Westport."

They smiled again; Telavel turned aside to take her place in the company. Aidris could hardly see where she rode. As they began to climb the hill, she turned her head but could not see him in the crowd of tumblers and village folk on the fairground.

"Trouble!" said Ortwen. "Talking foreign tongues. And now you're all of a flutter. That tall yellow-haired mountebank? Is he the one?"

"He is an old friend," said Aidris.

II

THE FIRST DAYS OF OAKMOON WERE VERY HOT AND clear. Aidris and Ortwen rode together as far as a crossroads north of Stayn.

"You are bidden to Cashcroft for the feast days and the New Year!"

"And your wedding!"

"If it comes to that!"

They leaned from their saddles and embraced. Aidris took the road to the west, and Ortwen went on northwards to her home.

The ride through Athron in high summer was like an old tale told over and over. She saw the same trees, the same ripening fields, the same brightly clad cheerful folk in the fields. Around every turn of the round, there was another vista of this lovely sheltered land, another high house in its park or another village dreaming in the shade of the Carach, the elm and the sycamore. By day she sometimes rested Telavel in a lane off the high road until the sun went down and then rode on at night, under the stars, with a few dogs barking from the farmyards as they passed by. Sometimes she was entranced, unthinking, simply breathing in the scented air, tasting the sweet wellwater, eating the fresh bread that she bought from the farm wives. Sometimes at night, as she came over one of the downs and saw a sleeping village, she felt alert, watchful, a traveller in a foreign land.

Nothing really prepared her for that late afternoon when she felt a strangeness in the air, a feeling that rain was about although the sky was cloudless. There was an unfamiliar smell, and she looked about for a smokehouse or a tannery. Telavel was restless. They rode over the brow of a hill, and it was the last hill. Before them lay the broad strand and the boundless sea.

Aidris felt her spirit leap out towards the far, misty horizon; it was not as if the vastness of the ocean made her small . . . rather she shared its greatness. She took in the nearness and the distances of the sea: the shadings and undulations far away, and the waves upon the shore. The long curve of the bay began with a rocky promontory that tumbled down into pools and shallows where the incoming waves boiled and spouted foam. The dunes and sea swamps flowed back to the north.

On her left was the manor farm, a typical Athron croft but made wonderful for her by its sea oaks and swamp alders. She saw where a road ran from the farm to another headland; beyond it lay Westport, the largest harbor of Athron, almost as large now as Port Cayl. Ships sailed from Westport to Eildon and the Chyrian coast of Mel'Nir and to the lands below the world.

Telavel pricked up her ears. There was a flurry of movement in the dunes. Ten white horses plunged into view, small, fine-boned, long maned. Their beauty was dreamlike, at a first glance unearthly, but the children of the sea, the Shallir, were of flesh and blood. The white stallion poised and reared on the crest of a dune and called to his mares. Telavel reared up and answered his call. Then they were gone, leaving a drumming echo of their hooves. Aidris saw that the beach was not deserted. There were nets being hung to dry at the south end and below her a solitary figure rose up off the sand.

She rode on down and dismounted when the sand became too deep. Then she and Telavel were right down, on the firm, damp sand, with shells and sea wrack in heaps. The solitary bather girded himself in a blue tunic and came on steadily. The dream did not end; perhaps it would never end. She saw that his skin was burned golden brown by the sun and his hair had bleached to that flaxen color she remembered. She ran a few steps and so did he, then they drew back, drew breath, not bold enough to run into each other's arms.

"Is that you?"

"I have been waiting..."

Who spoke first? Who answered? Raff Raiz bent down and picked up a turret shell and gave it to her. They walked to the very edge of the sea, and when a wave came, they ran back laughing. Behind them Telavel whinnied in excitement; she stood shivering in the foam of the breaking wave, stamping her feet.

Aidris was not lodged in the farmhouse; she slept in a little low cott with the Widow Mack and her grandchild, Edda. There was a pen outside and a stall that Telavel shared with an old grey donkey. The whole four-roomed cottage reeked of the sea. Widow Mack was the relict of a fisherman; her daughter and her daughter's husband had been lost at sea in a storm when Edda was a tiny child. The widow was not poor and not rich; she went every day to work in the fields of the farm or at the kelp works near Westport, and the child went with her, leading the donkey.

There was rivalry between the farm people and the fishers; when Aidris was invited to the farm for supper, they laid out their best linen and richest food . . . not a scrap of fish . . . to show that they were land-dwellers and proud of it. Her news from Kerrick was highly prized; they craved every detail of the royal visit, the marriage of Sir Gerr, and the state of the harvest.

Yet Aidris was always left to her own devices when she wished. She was allowed to sleep late: a bowl of milk and a piece of bread were left out for her breakfast. She went out, blinking in the bright sunlight, fed Telavel and groomed her, and then the pair of them ran down upon the sands, and Raff came to join them. He had a bunk at the south end in a humble lodging house for young fishers that had been made from the hulk of an ancient ship. There were no other persons at the beach making a holiday; now and then a few women would come and bathe for medicinal purposes. They saw only one beachcomber, and he came with his dark sack morning and evening at low tide.

She was struck by the absolute novelty of having no duties. Raff was much better at holiday-making. He knew the times to swim, the times to lie in the sun, the times to catch the sweet crabs that lived in the rocks and boil them up for a midday meal. He taught her not to sleep in the sun and found two woven reed hats, one for herself and one for Telavel, who looked as much like a donkey in it as she ever could. They took turns riding the mare along the water's edge and off into the dunes. The Shallir were very shy and quick. She never saw them again in such numbers, but their hoofbeats echoed sometimes around the sandy hills and through the brackish waterways.

They climbed up to the top of the rocky promontory which was called Nim's Head. Here, between sky and ocean, they began to talk of the world and of those they knew in the world.

"Werris has troubles," said Raff Raiz. "He has put himself too much in the hands of certain Mel'Nir landlords in the south. They harass the people. The rising will come there . . . the flame will rise there, to be fanned into life."

"You speak like my partisan," she said.

They sat side by side on the rounded summit of the rock; he bent and kissed her cheek lightly.

"*I* was always that," he whispered. "Since the day I saw you, so young and brave, stung by the arrow. Now I speak like my father. He has changed sides; it is a sign that Mel'Nir will lose the Chameln lands."

"Is he so changeable?" she asked. "Did Jalmar the Healer really have to do with those who attacked me and Sharn Am Zor in the wood?"

"No, but he knew Hurne the Harrier from Balufir, from

170

Rosmer's service. He turned the knowledge to his advantage. He was out of favor with Lien at the time and almost hiding in Musna."

"Did he know . . . does he know . . ." she said in a low voice, "anything of my parents' murderers?"

"No more than is generally known," he said solemnly. "Violence is not my father's style, though he has had resort to it. The assassins were what they seemed to be: two fanatical young followers of the Lame God, Inokoi. Even Rosmer's hand in the game could hardly be traced. He remains suspect, for he is one, with the Markgraf Kelen, who would see the Daindru broken, for his reasons, just as Werris and Mel'Nir would have it broken for theirs. My father had the wounded Heir of the Firn under his hand, and the Heir of the Zor, a child, within his reach, and I know he would not have dreamed of harming either of you."

"I sent for him to come to Achamar . . ."

"I know," he said. "I begged to go. I begged to be allowed to bring you word. I sulked and ran away, and he had me brought home again to Musna. He would not go because he knew the Daindru were in eclipse and must go into exile. He wanted to keep his irons in the fire with the rulers of Lien."

"How can he be . . ."

She wanted to say "so bad and so good" but did not dare speak so of the healer to his own son.

"My father has been dogged all his life by the success . . . if you call it that . . . of one man."

"What . . . of Rosmer?"

"Of course not. No, he suffers because of his elder brother. He has never come close to him in healing or magic or in breadth of soul," said Raff. "Our family comes from Nesbath; my grandmother and grandfather were both healers and lived by the healing springs. They had two sons, and the elder one was their favorite. He excelled in everything but was always something of a dreamer. When he was still young, he became bound in love and friendship to a maid of very high degree who visited the place to take the waters. He knew he could never be more than her servant, her healer. Yet he followed her to her home and served her faithfully, served her whole family, though they leave much to be desired in the way of honor or fine feelings. There he remains and does what he can to bring light into a very dark place. Meanwhile my father tried to find the same success. He went whoring after every ruler and every chance to gain power. He is a gifted healer. I am sure you understood that. But he cannot sit still. He married first of all a maid of Nesbath, and she died giving birth to Pinga, my brother. Then he wed again, a lady with connections in Lien, and I am her son. She died too. I hardly remember her. As a father Jalmar Raiz is as kind as any could wish; I feel love for him and for Pinga, too, although my father has always favored him. But we have led a strange unsettled life, driven on by his demon."

"Your uncle . . . who can he be?"

"His name is Hagnild."

She sat upright on the rock with a cry.

"He serves Ghanor . . . Ghanor, the King of Mel'Nir!"

"He has spent his life at the Great King's court," said Raff. "He serves the Princess Merse, his daughter, and his son, Prince Gol, and the terrible old man himself. They say he is the only one not afraid of the vile old tyrant. My father swears that Hagnild will bring down the Great King in good time. But who knows?"

"Hagnild saw my aunt, the Princess Elvédegran of Lien . . ."

"Hush," said Raff Raiz. "She has gone to the Halls of the Goddess . . . sixteen, seventeen years ago. Do not mourn for her. I know that my uncle Hagnild must have helped and comforted her in that place."

"My own family has its dark side," she said. "It was her brother Kelen who sent her into Mel'Nir. And Rosmer . . ."

"What an inflated reputation that man has." Raff smiled. "The bogey-man, the torturer, the wicked magician . . ."

"The night-flyer, the eater of souls . . ."

She shivered even in sunlight.

"He is growing old, too," said Raff. "His charms against age do not hold very long. He is like an old courtesan who must take every kind of disgusting treatment with mud and bats' blood and pigs' dung to remove her wrinkles. And he has a hidden enemy, crafty and strong, who thwarts him now and then and turns his art back upon the sender. At first one might think of Hagnild, but this is not his style at all: he could hardly do a harmful working. No, depend upon it, Rosmer's mysterious enemy is a magician out of Eildon or out of the Chyrian lands of Mel'Nir. Meanwhile he goes about very discreetly, proud but

172

not overweening, seemly in dress, not given to display . . . the model of a statesman. Yet he spends part of his life in fearful places where he works his spells or in dungeons listening to the cries and confessions of those racked and burned by his command."

"Is his parentage known?" asked Aidris.

"It is a secret," said Raff. "He lets it be given out that he is of noble birth or else a demon, a creature not of woman born. But he is of flesh and blood. My father has cut him for the stone, using charm of sleep to ease the pain. My father's guess is that Rosmer is of humble birth . . ."

"I have wished that I was . . . of humble birth," she said.

"It is not a comfortable state," said Raff, stretching out in the sun and grinning up at her.

"Look!" she said. "There is a merchant ship coming into Westport."

"Ah, perhaps it has come from the lands below the world."

They swam and sunned themselves until they were brown as the rocks. Telavel took to rolling about in the sea waves. They kissed, and she ran home at twilight when the lamps were lit, feeling as if her love and kissing showed in her face. The old woman and the child did not notice; they lived in another world; she was no more than a summer visitor. The days drew out; at Midsummer, fires were lit along the shore and the fishers and farmers danced together and made a feast.

She did not dare think of the end of the holiday. She looked at Raff Raiz, traced his brow and his mouth while he lay dozing in the shade and woke him up so that she could see his eyes, slate blue. They lay in the sea swamps and the dunes, held each other close, free from all hindrance, far away from prying eyes. She was still, peaceful, even the memory of Ric Loeke's roughness had been stilled. They held each other close, and his breath quickened, just as hers did, and he turned aside and sat up, almost angrily. They sat side by side, and she suddenly began to weep, and he held her and called her his true love, forever his one true love, and she was ready to die at that moment. The day ended in a thunderstorm; they ran home across the sands with Telavel galloping ahead and the lightning striking the top of the rock, Nim's Head.

The next day she left Telavel in her stall, for it was rainy though still warm. She met Raff on the beach and they walked about; even the old beachcomber did not come out. A light stinging rain was falling; Raff led her to a rock pool, and when they were in the pool, with the rain still falling, it felt deliciously warm. Raff began to take off her shift that she wore for bathing; he was already naked. She said no . . . began to struggle . . . but he begged her to trust him. So they embraced, half floating in the warm pool; he caressed her and put her hands on his own body. They were overtaken by a strong magic, the strongest magic, spreading through their bodies like the rings that spread through a pool when a stone was cast into the water. They came out and shivered and dried each other. The magic was strong because they were together, because they loved each other, that was clear to her. There was no shame or secretiveness between them; what they did seemed to be more than they might each have done alone, though perhaps it was a little like kedran love. Strangest of all, she was a virgin still, she had lost nothing but a certain innocence. She thought of Prince Terril and knew that she no longer kissed like a maid.

The summer came back; they swam and lay in the sun and talked and went back to the rock pool. But something worked in Raff Raiz; he was unhappy. On the first day of the dark of the moon, he met her on the shore dressed in his best suit of green with a velvet cloak. They climbed to the top of the rock.

"What is it?" she asked. "Dear love, what is it?"

"I must speak," he said. "Aidris, I must ask you . . ."

"What?"

He did not look at her but gazed out to sea.

"Come with me," he said. "Leave your life, as I will leave mine. You will not come back to the Chameln lands for years, perhaps it will never be. You have been orphaned and injured and driven into exile. You have wasted part of your life in waiting and hoping for a dream. Let Kedran Venn end her service. Come with me, and we will take ship to the lands below the world. We will stay together and live in a distant country and never return to Hylor. I will love and serve you my whole life long."

She thought of nothing, every thought was driven from her mind. She looked at the ocean and the sky and felt the immanence of the Goddess. This was her dream . . . to be with him forever. To be away from Hylor. To travel into a strange land, to lose her name and her heritage and all that had pained and troubled her for so long. She put her arms around him and bent her head against his cheek and let herself live in the dream. They were so close at that moment that Raff knew even before she did, even before her tears began to fall upon his face, what her answer must be.

"It is *your* dream," she said, when she could speak. "I would go with you over the whole wide world and be no one else but your love, your leman, but I cannot do it. I am the Heir of the Firn. I must work out that doom. I must do it for the people of the Chameln lands and for my father and mother who were struck down at my side and for the faithful followers of my house."

"You do it for yourself," said Raff Raiz sadly. "You are very stubborn."

She hung her head.

"If you will serve me," she said, "if you will help me bear our sorrow then pray you, love, sail to those lands alone. Let me think of you as free!"

"Perhaps I will do that, then."

He tried to smile and took her hands.

"I have nothing to give you," he said. "I have no jewels fit for a queen. Yet I will tell you a strange tale that contains a secret. It may bring hope and joy to your mother's house."

"My *mother's* house?" she said, wondering. "The royal house of Lien?"

Raff Raiz smiled this time and began to tell his story.

"I met my uncle Hagnild several times as a child when my grandparents lived and he still came to Nesbath. Then the brothers were parted for a longer time. Suddenly, two years past, my father had a grave falling out with the Markgraf Kelen. I do not know the reasons . . . it was a matter of money and the carrying of a message. We were all together in Nesbath, and my father had word that he would be arrested and brought to Balufir, and that Pinga and myself would be taken as well. I might have run off and tried for the Chameln border, a few days away, but Pinga, poor soul, is delicate, so my father says, and not so easy to hide as one might think. He had little time, and in his haste to protect us, he called upon his brother Hagnild. He did this with the help of one of his scrying stones, an heirloom called Galimar.

"He told us we must go into Mel'Nir to a hiding place. He would not trust me with the instructions for our journey; he passed them directly to Pinga with the aid of sleep magic, for Pinga is gifted in this way and I am not. We took a boat in the dead of night, and I rowed down the channel of the river Bal where it flows by Nesbath, out of the Dannermere . . . or Danmar, as it is called in the Chameln lands. You must know that the Palace Fortress of Ghanor lies not far from the shore of the inland sea upon a high hill, and below, beyond the hunting preserves of the palace, growing right down to the shores of the sea, is thick forest, part of the great border forest. It is called Nightwood. It is dense and old and full of magic. No ordinary folk of Mel'Nir would enter it willingly.

"We rowed far out upon the Dannermere, Pinga and I, and then came into shore and rowed some way up a dark stream. We were deep in Nightwood. We tied up our boat at a certain giant swamp oak and followed a difficult winding path. Pinga knew the way perfectly, and we were welcome guests, the very trees bowing down to let us pass, though Nightwood is a fearful place. We came at last to a clearing in the very heart of the forest where there stood an old brown house. The door opened before we knocked, and an old woman welcomed us in. She told us her master would come soon and made us very welcome and comfortable. We sat by the fire and told her all sorts of gossip out of Lien, which she was especially pleased to hear.

"Then there was a call, outside, and I thought it must be my uncle Hagnild, but it was not. A young man came in, about sixteen years old, and bade us welcome heartily and set down a bag of game that he had been hunting. He lived in the cottage too, and the old woman made much of him, they loved each other, as if she might have been his grandmother. Two things were remarkable about this young man at a first meeting: he was very frank and pleasant in his manner, I liked him at once, and more to the point so did Pinga, who has a gift for such things. But the most striking thing about this young hunter was simply his size. He was a giant, at least seven feet in height, overtopping many of Mel'Nir's large warriors, and built in proportion. He had thick reddish-brown hair, blue eyes, and one shoulder slightly twisted . . . it could hardly be noticed unless he took off his tunic. His name was Yorath. What does that signify to you?"

Aidris shook her head, mystified.

"I know the old tale," she said. "It is in a favorite book I had out of Lien. Yorath was a king's son who was hidden in a wolf's skin."

"We all sat there," said Raff Raiz, "and laughed and talked without a care, and Caco, the old woman, fed us dainties and called us her brave boys. Late in the night Hagnild came, riding Selmis, his pale mare. He was just as I remembered him, like my father but with sharper features, and his hair had grown pure white. His manner is rather grave, but he too looked on the young man Yorath with great affection. I would have said that the boy had been raised in Nightwood by these two, Caco the old woman, and Hagnild, the Healer and Magician from Ghanor's court. Yorath seldom left Nightwood, though he did speak of some time spent in the west of Mel'Nir.

"We spent more than a month hiding in that place and had a fine time with Yorath wandering Nightwood. Then my father sent word that the coast was clear again, and we rowed across the inland sea and met him in the Chameln lands. We were never sworn to secrecy by Hagnild, but he could see that we were children of a man who lived with secrets. I never spoke of my time in Nightwood to my father, but he could have had it all from Pinga.

"I heard nothing of Yorath's parentage, and of course I did not ask. But one thing told me the truth; I am sure it is the truth, and yet it is a great wonder. I went out alone with Yorath one day, Pinga stayed in the house. We went hunting with a boy called Arn, son of the nearby smithy, and then we had a swim in a forest pool. When we stripped off our tunics, I saw that Yorath wore a medallion around his neck. I had seen one exactly like it. You were wearing it that day in Musna village, and you wear it still. It is the silver swan of Lien."

Aidris felt as if the breath were being squeezed out of her body. The elements of the tale all came together in a rush: Hagnild, the secret house in the forest, even the hated size of the young man, Yorath. She seized Raff by the hand.

"Yes," she said. "It may be the truth. How it was done I cannot tell, but Hagnild is, after all, a magician. I feel it is the truth because of something my dear mother, Hedris, said on her deathbed. She said that she saw her dear sister Elvédegran, and that she held a male child in her arms and placed the silver swan of Lien upon its breast. This is that child, and Hagnild has saved him."

"It might be proved a little," said Raff. "I am sure the old woman, Caco, came out of Lien. Perhaps she served the princess. If Yorath *is* that child he will have a harsh fate..."

"He is the child of Prince Gol," said Aidris, "and must share his heritage."

"He is a marked child of the Great King's line," said Raff Raiz. "It has been written and prophesied in Mel'Nir that Ghanor will die at the hand of a marked child of his house. My father says that such prophecies may be no more than a wish to get rid of the Great King... but Ghanor takes no chances. He would have had a child with a twisted shoulder killed at birth."

"Oh, he is like a savage beast... they are all so cruel... how could your uncle stay in such a place?"

"They are men and women," said Raff Raiz gently. "And Hagnild is a healer."

Then she recalled why they sat there, and that Raff had told her the tale as a parting gift. She could have given him another secret to do with the House of Lien; but with a pang of regret for this failure of her trust, she knew she must not do it. She must not tell the name of Rosmer's secret adversary, the powerful magician who crossed his schemes, who lived for her in the world of the scrying stone. She thought of another scrap of knowledge that Raff and his father did not possess.

"I do not know if it will serve you or your father," she said, "but I have been told part of Rosmer's parentage. He is the bastard son of Prince Ross of Eildon."

"It is no secret, this claim of his," said Raff, "but my father does not believe..."

"He should believe it," said Aidris. "I have it from one who should know. From the prince himself."

He took it in bright-eyed. It was as if their talk of secrets had returned him to the world of intrigue and unrest that he shared with his father, Jalmar. He was as much bound to his father and to his brother Pinga, the poor greddle, as she was to her own house. For all his wit and his gentleness and his tumbler's grace, he was the servant of powerful masters, and she was a queen in exile, her fate undecided. They could meet as man and woman only upon this faraway beach or in the lands below the world.

They walked down from the top of Nim's Head and kissed and clung among the dunes. He turned aside with a gasp of pain and began to run. She did not watch him, but went a little further on to the beach and sat down on a little patch of seagrass where the swamp met the sand. She remained there so long that Telavel left her grazing and came and nuzzled her, feeling her sadness. When she raised her eyes, the beach was empty. She rode about until supper time feeling guilty because Telavel had not been part of her dream of freedom. She could not have taken her to the lands below the world.

In the night a wind sprang up; when she slept at last in her narrow bed, worn out with weeping, her sleep was broken by the drumming of hooves and the cry of horses. She thought of the wild white stallion of the Shallir and his noble herd galloping through the wild night along the sands.

Then it was dawn and the little maid Edda was in her room gasping and crying, "Oh, Kedran . . . oh, she is gone! She is gone!"

Aidris hardly took in her meaning until she saw the door of the stall kicked down and the rail of the pen broken. It had rained in the night, and the tracks upon the sand were clear enough: Telavel had run off with the Shallir, the children of the sea.

She ran out like one possessed, ran to the dunes and shouted and called for hours. She came back to the beach and lay on the sand like a sailor cast away, half-drowned, from a shipwreck. There was nothing to be done; there was no one to help her search for the mare. The old woman and the child were very gentle with her in her loss; they thought she wept only for Telavel.

Every day she went further and further into the sea swamps and sometimes came close to the Shallir, saw the mares and their foals whisking away with a swirl of water about their hooves. One afternoon she gave up the search to sit on the beach and watch the waves and wonder how she would come home to Kerrick Hall. She walked about collecting shells, and at last she brought out her scrying stone, which she had kept in her saddlebag at the cottage. She had not looked into the stone since Birchmoon when she returned from Wildrode Keep and told the strange tale of Sir Jared and Mistress Quade and their quest in Mel'Nir.

The light in the stone was summery and green. The Lady touched her eyes, drew her hands over her cheeks, asking why Aidris had been weeping.

"I have a tale to tell that will make you rejoice," said Aidris, not answering the question.

The Lady listened most intently, her image in the stone fading a little, then growing strong again. Aidris thought of Prince Ross and of Rosmer and of charms against old age. Then a cry rang out, faint and shrill, filling the world of the stone.

"Lady!" cried Aidris. "Oh, Guenna..."

The lady was there again laughing and weeping.

"The child," she said, "the child lives!"

She rocked an invisible child in her arms.

"He has grown as large as Prince Gol," said Aidris. "This cousin Yorath is one of the giant warriors."

The stone was filled with a glittering cloud, and when it cleared, there on the table or altar was a hideous poppet, old and wrinkled, seated upon a throne and wearing a tall, jewelled crown. It shook and toppled, its crown fell off, and so did its head. Ghanor, the Great King of Mel'Nir, fell down and died. The stone went dark. Aidris recalled that she had not asked for a spell to find Telavel. The beach was empty, and the evening wind had freshened. She took her net full of turret shells and went back to the cottage. Having lost all, the hope of future triumph or the death of her enemies did not comfort her.

Next morning Telavel came back. Aidris heard the old donkey snuffling and honking in his stall and went out at dawn after another uneasy night. There stood Telavel by the broken rail of the pen, exhausted and drooping. Her coat was mired with sand and saltwater, her mane and tail thick with burrs; she had hoofmarks and teethmarks on her flanks and neck.

Aidris could only weep and cling to her. She cleaned and soothed and combed and burnished the little mare, fed her hot mashes, took her to the manor farm for a cast shoe. Then, before time, the pair of them set out for Kerrick Hall again. She came to the top of the first hill and hardly dared look back at the ocean. When she did look, the beach was empty and so were the dunes. She and Telavel returned slowly and sadly through the summer countryside.

She came back to Kerrick late one afternoon and was glad, when she saw the kedran going about their duties, that she still had a day or two of her leave. She tramped into quarters, lugging her saddlebag. There on her old pallet sat a tall figure, drooping, just as Aidris's spirits drooped.

"Ortwen!"

Her friend raised a long face.

"Back in harness . . ." she whispered.

Aidris sat down and took Ortwen in her arms.

"What happened?"

The suitor, the handsome lad, had played Ortwen false with more than one of the village girls.

"Little weasel!" said Ortwen fiercely. "I could not take his lying talk of love. Once, twice . . . and that red-haired wench lording it over me . . ."

"What did you do?"

"Do?" cried Ortwen. "I threw him in the horse trough!"

She began to weep.

"Oh Aidris . . . I loved him so . . ."

It had been a summer for love in Athron, but for love that did not or could not last. At Kerrick the harvest came in; Sabeth sat in the gardens and stitched at long robes. Her child was expected during the feast days at the year's end. The midwife swore she would come to term and that a winter's child had a summer life.

Telavel was collicky; she clubbed Grey Company when they drilled by turning the wrong way. Aidris had her to Sergeant Fell, and one morning Hanni, the ensign, raised a laugh in the stable yard.

"Venn . . . I don't know what *you* did on your long leave, but your horse is in foal!"

Sergeant Fell was distressed.

"Dear Goddess, Venn . . . did a farm horse get to her? Or a donkey? Would you breed a mule with this lovely Chameln grey?"

Aidris held her peace. Telavel rounded out slowly, but in the new year she would have to be quartered with the stud mares. Aidris would have to change her life; she would have no horse to ride, grey or otherwise. When the feast days came, Megan Brock spoke to her in quarters over a glass of good wine. She agreed to do the ensign's test in the new year and ride a certain black house gelding in New Moon company. A recruit had come with a new grey to take Telavel's place.

The feast days were very quiet. Lord Huw and Lady Aumerl did not keep their usual state. Then at New Year the bells rang and fires were lighted: the Lady Sabeth of Kerrick had borne Sir Gerr a healthy girl child. Aidris was able to watch the birth customs of Athron, and she did not find them so very strange. They were more kind than those of Lien, but not so ancient as those of the Chameln lands.

There was the "long vigil" before the birth — and with a young mother it might be very long — during which she might have comforters in her chamber, a man, a mother and a maid. She sat the vigil with Sabeth and so did Lady Aumerl and Sir Gerr. It was plain from what the midwife said that she was already regarded, at the beginning of her twenty-second year, as an *old* maid. There were jokes about certain landowning families where a maiden aunt was kept expressly for this purpose. Sabeth was in good spirits, and her comforters got along well enough together.

"This was never my thought," confided Lady Aumerl to Aidris at the fireside. "To sit the long vigil at all would have bored and frightened me as a girl. I longed to be a true kedran and ruler of my own house."

"Who sat vigil with you, my lady?" asked Aidris.

"For Niall, the firstborn, it was Huw, of course," said the lady, remembering fondly, "and my old Aunt Drusse, come out of Mel'Nir, as a maid, and for a mother I had my friend Margit, the reeve's daughter of Parnin, who married a knight, Sirril of the Green. I travelled there to sit vigil with her in the following year, and she bore a dead child and the next year so did I. We should not speak of it, I suppose. But all has not gone badly: she has two daughters and a son and I have my two boys and now I have Sabeth, for my daughter-in-law. Will you come to it too, my dear? If all goes well in the Chameln lands? Sabeth has told me you are betrothed."

"I must," said Aidris. "For a matter of inheritance."

She watched the Lady Aumerl stretched out warming her feet at the fire while Gerr sat by the big bed murmuring to Sabeth. She realised just how discreet and kind the lady was, an excellent mother-in-law. She wondered about that Chieftainess of the Nureshen, Gezi, Bajan's mother, who had dressed her in the ceremonial lodge long ago and who would help her give birth.

Then the time was ripe, and the comforters went away and their places were taken by three midwives: the Garth midwife who was in middle-age, her young daughter and a very ancient creature from Stayn. This triad proved the rank of the mother, a lady of Kerrick Hall. The Garth midwife bade Aidris stay and watch the birth; she wanted her magic, her scrying stone close at hand. So she went to the head of the bed where Sabeth, rosy-faced, panted and asked what time it was.

"Lamp-lighting time," said Aidris, smiling. "And it is snowing again. Tomorrow is the New Year."

"So long . . . we have been so long in Athron . . ."

Then Sabeth's breath was caught, and the midwives held and instructed her and with a last struggle and a cry that was hardly a cry of pain, it was done. The crone held a rose-red, wrinkled newborn child that moved all four limbs like a reluctant swimmer and let out a gusty shriek. The three midwives cried out in triumph.

"There now, a girl," said the Garth midwife. "But it was well done, my lady, well done. See there . . ."

Aidris watched, she could not help watching, the art with which all was staunched and cut and the afterbirth carried away. She hated the bright blood that had been spilt. The child, in its blessed cloth, was laid on Sabeth's breast, and she showed it to Aidris. They stared and laughed. For the creature, with quantities of black hair and wide-open eyes, looked exactly like Gerr of Kerrick. For the first and last time, the look of the young knight was stamped upon the face of his infant daughter.

"Ah," cried Sabeth, "how will she be called Imelda, as her father wishes, if she has this black hair?"

"Pff . . . it will fall out, my lady," said the old woman. "Depend upon it that is falling hair, pillow hair. By the time she is two years old, she will have your own lovely golden locks."

"Run along," said the Garth midwife to Aidris. "Bring the word, Kedran . . ."

So Aidris bent to kiss Sabeth, who lay in a dream, cradling the child.

"Wait," said Sabeth, "it is snowing. Take your cloak, your beautiful fur cloak, from the press . . ."

"I will," said Aidris, "but you must not weep . . ."

She saw that Sabeth's eyes were suddenly brimming with tears.

"I remember when I was cold and afraid and you gave me the cloak," she said. "And now I have so much. I have all that I could wish for."

"Hush," said Aidris. "Rejoice. We all rejoice with you. One day, one day I swear to you, our children will play together in a garden!"

So she ran and brought word to Gerr in one bower with his male companions and to Lord Huw and Lady Aumerl in another and to the company in the front courtyard who rode into Garth. Then, slipping on her cloak, which smelled of sweet Athron herbs from the press, she crossed the north court, calling the word to any who were about, and climbed the hill to the Carach tree. She came to the top of the hill and called to the men at arms who waited there, beside a brazier and the unlit pile of the bonfire.

"Light up! Light up! The Lady Sabeth has borne a daughter, and all goes well with them both!"

There was a cheer . . . the men had had something to keep out the cold . . . and the cover was reefed from the heap of dried branches and a torch set to it.

"Kedran Venn!"

A tall muffled figure lurked by the trees; Crib, the black dog, bounced over the snow to Aidris and leaped up cheerfully.

"What then?" she said to the dog. "Do you like my cloak?"

Niall of Kerrick looked at the winter sky covered with low-hanging snowcloud.

"In this new year I will travel to Eildon," he said.

The flames of the bonfire cast strange shadows on his face.

"Have you come so far in your studies?" she asked.

"Yes," he said. "I have not your natural gift for magic, but I have applied myself."

"You make too much of my gift," she said.

"Do I?"

He smiled and flicked his fingers at Crib, the black dog, who stood looking expectantly at his master. For an instant the dog was gone, it had vanished away, leaving only its shadow on the snow. He flicked his fingers, and the dog was back again. Aidris laughed.

"Chance has played a part in all my workings," she said.

"Will you come to Eildon then, as part of my escort?" he said lightly. "Or does chance bind you to Kerrick Hall?"

"It is the place where I can be found," she said. "When the time comes for my return."

"And if the time never comes?"

"I will go anyway," she said. "In two years or a little longer."

"I would rather Gerr and his lady had had a son," said Niall suddenly, "to inherit this manor."

"What, will you never marry? Never have sons?"

"I may never inherit," he said. "I may give my brother the right. How is it with inheritance in the Chameln lands, Kedran Venn?"

"A woman may inherit in her own right, as first born," she said. "Surely you know that? I am sure that your brother knows it, although he has not made much study of Chameln life."

"I know something of his foolish notions," said Niall, "but we are not as close as brothers can be, and he cannot confide in me. I know that someone bound him harshly with an oath, more than one. He may not question, so he is driven into all kinds of imaginings. His fancy fights with his honor. For a nature such as his, these oaths are plain cruelty. What would drive anyone to demand them?"

Aidris stared at him angrily.

"Fear," she said. "Your brother was already full of foolish notions when I first set eyes upon him. He deceived me and deceived himself. And I was afraid, Master Kerrick, afraid for my life."

She turned her back on the bonfire, and the pale winter shape of the Carach tree, and strode off down the hillside.

"Wait!"

He ran after her, and the dog Crib danced ahead of him and sat in her path.

"Kedran . . ." said Niall. "Aidris! My dear friend! You were unprotected then and you were very young, I know that. But to come as a kedran is one thing, to marry into our family is another. What have you brought to us? Who is the lady Sabeth? What manner of person is she, if she is not . . ."

"She is an orphan out of Lien," said Aidris. "And you see very plainly what manner of person she is. She is most true and lovely and kind."

"I do see that," said Niall, "but her estate . . ."

"She is my friend," said Aidris, "and so is Gerr."

"This is all you can offer?" He smiled.

"My friendship will be enough!" she said.

He stared at her where she stood, wrapped in her cloak, and she saw that he had begun to unravel the long, tangled thread. She turned again and walked off down the hill.

CHAPTER
VII

THE WHEEL OF THE YEAR TURNED; SHE RODE out in the first days of the Willowmoon as Ensign of New Moon Company under Lieutenant Yeo. They came to Varda with the lord's tribute, and Aidris saw Nenad Am Charn again. The city was as strange to her as before; she felt again that sensation of being in a foreign land as she looked up at the tall house with the sign of the double oak. It was Mid-week, a market day in Varda, and at this time, early afternoon, the trading room was busy. A party of Varda ladies were buying furs; there was at least one customer, tall and burly, who might have come from Mel'Nir. As she waited at a dark table for one of the shopmen, there was a commotion upon the stairs. A party of people were descending with much ceremony, and she saw that they were all from the Chameln lands.

A thin elderly man came briskly down the narrow stairs of this townhouse; he wore the beaded tabard of a page or cup-bearer, slightly motheaten, and had a Chameln lute, a tarika, slung over his back. At the bottom of the stairs, together with a younger woman, he unrolled a strip of woven carpet. Aidris did not know whether to laugh or cry: they were performing the old and uncomfortable task called "smoothing the way." She had last seen it done when she was nine years old and walked through Achamar with her mother in the Fir Moon to lay branches upon the sacred stones in the south wall. A score of citizens, sweating in their furs, had unrolled and unrolled the heavy leather-backed carpet, stiffened with wooden battens and embroidered with birds and spring flowers, where their feet touched.

Now the carpet strip was unrolled for an old lady, stiff as a poppet in her long beaded robe and her "star-maid" headdress, with its two thick plaits of horsehair trimmed with brilliants. Her face, under the coif, was lively and proud, with snapping black eyes and a nose like an eagle's beak. She cried out in the Old Speech, *"Are those two Athron lackeys come with our carriage?"*

A middle-aged waiting woman soothed the old dame, and her progress through the trading room continued. At the door, the lady and her retinue stood still, and the elderly page or minstrel called in a strong voice for a cheer. The double cry rang out "for the two oaks, the Daindru and the blessing of the Goddess" and then, the Athron lackeys having arrived with the carriage, the old lady was laden in with her servants and driven away.

Aidris saw that Nenad Am Charn stood upon the landing of the stairs with a lady in a plain Vardan cap. She stood looking up at him and saw his quick movement to take the arm of his wife. So she came up to them, smiling, and he bowed and his wife sketched a curtsy.

"You have visitors who stand on ceremony," said Aidris, unable to keep from smiling.

"Exile is hard for them to bear," said Nenad Am Charn. "Our house is honored by your presence. My wife, Lallian Am Charn . . ."

"Come up, Dan Aidris," said the envoy's wife in a low voice. "Come Nenad . . . let us get off the stairs . . ."

So they went up and stood at the door of a room with books and papers where Nenad had been receiving the strange visitors. A young man was inside gathering together a heap of parchments. He came out briskly, his Firnish brows twitched together in a frown, which hardly lifted when Nenad Am Charn presented him.

"My son . . . Racha Am Charn. Kedran Venn, also from the Old Country."

"Ensign Venn," said the young man. "Isn't that an ensign's shoulder knot?"

"Yes, I have made ensign," said Aidris.

"Bravo!" said the young man. "How pleasing to see an exile who does not look for charity."

187

"For shame," said Lallian Am Charn. "You must forgive my son, Ensign Venn. His manner is too harsh."

"I am an Athron lackey, Mother," said Racha Am Charn as he hurried off down the stairs.

The living rooms of the house were full of music and cooking smells, and she glimpsed young girls in Athron dresses. Nenad led her into the study and shut the door.

"I must say again 'forgive my son,' Dan Aidris," he said. "He knows nothing. I have confided only in my dear wife."

"Who were those people?" asked Aidris.

"Exiles," said Nenad Am Charn heavily. "The Countess Palazan Am Panget, relict of a southern lord, has gathered about her a little court of loyalists. They live in House Imal on Goose Lane in a pleasant quarter of Varda."

"And they are poor? They make demands upon your charity?"

"They are indeed . . . pensioners."

"Are there other exiles from the Chameln lands?"

"Not too many," said Nenad. "Some mining families from the Adz, who have settled in the south by the Grafell Pass. A trickle of folk from the Chameln lands always crossed the mountains, Dan Aidris, seeking their fortune . . . going away to Cayl, to the sea. The number more than doubled for a short time after the fall of the Daindru, even though the borders were closed. Now things have settled a little; some exiles have simply gone back home, others have found a place in Athron. I send what help I can to any who need it: the miners for instance and that household in Goose Lane. My son does not understand the ways of the Chameln and the claims of hospitality."

"I have heard of the old lord Panget," said Aidris. "Perhaps I saw him and his lady at court."

"Dan Aidris," said the Envoy most earnestly, "do not be tempted by these people!"

"I would not fail in my duty to any folk of the Chameln," she said. "I have left you to carry all the burdens, good Nenad, while I was far away at Kerrick."

"It has not been a heavy task," he said. "Do not trouble yourself, my Queen. It would be reckless for you to mingle with these people here in Varda. They live out their lives in a dream of the old ways . . . as you saw from this ridiculous procession. Oh, you might have been Queen in Goose Lane and kept a maimed court in exile, with empty ceremony and intrigue to pass the time, but you have chosen a better way, however lonely. You are still young; you will come into your kingdom."

"If I hold fast to my hope," she said, "it is because of the great joy it will give me to reward those who have been as faithful and steadfast as yourself."

"I must not give you any false hopes," he said, "but I have heard that the Chameln lands will have a rising, an insurgence . . . more than one. I will be travelling this year to Achamar for the first time since the troubles. Be sure I will find out all I can."

"Pray take care," said Aidris.

"I will."

"Has there been any word of Nazran Am Thuven and the lady Maren?"

"None, Dan Aidris."

"I pray you, do not spare me the truth. I know that their manor house was destroyed and they were rumored to be shut up in Ledler."

"That is all I know myself," he said. "Hope cannot be too strong in this case. Old Nazran wrote once, and his letters were smuggled from the fortress. Since then there has been no word. But there was a disquieting whisper over your aunt, the widow Micha Am Firn . . ."

"So disquieting that you did not tell me?"

"It is better so, my Queen. You have chosen silence . . . it is better so, believe me. If I repeated every foolish tale . . ."

"You are right." She sighed. "But tell me now. What has been done to my poor aunt?"

"Not any usual form of torture," said Nenad Am Charn with a grim smile. "Werris would have married her."

She thought of Lord Werris, handsome, correct, civilised, a dry and distant man when she knew him.

"We have all underrated Lord Werris," she said. "He has shown decision, now he shows ambition. What of my aunt? Did she take his offer? Was she brought to it?"

She remembered the quiet, dark, pleasant-voiced little woman, going about in her stone rooms, stricken by her widowhood. How long ago? Eight years?

"We do not know," said Nenad Am Charn.

Varda in early spring was bustling and pleasant. As she walked the streets, invisible, she tried to recall Achamar but could only remember bright pictures like illuminations from a book of seasons. At the palace of the princes, when they left the tribute, the kedran troop were entertained well below stairs. She had no glimpse of Prince Terril. The news of the royal household was that the heir, born to poor Princess Josenna after the royal visit to Kerrick Hall, was dropsical and did not thrive. So New Moon Company rode back, with Aidris riding second on Dusk, the handsome, ill-natured black house nag that Megan Brock had given her to manage.

"For Old Hop's sake, Ensign Venn," said Marten, a red-haired woman who rode behind with her friend Farrer, "Keep that vicious brute in order. If he side-skips again I will run mad."

"Ease up," said Farrer. "If anyone can ride him, Venn can."

Dusk lugged badly, as if he knew he was being talked about, and Aidris wrestled with him and scolded. She was embarrassed when the kedran complimented her on her riding: it was as if one said she breathed well or knew how to eat her dinner. The likeness to table manners held good: her style, even after five years, was different. She did not come naturally to the dressage, her talent was rather for staying on. Raff Raiz had said she rode like the jockeys, the prize riders of Lien.

When they came home to Kerrick, she made haste to visit Telavel, out in the paddock with the brood mares. She counted again . . . Willow, Birch, Elm, Oak, Apple . . . it seemed like a life sentence. She traced a few white hairs on Telavel's nose; the mare was ten years old.

Ortwen said she was pleased to hear that Aidris had kept out of trouble in Varda.

"New Moon . . . do they suit you, those hearts?" she asked slyly.

Grey Company had had no pairs of kedran lovers, but in New Moon only Aidris and the Lieutenant were unmatched, and Yeo was the friend of Megan Brock. She found them no better or worse to ride with than other soldiers.

"Everyone will have a friend if she can find one," said Aidris. "It makes no difference if some of these are lovers too. Remember how I was called your dear and your kedran wife?"

"Gossip," said Ortwen, "'maids' talk. But what of your lady at the hall?"

"I love Sabeth," said Aidris. "She is like my sister. I would say I loved you too, except that you would throw me in the horse trough . . ."

She ducked under Ortwen's arm as it swung over her head. The tall girl blushed and smiled.

"We are too shy, maybe," she said, "or it is simply not in our blood."

Sergeant Fell kept a close watch on Telavel and believed she would come to term early because of her small size. The little mare, who had been late to show, rounded out like a tun. Aidris had a nagging worry. She thought of a foal's birth as more painful and dangerous than the birth of a child. In the middle of Lindenmoon, Gavin woke her early; she scrambled into her gear and ran to the birth stall. The old sergeant stood in the doorway, and Aidris saw that her eyes were full of tears.

"Oh tell me . . ." she cried out.

"Oh Goddess!" said Sergeant Fell. "Oh heaven and earth! It is a dream, a wonder! Venn, why did you not tell me!"

Aidris ran to the stall, and Telavel was on her feet, snorting and sweat-streaked. The foal lay in the straw, and it was pure, pearly white, more beautiful even than the foals of the Chameln grey: it was a colt foal of the Shallir, the children of the sea. The Sergeant and Aidris knelt and soothed and praised Telavel like two fools. Telavel nudged the foal to its feet, and it stood with splayed legs nuzzling for her milk, while Sergeant Fell extolled all its points.

"So rare . . ." she said at last. "I have heard of mules, marked with grey, from the donkey mares, but this is a wonder. I tell you they never breed in captivity. Venn, Venn . . . you could sell this lovely thing for a king's ransom!"

"Never," said Aidris. "It is Telavel's child."

"Name it . . . think of a name. Take your time."

"I have a name," said Aidris. "He will be called Tamir, which means Sea Oak in the Old Speech."

The news of the wonder spread far and wide. The kedran and the housefolk and all the men and women of the countryside for miles around found time to come and watch the foal of the Shallir running beside its mother in the paddocks.

"Trouble," said Ortwen. "A moon at the seaside, and here is a miracle to show for it. What will you do with this lovely prize?"

"Bring him home to the Chameln lands."

It was easy to say this, but she knew that the way had become longer than ever. She was, for the first time, putting off her return instead of looking forward to it. She must remain in Athron for two years, three, until Tamir was full-grown, until he was broken in. What year was this? The year of young things, of the white foal and the baby Imelda.

From the first when her black hair fell out in handfuls upon her lace pillow and grew in bright gold, Imelda was a forward child. Sabeth and the new waiting-women and Amédine, a young matron from a nearby manor with babies of her own, could only marvel at her. She walked before she was a year old, ran soon afterwards. Kerrick Hall was like a barnyard, complained Lord Huw, with all the hens ruffling after one chick.

Niall of Kerrick had gone into Eildon alone and on foot, with only his dog for company. Sir Gerr rode out to a tournament, then on a longer journey, almost a quest, to the north, near Parnin, to help Sirril of the Green against certain cattle thieves who had driven his herds into the Black Plains. He took Rowan Company, whose horses were of the Kerrick breed, and two companies of men-at-arms. The kerns and kedran remaining were busy with the harvest and with autumn floods when the river Flume spread over the meadows and carried away its bridges.

Aidris was out of quarters now and lodged on the second storey of the barracks in the small cell-like room of an ensign. It seemed to her a wonderfully pleasant and comfortable place, with a tiny mullioned window that overlooked the house paddocks and the river, further off. She made her room fine with her fur cloak on the pallet bed and an embroidered picture of a Carach tree that Sabeth had given her. She had a wine cask cut down for a desk and sat looking out at her two darlings, Telavel and Tamir, racing about the nursing field.

At the New Year for the first time there was no gift box for Sabeth and herself from the faithful Nenad Am Charn. Aidris was disappointed and vaguely alarmed; she recalled that the envoy meant to go to Achamar. She was glad to ride out again with New Moon Company for the taking of the annual tribute. It was a long and troublesome duty this year with a visit to a horse auction, and she did not come to the house in Tower High Street until her last day in Varda.

The spring weather was cool and showery; under the sign of

the double oak there stood a minstrel in a threadbare cloak who strummed a tarika. He sang a melancholy strain from the northern tribes; she recognised the elderly page of the Countess Palazan Am Panget and flung him a piece of silver. The trading room was empty except for four Melniros at a table drinking apple brandy and Racha Am Firn at a counter.

The envoy's son smiled at her approvingly.

"Ah, Ensign Venn. I have your New Year's box. My father left word..."

"A letter?"

"No. He is still in Achamar with my mother and sisters."

"He is well? No harm has come to the family?"

"None!" said the young man with a glance at the men of Mel'Nir. "The borders are open. He is a loyal servant of the Protectorate."

"I am not!" she said sharply.

He flushed and lifted the gift basket down from a shelf. Outside in the street, the voice of the minstrel rose in a song she had never heard before; its words were in the Old Speech.

"The Winter Queen and the King of Summer
Will cast them down.
The men of Mel'Nir are tall as trees,
They will lie dead on the plain.
Proud Lord Werris,
Where are your warriors?
The Queen has come and the young King at her side,
O ancient land, rejoice!"

"Do you have the Old Speech, Master Am Charn?" she asked.

"No... Yes, a little," he said. "It is treasonous rubbish. The old fool sings to vex me, Ensign. I have stricken the charity lists for those beggars on Goose Lane."

She felt a dull sadness.

"Exile is long," she said. "Have the Chameln lands become so poor and their envoys so niggardly that they have no pensioners?"

"I am accountable," said Racha Am Charn. "I have to balance the books!"

Aidris went out into the street; her frail link with the Chameln lands had snapped. There was no one in Varda who knew her true name or where she could be found. She stood beside the old minstrel. He had a dark, bony visage like a carved mask upon a spirit tree; he began to sing again:

> *"Far off, far off in Achamar*
> *The fires are lit,*
> *The King and the Queen have come home,*
> *O let me live till that moon!"*

"A *fine song!*" she said in the Old Speech. *"Is it of your own making?"*

He bowed his head and smiled, rather distantly. She thought she recognised the arrogance of a senior servant, a butler or major-domo, who made small talk only with persons of equal rank.

"I pray you, good sir," she said, "bring this gift basket to the Countess Palazan Am Panget at House Imal on Goose Lane."

She wandered off into the streets of Varda and sat in a small park with a Carach tree before returning to New Moon Company. She began to smile, thinking of Nenad Am Charn and his advice to her. The proud old minstrel had really done her a service. If he had spoken kindly to a fellow-exile, she might have been tempted to visit House Imal, to be among Chameln folk, even to be queen for them for an hour. So she resigned herself to ride out of Varda again, and she was glad not to visit the city next spring.

Before the winter Telavel was back in training. Aidris returned to Grey Company as ensign, and Hanni went home to Westport with her friend Rigg, the man-at-arms. Word came back that they had sailed on a trading vessel.

The wheel of the year turned; in the first days of the Thorn-moon, the month of sacrifice, she woke at night in her friendly room and fumbled under her pillow for the scrying stone.

"I had forgotten the day," she said hoarsely. "May the Huntress forgive me . . . I had forgotten the day!"

In the world of the stone, there were two golden crowns and a bunch of oak leaves. The voice of the Lady said, faint and soothing: "The day is not yet done . . ."

Then the stone was filled with glittering mist and when it

cleared she saw a blaze of candles and a festive table. The luxury that she saw, the slashed and puffed satins that the guests were wearing and the brilliance of their jewels, aroused in her a kind of squeamishness. This was how Athron folk looked upon the ways of Lien. She concentrated upon the young man at the head of the table.

The chair he sat in was tall and grand as a throne, and she could see that he himself had grown straight and tall. Sharn Am Zor was more than ever the model of a prince: his bright hair had not darkened, his features combined the strength of Esher, his father, and the striking beauty of Aravel, his mother. His eyes were a deep and brilliant blue. If Aidris found any fault with him, it was that he did not smile enough and looked out upon the world with a hint of his old petulance.

Behind him and over his head as a canopy hung two cloths of state, richly embroidered with the crests of Lien and of Hodd, Chernak, Winn, Farsn, of the mountain feoff of Vedan, of Radroch and Nevgrod, the crests of all his possessions and offices, and in the midst of these smaller crests the twin oak trees of the Daindru. Sharn Am Zor had this day come of age. He was King of the Chameln lands, her co-ruler; and by these rich banners, she knew he held to his right and to hers.

She had time to look quickly at those who joined the new king in his celebration. They were all strangers. Aravel was not to be seen, the Markgraf Kelen and his lady were not present. There was no one who could be singled out as a relative, still less as a teacher or governor or even a steadying influence. A man of about thirty with brown hair sat at Sharn's left hand, and a lovely young woman on his right. The guests raised crystal goblets filled with the red wine of Lien, and as they drank the stone became dark.

Sir Gerr of Kerrick, back from the north, tended to the running of the estates while his father Lord Huw sat with a leg in splints from a fall in the hunting field. Aidris perceived that this suited the young knight very well; he was busy and carefree, without any hint of a tormenting ambition. At New Year, Niall of Kerrick returned, "quiet and full of secrets" as Sabeth put it, after his stay in Eildon. He came like a pilgrim, walking back through the snows in a long, dark cloak, with his black dog at his heels, and shut himself up in his rooms in the north wing. Ortwen Cash came back after New Year, betrothed again, this time to the smith's son, the steady fellow she had thrown over once before.

"This time," she said to Aidris, "I'm tired of quarters."

"Do you like him? Is he your friend?"

"Surely," said Ortwen, smiling. "And he *is* a gurt big fellow. We're suited."

They sat in Aidris's room eating dried fruit from the gift basket. It had come from Racha Am Charn. He went so far as to inform the ensign that his family still remained in Achamar; the borders had been closed "on account of some unrest." Aidris remembered the words of Nenad: "There will be an insurgence . . ."

Down below in the house paddocks were the foals and their mothers, and over the fence six or seven colts and fillies. Brown, bay, red-roan. One, not the tallest but the most spirited and striking, was white.

Tamir was all her joy. She had him hand-tame, spoiled him most tenderly. In the spring he wore his headband, then he ran the circle in the training field with Aidris holding the long rope. She had good advice, too much of it, but she went on steadily, by herself, often with only Telavel to encourage the pair of them in their antics. The blanket, which he took to at once; the bit which he could not abide. Aidris would watch him circling, giddy with concentration.

In the long summer evening Sabeth came down with the child running ahead, to see the white horse. Imelda cried out, and Tamir put on a show for her, flinging off his blanket, kicking up his heels, thcn suddenly all charm and docility when he saw that Telavel was getting a piece of apple.

"He is a child," said Sabeth.

Aidris felt pity in her glance. Sabeth hoped for a son at the year's end.

"Venn, Venn," said Megan Brock, strolling through the twilight. "He is two years old. Are you one of these spidery little wights who ride for gold in Balufir?"

"I weigh no more, Captain."

Still, she took her time. She spent half of her stored soldier's pay, half a dowry, at the saddler's shop in Garth. The copy of Telavel's saddle was excellently done but much plainer.

"My Goddess, lass," said the saddler, "this foreign thing was most fancily wrought, with the tooling and the runes, are they, and the gold and the green. Fit for a queen, when it was new!"

Now Telavel's saddle was worn and faded. They carried the new saddle back to Tamir and let it lie in his stall. He gave it a kick, as if he knew very well what it was for.

"For shame!" she said fondly. "For shame, Tamir!"

She was alone in that wing of the stable with only a few loose boxes tenanted. Outside the summer night came down. She picked up a shell that hung on the rail of Tamir's stall and listened to the ocean. How far to the lands below the world? How long to sail to those lands?

By Carach Troth at the summer's end, she was riding Tamir every day for exercise. He learned quickly, but she sensed a wildness in him, an unquenchable spirit.

"You have done the right thing," said Sergeant Fell. "He is as well-broken as he can ever be. He loves you, and he loves to parade about, to lead the field. And maybe, if you had left him a little longer . . ."

"What then?"

"He would have led all the fillies away to the woods," replied the old horse-doctor.

They rode in the river fields with Sergeant Fell on Telavel. At full gallop, feeling the strength of Tamir, she tried to recall the plain, the endless silver grass of the plain and the long hair upon the spirit trees, but her memory had grown faint.

"This one," said the sergeant, "this little mare is a wonder as much as your white king, her son. What I would give to see a full troop of these sweet souls."

"Captain Brock has hopes of another White Company," said Aidris.

"Not with Tamir!" said the sergeant. "He is not the lad for it."

The harvest came in, and Thornmoon was unusually hot. There were fistfights in the stableyard, and the new recruits, kerns and kedran alike, led to a lot of head-shaking from the veterans. Niall of Kerrick, going about again, began to plan a pageant for the Winter Festival, with music, maskers and dancing. In the dark of the Thornmoon Aidris had a strange dream: she was riding through a dark wood, among a press of other riders, all silent, and they came to the edge of a precipice. She felt a cold wind and looked down into a deep gulf. An old man spoke up in her dream and said, ". . . many hundreds, but it will not serve them, poor devils."

Then a woman laughed aloud; it seemed like the captain, Megan Brock, and she whistled a tune, there in the darkness. Aidris woke shuddering at the dream, though she could not explain it. She looked into her scrying stone, and it was dark; it had been dark for many days.

Aidris came back from the stableyard still wet from the pump and began to climb the stairs to her quarters. Half the troop had ridden to Stayn for the raising of a roof-tree, but Grey Company had a free day and were all off on their own occasions. She was tired and dusty from exercising both her horses. It was early afternoon with a first breath of autumn in the air.

"Aidris!"

Niall of Kerrick stood by the stairs looking up and with him old Gavin the Waker. She stared at them and was afraid of the way they looked at her.

"Riders," Gavin was saying. "Riders have come . . ."

"Riders from the Chameln lands!" said Niall of Kerrick.

She felt something that was close to panic. She ran just as she was out through the stableyard towards the front of the Hall. A crowd had collected at the end of the avenue. She pushed her way through. Ten riders were dismounting; there were tall banners.

Bajan stood in the courtyard. A tall man, Lingrit Am Thuven, had approached the steps of Kerrick Hall, and Nenad Am Charn stood beside him. The trading envoy was the spokesman, and he cried out in a loud voice to Gerr of Kerrick, who waited before the doorway.

"Good Sir Gerr . . . we have come out of the Chameln lands with this worthy company of noblemen and servants of the double throne. We are seeking that lady who came through the mountains with your help some seven years past and who has been sheltered at this your noble father's house. We are seeking our queen, to bring her home again."

Then Sir Gerr, smiling, as if he might be puzzled by this display or simply modest said, "Good Envoy, the lady who came with me to safety is now my wife . . ."

There was a slight hiss of unbelief from the newcomers, and Aidris saw Bajan lay a hand on his sword. Before Nenad Am

Charn could speak again, Sir Gerr reached a hand into the darkness of the portal and led out the Lady Sabeth, blushing, in her long robe.

"Here she is," said Sir Gerr. "The Lady Sabeth, whom I brought to safety . . ."

This time there was a murmur of impatience. Lingrit and Nenad bowed to Sabeth, and the trading envoy said, "We are pleased to know your lady wife, but she is not . . ."

Aidris walked steadily out into the courtyard and stood before Bajan. A young girl in a fine red tunic uttered a glad cry. Bajan smiled. He knelt down before Aidris in the dust of the courtyard. All the riders turned towards her and knelt down: she saw Jana Am Wetzerik and old Zabrandor, who had been Esher's Torch Bearer. A kedran had sprung up again to give a signal: the wooden trumpets of the Chameln lands blew a wild blast, and a herald began to cry out in a mighty voice. She heard nothing but a string of names, and they were all her names.

"Keeper of the Keys of Achamar, Lady of the Groves, Countess of Vule, Lady of Shorr, of Grunach and Ez, Landgravine of Ringist, Ruler of the Chameln lands, the Queen who shares the double throne, Dan Racha Sabeth Aidris Am Firn . . ."

She raised up Bajan: he led her quickly through to the steps of the hall, raising up the others as she went. She pressed the hands of Lingrit and of Nenad; she was urged up two or three steps, and the company cheered aloud. She put up a hand for silence and turned to those above her: Gerr and Sabeth, Lady Aumerl, Niall of Kerrick.

"Aidris, dear child . . . what is this?" cried the Lady Aumerl.

"Hush, Mother," said Niall. "She is their queen."

"Queen Aidris," he said, so that those waiting could hear, "you have lived among us in a humbler estate, but now we welcome you and all your followers to enter Kerrick Hall and accept our poor hospitality."

Aidris came up and stood beside them.

"Nothing in my life is sweeter than this hour," she said. "I see loved faces again, and I promise that all your steadfastness will be rewarded. Let me express my love and duty still to the master and mistress of Kerrick Hall and to Niall of Kerrick, who has welcomed us."

The Chameln cheers were loud. They were, she perceived, a noisy folk who cried out and wept and sang and shouted more readily than Athron folk. She had been too quiet, but it was often a queen's part to remain quiet in the noisy throng, to raise a hand . . . as she did now . . . for silence.

"Before we go in," she said, "I will perform my first action as your proclaimed queen. I can never repay all that I owe to these two dearest friends who brought me to safety in Athron, but I will beg them to accept what I have to give, straightaway, in the way of honors. Let Sir Gerr of Kerrick, that true knight of the order of the Foresters, and his lady Sabeth, my dear friend, be Count and Countess of Zerrah, and enjoy forever, with their heirs, the possession of the manor of Zerrah, in the mark of Ez, in the Chameln lands."

Under cover of the cheering, as she led them forward, Sabeth whispered, "Oh, what have you done to us . . . there I am all unprepared and pregnant too, in an old gown . . ."

"Well, you have your manor house," said Aidris, smiling, "and can rebuild it finer!"

"I can only believe it of *you*," said Sabeth, smiling all the while and acknowledging the cheers. "A girl who could keep quiet about her own betrothal. Is he that handsome one with the brown beard who looks at you so warmly?"

"Yes, that is Bajan."

Aidris turned her head at last and dared to look at Gerr of Kerrick. He smiled, too, but in his eyes she read a hint of bitterness.

The chambers in the south wing, hastily aired, smelled of thyme and rosemary. She was bathed before the fire with three waiting women and Sabeth sitting nearby with her embroidery frame. It was like the lodge of the Nureshen at the Turmut, for all her dusty kedran gear had been taken away in a heap. Her two women from the Chameln lands were Millis Am Charn, the young girl in red, and a thin dark woman whose name was Yvand, and the third was Therza, who had returned with Gerr and Sabeth from Eildon. Yvand was the only one who knew how to serve a queen, and she directed her two companions in whispers.

When Aidris was dressed from head to foot in fresh Chameln raiment, Millis and Therza fetched a long glass, just as two girls of the northern tribes had fetched the brazen shield. The long tunic of green velvet and brown doeskin was beaded with jade and lake pearls and embroidered with gold thread. Her breeches were of darker brown leather, and her boots were green, with gold tassels. The air of Athron had changed the texture of her hair; it curled more softly. Her skin was pale, with cheeks lightly flushed. She held herself very straight, always, but she had hardly added an inch to her stature in seven years. She was a woman of the Firn, just over five feet in height.

"If the countess would come . . ." beckoned Yvand.

Sabeth came and stood behind Aidris, and all four women looked approvingly at the picture the queen made in the glass.

"Green is your color," said Sabeth. "What must I call the queen now, Mistress Yvand?"

"She is your close friend, Countess," said Yvand, "so you may say simply "my Lady." Others will say "my Queen" or "Dan Aidris." We have no usage such as Majesty, but foreign persons do use this word."

Yvand held out a leather case to Sabeth. She reached in and took the circlet of gold, set it on Aidris's head and adjusted the fine strap of plaited horsehair that held the simple coronet in place.

"Yvand," said Aidris, "who had my measure for these clothes?"

"The women of the northern tribes, Dan Aidris."

"Where have I seen you before, Yvand? In Achamar?"

The dark woman smiled at last.

"I was a seamstress, Dan Aidris, assisting Lady Maren Am Thuven, as Keeper of the Robes."

"Of course. And have we news of Lady Maren?"

The young girl, Millis, began to speak, but Yvand gripped her arm.

"There is nothing certain, my Queen," she said. "It will come from one of the Council lords."

Therza who had been standing at the door called softly, "The Count! Count Bajan!"

"Great Goddess!" murmured Sabeth in the ear of the queen, "We are all counts and countesses now!"

The room was cleared in an instant. Only Sabeth remained at her embroidery frame, a most blooming young chaperon. Bajan came in and strode impatiently the length of the chamber, as if he would take up all the years in this distance. She strained to see him in the candlelight, to find a man that she knew in this heavily muscled, middle-sized, dark-browed Chameln lord.

As he passed through some shadow and then came into the light of the fire, she saw the tilt of his head, his smile, and was able to give that old, glad, cry, "Bajan!"

He took both her hands. They kissed gently on both cheeks. He looked at her, as Sabeth had said, warmly; then took her in his arms, and they kissed for so long that Sabeth gave a discreet cough. They drew back and stared at each other, half-amazed. Aidris saw that she had grown beautiful in his eyes. She was twenty-four, and he was thirty-three, and they had been long betrothed.

"Lady," said Bajan, "I have found you, and I will never let you go far from my side again. But the way to Achamar is long, and I fear it will be stained with blood."

"You have my ring," said Aidris. "How did it come to you?"

"Mysteriously," said Bajan. "Three strangers found me out at a mountain camp. Where did you conjure up such creatures?"

"They are the messengers of Prince Ross of Eildon," she said. "Come, sit down and tell me the state of the lands."

"The councillors are waiting."

"Then tell me only two things. First, where is the king? Where is Sharn Am Zor?"

"He has landed at Winnstrand on the Danmar and taken command of a large horde of the folk, risen against their Mel'Nir landlords."

"Good news. But tell me now . . . what is known of Nazran Am Thuven and the Lady Maren?"

Bajan put an arm about her.

"The Lady Maren is long dead," he said. "She died in Ledler Fortress in the first year after you had gone into exile, from an ague. Nazran survived in Ledler for two or three years; now it is believed that he is dead. He would be far gone in years . . ."

She bent her head. They had gone, both of them, to the halls of the Goddess, and were more certain to find peace because of the pain of their going. She remembered Nazran speaking to her in a darkened room: "In those bright halls we are all made whole and sound . . ." Yet in that memory was a perverse hope, for he had spoken of Elvédegran's deformed son and it seemed that this child had lived and flourished.

"I will go to the Council!" she said.

She led Bajan to Sabeth and presented the new Countess of Zerrah.

Old Zabrandor unrolled a map as large as the table and weighted its edges with wine beakers and candlesticks.

"Werris holds the center and Achamar," he said. "The Melniros are hard-pressed in the southeast where the folk have risen. I will not say how this has come about, but it has happened, and the king has come to lead them."

"You saw him?" asked Aidris.

"I did," said the old lord. "He is a most brilliant king, proud and wise beyond his years. He bade me come to meet the northern tribes because my lands lie about the plains by the Nesbath road and I know the best way to come through this country even when it is thick with the Melniros."

"See here, my Queen," said Jana Am Wetzerik, taking up the tale. "I have been keeping a troop of my battlemaids and housekerns together in the north at a camp of the Durgashen. When word of the rising came, all the tribes took up arms; Count Bajan, together with Ferrad Harka of the Durgashen, led them to Thuven, then captured Vigrund. We hold the mountain passes into Athron. The plain lies between us and the army of Sharn Am Zor. Lord Zabrandor came through alone with some difficulty. Werris in Achamar and the King of Mel'Nir will try to bring in new warriors and keep our two armies parted. I use the word armies, it is not a good word. These are folk hordes who need a greater stiffening of trained soldiers."

"There is some danger from Lien," said Bajan. "If the Markgraf Kelen allows Mel'Nir to come in along the forest border or to hire mercenaries to seize the Adz . . ."

"Lord Lingrit," said Aidris, "how stands Kelen with Sharn Am Zor?"

"They have no love for each other," said Lingrit. "The Markgraf has done all he could over these past years to win the love and the loyalty of the prince. He has failed. His bullying did not serve and neither did his kindness nor his seductions of various kinds. The young king, once come to his majority, pretended to be more reasonable, went about at court and so on, but when the news of the two pretenders came from Dechar and the countryside flocked to their banners, he escaped. He sent word to me, and I travelled through the Adz and came to Vigrund. The king came secretly out of Lien and landed at Winnstrand with a small band of followers."

"*Pretenders . . . ?*" said Aidris softly.

The councillors looked rueful.

"If it please you, I will tell the queen," said Nenad Am Charn.

The trading envoy had been sitting quietly during the talk of armies, but now he bent forward across the table and poured himself some more wine at the eastern end of the map.

"In past years, Dan Aidris, there have been many legends and tales come out of the Chameln lands concerning the fate of yourself and of the king, Sharn Am Zor."

"I have heard some of these tales even here in Kerrick Hall," she said.

"I noted them all," said Nenad Am Charn. "I was one of the very few privileged to know the true whereabouts of our queen, and I could judge if anyone had stumbled upon the truth. These sightings of a princess or a prince were mainly the wish dreams of a simple folk. At Midsummer, six years past, a young maid clad all in green and wearing a golden crown appeared to a group of poor miners in the Adz. She cried out in the Old Speech: '*I am the Oak Maid!*' and disappeared into the forest.

"More than once the royal children appeared together: a golden-haired boy and a dark-haired girl, sometimes wearing fine clothes and golden crowns, sometimes poorly dressed, asking for succor. In the Hain by Achamar, the royal hunting preserve, a huntsman of Mel'Nir and his Chameln servants saw a bright light in a glade where they had a stag at bay. When they came up, a young dark-haired girl in a white tunic with an arrow protruding from her left side bade them stop and let the stag go free. This last, though a very striking vision, was not a hopeful one for those who remained loyal. It seemed to say that the Heir of the Firn was dead and walked as a ghost in that wood.

"These tales were very different, especially when one asked more questions, from any real attempt to set up a pretender to the throne. I think the councillors will agree that pretenders . . . and many have been seen in the lands of Hylor . . . are the tools of those who would come to power."

"The False Markgraf Robard ruled in Lien for ten years," said Lingrit Am Thuven. "In the service of the Denwicks who raised him up."

"There was a False King of the Firn . . . Védor or Védoc," said Aidris, "and a false Heir of the Zor, Princess Zenia, raised up so that a Count of Storr might marry her. But these are far in the past."

"The present insurgence began in the south," said Nenad Am Charn, "and centered upon the ancient town of Dechar, not far from Winnstrand. It has a large community of the Moon Sisters, the largest in the Chameln lands . . ."

"Why, I have visited that place," said Aidris. "I think the general will remember. I went there with my father and mother long ago, on the way to a holiday by the Danmar."

"By the Goddess, of course!" said Jana Am Wetzerik. "What a blessed time that was. We came by the Dechar citadel and were entertained by the Moon Sisters."

"I am not sure what that means in the context of this present strange tale," said Nenad Am Charn. "The sisters are well beloved and peaceful. The Mel'Nir landlords around Dechar have shown themselves at their worst . . . even Werris fell out with them over their greed and their cruel treatment of the tenant farmers.

"The Moon Sisters helped the poor and tried to mediate between the men of Mel'Nir and the folk. There was some dispute over a levy of grain from the remaining lands of the citadel. The sisters refused to pay and refused to allow the soldiers of Mel'Nir to enter their sacred halls. When at last they forced their way in, the folk rose against them.

"The sisters not only resisted Mel'Nir, they brought out of hiding a young woman and raised her up as Aidris, Heir of the Firn. The countryside was alight with loyal feeling for miles around; the landlords were set upon, many lost their lives as well as their ill-gotten holdings."

"It is strange to hear of this pretender," said Aidris. "Who could she be, this queen? Who has taught her to do this? The Moon Sisters are good women and known for sound sense rather than flights of fancy. Does anyone know what this false Aidris looks like?"

"I have seen her," said Zabrandor. "I was living hidden away at a manor not far from Dechar, a long way from my own lands, which had been gathered by Mel'Nir. For a time, forgive me, my queen, I believed it might be yourself. Then for a little longer I rallied all the people in the name of this imposter.

"I met the false Aidris in the citadel at Dechar about two

moons past. Of course I knew the moment I came into her presence that she was a pretender. She is slender and darkhaired. Her face is pale, with eyes of a hazel green, a pretty and pleasing face. But she is ill-made or injured, her left side twisted. This is supposed to be a mark of her royal identity, the wound made by an arrow in the wood near Musna. Her manner is sweet and childish at times; she speaks well, with a Lienish accent. Sometimes she becomes very haughty and wayward, as if she believes this is how a queen must be.

"Dan Aidris, I was the only person far and wide who knew the true queen, yourself, and took this creature aside and spoke with her very sharply. I came away almost convinced of her innocence. I would say that she is some kind of foundling, that she has lost all memory of her true parentage if she ever knew it, and that the Moon Sisters or some others have taught her that she is the queen. I could not penetrate her disguise or learn of any power that might have raised her up."

Aidris could not repress a shudder.

"I hope our paths do not cross," she said. "I would not know what to do with her."

"There is more to tell," said Nenad Am Charn. "When Dechar was fully in the hands of the Chameln, it had to withstand an attack from the warriors of Mel'Nir. A young man on horseback with a few attendants entered the city and gave it out that he was Sharn Am Zor. The folk accepted him; the newcomer busied himself with the defences of the place, and Dechar held firm. The false Sharn met with the false Aidris before the citadel; they recognised each other at once. The rule of the Daindru was proclaimed in Dechar."

"Lord Zabrandor?" said Aidris.

The old lord sighed and ran clawing fingers through his beard.

"Yes," he said. "Yes . . . I have seen him. I was not at all ready to believe. I knew very well that King Sharn was in Lien. But this fellow, at a distance anyway, played his part very well. Too well. The young king was never much of a horseman. The pretender did more than act the king . . . he defended the city. But he is an impudent imposter, nothing more nor less. Once again I had the notion that he came from Lien. He wore fine Lienish clothes. He was by no means as handsome as Sharn Am Zor, but after seven years, with a child growing into a man, he could have deceived many people.

"He tried his best not to meet me face to face. He knew well, as the poor false queen did not, that I would know him for a pretender. I found myself sorely tested. I left the city, and since the countryside had risen, I was able to gather about me certain other lords and ladies come out of hiding or retirement. We proclaimed the Daindru far and wide.

"Then at last, and to our great joy, the true king landed at Winnstrand. With our help he was recognised at once; he led our army. Old Gilyan marches with the king, Lady, and Count Barr and the Countess Caddah. We skirmished with the Melniros on the shores of the Danmar. King Sharn, jealous of his right, sent a troop of kedran back into Dechar, seized both the pretenders out of the citadel and held them prisoner. Only then, with those two outside the walls, would he consent to enter the city. Since then we have marched many leagues beyond Dechar, gathering strength, but we are still not prepared to strike at Achamar."

"You have done bravely," said Aidris. "I cannot see that the pretenders threaten our rights any longer."

"My Queen," said Bajan, "your rights must be proclaimed in the same way. There are landholders in the hills between Zerrah and Achamar who have lived quietly in accord with Mel'Nir. They will not risk their forces except for a true queen and a certainty of victory."

"You have not spoken of the greatest pretender of all," said Aidris. "How does Lord Werris? What of his marriage plans?"

"He has not married the Lady Micha Am Firn," said Nenad, "but she has been brought to Achamar. Werris denies the right of princes and pretenders alike. He is fighting for his life. He goes about in fear of assassins."

"We will send none," said Aidris, "yet he may not escape."

She rose up from the table.

"We must ride out of Athron boldly and without secrecy," she said. "I will be seen far and wide, and it will be known that I am the queen. I will make myself known to the princes in Varda, my cousins. I will write at once to my uncle the Markgraf Kelen asking that he help my right to prevail. I will go further . . . I will send letters proclaiming the Daindru to the so-called Great King of Mel'Nir and to his son, Prince Gol. I will ask them to abandon Lord Werris."

"This might all be done," said Lingrit, "but it is difficult to get a message to the rulers of Mel'Nir."

"The Healer at the court of Mel'Nir is called Hagnild," said Aidris. "I believe he would deliver my letter."

"This is all bravely said," put in Jana Am Wetzerik, "but the queen must be closely guarded. We would not lose her now that she has been found again."

"Dear General," said Aidris, "I have been invisible too long. All men must know that the queen has come again."

Then Zabrandor uttered a rumbling cheer, and the councillors saluted her and drank her health. The steward of Kerrick Hall looked in at the fierce Chameln folk and bade them timidly to come and dine with the lord and lady of the house.

Towards the end of the long dinner, there was a noise of singing and drumming in the north court. The captain Megan Brock came into the room where they were dining; Jana Am Wetzerik stood up to take her salute.

"It is the kedran, my lord," said Captain Brock, in answer to Lord Huw's question. "They are making a drum parade for the queen. If she would be so gracious as to step out on the balcony..."

Aidris crossed the long gallery with the two tall kedran women behind her and stood on the balcony beside the blue fir trees. Down below all the kedran drummed and shouted and waved torches. She felt foolish tears sting her eyes as she waved to the upturned faces.

"Well, Brock, my dear old comrade," said Jana Am Wetzerik, "this is a far cry from the Chyrian lands. What have you to report of this recruit that came to you?"

"I am loath to let her go," said Megan Brock. "Where else will I find an ensign who writes in two scripts and has the Old Speech? And she rides well, I will allow."

"What veterans have you?" murmured the general, as the kedran waved still and began to march off, cheering for the Queen of the Chameln.

"Enough," said Megan Brock. "Some of the younger ones would be keen to see action. There are kerns who could be mounted..."

As they went in, Aidris said to the captain, "My room in the barracks must be cleared, Captain. I would have my comrade Ortwen Cash bring all the things to me in the morning."

The captain saluted. In the brightly lit dining chamber, at the head of the table, with Bajan on her left hand and the Lady Aumerl on her right, she remembered suddenly her dream of the forest. The darkness, the movement through the woods on horseback, the melody the captain had sung.

"The Winter Queen and the King of Summer
Will cast them down.
The men of Mel'Nir are tall as trees.
They will lie dead on the plain."

The wine in her goblet was red as blood. She had as little stomach for the rest of the dinner as she had for a battlefield.

"You are tired," said Bajan.

"No!"

"The queen may not be tired," said Lady Aumerl, smiling, "but Ensign Venn has had a long day. Let Count Bajan escort you to your chamber."

So another toast was drunk, and Bajan led her down the table to bid good-night. She came to Lord Huw at the table's end; the Lord of Kerrick looked hale enough, but he was still lame, with a basket frame to support his leg.

"Forgive me," said Aidris, "for entering your service under a false name and for leaving it so suddenly."

"Majesty," said Lord Huw, "I do not know when Kerrick has been more honored."

He smiled at her with a perfect understanding, as if he knew the long way she had come and the long way still to travel. On an impulse she stepped forward and gave the Lord of Kerrick a kiss upon his cheek.

"I will pray that your leg heals perfectly," she said.

She sat with Bajan at the fireside in the guest chamber, the same where Prince Ross had been lodged. Yvand and Millis moved about in the shadows. The room was high and shadowy, with fine hangings . . . almost, almost they might have been in the Palace of the Firn at Achamar. It needed a smell of fir and dried rose petals, the rose petals sent from Lien for Queen Hedris to scent her linen. She drew out the scrying stone from her new tunic.

"Has your mother's gift been a comfort in exile?" he asked.

"More than that," she said. "It has helped me to work magic."

"The tribal shamans by Vigrund are beating their drums night and day," said Bajan. "If it were only magic we needed!"

"Let us 'see if the stone has any message."

For the first time in ten years she let another person look into the stone. She remembered the wood where she had crouched with Sharn Am Zor, in peril for their lives. Bajan gasped.

"I see . . ."

"What? Tell me!"

"A crown, two crowns linked, lying upon a green cloth, and near them a bunch of oak leaves."

"The Daindru has come again," she said. "Do you see anything else?"

"Now the picture is different," he said. "A silver coronet and an eagle's feather."

"For you," she said. "Your crown and the eagle feather for the crest of the Nureshen."

"What place is that we see?" he asked.

"I call it the world of the stone," she said. "There is a being there, a Lady, who watches over me. She is my witch-mother or my wish-mother as they would say in Athron."

She looked into the stone herself and saw only a bunch of nettles.

"We must take care," she said. "There will be danger."

Bajan smiled with his head on one side as if to say that they did not need a scrying stone to tell them that.

"I must do all," she said. "I will speak further with Lingrit, prepare the letters . . ."

"Hush," he said. "Rest now. We have a lifetime. This is only the first day."

She slept late in the huge soft canopied bed and woke with Yvand holding a milk posset, the first in seven years.

"There is a big Athron wench waiting, my Queen," she said. "She has a pass from the kedran captain."

"Let her come in," said Aidris.

Yvand showed her disapproval. Aidris set the half-finished milk posset back on the tray and said, "Ortwen Cash is my comrade. She may come to me whenever she will. And I have lost the taste for milk posset. I will drink rosehip tea in the mornings."

Yvand went off, and presently Ortwen came peering round

the door of the bedchamber. She carried the fur cloak and a small bundle of Ensign Venn's possessions. Ortwen looked shy and sad. Aidris was ashamed of her long masquerade. How was it when a close friend was proved to be of high estate? Sabeth could become a countess in the twinkling of an eye, but Ortwen had to endure the teasing of the stableyard.

"I am still the same," she said.

Ortwen laid her burdens aside and perched on the edge of the bed where Aidris patted the quilt.

"Trouble," she whispered, trying to smile.

"Forgive me," said Aidris. "I told no one. Not Sabeth. Not Sir Gerr or the lord and lady. Terril of Varda did not know, although he is my own kin. Only Niall of Kerrick guessed, I think, and Prince Ross of Eildon knew me because of his magical powers."

"It was plain from the first that you were some lord's daughter," said Ortwen with some of her old humor. "The book-learning. The queer fine clothes . . . linen underdrawers!"

Then they laughed aloud, and Aidris said, "How we will laugh and cry when we think of these seven years!"

"The barracks is in an uproar," said Ortwen. "Nothing to match it since the Carach came back. Lord Huw has spoken with your tall general, Brock's old comrade. A company of volunteers will follow you home. It is all settled."

Aidris stared at her friend.

"Ortwen," she said, "dear Ortwen Cash . . . will you do one thing for me?"

"Surely," said Ortwen, wondering.

"Do not ride with me," said Aidris earnestly. "I pray you . . . do not ride to battle. Go home to Cashcroft and be married to Han the Smith."

"But why . . . ?"

"I am the queen; I must go," said Aidris. "But I cannot lead you to blood and death. I would be a false friend indeed."

"Others will go," said Ortwen stoutly.

"No, they will not," said Aidris, making the decision. "I will not have them. If the veterans, the true kedran and kerns . . . Brock and Yeo and Wray and Lawlor and the rest . . . make up companies I will not object; but no untried soldier of Kerrick Hall will ride with me, I swear it."

Ortwen sighed.

"They will never believe, back home, that I rode seven years long with the Queen of the Chameln lands."

"My friendship lasts forever," said Aidris. "We will meet again and ride together and speak of old times. You will have all that remains of my soldier's pay to buy that south field your father likes."

"Would you do that?" said Ortwen. "Truly, it is a good field, but you have no need..."

"Let me," said Aidris.

When Ortwen had gone, Aidris stood at the window in her nightgown looking at the gardens of Kerrick Hall, which she had never seen from the south wing. The women were waiting to dress their queen. Bajan and the councillors were waiting. The queen's horses were waiting to be exercised. She looked at a few of the tokens that had sustained her during her time in exile: the sword of the Firn, the beloved book *Hazard's Harvest*. Unexpectedly Yvand gave a loud sob: she was holding up the white tunic, Aidris's good white that she had worn perhaps nine times in seven years.

"It is still good," said Aidris. "Hardly a bead has been shed."

"We sewed it together," said Yvand, "the Lady Maren and myself."

Aidris slipped under the rail and knelt beneath the Carach tree.

"Carach," she said, "*the time has come. Give me your blessing once again for my journey back into my own country.*"

"*Oak maiden,*" said the Carach tree, "*Your own trees will give you that blessing.*"

"*Carach, we speak in the Chameln lands of lost Ystamar, the Vale of the Oak Trees. Is there such a place?*"

"*No one knows where it lies,*" said the Carach, "*except the wild creatures, the wolf and the wild swan.*"

Three leaves of the Carach, just turning to gold, dropped down upon her, softly as bird's feathers. She gathered them up and bade farewell to the Carach tree. She had come alone to the top of the hill, but when she turned, Niall of Kerrick and his dog Crib stood waiting.

"The Carach honors you," he said. "Go well, Queen Aidris."

"Watch over me, I pray," said Aidris. "You are far beyond me in magic, Master Kerrick, since you went into Eildon."

"My brother rides questing to help regain your throne," he said.

"It is not a quest!" she said.

Niall of Kerrick smiled at her, but his eyes were solemn. For a moment, holding the Carach leaves, she knew what he had wished to say to her for so long, which now could not be said. They clasped hands, and she went down the hill to the point where her kedran were waiting.

There was a brief leave-taking. Lord Huw and his lady stood at the door of Kerrick Hall, but Sabeth stood at her chamber window, her golden hair unbound, holding the child Imelda. She called a farewell to Gerr and to the queen.

"See there," said Millis Am Charn, riding in the escort, "the Countess of Zerrah is lovely as a princess from some old legend!"

Ten kedran and ten mounted men-at-arms, all veterans, rode with the escort of the Chameln. Sir Gerr, in the panoply of a knight Forester, led them down the avenue. Sergeant Lawlor led a second horse, Telavel, skittish and excited by the presence of six other Chameln greys.

As they came through Garth and turned to the east, Aidris looked up and saw that the sky was covered with mares' tail clouds. She rode in the midst of a company of Chameln lords in dark cloaks. She was dressed in white and mounted upon Tamir, the white stallion. Turning her head, she saw the hulk of the old mill looming among the trees. She waved her hand to Kedran Venn, watching through the eastern window; then the mill was lost to sight behind the hedges of the Varda road.

CHAPTER
VIII

THE NEWS OF THE QUEEN'S COMING RAN AHEAD of them through the autumn countryside. The people of Athron came to wave and cheer; the maple, ash and Carach blazed scarlet and gold beside the strange banners from the Chameln lands. Those who saw the queen riding past, a young girl, dark-haired, sitting her magical white horse so well, swore that she was beautiful, her complexion delicate as a wild rose, her eyes green as oak leaves. It was clear to them and to the bards and story-tellers that this was how a queen was meant to look.

As they came to Varda, there were many banners hung out, and the gates of the city had been shut but only so that they could be ceremonially opened at the queen's approach. When the trumpets had spoken to each other, the gates parted, and there before the assembled citizens and the lord mayor was a solitary horseman in green and gold, upon a roan mare. He came out of the city and doffed his plumed hat to the queen. They touched hands.

"Dearest cousin," said Terril of Menvir, "welcome to Varda."

"Dearest cousin," said Aidris, "I thank you for this fine welcome!"

They smiled at each other most warmly and rode side by side into Varda.

"I was forewarned," said Terril. "There was word that the Queen of the Chameln had been living at Kerrick Hall."

"And this told you all?"

"I swear it!" said the Prince gallantly.

The ceremony went forward. It was a clear cool autumn day, and the queen's party and their escort rode right through Varda to the palace where it stood among the gardens of the city.

Riding down Tower High Street, they drew rein at the sign of the double oak, hung with more flags, and Aidris gave a friendly greeting to Lallian Am Charn and her younger daughters and to Racha, the envoy's son. The young merchant of Varda looked more worried and disapproving than ever.

As they came through a certain quiet square, Aidris sent word to the heralds, and the whole procession turned into a quarter of Varda with large, old-fashioned houses that had seen better days. They came to a rambling mansion, somewhat decayed, but now hung with banners and evergreen from all its musty turrets and crumbling balconies. There in its garden was raised a spirit tree, a totem of the Chameln lands, crowned with long tresses of human hair.

The inhabitants of House Imal to the number of forty or fifty persons, mostly of humble estate, came streaming out cheering loudly when they saw the queen. The front door of the house flew open and down the path came the old Countess Palazan Am Panget in all her finery, accompanied by the elderly minstrel and her two waiting women.

Here for the first time Aidris saw green branches raised in almost every hand; these were not only her poor subjects, they were petitioners. She would be whipped to death by their green branches; she shrank away from such a tide of human wishes. She said to Nenad Am Charn who had come up to her left hand, "What can we give them?"

"Silver, for their feast," he said. "Their exile is not yet at an end."

So she rode forward and addressed the crowd saying:

"Good people of the Chameln lands . . . take a gift in my name! But you must wait with your green branches till I rule again in Achamar with the king, Sharn am Zor!"

The cheers redoubled. The old countess held out her arms on either side, her two waiting women took hold of her by the arms, lowered her into a curtsey, then hoisted her up again. The elderly minstrel came forward and bowed. He was proud and unsmiling as before; she could not tell if he recalled their last meeting.

"My greetings to the countess," she said, "I hope she is well."

"The countess greets the queen," intoned the bard, "and begs for news of the king, Sharn Am Zor."

"King Sharn leads an army by Winnstrand."

215

He bowed his head.

"The countess begs the queen to accept a humble gift."

He held it up for her upon his tarika a large unpolished gemstone, dark red in color, with flashes of hidden fire. It was not pierced but hung in a net upon a simple plaited thread, Aidris took the stone and stripped off a large, new ring with a pearl, and had a kedran bring it to the countess.

"Good minstrel," she said, "to celebrate my return pray sing your song again . . . of the Winter Queen and the King of Summer."

Again he bowed gravely, struck a chord, and began to sing. Aidris spoke the words in the common speech to Prince Terril, and those listening so treasured up the words of the queen that they sang the song again with these words. It became a riding song for the kedran, and they carried it back into the Chameln lands:

> "Far off, far off in Achamar
> The fires are lit,
> The King and the Queen have come home.
> O let me live till that moon!"

They were received at the palace entry by Prince Flor and his Princess and their son and heir, the young Prince Joris. From a dropsical infant this child had grown into a healthy and handsome little prince with chestnut hair and blue eyes. His mother, Princess Josenna, had become pretty and agreeable from sheer relief. She smiled warmly at Aidris, gave her a cousinly embrace, laid on ceremony, enough and not too much, for the royal party.

They rested briefly from their journey and then went in to dine. The palace was refurbished with a new front of white stone and a wide terrace before the chamber where they dined.

"Well, dear cousin," said Terril, "I have some notion that you will ask a favor. I promised to grant you one when we first met."

"Cousin," she replied seriously, "I will not ask you or your noble brother to send troops with me. If you own that I am the queen and Sharn Am Zor the king, that will be favor enough."

The prince looked relieved.

"Certain knights and battlemaids will go along anyway," he

said cheerfully. "You have persuaded Gerr of Kerrick, the new Count Zerrah. The Foresters are always ready for a quest."

She held her peace. The idea of questing still seemed frivolous to her and to have little to do with the perils that lay ahead.

"Tonight there will be fireworks in the gardens," put in Terril. "Green-fire out of Lien, dear cousin."

Aidris looked out into the gardens of the palace and beyond them the public gardens of Varda.

"Cousin Terril," she said, "I have never heard the name of that mountebank who taught you and Master Fantjoy a certain spell."

"Oh, he passes through," said the Prince. "He is a healer too, and a herbalist. His name is Jallimar."

"Does he travel alone?"

"No, with a greddle of all things. Some say it is his own son."

"Where is he now?"

"I think I know that too," said the prince. "He is far off in your Chameln lands, in the service of the young king."

After three days and nights in Varda, the queen and her escort rose to the Rodfell Pass in bright sunshine and crossed into the Chameln lands. With the queen, besides her Chameln lords and kedran, there rode certain knights of the order of the Foresters. Gerr of Kerrick, the new Count Zerrah, rode in the van, and with him, Sir Jared Wild of Wildrode and his cousin by marriage, the battlemaid, Baroness Ault, and Sir Berry Stivard of Blane, who had married the fair Amédine, and Frieda, the Lady of Wenns, and all their kerns and kedran to the number of a hundred and ten.

The Rodfell was a low-lying, easy pass, which rose up gently, with the mountain wall to the south and the peaks of the Four Sisters to the north. Aidris rode at the head of the company, behind the kedran general and Captain Brock and a pair of officers. She rode Telavel, and far back, behind the proud display of the Foresters and the dark cloaks of the Chameln lords, Sergeant Lawlor had the task of leading Tamir into his new homeland.

So they came to the top of the pass in midmorning and looked down a long, gentle slope to the border town of Vigrund. Mist still shrouded the valley and swirled around the lower branches of the trees. The road ran through the midst of the forest. Just over the crest Aidris called a halt. On the south side of the road was a clearing with a pair of spirit trees; she dismounted and walked alone into the clearing, with Bajan and the Herald of the Nureshen following at some distance. She knelt by the taller spirit tree, then stood still observing the signs of the forest. She summoned the herald, a tall man with white-blond hair, and said to him, "They will hear you!"

So the herald lifted up his mighty voice and cried out in the Old Speech, *"Tell Tagnaran, the Balg of the Tulgai, that Aidris, the Queen, has come home again. She will have her lands and her throne, the double throne that she shares with Sharn Am Zor. She will reward the Tulgai for their help and receive their fealty at Vigrund. Tell Tagnaran! Hold high the Daindru!"*

The ringing sounds of the herald's voice fled off into the misty depths of the forest. There was a moment of silence, then a single bird call and another and another; then the silence flowed back again.

"By the Goddess," said the Herald, surprised. "The wee devils *are* about!"

"Hush," said Aidris. "They will hear you!"

"Pardon me, my Queen."

She smiled at the herald and at Bajan; she could smile at everyone that day.

"You are awaited . . ." said Bajan.

They mounted up, and as the whole company moved off, she saw shapes in the mist upon the road. In a short distance they became clearer: ranks of dark riders, with here and there the colored cloaks of the youths and the maidens and the blonde hair of the Zor. A few whooping cries came out of the mist.

"Come then, my Queen!" cried Jana Am Wetzerik.

Aidris pressed forward on Telavel and cried out to Captain Brock; the standard-bearer followed too, and they rode to meet the northern tribes. They were surrounded, the shouting and wild cries echoed up to the mountain wall. Aidris saw Megan Brock crying out amazed at the welcome, but her words were lost in the tumult. The pace of the ride had not slackened; a double file of riders went ahead; the cheering did not stop all the way to Vigrund. And so the queen was brought home again.

* * *

There were signs of fighting in Vigrund: broken shutters on the houses and the remains of a barricade that the citizens had thrown up against the garrison. The garrison of a hundred men of Mel'Nir had been surprised; messengers had been ambushed on their way to the town so that the captain did not know the strength of the Chameln rising until too late. The townsfolk held the soldiers at bay until the northern tribes came down and finished the work.

"There are twenty survivors," said Bajan in answer to a question from Aidris. "Some are wounded. They lie in the old gatehouse yonder, which they used as a prison."

Now there were cheering crowds in the streets. The queen was lodged at that excellent inn where Sir Jared Wild and Mistress Quade had rested on their way home. The landlord, Master Keel, and his wife stood beaming in their best clothes to welcome the queen and her followers. There were few green branches to be seen in Vigrund—it was not a custom of the northern tribes. But Aidris looked down an alley as they passed by and saw a woman with a green branch running towards her. A beefy citizen took the woman by the shoulder and deliberately threw her to the ground. Aidris drew rein and shouted. A kedran of the escort brought the woman through to stand beside the queen. She was a woman of about thirty with a widow's scarf; she hardly dared to raise her eyes.

"Come," said Aidris. "What is your name? What will you ask of me?"

"I am called Mattis, my Queen," she said in a sweet, soft voice, regaining her courage. "I ask leave to tend a wounded man called Dal, Sergeant Dal."

"A wounded man?" asked Aidris sharply.

"He is a man of Mel'Nir, my Queen," said the woman, looking her in the eye. "He was billetted in my house for six years. He is my husband now; we were married by his captain, according to Mel'Nir custom. He is sore wounded and may not live."

There was a silence in the street, and Aidris caught a quick, questioning look from Bajan. She looked about and said, "Who answers for the prisoners in the gatehouse? Who has the duty?"

A foot soldier of the Nureshen in bronze strip mail came out of the crowd and saluted the queen and Count Bajan. He explained that the watch captain of Vigrund had the duty and he was in the relief troop.

"Let this woman come to the Mel'Nir sergeant," said Aidris, "and any other woman in her plight. But see that the prisoners stay closely pent up."

The man bowed low; the woman, Mattis, gasped out her thanks and kissed the hem of the queen's tunic. A murmur, the ghost of a murmur, came out of the crowd. Aidris said loudly, "This is the mercy of the Goddess, which I will bring to all those wounded in battle. My will, the will of the Daindru, is just as strong in this as it is strongly bent to drive the Melniros from our Chameln lands!"

The crowd cheered her to the echo. She went into the inn to rest, but there was no rest for the queen that day. She went in to dine with the Athron knights, all in high fettle, burning to ride further and look at the encampment of the tribes and the lines of Mel'Nir. They had heard talk of skirmishing and single combat. When dinner was half over, there came the tribal leaders, the Dencha, the Little Kings and Little Queens of the Durgashen, the Ingari and the Oshen. She received them in another room of the inn, and Ferrad Harka, Chief of the Durgashen, came with her to the war council of the Chameln lords.

Old Zabrandor unrolled his map again, and without palaver, Chief Ferrad, a grim-faced man with long moustaches and stinking black furs, said, "We have lost ground in the few days since the lords went to fetch the queen. The Melniros have cut the road to Zerrah, beaten off the riders of the Ingari, and thrown up more earthworks on the plain."

"What is the strength of Mel'Nir?" asked Aidris.

"We have no certain numbers, my Queen," replied Ferrad Harka, "but the warriors of Mel'Nir number upwards of a thousand, more than half of them mounted. Then they have mercenaries, two hundred bowmen."

"What, have they come out of Lien?" she asked.

"No, my Queen," answered Bajan. "They are most of them men of Lien, but Werris has had them in Achamar for some time."

"They have been marched here, poor brutes." said Jana Am Wetzerik, "and for little pay."

"We have more than four thousand of our folk ready to take the field," said Ferrad Harka, "and of those a thousand are mounted. We should gain the victory over Mel'Nir if we could come to them in the right way."

220

"As Dencha Harka has said," murmured the general tactfully; "but we have all the swiftness on our side and none of the weight."

"How is the water supply for the horses?" asked Aidris.

"It stands much better with us than it does with Mel'Nir," said Bajan, "but we are ravaging the lands of our comrade Lingrit Am Thuven."

"The cause is good," said Lingrit sadly. "Thuven Manor is there, such as remains of it, only to serve the queen."

"A place has been kept for you, my Queen," said Ferrad Harka. "Your own royal lodge is being built among the tents of the tribes."

"Let us ride out at once," said Aidris, "and see the encampments."

The road through the forest from Vigrund was lined with cheering tribesfolk and kedran on watch. She looked into the South Ride and wondered if it might be a place to exercise Tamir. Then the road wound out of the trees, and she saw the plain. She had hardly seen it from this vantage point but only from Thuven. There to the southeast were a few small villages and sheep folds of the plains, breaks of trees, and all among them the whitish tents of Mel'Nir, made of thick cotton cloth. The road was cut less than three miles away, and earthworks had been thrown up on either side, made higher by screens of brushwood.

She looked at the brown hide tents of the tribes that clustered all along the edges of the forest on both sides of the road. There were pickets for the horses and several railed pens. Cooking fires burned before the tents, and beside the lodges of the chieftains there were storehouses upon stilts like the houses of a lake village.

She looked fearfully towards Thuven and what she saw was a more sorrowful sight than ruin and waste. The trees and the lake were as beautiful as she remembered them; behind the trees the beloved house rose up as it had always done, and the setting sun of autumn put a light in the staring dark windows. She gave the excited Telavel her head a little and rode along the front of the camp with Lingrit after her on his tall brown gelding. The wind that always lived there turned the grasses to silver, and she and Telavel both remembered that this was the plain at last, only the sea more boundless. A cry reached her. She saw a movement be-

hind the earthwork and turned Telavel towards the barrow before
the watchers of Mel'Nir could undertake anything against a solitary outrider.

She waited now and did not ride up onto the barrow; Lingrit
came up, followed by Bajan and the other councillors. She could
look through the windbreak of dark trees to the overgrown drive-
ways and the lake shores. Folk were coming and going with
leather buckets and waterskins. The house was an empty shell
with trees and vines growing up inside the ruins.

Bajan pointed to a fine lodge against the forest fringes.

"That is the guest lodge," he said. "It could be finished in
the night if you wish it, my Queen."

"Let them take their time," said Aidris. "I will stay one or
two more nights at the inn."

They stood looking back the way they had come and beheld
the Athron knights on their chargers dancing about down the
road. One of them, surely Sir Jared Wild on Snow Cloud, made
a foray to the southeast. His boldness did not go unnoticed; two
armored men of Mel'Nir on their war horses appeared upon the
plain, their panoply glowing in the light of the setting sun.

"Fools!" swore Ferrad Harka.

"Not so," said Jana Am Wetzerik coldly. "That is what these
rash painted knights are for, noble Ferrad. They will draw out
the mounted lords, challenge them by name, joust with them."

"Then they must be prepared to joust indeed," said Lingrit
Am Thuven, "for there are no knights in Mel'Nir, no knightly
orders. They fight to the death, if they choose, and without
quarter."

"So do we!" said Bajan.

He drew his own horse, a new grey called Rastha, up beside
Telavel, and the young stallion widened its nostrils and forgot
its manners so far as to nip and nudge at the little mare. Bajan
smiled at Aidris. As they rode back, a small drum began to
sound.

"A shaman is praying for our enterprise," said Bajan.

"We need his prayers," she said. "Which is your lodge? Are
your brothers and sisters here, too?"

"I share the lodge of Batro, you remember, Batro with the
yellow hair, my sister Ambré's husband. My brother Abrajan
lodges with the young men. See . . . there is Batro's lodge, with
the eagle banner for the Nureshen."

By the time she came to the inn again and sent Telavel to the stable, Aidris found she was so weary she could hardly climb the stairs of the inn. She almost fell asleep in her bathtub before the fire.

"No, my Queen," said Yvand, "it is not charm of sleep that has smitten you, it is the people."

"I rode all day as a kedran," said Aidris with a yawn, "and tired as little as Telavel."

"A kedran does not have the duties of a queen," said Yvand, "to smile and wave and talk with lords and commons."

"Who keeps the watch?" she asked. "See that they bring me word if Mel'Nir begin mustering."

"Sleep, my Queen," said Yvand. "You will be summoned."

Vigrund still rang with voices. Fires had been lit in the marketplace and there was dancing in the streets. High up in the best room of the inn the queen fell asleep.

She had fallen asleep before supper, and she woke hours later when it was still very dark. For a moment she thought she was in her dear, narrow room at Kerrick, then she remembered: "I am queen and come to the inn at Vigrund." She saw the glow of the banked fire; she slept alone in the big room, with Yvand and Millis off in a little dressing room. She could not tell what had awakened her: a cry? a clattering in the dark street? Now all was still.

She had been dreaming, but nothing remained of the dream except a voice crying out her name, crying out for the queen. She tried to forget this dream, but another image from the dream took hold of her. A beating of dark wings, black feathered pinions beating and beating, blotting out the light as they passed over the forest and cast a shadow upon her upturned face.

She sat up, pushing aside the featherbed and held up the scrying stone. It gave off its soothing light. In the world of the stone there was a brown cloth and on it a bunch of mistletoe. The message of the magical plant was one of peace and protection, but it could not drive away her dream. Then, from one heartbeat to the next, the light was snuffed out in the world of the stone; it became a cold dead thing in her hand.

She was afraid then and angry, because there was nothing to fight against, no reason for her fear. The room was quiet, nothing moved in the shadows, nothing stirred outside her door or scrabbled at the windows of the inn. If she cried out, she would only wake her tired servants from their earned sleep. She sat still, hardly breathing, resisting the insidious fear. What made the stone so dark? Why was her protection withdrawn? She knew the answer, and it filled her with fresh anger and with despair. The Lady herself was afraid, and of their oldest enemy: the night-flyer, Rosmer, the sorcerer who had looked out from the forest stone. The fear, the night alarm were his presence.

She shouted at the intruder in her mind: "You shall not have me! I am not your creature, not Aravel nor Kelen nor any that you can bend to your will. Go back old man, old Eildon bastard, shame of a noble house! You are wrinkled and hideous, your gimcrack spells have not worked. You have a pain in your side . . . you must be cut for the stone!"

She sat in silence, shrieking this childish raillery, feeling the presence of her enemy grow and grow, as if she conjured him up, dragged him into the light, made him palpable by her taunting. A gust of wind struck the mullioned window; a log crashed down in the fireplace and the sparks rose. Yvand called sleepily from the next room, "My Queen? Dan Aidris?"

"A gust of wind," she said. "Sleep, Yvand."

The old one had come and gone. What was it Nazran had said? "Dark magic festers in the mind like fear."

Aidris slept again and woke with the first streaks of dawn lightening the sky over the plain. At last the streets of Vigrund were empty and quiet; she found she loved this stillness and emptiness. The escort went with her to the stables where Sergeant Lawlor had the two horses saddled. Tamir was very restless.

"He misses you, Dan Aidris," said the sergeant. "This ride will settle him a little."

The sergeant mounted Telavel, and with the escort of six kedran from Wetzerik's troop, they rode out of Vigrund down to the South Ride. A few townsfolk saw the queen go by in the morning mist. A kedran rode on ahead, and when they came to the wide grassy bay in the sea of trees, larger by far than the exercise paddocks at Kerrick, a few old friends came up from the kedran camp. She saluted Captain Brock and Lieutenant

Yeo, then began to put Tamir through his paces and show him the Ride.

He was baulky at first, but she knew the reason. It was not only the nerve-wracking ride over the pass, the hordes of shouting people, that had upset him.

"Ah, my dear," she said, coming back up the ride. "The trees will not harm you. You must learn to know the forest and the plain. This is your mother's country . . . you are Telavel's child after all. See how well Telavel goes, close to the trees!"

Tamir allowed himself to be persuaded to come closer to the forest trees; he began to enjoy the South Ride, plunging through its open spaces and wisps of low-lying mist. In the center of the Ride, Aidris took him through the very beginnings of dressage, all that he had been taught. He walked, he turned, then before he was asked to trot, Tamir pranced off into his own parody of the difficult groundwork of steps that Telavel and Yeo's splendid black mare Nightbird were performing nearby. The kedran laughed at his antics, and he rocked delicately for them, acknowledging their laughter. Aidris realised that she was happy, as happy as she might be, as queen, in the midst of an armed host, preparing for battle.

Tamir checked nervously just at the entrance to the forest, beside that broad path she had followed, with Sabeth and Ric Loeke riding ahead, years before. With a thump of fear she saw that there was a dark figure standing in the shadow of the mighty trees.

She swung away, and Sergeant Lawlor cried out, "Who's there? Come out, damn you, and show yourself!" She said to Aidris, "Get further back, Dan Aidris!"

A wild and desperate cry came from the forest.

"Queen! Queen Aidris Am Firn! O save me . . ."

They both saw the man, if it was a man, hold out empty hands and fall down upon the path. Captain Brock rode up with some of the escort.

"Stay back, Queen Aidris," she said. "We'll have this prowler out in the daylight or drive him away."

She rode off down the path with three other officers, and the man fled away before them. Again he cried out, "The queen! I must speak to the queen!"

Then the kedran and their quarry were lost to view. Aidris

watched, thinking of treachery, of the arrows that might fly from every bush and tree. Was it some trap? Could that lone suppliant harm his pursuers?

"It is some mad hermit," said Lawlor. "Everyone seeks to come to the queen."

They waited, and soon Captain Brock and the others rode back empty-handed.

"Truly," said Megan Brock, "I have seen some strange sights since I came into the Chameln lands, Queen, but this beats all. The man was a scarecrow in ragged clothes and animal skins, ill-cured and stinking. Yet I swear he spoke in the accents of Lien."

"What did he want of me?"

"He begged for you to step into the shade of the trees to speak to him. He said that he cannot leave the forest. He has wandered there for seven years; his master had him under a spell. If he once goes beyond the boundaries of the woods, he will die."

"Did he give no name?"

"When we refused to bring you into the woods, he ran off, but first he bade us bring you a token."

"What is it?" asked Aidris.

"The maddest thing of all," said the captain. "He plucked out a great handful of his own long beard. Here it is!"

The bunch of hair that she laid in Aidris's hand was fine and silken, twined with a scrap of fern. It was of so bright and unmistakeable a color that it glowed in the pale autumn sunlight: a hard, foxy red. Aidris felt a thrill of terror and then of pity. Seven years! She rode Tamir at once to the path and peered into the shadows of the forest.

"Hurne!" she cried out. "Hurne!"

There was no answer; the wild man had gone. She turned aside, ready to toss away the handful of bright hair, but then thought better of it and stowed it in the pocket of her tunic.

"I know him," she said to Captain Brock. "He was a mercenary out of Lien. He twice was sent to kill or capture me and twice failed."

"And his master?" asked Megan Brock.

"I know him too," she said. "But I will not speak a name of such ill-omen on this day."

They heard the sound of trumpets and drums.

"What does that mean, Captain? Will Mel'Nir give battle?"

"The tribes are mustering, Dan Aidris. Will you return to Vigrund?"

"Not I," she said. "I will watch from the barrow with certain council lords. But first . . . let me breakfast at the kedran camp."

The captain smiled. Her hard blue eyes could still see into a kedran's soul even if that kedran had become a queen.

"I have never watched a battle," she said, "but it is as difficult as any duty. I am sure you will learn much, Dan Aidris."

Aidris bade Sergeant Lawlor bring Telavel back to Vigrund, and she followed the escort down a bridle path that led to the kedran camp. It was well placed on a mound before the trees on the south side of the road, in the midst of the camp of the Durgashen. There was movement all through the tribal camps, and far away by the barrow she saw a body of dark riders. A party of Athron knights came down the road and hailed the queen; Frieda, the Lady of Wenns, a stout old "battlemaid," came to join the kedran, but the Baroness Ault rode out with Sir Jared as his shield-bearer.

There was movement too in the camp of Mel'Nir. Thick ranks of mounted troopers could be seen behind the barriers in the center. Aidris remembered the sound they made, like a mighty war engine. Jana Am Wetzerik sat at the open doorway of her tent at a table with her officers, and they gave the queen and Lady Frieda a hearty welcome. There was a most comradely time spent eating and drinking and watching the weather and making scornful comments on the arrangements of Mel'Nir. Yet she looked at all the women with a cold knot of fear in her chest and knew that they were all afraid, as she was.

The horde of the Durgashen and the Ingari were massing all around them, more than a thousand, with banners. They wore padded leather greaves and breast plates of bronze, and they carried long spears. There were mounted archers among them, young men and women in small companies.

A prolonged and strange trumpet call rose up out of the din and the general said, "They will come to parley. They know the queen is here."

Two riders broke out from the barriers and came up the road; one was a herald with a long pennant, and under it a flag of truce. The herald of the Nureshen rode out and met them midway between the lines and brought them in. Aidris saw them dismount among the bristling warriors of the Durgashen; she stood at the front of the mound waiting until Ferrad Harka led up the two men of Mel'Nir.

The herald was a model of his kind, a huge man, fair-haired and blunt-featured, whose cheeks drooped a little from blowing his own trumpet.

The officer with him was shorter, thick-set and dark with a handsome open face and fine teeth. Aidris was impressed by their heavy boots and strip mail, the herald's painted, the officer's a plain, polished grey. They both covered their armor with a long, belted cotton robe that reached to mid-calf.

The officer saluted:

"Brond," he said. "Marshal of the Army of the Protectorate. I come under truce to bring a message from our commander, Hem Allerdon, to the queen."

"I am listening, Marshal Brond."

He smiled and drew himself up.

"Hem Allerdon bids Queen Aidris of the house of the Firn to yield herself up and go with his escort to Achamar to the Protector Werris, who rules in the Chameln lands for the Great King, Ghanor of Mel'Nir. She will be kindly treated and restored to her kingdom under the continued protection of Mel'Nir. Hem Allerdon commands the northern tribes of the Nurashen, the Durgashen, the Ingari and the Oshen to get themselves back home again before the winter comes. The northern tribes cannot stand against the forces of Mel'Nir. They will be cut down, be they as thick as swine grunting about our feet. We will spurn them out of the way."

Ferrad Harka allowed himself to be drawn. He gave a roar and moved towards the men of Mel'Nir. She saw that Lingrit Am Thuven and Old Zabrandor had joined the watchers; now Lingrit laid a restraining hand upon the chieftain's arm. Brond did not flinch.

"It is the custom in Mel'Nir to let an envoy speak," he said. "And to understand that he brings a message from another."

As it was her turn to speak, she found that she was able to look about, see her listeners, control her words and gestures like a player in a masque. She was conscious of all that had gone into her brief reply: the helpful phrases that Lingrit had written out for her to study, the speeches of other rulers that she had learned from Nazran, even the poem, "Queen Negartha Hurls Defiance at Her Enemies," from *Hazard's Harvest*. The

228

ringing tones of her voice she owed to Megan Brock.

"Marshal Brond," she said, "hear my words. My herald of the Nureshen will bring them to Allerdon, Commander of the invading army of Mel'Nir. There is no Protectorate of Mel'Nir in the Chameln lands. Lord Werris is no protector but a usurper, and he serves a foul master, Ghanor of Mel'Nir, no Great King but a tyrant grown old in deeds of blood, who will die by the hand of his own kin. Werris is too proud. If he comes before me, he will have to answer for the deaths of my two trusted friends, Nazran Am Thuven and his wife, the Lady Maren.

"I charge Hem Allerdon and all the men of Mel'Nir and the mercenaries of Lien under his command to take themselves hence, to get themselves back home again before the winter comes. Because they may be sure that for them, for those who invade our Chameln lands, a terrible winter is coming. The power of the Goddess is in my Chameln warriors, and they will hurl back the might of Mel'Nir. The Daindru rules in these lands, as it has done for a thousand years. I speak this in my own name as Aidris, the Queen, and in the name of my cousin, who shares the double throne, King Sharn Am Zor."

When the cheering had died down, the Marshal bowed low to her.

"Majesty!"

She gave an encouraging word to the herald of the Nureshen, then the three men mounted up again. She watched them riding at a rolling gallop towards the Mel'Nir lines. The Marshal and his herald, on either side of the herald of the Nureshen on his tawny mare, rode monstrous chargers with plumed hooves. The long banners of the heralds snapped in the wind. The day was grey now, with a weak radiance where the sun was shining behind the clouds. A kedran cried out, "See there, my Queen! The Athron knights have engaged the knights of Mel'Nir!"

"Come, my Queen," said Lingrit, "let us make the ride to the barrow."

So she mounted Tamir again, and the men and women of the Durgashen cheered her round about. She saluted the general and the ranks of the kedran, and came with Lingrit and her kedran escort along the road. She saw how three Athron knights rode against three noblemen of Mel'Nir, midway between the opposing hosts.

"The Melniros wear crests and armor like the Foresters or

229

the Questors," she said to Lingrit, "but you have said they are not knights."

"They have no history of knighthood," he said. "It comes from Eildon. Those are young nobles, sure enough, their fathers the war-lords of Ghanor, the king."

As they watched, an Athron knight unhorsed his opponent and gained a cheer from the Chameln camp. She saw that it was Gerr of Kerrick. She turned off the road now and rode along the front of the camp, close to the ranks of the Nureshen. She came to Bajan and his lesser chieftains, all armed and fierce; the whole host of the Nureshen cheered for the queen.

They leaned from their saddles and embraced. Bajan clasped her gloved hands tightly. They could do no more than this; she was stifled with pain and fear.

"My love..."

"Come back safely..."

There was a flurry of trumpet calls from the camp of Mel'Nir, and the escort called for her to make haste. She bent low on Tamir, and they rode round the massed riders of the Nureshen and the Oshen and sped on towards the barrow.

The way had not changed. She looked at the ruined manor house and the untended orchards with the trees bare. The wind was from the north and blew over the barrow with an icy breath, stirring the long grass. A stockade of logs and brushwood had been freshly built to shelter the queen and her attendants. As she came round it, she gave a glad cry. There in the shelter stood a young oak tree; in seven years it had grown waist high.

"An oak tree is a good omen," said Lingrit with his wan smile.

"I planted it myself," she said, "in the year that I went into exile."

The kedran were pleased and said that it would be called the Queen's Oak. She got down and let Tamir graze on the hilltop with the other horses. There was a sudden movement near at hand, and the riders they had just passed of the Nureshen and the Oshen gave their battlecry and rushed down upon the earthworks of Mel'Nir.

Watching was more terrible than she had imagined. She saw the arrows fly out in a cloud and saw the foot soldiers taking the charge. There was a dull noise of bodies hitting together. Horses screamed and fell down; a horse ran out of the mass dragging a rider by the stirrup. The foot soldiers of Mel'Nir

were not broken, but she saw them fall, thought she saw blood
even at this distance. Then the riders wheeled away, in a movement worthy of kedran cavalry, and went back to their lines.
The plain was covered with dark clumps; horses ran riderless.
Then a score of runners hurled themselves on to the field, half-
naked runners shouting to each other.

"There go the gleaners!" cried the kedran.

The runners caught the horses or turned over the fallen
riders. A pair of them caught up one who still lived and ran
back. A runner was shot down by a solitary archer of Mel'Nir
mounted upon the earthen rampart. Lingrit gave a shocked
exclamation.

"It is a tribal custom," she said. "They make it a test of speed
and strength."

"Other folk wait until the battle is over," he said.

Before the gleaners had done their work, a second wave of
riders rode at the earthwork a little further south, and behind
them came a mass of foot soldiers. Aidris watched with her
teeth gritted and felt a kind of relief when the battle was joined,
when the riders whirled away again, leaving the two groups of
foot soldiers locked in combat upon the earthwork. Far down
the line, she saw the banners of the Athron knights retiring.

"They need more cavalry in there," she said, "to secure this
damned earthwork from the south."

Slowly a white wall moved across the road in the center. It
began to move forward, just as slowly, then with a quickening
pace and at last the earth shook and with a noise like thunder
the mounted troopers of Mel'Nir charged down upon the horde
of the Durgashen. The noise of their coming together was thick
and metallic. All those watching upon the barrow rose and cried
out. The Durgashen, horse and foot, flowed out and round the
heavily armed warrior on their warhorses. Soon there was little
to see, a dust cloud had arisen, yet she knew what was hidden
by the cloud. She felt the deaths of those who died beneath the
hooves of the horses, of the rider unhorsed and gored by the
spears, of those packed sweating and bleeding in a narrow
space.

She turned aside and went forward a little on the barrow and
looked down into the camp of the Nureshen. She looked for
Bajan's standard. She felt another surge of anxiety; she was
angry with Bajan because he did not send word that he was

231

unharmed. Lingrit came after her and pointed down into the ruins of the manor house.

"We can go down, my Queen. There is shelter there."

"Would it not cause you pain?" she asked. "It is a sad place."

"I have hardly lived in Thuven," he said, "and I do not believe in ghosts."

"You have lived in Lien," she said.

"Yes, I have lived in Lien almost as long as I have lived in the Chameln lands," said Lingrit with that wise look that reminded her of his father. "It is more civilised than any other place, even old Eildon, and it is more cruel and savage."

"Was there a change in your estate when Mel'Nir seized the Chameln lands?" she asked. "Did Kelen receive some envoy of the protectorate?"

"He despises Mel'Nir," said Lingrit, "but he did receive their envoys, and he made much of Prince Gol."

"Has he forgotten the sufferings of his own sister, Elvédegran?"

"He has other marriage plans for the prince."

She stared at him.

"The Princess Merilla Am Zor," he said, "sister of King Sharn, is well-grown and accomplished."

"She is a child!" cried Aidris. "I cannot believe this even of Kelen and his foul shadow Rosmer."

"The Princess is fifteen, and Prince Gol a widower for the second time at forty-four. Ghanor will die . . . in his bed at the Palace Fortress, I would say, and not by the hand of any grandchild. Your cousin could be a queen."

"May the Goddess preserve her!"

There was a shout from the kedran watching; the dust had been laid, on the plain, by a cold light rain. In among the Durgashen the troopers of Mel'Nir could be seen now as a solid body. They were steadily gaining the advantage, pressing the tribes back along the road to Vigrund. Some of the Durgashen, hard-pressed, had begun to fly the field.

Nearer at hand the cavalry of the Nureshen had reformed, and they charged again, a last charge, at the earthwork, which their foot soldiers had almost been able to hold. Now they were bringing out those who were left, saving what could be saved.

Aidris said to the young kedran officer whose name was Gefion, "The battle is lost!"

"Not so, my Queen," she replied seriously. "Undecided. Mel'Nir have their flank unprotected . . . see there, can you see?"

Aidris could see the beaten horde of the Durgashen and the Ingari flow away from the southern flank of Mel'Nir. The kedran charged at last. It was too far away for the watchers on the barrow to see clearly. The kedran, fresh and disciplined, came down upon the troopers, tired from the close combat. The white ranks of Mel'Nir bulged and heaved, trying to turn and reform. Those who had pursued the Durgashen too far along the road to Vigrund were surrounded and brought down. She saw the great battle horses for the first time running riderless upon the plain. When one broke down to its knees, the gleaners rushed in at once and killed it with axe and sword, then ran back to their lines drenched in dark blood. She watched still, lips drawn back in a grimace. The troopers did reform and rode back to their lines. The kedran charged at their flanks again and again, then they came under a rain of arrows covering the retreat of Mel'Nir, and the action was broken off.

She stood aching in the rain and cold and drank apple wine that the kedran handed to her. Riders came up onto the barrow. Before she could cry out for news, Old Zabrandor had flung himself from his horse and come to her side.

"Count Bajan sends greetings, my Queen. He will come to the inn at Vigrund."

Aidris felt relief so keen that she could have sunk down on the cold hillside. She put a hand on the old lord's arm and thanked him. The cavalry of Mel'Nir had drawn back behind their barriers. Far away at the very southernmost end of the field, there was a last skirmish between riders of the Ingari and a band of archers from Lien with a war machine, a wooden platform, which they pushed forward for a shelter.

"There is not much more to be seen, Dan Aidris," said Zabrandor.

"My lord," she said in a low voice, "after what I have seen today, I am not hopeful of coming to meet Sharn Am Zor. Mel'Nir will drive the tribes back."

"I fear it," he said. "It goes better with the king's army, but there is the risk that Mel'Nir will bring in fresh troops over the Danmar."

There was shouting and laughter behind them where three

Athron knights, elated with battle, were planting captured banners of Mel'Nir inside the enclosure. She was pleased to see that they had come back unharmed from their joust with the young nobles of Mel'Nir. She tried to smile and receive them pleasantly.

"Yes," she said to Sir Jared Wild, "I planted the oak myself. But I know you heard a strange lying tale that the Heir of the Firn lay buried here on the barrow."

"Queen Aidris," he said gallantly, in his big untuned voice, "I fear we all serve the queen very ill to let her stand here in the rain and the cold."

"Majesty, ride with us," cried Sir Berry Stivard. "Ride with us to our Athron tents now, on your way to Vigrund."

"We will give you and Lord Lingrit and your kedran here a cup of mulled Athron wine to keep out the cold," said Gerr of Kerrick.

She saw their handsome Athron faces and felt a sudden longing for Kerrick Hall with the lamps lit. The orders were given and the whole party mounted up and rode down off the barrow. It was not much past midafternoon, but the late autumn day seemed already far spent; fires were being lit along the edge of the battlefield.

They rode back behind the lines of the Nureshen, and she saw sights and heard sounds that could not be borne. She spoke to many of the tribesfolk, but could not remember afterwards what she had said to comfort them. She looked about for Bajan, but could not see him and wondered if they had lied to her and he was among the fallen. It seemed to her that the Heir of the Firn, that green girl, *was* dead, dead long ago and buried upon the barrow, by the oak tree. Now there was a woman who passed by on a white horse, a woman in whose service others died and were maimed; now there was only the queen.

CHAPTER
IX

T HE COLD RAIN DID NOT STOP. IN THE NIGHT
after the battle, a strong wind sprang up and the opposing armies
were lashed by the storms of autumn. Aidris had forgotten how
hard it could rain, how hard the winds could blow in her native
land. Both camps became a morass; tents were blown away;
there was no thought of fighting. The queen sat in her warm
room at the inn, and Bajan came every day to join her at the
fireside. She began to recover from the shock of her first battle,
her first battlefield.

There were things that could not be borne, yet all must bear
them. Lieutenant Yeo was dead, killed in the first kedran charge;
Megan Brock, as the kedran said, had been wounded and widowed in one day. Bajan's young brother was sorely wounded,
might not recover. The losses, everyone cried at the council
board, were light. The prospect was hopeless. Winter would
come down, the forces of Mel'Nir would become more and more
restive in their exposed positions on the plain and would press
the tribes closer.

There was a hectic spirit abroad; the tribesfolk and the kedran
found themselves a warm fire or a billet in the town and got
drunk. Aidris heard the Athron knights, come up from camp,
roistering in the dining room of the inn. She came upon Nenad
Am Charn and Old Zabrandor the worse for wear over a game
of Battle. She came unheralded to call upon Lingrit Am Thuven,
whose servants and baggage had lately come out of Lien, through
the Adz. That pale and melancholy man sat by his fire in a
silken robe; one handsome young man played upon a dulcimer,
another served Lienish wine and dainties. With the charm of
Lien still upon her, she followed Yvand up the stairs again and

found Bajan sunk in gloom by her fire. She dismissed Yvand and prowled the room and cried out, "This is mere foolishness..."

She went to Bajan and kissed him. She smoothed back the thick brown hair from his brow and found a long healing scar where he had been grazed by a spear.

"Lady," he whispered, beginning to understand, "what would you...? I should ride back to camp."

"No!"

"It *is* a rough night..."

They kissed again, kissed and clung until they were robbed of breath and fumbled their way to the big welcoming curtained bed.

"I have thought of you..."

"Now I am here!"

The maids' gossip was all wrong; perhaps the Lienish wine was a specific. She felt no pain to speak of and no fear. A strong magic bound them together, a magic of the Chameln lands. The dark huntress sought through the forest and found her hunter who lay with her; the young men and maidens lay down together in the fields at midsummer. They were nameless lovers; they were Count Bajan and the queen. The night drew out; they fell asleep, and Aidris woke when Yvand came in to make up the fire, She put a finger to her lips; Bajan was still asleep. Yvand, who had been twice wed, raised her eyes to heaven and blushed, and smiled.

The storm continued; the weather was so rough they did not take out the horses, and the shamans predicted that it would continue so for at least five days more. Yet on this third night, past midnight, they woke with strange voices crying out in the street below and sounds of a crowd gathering, in spite of the foul weather. Still the voices howled for the queen, the queen.

Bajan rose up cursing and put on his breeches. He went to the far window overlooking the street and cried out, "Look! Come love, here is a sight to behold!"

She came in her furred bedgown and peered through the shutters. In the street stood ten, twenty, a whole troop of warriors, long-haired and ferocious, with the rain streaming from their leather cloaks. The leader of the Tulgai stood proudly in the light that shone out from the inn door. Aidris flung wide the casement and leaned out into the rain.

"*Akaranok, my good friend!*"

Then Akaranok cried out in joy, and all the Tulgai shouted for the queen.

"*My Queen!*" cried Akaranok, "*I bring greeting from Tagnaran. Speak with me, I pray, though the hour is late. I have important news!*"

The inn woke up again and received the warriors of the Tulgai, who feasted until dawn. So many of their kind had not been seen in Vigrund since the coronation of the Daindru, Esher and Racha, years before. The queen was dressed again and received Akaranok and two of his followers by her fireside.

Count Bajan was presented and a health drunk, but Akaranok came swiftly to his news.

"*My Queen,*" he said, "*this man is called Beregun, and he lives far to the southeast. He is a hunter of the Kelshin, the dark ones, our blood brothers who have their home in Nightwood in the kingdom of Mel'Nir.*"

Beregun was like and unlike the true Tulgai. He was more lightly built and in fact fairer of complexion, though his hair was black. He said in a firm light voice, "*Queen Aidris, I hunt between the great forest and Nightwood, and in the hunting preserves of King Ghanor. I hunt the high trails, as we say, and I can travel swift as a bird through the treetops. I came from the woods by Nesbath in one day and a half...*"

"*Truly, good Beregun, you travel like the wind,*" said Aidris.

"*Armies are gathered in Nesbath, and they are the Red Hundreds of Ghanor, the King.*"

"*So they are coming,*" said Bajan. "*We have feared as much. Will they take ship from Nesbath?*"

"*No, Count Bajan,*" said Beregun. "*They come by land. I believe they will ride tomorrow, and in three days they will reach the Adderneck Pass on the Nesbath road into the Chameln lands.*"

Aidris put out a hand to Bajan. It seemed afterwards that the whole fateful outcome was in their minds at this moment. She did not see the way clear, but she knew there must be a way to turn this knowledge to advantage.

"*Beregun,*" she said, "*I thank you from my heart for bringing me this news. I pray you stay here and eat and drink your fill. You must speak this news again.*"

Bajan sprang up, as she did. Yvand came from the shadows where she had been watching the Tulgai.

"The council," said Bajan, "at once and secretly, Yvand, fetch those who sleep in the inn. Make tea . . . sober them if necessary. I will ride to the camp and bring Harka and the general."

So Lord Zabrandor unrolled his map on a hasty assemblage of tables in the queen's chamber, and even before Bajan returned with the others, the force of the news was plain.

"There is Adderneck," said Lingrit Am Thuven. "There is the last known front of the King's horde, the army of Sharn Am Zor. If the Red Hundreds come through and meet the men of Mel'Nir who are already here, they will divide our forces forever."

"By the Goddess," said Zabrandor, "they are too proud, committing themselves to that pass. They must not come through."

"How can they be stopped?" asked Lingrit. "Can we warn the king? Can we bypass Mel'Nir and send our own tribesfolk over the plain?"

Aidris looked at the map. She spoke and so did Nenad Am Charn, with one voice.

"We might go through the forest!"

They stared in silence at the black curve of the forest painted upon the old seamed parchment of the map and knew that Mel'Nir had been delivered into their hands.

"A force of cavalry," murmured Lingrit, "Three hundred, five hundred . . . is it possible?"

"We would need guides," said Nenad. "The guild house is shut down. The forest guides quarrelled with the garrison."

"We have guides, the finest in the forest," said Aidris. "The warriors of the Tulgai."

So the others came, Ferrad Harka with a bloody bandage on his arm and Jana Am Wetzerik alert as if she were on parade, crying, "Well, have you seen it? Do you have the answer?"

They did have the answer; the plan was like a live thing.

"Secrecy," said Bajan. "We move tomorrow while the rain holds to cover all. It is given out that a troop is marching to the Adz."

"These hundreds are expected," said Wetzerik. "The Melniros in the south know they are coming, and so do our own opponents here. Count Ferrad, Count Bajan . . . you will see these bully boys break off soon and march south to join their expected reinforcements. But you must hold them until that time."

Lingrit said drily, "The queen must go south with the troops of the great ambush. She will be brought safely to the king's army, and the Daindru proclaimed. I will go as well to protect her interests."

She thrilled at the promised activity and at the same time shuddered. She would be parted from Bajan.

"The queen will be missed," said Nenad Am Charn. "It may upset the morale of the tribes."

"No," said Aidris, considering. "No, I see how it will be done. I will pack up at once to move to my lodge at the camp. That will explain my absence from Vigrund. At the camp, my place will be taken by the lady Millis Am Charn, riding Tamir, my white horse, behind the lines. The tribes can share the secret a little . . . they can cheer the queen's horse instead of the Queen."

"Who will lead the ambush?" asked Zabrandor.

"You must take the command, Lord Zabrandor," said Jana Am Wetzerik, "for your lands are there by the Nesbath road, and you know the terrain best."

"I will do it with good heart," said the old lord.

Then when they had all thrashed out the question of the riders who might come along, and had chosen as troop leaders Brock for the kedran, and Batro, Jorgun and Vadala for the tribes, Zabrandor said again, "All who go along must be prepared for bloody deeds rather than knightly courtesy. We do not go to ride brave figures upon the plain but to fall upon our enemy secretly and kill him."

There was a burst of savage laughter from the warriors of the Tulgai who followed the common speech well enough, even if they would not speak it.

"There you have our name," said Aidris. "We are the Morrigar, the Giant-killers."

They drank a health to the enterprise and discussed the question of their allies, the Athron knights.

"They must all be trusted," said Aidris. "We are taking some of their veteran troopers."

"It would be no bad thing," said Lingrit, "if the new Count Zerrah came along, if he could be persuaded to leave the field of honor. There are many new men, you will admit, Lord Zabrandor, surrounding the young king. I serve the queen and like to see her interests well represented. She shall have the new-made count along, too."

So it was agreed, and a lot more beside. The preparation went on in secret haste everywhere; it was already daylight, but the rain went on unabated. Aidris packed and waited; Yvand made it clear without a word that she intended to ride with the queen. At last, not more than half an hour before she left the inn, Yvand came to her and said, "It is the innkeeper's wife, Mistress Keel, my queen. She knows that you are moving to the lodge. She begs most earnestly to be allowed to speak to you."

"I will see her," said Aidris. "Will she ask some favor? We have certainly made a battlefield of her inn. We owe the poor woman a good deal."

The woman came in briskly; she had arranged to see the queen alone. Aidris looked at her closely for the first time and saw a handsome, dark, lively person about forty years, with a suggestion of city manners that she could not have gained in Vigrund.

"Queen Aidris," said the innkeeper's wife, "I could not help hearing from the kedran that you were once a kedran yourself."

"That is true, Mistress Keel."

"I think you took the name of Venn."

Aidris nodded, with a very first inkling of what was to come. The woman took a letter from her pocket, a faded letter, which she handed to Aidris in silence. Aidris read a few lines and looked up amazed. The woman smiled sadly.

"I have been married to Keel the innkeeper for some years," she said. "I was the widow of a Lienish riverboat captain, name of Lorse."

The Widow Lorse had haunted her dreams a little in former years, but she had seen her as blowsy and high-colored. She looked at the letter, written on paper from her own writing case in the glade by Lake Tulna. Sabeth had a fair rounded merchant's script, taught her by the Moon Sisters. She had witten without superscription or signature:

"You will know Loeke is dead, from a fall, and his horse brought home to Vigrund. Do not worry or fret yourself. I am travelling on into Athron and I have *guides* and *gold* and I am not alone. Loeke, not to speak ill of him, was rough work and a boorish fellow. I have a friend who travels with me, and she is a little kedran maid who calls herself Venn, though I doubt that is her real name. She is of a rich Chameln family, and they are sending her into Athron because of the Melniros in their lands. She is brave, far braver than I, in the forest, and fears neither fairies nor demons. I think she will prove my *true friend*. I have even thought we might stay together in Athron and I take a *respectable place*, as for a waiting woman with an *envoy* in Varda, where she is going, rather than the other, the Countess P. For you have always said I must look for good fortune wherever it beckons. If you do not hear from me, you will know this is what has happened. *Do not worry*, my dear, and know that I will always think of you kindly."

Aidris could have wept at this artless letter. She looked at Mistress Keel and again the woman smiled sadly.

"I did worry," she said, "but I told myself that Sabeth, my beautiful one, had indeed found good fortune."

"Yes," said Aidris. "Yes, the greatest good fortune. I like to think that I helped her to find it. She is married for four years now and has borne a daughter and will soon bear another child. Some time after she wrote this letter she met a young man of good family who later became her husband."

"I am pleased to hear it," said Mistress Keel.

"It would be easy for you to find out the name and estate of this man," said Aidris, "but I must beg you not to do it and to keep your own counsel."

"She has your friendship..."

"Forever!"

"Delbin was a soldier," said Mistress Keel suddenly, "and married to a farmer's daughter. I never told her that I found this out. She liked to think that they were finer. But they were a pair of young country folk, alone in the world, without family. They died when their cart overturned crossing the Ringist. The baby was rescued, floating, and brought to the Moon Sisters. The trick of fate was that she was beautiful, lovely as a princess, and turned out upon the world alone at sixteen. It might have gone much worse for her in Lien..."

For an instant Aidris was tempted to ask the woman about dark matters, about Hurne the Harrier and his master, but she would not get in deeper.

"Will you keep this letter?" she asked warily.

For answer the woman reached out and took it from her hand. She smoothed it out and held a corner of the paper to the last coals of the fire. They both watched in silence as the letter burned to ashes.

"Thank you, Mistress Keel."

"The Goddess is kind," said the innkeeper's wife. "My prayers have been answered."

"You and your husband will be well rewarded for the use of your inn and for your good service."

"My Queen . . ."

The woman curtsied low and went away again. Aidris, in the few moments alone that were left to her, pondered, on this special day, on the lives of women. Her own life seemed to her hardly a woman's life at all, with none of the softness that women were supposed to enjoy and, thank the Goddess, not much of the shame and violence to which they were subjected. She drew out the scrying stone and saw the Lady at once, looking out with a fierce expression.

She said, "Is it well? Do you know our purpose?"

For answer there was only a whisper.

"Go swiftly!"

A hand held up a snake very tightly, behind its head, as if to squeeze the creature to death. The sign was plain: Adderneck. So from this lady, whom she thought of as having been "a true woman," loving and being loved and fighting for those she loved with "a woman's weapons," including magic, she received, on this day, only a call to battle.

Then it was time. Yvand, dressed for the journey, came in with Aidris's fur cloak, and, shining-eyed, slipped around the queen's wrist a wreath of ivy leaves, wet from the rain. They went down the stairs, and Telavel waited with the escort. She took some time to visit Tamir in his stall and bid him farewell. Then they rode to the South Ride in the steady rain, and there she parted with some of the escort, chosen by lot, for they would all have ridden with the queen.

The South Ride was packed with mounted troops, eerily silent, riding off by companies into the forest, with order kept by a few drumbeats and muffled shouts. There was a shelter, hardly a tent, set up on the right of the broad field, under a large oak tree. Bajan stood waiting with a tall woman, his sister Ambré, whose husband led one of the companies of the Morrigar. There was a shaman, a holy man, brought from the camp of the Nureshen, and Lord Lingrit and Nenad Am Charn to see that all was done well.

So, in the rain, with the movement of the army all about

242

them, she took Bajan's hand and they spoke to the priest and were married. The shaman, a mild-eyed man, not impossibly old, with a long braid of hair looped over his shoulder, invoked the blessing of the Goddess. Bajan gave her a heavy silver ring with a fire opal, and she gave him a gold ring. They kissed. She was numb and cold and wished they were in bed at the inn, or in some mountain camp, in the bridal tent, where none came except to leave food at the door.

She tried to smile for his sake, but when she embraced Ambré, her new sister, they both shed tears. Lord Lingrit had one of his servants stand forth with a stirrup cup for the whole party, of strong fine brandywine out of Lien. So they gulped or sipped the fiery spirit and healths were drunk to the queen and to Danu Bajan, the new consort. Then Gerr of Kerrick, Count Zerrah, was there, mounted upon Firedrake, ready to ride with the queen. She kissed Bajan once more and mounted and rode off in the midst of the kedran company with Lord Lingrit on one side and Gerr on the other; so they entered the forest. There was a bird call from the mustering tent, and Akaranok swung himself up on to the front of the queen's saddle.

"Straight on for two leagues, my Queen," he said, "then we turn southeast for Aldero."

The pace was fast for the whole of the first day. The six hundred riders of the Morrigar swept down upon Aldero, drank it dry and swept on again, by smaller trails, bearing always southeast. The way was downhill; the kedran company, with the queen among them, camped in a clearing that the Tulgai called Six Ways. Megan Brock, wearing a hood to protect her stitched cheek, went about inspecting the horses, trying to cheer the women in their cramped quarters. There was one fire for twenty riders that night, and they knew they must soon turn to cold food as they came nearer to the pass.

Aidris broke off her dice game with Lingrit and Gerr and walked out to find some air. The crowded camp reeked of damp horses and burnt broth. Not far off she heard other riders passing by; an owl called, a true owl, not one of the Tulgai. She managed to sleep a few hours on this first night and in the dawn rose up with the wakers going about.

The going became harder. They rode uphill, the forest trails were narrow, the rain and cold unceasing. There was casting about and cursing when the company of the Nureshen failed at a meeting point. Aidris became aware that many of the ked-ran, whether from Athron or the Chameln lands, did not love the Tulgai, hated to be directed by a dwarfish creature that swung down whistling from a tree. Yet Megan Brock held them together, and the little men did their work marvellously well. After the long day riding, with her legs ready to fold under her and her body aching, she groomed Telavel as she had always done and fell into an exhausted sleep.

Akaranok said, breaking into the difficult morning hour before they rode off, *"There is one who follows, my queen. He catches up in the night. He runs the trails like a wild beast. He cannot come out of the forest."*

"Can he be caught, Akaranok?"

"Only by the longshanks," he said. *"These warrior women could hold him, but it would take many of our Tulgai to do it, and they are needed to show the way."*

"I will give you a detail one night."

Time was pressing. The forest had swallowed them up. Were they more than a day's ride from the pass? Zabrandor appeared at midday bristling and alert while she and Lingrit and Gerr felt themselves very grey and downcast.

"We make good time," he said. *"My Tulgai have flown ahead and spied out the hundreds."*

So they rode on, down a gentler slope, packed with the loose, green pine that told them they were approaching the Adderneck.

Gerr of Kerrick, at least, had his second wind. "An adventure," he panted, "a great saga, my Queen. The Forest Ride of the Morrigar. The Great Ambush."

She spoke at last to Lingrit about the one who followed. He was grey with fatigue; she knew that his joints ached in the damp.

"Hurne?" he echoed. "Hurne of Balufir? No wonder he disappeared from his city haunts!"

"He was so well-known, then, in the city?"

"He became well-known through his disappearance. Rosmer set up a search for him . . . made it an excuse to bring down some of his enemies with talk of corruption and murder."

"Yet Rosmer keeps him here in the forest!"

Lingrit rode on in silence, then spoke to her most seriously. "My Queen, this is a great enterprise. We must come through.

Even if the ambush fails for any reason, you must be brought to safety with your cousin the king. We have no time for diversions. Let Hurne run or have him swiftly dealt with."

"What could we learn from him about his master?"

"Why would you spare him . . . if this is a man who tried to capture or kill you?"

"He has paid for this," she said. "I think I can break the spell that holds him."

"But what then?" he demanded. "Add him to your train? Send him back into Lien or some other land to do deeds of villainy?"

She shook her head. When it was night, they halted not twenty miles from the Adderneck Pass and made their final camp. She fumbled about with a handkerchief and then said to Yvand, privately, "Make me a poppet, Yvand. I have need of one."

So Yvand, with a sidelong glance, took the piece of cloth and, with sticks and a pine cone and thread from her pack, quickly made an excellent poppet. They wrapped it in a piece of dark blue silk and blacked its cloth legs for boots. Aidris drew out at last the handful of red hair that had been brought to her, and Yvand stitched it on to the creature. They stared at the thing in the half light and smiled squeamishly. Aidris thought it already had a look of Hurne.

She did not summon Akaranok or her escort or make any move to take Hurne, if indeed he followed them, but went off behind the tent where the faint light of the Huntress Moon, an extra moon edging into the calendar, came down through the pines. She knew the words very well, and added new ones of her own. She named the poppet Hurne and kept it by her and bade it come out of the forest when she told it to. It was a working that she might not have done with much conviction at any other time, but the long way riding had told on her. She was lightheaded. She could not sleep for a long time and then slept too deep and woke unrefreshed.

For the first time on that day she saw the whole troop, rippling a stand of young pine, where a fire had gone through four summers past. Standing on a low bluff with Gerr, she could also look back and see a part of the long way they had come. Now was a time of waiting. They must time it just right and be silent and wait for the news brought back by the Tulgai and the mounted scouts. So she was allowed to ride through all the troops, greeting the tribesfolk, showing that the queen had kept them company.

They rode then across a plateau, a high shelf thickly covered with pines that dropped suddenly into the gorge. The way down was steep, but there were good trails. A special hundred, drawn from all the Morrigar, had ridden on ahead with their guides. They would go down in daylight and cross the Adderneck. It was hazardous. No one lived in or near the pass, but patrols from Mel'Nir might be about. If it was watched or guarded, the orders were for them to stand firm and send word back. By midday they had not returned.

The weather, here in the southeast, was clear at last. Aidris longed for rain and mist; the pine woods were too open. At any moment a troop of Melniros, come by chance to the plateau to hunt, might see the riders among the trees and give warning. At dusk of the long day, the scouts from the southern road returned, and there was a last quickening of the pace. Riders poured through the pines and spilled down the side of the pass. Aidris went to a point where she could look down and see the Adderneck spread out before her in the twilight. The broad road flowed in from the south into a valley with high wooded sides, then for half a mile the valley narrowed and was clamped between high rocks. The road flowed out again and wound off another mile or so to the plain, still between high bluffs. Word had come from the northern scouts: a camp of Mel'Nir was just visible by a village called Folgry, due north on the plain.

There was nothing to do but wait, in darkness. Aidris put her head down on a folded blanket on the pine needles to rest her eyes for a few moments, then Yvand was shaking her. She had slept deeply; it was time.

She mounted up and came with part of her escort to the place that had been chosen for the leaders to watch the ambush. Presently Batro of the Nureshen came up and promised that the wait would not be long. She soothed Telavel and gave her pieces of apple to keep her quiet. The place where they stood was narrow; the escort and a whole troop of the Durgashen pressed closely round about. Megan Brock came up, and then Old Zabrandor himself squeezed his tall horse through to the queen's side. Aidris looked down into the blackness of the pass and felt the wind blow cold.

Old Zabrandor said, "You'll hear their scouts soon, my Queen. They are coming on in full array, these hundreds, but it will not serve the poor devils!"

Megan Brock gave a soft laugh and whistled the riding song of the kedran:

> "The Men of Mel'Nir are tall as trees,
> They will lie dead on the plain."

The night was not silent but full of movement: a cough, the creak of leather. Then she heard it: hoofbeats in the pass, one rider, then another. The outriders of Mel'Nir came through and hard on their heels grew a mighty metallic wave of sound. The Red Hundreds, the crack troops of the Great King, the scourge of the warlords, the pride of Mel'Nir, rode boldly into the pass, talking, laughing and singing their own bouncing saddle-songs. They wore their white surcoats, and on their helmets were yellow and white plumes, clearly visible in the night. They came on, invincible and proud, and Zabrandor had gone to begin the work.

When the narrowest part of the way was full, the mounted archers of the tribes shot from ambush at those following, still in the broader part of the valley. They uttered no battle cry, only the arrows came whirring out of the dark, and the men of Mel'Nir fell down, shouted, died. Those in the narrows, pressed ahead in terror, three, four, six abreast through the gap, and were struck down with axe and spear by those lying in wait. Still they pressed through, roaring and hacking with their broadswords, but the narrow way was slippery with blood and packed with dying men and horses, and they could not pass.

Behind them, in the broader way, the hundreds following quickened their pace to help their comrades and were soon all in the pass. Fires sprang up behind them on the Nesbath road, and the remaining forces of the queen rushed upon them, howling their battlecries. In the narrows and elsewhere companies of the giant warriors packed together, against a rock wall or a rampart of baggage wagons and were steadily cut down by the lighter warriors, riding out of the dark or shooting arrows from ambush. Many of the braver spirits . . . and indeed all the men of Mel'Nir were brave . . . tried to ride up the cliff trails and come out of the deathtrap, but their horses could hardly do it.

They fought their way up to the plateau on foot, and those who were not overwhelmed or dashed to death upon the rocks, a very few, ran off into the pine woods.

Too late the General of the Hundreds, Kirris Hanran, known as the Lynx, who had ridden at the head of the last cohort, the honor guard of fifty picked men, saw that nothing would serve and called the retreat. He hacked himself from the pass with a handful of men, came past the bonfires and fled back along the road towards Nesbath.

After the silence of the forest, the din of battle split the night like thunder. The clash of arms, the cries of men and of horses, all echoed from the walls of the pass. It seemed impossible to Aidris that these desperate sounds could not reach across the plain to the sleeping village of Folgry. Yet the pass enclosed the sounds, and the troopers of Mel'Nir, in their camp, slept sound while the Red Hundreds died.

The magnitude of the disaster for Mel'Nir was so great that legends sprang up making it greater still or explaining it away. So it was given out that many of the giant warriors fell upon their swords or did to death their own horses, but this was not the truth. Then it was claimed that all the Morrigar, the Giant-killers, were kedran, a thousand female warriors, and that they were aided by the hosts of the Goddess, in particular the pack of savage spectral hounds that the Dark Huntress leads across the sky.

The truth was grim enough; men had died in curious ways, trampled to death by their horses or suffocated under the press of the dead and dying in the narrows. Booty was taken, not only in the form of horses, weapons and armor but gold coin to pay the warriors of the Great King and the mercenaries of Lien who fought for him.

When the fires had been lit the whole length of the pass, the gleaners of the tribes went to work and counted. For one hundred and sixty dead of the Morrigar, the men and women of the Great Ambush, more than a thousand men of Mel'Nir had died. They were laid out in the pass, unhallowed, in the cold of the approaching winter, for the tribes and the kedran could care only for their own dead, who were buried in the forest round about.

* * *

Before morning broke, while the gleaners were still at work, Aidris was brought down a long, easy trail to the head of the pass, where it met the plain. She rode with Lingrit and Yvand and her own escort; the Morrigar would be mustered at first light and follow to the east. Their meeting place was Radroch Keep, a hunting lodge of Lord Zabrandor on the plain by the town of the same name, now within easy reach of the army of Sharn Am Zor, if it had not already been taken.

So she took her leave of the forest and of the warriors of the Tulgai, without whose craft the Great Ambush would never have been planned or carried out. She could hardly reward these allies; all that they wished in the way of booty was theirs. She sent word to Tagnaran, the Balg of the Tulgai, that his tribute to the Daindru had been paid forever and that every year in the first days of the Aldermoon gifts would be sent to his people.

"My Queen," said Akaranok, "we are rewarded. The giant warriors were no friends to our people or to our blood brothers of the Kelshin."

So she bade farewell to them all, and they took to the treetops, eager to bring the news of the victory to their own people and to the waiting tribes at Vigrund. Aidris and her little party of riders stepped out cautiously upon the plain. She turned Telavel aside and stared at the slopes of the forest and the plateau, then took the poppet from under her cloak and let it fall gently into the grass. "Come then," she said in her mind, "come out. Go free. Trouble me no more. You have had no luck hunting in the Chameln lands." Then, with this act of mercy, if that was what it was, she rode away from the scene of what would be accounted her greatest triumph.

A soft hail came through the morning mist, and Gerr of Kerrick rode out of the pass and joined them. Her own feelings for the thing that they had done were reflected upon the young knight's face. He had a look of acceptance, even of satisfaction, but could not hide the weariness and horror that accompanied the art of war.

The sun was just rising, sending long fingers of light across the plain; not far to the southeast they could see the shores of the Danmar, where lay the largest camp of Mel'Nir. The riders kept together, and the five kedran were watchful. Aidris felt a shred of worry when she looked at Lingrit Am Thuven, more grey and ill than ever. He caught her eye and smiled.

"We are covered with glory, my Queen," he said wryly.

"My Lord," she said, "how do you fare? I think you are not well."

"Well enough, my Queen. But surely Sir Gerr has taken some harm to his leg?"

"A scratch," said the knight. "By the Carach and the Morning Star, we *are* a sorry lot to ride with the queen!"

Gefion, the kedran officer, cried out. At the same moment that she saw the riders coming in on their left from an old sheepfold, Aidris saw the tower of Radroch caught by the sun's rays. They urged their horses forward, and they were fresh enough, all except Firedrake, for they had taken no part in the fighting. Aidris whispered to Telavel, and they sped over the endless silver grass of the plain. She looked for their pursuers: two familiar shapes, troopers of Mel'Nir, and other riders on lighter horses, mercenaries. Firedrake trailed, and she heard Gerr give a cry and wheeled to help him. Yvand had checked too, but she saw Lingrit flick the rump of her horse; it bolted for the tower.

Lingrit called, "Go on! Ride on!"

Aidris knew that he did not want to utter her name. She reached Gerr and found him standing; Firedrake was lame. A kedran had turned back to help them. Aidris saw another man, a stocky man, running up on foot from the sheepfold. He held up a weapon that she did not recognise at first; she heard one heavy sound, Telavel fell down, fell to her knees, crumpled without a sound. She was dead before Aidris dragged herself free. The bolt of the crossbow was deep in her chest, and the archer was running away, winding his weapon.

Aidris gave a loud screaming cry of rage and pain. She drew her sword and ran for the stocky man. She ran very fast, caught him up, saw his look of surprise. She kicked him in the groin, wrenched the weapon from his hands and drove at his face with her sword. He fell down, bleeding, and she drove the sword into his throat and wrenched it out again. The kedran came up and held out a hand, and she sprang up behind. The kedran's grey went wide, far away from the troopers who were hesitating in their pursuit because the small party had divided.

Gerr had mounted up again, but was not running Firedrake. The kedran turned again, heading in for the keep. Lingrit and Yvand were at the wards of the tower, she saw them shouting and waving to those within. The other kedran had engaged the riders, and Gerr was bringing Firedrake slowly, with painful slowness, to help them.

She slipped to the ground and said to the kedran. "I am safe. Tell them to break off . . . break away and bring in Gerr, Count Zerrah."

The kedran whirled away, and she went stumbling to the base of the tower. Yvand was weeping. Lingrit said, "My Queen . . ."

They stared at her blood-stained sword.

"Can you get any help from the tower?" she asked.

"They are a Chameln garrison, at least," said Lingrit. "The King holds Radroch Town."

There was movement overhead on the battlements of the ancient keep. The garrison had read the skirmish well enough to begin firing arrows at the riders of Mel'Nir. When the kedran of the escort broke away, taking Gerr with them, the pursuit was broken off too, although none of the arrows had found their mark. Aidris bent down and wiped her sword upon a tussock of silver grass and looked at the plain. Telavel was dead.

A man had come out of the tower. He put his hands on his hips and surveyed the company.

"What in the name of the Goddess are you kedran doing so far from Radroch Town at this hour?"

"Are you Lord Zabrandor's steward?" demanded Lingrit.

"Sansom, Warden of Radroch Keep," said the man, "Our lord is not here,"

"He will be within the hour," said Lingrit. "We must bring this lady in to rest and send word to the king."

"Lady?" echoed the man.

"The queen."

"I don't know you," said Sansom. "I don't know any of you. Lord Zabrandor is far away. What queer trick is being played here?"

"Mind your manners," said Ensign Gefion. "Let the queen come in!"

"Another one," said Sansom, grinning.

"No," said Aidris, "the only one. I will go in and wait for Sharn Am Zor."

"What have you been doing with that sword?" asked Sansom.

"I killed a crossbowman who killed my horse," she said.

She walked past him into the tower. There was a big comfortable hall hung with trophies of the chase and the crossed spears that were the arms of Lord Zabrandor. To one side was a small guardroom with a fire. She went in and sat in a settle near the fire. The warmth began to seep over her, to dry the dew on her cloak. Soon, she thought, soon I will be warm, the warmth will reach my heart, I will begin to feel pain again.

There were voices in the distance, coming and going through the old keep. The door of the guard room was shut, opened again. Yvand brought her a beaker of sweet apple wine and a piece of bread. She ate and drank and leaned her head against the chimney piece and fell into a dreamy state, more sleep than waking. The door opened gently now and then as if someone looked in on her, but she was too tired to raise her head. She slept and dreamed that she was riding across the plain, and thought, in her dream, I will be sad when I wake, for Telavel is dead.

Then at last she woke, feeling that a long time had passed, but she saw that the fire had burned down only a little. She tried to rouse herself, shrugged off her cloak. There was a silvery trumpet call, loud voices and heavy footsteps echoed in the hall. The door of her hiding place was flung open, and Lingrit came in with Gerr. Her escort were there, too, packing around her at the fire as if to protect her. Yvand came and knelt at her feet and wiped her face with a damp cloth and combed her hair.

In the hall a voice rang out like the voice of the silver trumpets, "Thuven must do better than this! I might believe Zabrandor. I have received no shred of help from the northern tribes. We will make a vile winter of it here on the plain with not a drop fit to drink and no decent quarters, eh Zilly, my lad? And to top it all . . . the queen? The queen? Is it the queen? Or another of these Chameln pretenders?"

Two courtiers appeared, strangers in Lienish dress, puffed and slashed, in bright spring colors. Sharn Am Zor came forward, tall and beautiful as the morning in a sky-blue doublet and a golden cape. Aidris, watching him, saw a pride of the flesh, an arrogance that stemmed from his unmatched physical beauty. Yet *her* true servants clustered about a short dark woman, weary from campaigning, stained with blood, bereaved. She sprang up, pushed past her followers, and strode out to confront the king.

"No, cousin," she said firmly. "I have come home!"

Sharn Am Zor stared, and she stared him down, just as she had done when they were children. The arrogance drained away from his face, leaving it vulnerable and soft.

"Oh, Aidris . . . oh, is it you?"

"Yes, my dear!"

They embraced, held each other close. She glimpsed in the face of one of the courtiers an agonised relief. The silver trumpets sounded a wild call, and those within the keep all hailed the Daindru. With the perfect timing of a good omen, there came another trumpet call from outside; Zabrandor had come with his victorious warriors of the Morrigar.

CHAPTER
X

"FROM THAT HOUR," WRITES A CHRONICLER, "it was but a step to Achamar." The step took six moons and cost more lives. Yet Ghanor, the Great King, sent no more troops into the Chameln lands, and those lords and their followers who upheld the Protectorate of Mel'Nir were abandoned to their fate. The Daindru was proclaimed throughout the lands: they could be seen going about together, the Winter Queen and the King of Summer, by Radroch on the plain, at Nevgrod, Grunach, Zerrah, and at the seige of Ledler and at Achamar.

But from the hour when she reached Radroch Keep, Aidris felt that she campaigned no more; she made no more forced marches through the night and watched no more battles. She was, like Sharn Am Zor who hated to ride, "brought through" to the battlefront, then returned to some safe and comfortable place behind the lines. For more than a moon she lived in the tower of the keep. She did not ride, although half a dozen fine horses . . . from Sharn, from Zabrandor . . . were paraded temptingly below her windows in the inner court.

Her chamber in the tower was comfortable enough, even if Sharn thought it a dreary hole without good hangings. He sat with her after dinner on the second night when she had recovered a little and they heard music and played at dice. They leaped about in their topics of conversation, their sharing of their exile.

"Let me show you these two," he begged. "We can watch them unobserved . . ."

"No," she said, "I cannot bear it. Wait a little."

She felt too much like a pretender herself. Then, watching him rattle the dice in the cup, she said, "You mean the pretenders are *here?* In the keep?"

"Where else?" He grinned. "Come, see them. It is great sport!"

She shook her head. He was cruel. It was the bad influences of Lien.

"Kelen is a fool," he said in answer to her question. "He drinks too much. Have no fear, Rilla will never be tied to Prince Gol. I have other plans for her."

Then seeing her look of fear, he smiled.

"No, truly," he said. "I was thinking only of bringing her to Achamar. I am not such a monster. Look, if you beat me on this next pass, I swear I will let you find her a husband when she is of age."

It was foolishly easy; she had only to wish on the dice in a certain way, and she won the throw.

"I must find you a wife first of all," she said.

Sharn made a gesture of resignation.

"You could not wait to be wed to good old Bajan."

"We did not wait, dearest coz." She smiled. "I think we wed to please Yvand . . . or to safeguard any child I might have."

The king blushed.

"I think you have learned coarse ways from the Athron kedran," he said.

"Lien is a debauched place," she teased. "Everyone knows that."

"Athron is a backwater."

"Yes," she said, "but it is a kind and lovely land. Not so beautiful to me as the Chameln lands, and not so fine and highbred as Lien, but full of peace, and its own magic. I will go there with you on a progress one day. Would not that be a pleasant time . . . we could go to Kerrick . . ."

"That *would* be amusing. To see Terril of Varda and the talking trees. I like your new man, Zerrah, the son of Kerrick."

"I like your new man Denzil of Denwick, although his name is foolish."

"What, old Zilly? Yes, he is very loyal. Mind you, he owes me a lot."

Sharn's face darkened; he looked about the plain room as if testing the shadows. She thought of Aravel, of whom he would not speak.

"Lien can be a dark place," he whispered.

"Rosmer?"

He nodded, lips compressed.

"He tried to destroy the Daindru," she said.

"He gave me bad dreams," said Sharn.

That night, when the king had ridden with his court back to the comforts of Lord Zabrandor's Great Hall in Radroch Town, Aidris could not sleep. She sat up sweltering in the Chameln feather quilts, then went back to the fireside. The door of the room where Yvand slept was ajar; she closed it before she stirred up the fire. She sat grieving for Telavel, thinking of the new grey, the colt that had been paraded for her use that morning.

There was a breath of wind in the room, and she saw that beyond the chimneypiece an old hanging stirred. She was alarmed, ready to cry out. A young girl came into the room from behind the curtain, moving so lightly and gently that Aidris wondered if she were dreaming. The girl was very small and slight, with dark, straight hair that hung over a high forehead. She had a pale, pretty face with full red lips and large eyes. She was dressed in Chameln fashion, in a long beaded tunic of blue velvet, grey doeskin breeches and handsome boots of crimson leather. Her rich clothes were rather new, but not well kept, the beading ripped, the boots scuffed. The tunic almost hid some injury to her left side; she held her left shoulder too high; her slender neck was crooked. Aidris thought: her ribs have been broken and not properly set.

The girl stared shyly at Aidris and stretched out her hands to warm them at the fire.

"They say there has been a great victory!" she said in a sweet, rich voice.

"Yes," agreed Aidris softly, not breaking the spell, "a great victory!"

"I won a great victory, too," said the girl, "but they have put me in prison."

"How came you here," asked Aidris, "to this chamber?"

"I am allowed out, sometimes, at night," said the girl sadly. "Sansom lets me go up and down this little secret stair. To his bedchamber."

"Sansom!"

"You should address me by my title," said the girl. "You should say 'my Queen'!"

Aidris shook her head.

"I could not do it," she said. "I know you are not the queen."

"You know, indeed . . ." said the girl, tossing her head. "Who has seen the queen? How could you . . ."

She broke off and stared at Aidris. She came nearer with her particular light and graceful step and laid a hand on Aidris's hair.

"Your eyes are green," she said. "You are a little older, I think, and your hair curls naturally. I curled my hair every night, as I was taught, but the curling rags are all used up."

"*Who* taught you?" asked Aidris, still very soft.

"My waiting women, of course," said the girl. "Seffina, Riane and Fariel and Tylit and the rest . . ."

"Tylit was the queen's nurse," said Aidris, "never her waiting woman. She married a gardener and went to live in Lien."

"*I remember,*" said the girl. "I remember little else. I even have the queen's dreams."

"You have been cruelly deceived. Someone has stolen your own life and your own dreams."

"No!" said the girl. "No, I still have one dream . . ."

"Tell me . . ."

"It is always the same," she said. "The candles are lit. I step out upon the balcony and it begins to shake, it cannot hold me. I see Hazard, my poor Hazard, waving his arms and shouting . . ."

"Hazard? A person named Hazard?"

"Of course," said the girl. "Don't you even know that? You

are no queen at all, only a pretender. Hazard, Robillan Hazard, is the greatest poet in Lien."

"I have his book," said Aidris, *"Hazard's Harvest."*

"An early work," said the girl, "with a private copying done for a royal lady. It is very strange that you should mention it. The king has seen that book."

"The king?"

"You must not be confused," said the girl kindly. "There are two kings. One is handsome and one is gentle. They are not in the least alike. One is here in the tower, deep down. One rides about, free, and says that Hazard is his friend, but he lies, he is not to be trusted. The other knows only Hazard's writings. And see . . . this other poor king, this pretender, he has given me this token . . ."

"Oh stop!" cried Aidris, half laughing and half weeping. "I cannot bear any more . . ."

"You see," said the girl, "how hard it is to be a queen. Everything in your life becomes twisted and confused."

There was a sound in the next room. The girl took fright at once; she was gone as quickly as she had come by the secret stair. Yvand opened her door.

"My Queen, I thought I heard voices!"

"It was nothing," said Aidris. "I was talking to myself."

"Shall I make tea, my Queen, to help you sleep?"

"Yes please, Yvand."

She saw herself as a very old woman, years hence: the Old Queen, crouched by her fire, drinking tea in the night hours. She felt pain and revulsion and wondered if this was how Guenna, her grandmother, had felt when she was betrayed and disgraced. The token from the gentle king, the one who lay deep down in this very tower, the token that the False Aidris wore on a string around her neck, was a turret shell from the ocean shore.

She bided her time; she had learned patience in Athron. The Morrigar were encamped all about Radroch Keep, and the officers lived in the inner bailey where Zabrandor had housed his hunt servants. An encounter loomed before the winter with the remaining warriors of Mel'Nir, those from the southeast and those marching down from the encampment before Vigrund. There was a war council of the Daindru in the hall of the keep, and here Aidris met again her father's fourth Torch Bearer,

Gilyan, no "new man" but an old man, white-haired, looking older than Zabrandor. He presented a shy girl in kedran dress: His grandchild Lorn Gilyan; and Aidris, knowing what was expected of the queen, took her at once into her service.

She watched the young king and his advisors at the council board: Old Zabrandor, the Countess Caddah, a dour Firnish woman whose lands lay further east on the Danmar. Then there were the newcomers: Denzil of Denwick, younger son of a Lienish duke called "the richest man in the world"; Seyl of Hodd, a family connection, as darkly handsome as his master was fair; and Engist, the king's master-at-arms, a gnarled veteran soldier.

Aidris found herself striving, as they strove, to make all plain to Sharn Am Zor, to hold his interest. He was clever and quick, but he could not put his mind to anything for very long. His gaze wandered from the map, he began to gossip with Zilly of Denwick or turn to the others in his train, Seyl's beautiful wife, her waiting women, all eager to pander to the humors of the Summer's King.

She looked with fond irritation at her own followers: Lingrit, that grey and melancholy man, old Gilyan, Gerr, Count Zerrah. She added to them, mentally, Jana Am Wetzerik, Nenad Am Charn, Bajan. She longed for Bajan, clenching her hands to feel his two rings cutting into her fingers, the small gold ring that he had sent to her in exile, the new silver ring with a fire opal, her wedding ring.

"My Queen . . ."

It was Lingrit, prompting her to answer some question. Her attention had wandered just as the king's had done.

She bided her time. The Morrigar rode off to drill with the king's army camped about Radroch Town. She went down to the hall with the young officer Gefion from her escort and found Sansom, the warden.

"I will see your prisoners," she said.

Since his ill-mannered reception of the queen, Sansom had worked hard to make amends. She tried to see what manner of man he was; he looked solid and commonplace.

"Come, my Queen," he said. "This is a good time for it. Come and take a look."

He led the way down a winding stair in the inner bailey, at

the base of the tower. A landing ran off unexpectedly like a shelf. He led Aidris and the ensign along it and into a round room with a few padded settles as if it had been used by gentlefolk. There was a stone grille set low in the wall; between the ornamental leaves and flowers of the stonework, the watchers could look down into two large cells, whitewashed, windowless, lying about four feet below the round room.

"The true dungeons are lower still," explained Sansom. "They are no longer used. This place is the menagerie where Lord Zabrandor kept strange beasts. He had a black bear once, from the northern mountains, and a lynx and a white deer."

Aidris looked with numb foreboding. In one cell the false Aidris lay asleep on a bed of straw. There was a large mirror in her cell and a high-backed chair tied with bedraggled red ribbons.

"She has a pretty face," said Aidris. "What do you think of this poor false queen, Master Sansom?"

If she thought to trap the man into some heartless words, she failed for he answered, full of pity, "Someone has filled her head with all this mummery and pretence, my Queen."

In the neighboring cell Raff Raiz sat quietly reading a book. He wore a suit of Lienish satin, ill-kept, in bright spring-green and yellow.

"And the false king, Master Sansom? What of him?"

"He knows what he has done, poor devil," said Sansom. "He expects . . ."

"What?"

"The punishment for high treason. It can only end one way . . ."

His voice trailed off as if he recollected that he was speaking to the queen.

"Take me down," she said. "I will speak to the false king."

The warden and the young ensign stood at the door of the cell, but she went in alone and pulled the door to behind her. Raff Raiz stood up, as if his joints were painful, then he knelt down at her feet. She experienced the death of love, an unreasoning bitterness that made it difficult for her to speak.

"Jalmar Raiz did this," she said. "Has he left you to your fate?"

"He came out of Dechar with my brother."

Raff did not raise his eyes.

"Who is the false queen? Where did he find her?"

"I do not know her true name," he said. "She is a player, a player's wench, out of Balufir. She is innocent. She should be spared."

"And you?"

He sat down on the floor of the cell and stretched his legs. He still did not look her in the face.

"The plan worked," he said. "Dechar was held. Sharn Am Zor rose to the challenge. I risked my life. I risked . . . your displeasure."

She had nothing to say to him. She knew what must be done and done quickly, but she could not consult with him. She said, with an effort, "I will do what must be done."

She went out of the cell, her face stiff with disgust.

"Fetch the prisoners a change of clothes, Master Sansom," she ordered. "Plain soldiers' dress. Their royal raiment has grown foul. Wait upon me in my chamber when it is done."

Then when they had climbed out of the menagerie into the courtyard, she said to Ensign Gefion, "Send Sergeant Lawlor to me as soon as the Morrigar return from their drill."

There was a need for haste because the king was coming that night. Zabrandor was entertaining the Daindru in his lodge; his servants were already busy in the kitchens. Aidris sat in her chamber and plotted like a witch.

Outside, the sky over the plain had grown white; the first snows of winter had begun to fall. She looked out at the whitening plain and saw the snow covering a heap of evergreen, far off by the old sheepfold. The kedran had buried Telavel and laid pine branches upon the grave. She thought of the forces of Hem Allerdon marching south, harried by the tribes, and wondered if he had had word of the disaster at Adderneck.

Sansom, when he came to her, already had a gleam in his eye that she recognised. He was afraid; he did not know what the queen was planning.

"Master Sansom," she said, "the prisoners give me no rest. I must take care of them."

He stared at her, moistening dry lips.

"My Queen . . ."

"I mean to set them free."

He shook his head in unbelief.

"The king," he said, "the king brought them here!"

"I will answer for the king," she said. "You must deliver up the keys of the menagerie and of their cells."

"My Queen . . . I dare not . . . the king . . ."

"You must give me the key of that secret stair," she said. "The one that the poor false queen used to come to your bedchamber, Master Sansom! Would it please the king to hear of that, I wonder?"

He had been standing before her, awkwardly; now he forgot himself and sat down on a stool by the fireside. He was sweating.

"She tempted me," he said. "It is not as bad as you think . . ."

"Do not blame that poor girl for what you have done," she said.

"I am not a gaoler!" he burst out. "I am . . . I was an honest man. I did not hurt her. I helped both prisoners, to food and comforts. She is some kind of singing-girl—the king himself, the king . . . talked to her privately . . ."

His voice trailed away. Aidris sprang up angrily, and Sansom fell to his knees before her.

"The keys, Master Sansom," she said, controlling her anger. "Get up, sit on the stool. I think I have a commission for you that will take you far from the keep for the rest of the day."

"Yes, my Queen," he said thickly, "a commission . . ."

He was fumbling the keys from the iron ring that hung at his belt.

"You must ride into Radroch Town to the cloth merchants there who were given the work and bring back the new hangings and rugs for this chamber. I wish to be fine when the king visits me this night after the feast."

It was a most royal commission . . . the kind of hasty demand that kept servants working while others sat down to feast. She watched from the south window of her tower as Sansom galloped away with two of the garrison, headed for Radroch. The Morrigar were already riding back to their quarters; she received Sergeant Lawlor before she ate her midday meal.

Her officer from Grey Company had caught wind of the queen's strange humor. Aidirs had a longing, as she saw Lawlor's homely face, for the security and order of the kedran barracks. Now she was carried by events, by the movements of armies, like a leaf on a stream, or she set intrigues in motion, like this one. Yet she must see it through to the end, and the end was good.

"Sergeant," she said, "you must help me. It is a matter of

the highest secrecy and trust. Take three or four kedran from Athron."

Through the long wintery afternoon, the queen was sociable and kind. She walked upon the battlements of the keep with Lingrit and Gerr of Kerrick, listened to music with a merry company of her two waiting women, Yvand and Lorn Gilyan, and Master Carless, her lute player, borrowed from the king. The court of the Zor arrived at dusk from Radroch Town; there was a great coming and going throughout the keep, and at last the Daindru sat down to feast. The talk was all of preparation for the next encounter with Mel'Nir; the king's generals, Seyl of Hodd, Anke of Caddah and Old Zabrandor, felt victory very close.

The hour was late when Aidris and Sharn left the hall and went up to the queen's chamber. The new hangings and rugs were in place, and even the king found them very fine. The fire was pleasant; Yvand had brewed tea.

"Can you talk of a matter close to my heart, dear cousin?" asked Aidris.

"What would you have?" he asked, smiling.

"The prisoners, the false Aidris and the false Sharn. They will not let me rest."

"What, have you not seen them yet?" he cried. "Come . . . we'll wake them . . ."

"No," she said. "I have seen them. I have spoken with them. I know who or what they are and who set them up."

Sharn gulped a mouthful of tea; he stared at her, still flushed and bright-eyed from the Lienish wine at the banquet.

"You know more than I do, cousin," he said.

"I doubt that," she said. "Could you forget a man who saved my life at least? Do you know nothing of Jalmar Raiz, the Healer, the turncoat Lienish spy, and his son Raff?"

"Oh, it is the false king you know," said Sharn.

"Not half so well, dearest coz, as you know the false queen . . ."

"Tush," he said, flushing darkly. "Is there backstairs gossip even in this wretched keep? What ails you, Aidris? Will you teach me my duty? The false queen is a poor poppet."

"She is Hazard's friend . . ." said Aidris in a moment of intuition.

Sharn Am Zor turned pale; he went from red to white and was completely sober on the instant.

"What do you want?" he asked. "What will you have me do with these creatures?"

"They have played their part," said Aidris. "They must trouble us no more."

"You mean to kill them?" he snapped. "To have them put down, secretly or openly?"

He struck out at her, she knew, for that one word . . . Hazard.

"No, cousin," she said. "I mean that we must set them free."

He sat in silence, drinking his tea, and looked so young, a child at the fireside, his silks and satins some player's dress worn for the winter festival.

"They committed high treason," he said. "They struck at our sacred right. The man, Jalmar Raiz, who went about with them in Dechar, is a notorious intriguer, a creature of Kelen's, a thief."

"Dechar was held," she said. "Our right is secure. I do not know what Jalmar Raiz really planned. He drew you out of Lien to uphold the Daindru. I believe he knew where I was hidden and did not betray me. He had our lives, both our lives, in his hand that day at Musna and had no thought of 'putting down' those two children, the Heir of the Zor and the Heir of the Firn. Now he tests our feelings, cousin. We are each bound in friendship to those pretenders. If we kill them, we kill ourselves. We kill the mercy of the Goddess that should live in the heart of every ruler."

"You speak like a Moon Sister," said Sharn. "There is no mercy . . . for us, for anyone. You can have your wish. The pretenders . . . Hazard's light o' love, and Raff Raiz, the magician's son . . . they can be released from their captivity."

He smiled at her.

"Let us send for Carless, the lute player," he said.

He walked to the door, and she heard him talking to his escort, the King's Guard, tall mercenaries of Lien, for he no longer seemed to trust the traditional royal guard of kedran. He was gone for only a few seconds, and then they waited until Carless came in. He was a beaming, pleasant little man with a warm, sweet voice, and he sang a song that Aidris recognised from her book, a song by Robillan Hazard.

> "O Taranelda, my true love,
> I love you better for this pain,

This absence from your presence, sweet,
This silence in our love's refrain."

Sharn relaxed, dreaming by the fire; the candles burned low.
When he moved a hand to brush the hair from his eyes, the
firelight caught his rings and sent points of light scurrying about
on the new hangings. Aidris remembered Aravel, his mad mother,
in the palace of the Firn, at Achamar.

"Come harp and lute and lovely flute,
With lilting flight of harmony,
To render all my longings mute
And bring my dear love back to me."

The song was sweet, but she was far away from any thoughts
of love. If she longed for anything, it was for peace. As the last
notes faded into silence, there were heavy steps and raised voices
outside the door, and she heard Ensign Gefion shouting angrily.
Engist, the king's master-at-arms, burst into the room with a
drawn sword.

"Remember where you are, man!" said Sharn Am Zor.

The old soldier did not even sheath his sword.

"Majesty," he said, "the prisoners are gone! The cells are
disordered . . . their clothes lie there . . ."

Sharn sprang up. His rage would have been more frightening
to Aidris if it had not so perfectly resembled the rage of Sharn
the child.

"Treachery!" he said hoarsely. "Firnish treachery . . ."

"Get your henchman out of my chamber!"

She raised her voice, and the man slunk away. Sharn continued to rave and swear.

"You talk of mercy? Are they dead then? You have done this
thing, Aidris. They say you are a witch. Must I rule with a
damned Firnish witch queen? Did I suffer all my life to be
crossed and cozened by a woman now that I am king?"

"You are found out, cousin," she said. "You sent Engist to
kill the prisoners!"

"To fetch them!" he said angrily. "To bring them up the
secret stair to this chamber."

"Engist . . . your master-at-arms?"

"Believe me," he said. "Aidris . . ."

He sat down again, his whole body shaking. She did not know the truth; she would never know it. She stood beside him and put her arms about him.

"They are safe," she said. "We are safe. Your suffering must have an end. You have come home again, Sharn. You are king in the Chameln lands, and I am queen."

She thought she saw those two, Raff Raiz and the nameless girl, the players' wench, wandering about in the snowy night. Yet this was only her cruel fantasy; Lawlor told her a different tale.

"It worked like a charm, Dan Aidris. We went down to the cells, muffled up that precious pair a little and came out with them. The yard of the keep was full of soldiers and house servants . . . who counted heads? The false queen was frightened at first, but we told her to be a good girl and go into exile like a true queen. No shortage of horses—we set her up behind the false king on a big charger captured by Adderneck. We brought them past Radroch Town, as you said, all the way to the shore of the Danmar, within the king's territory.

"There was some magic in all this, I think, for they were awaited. We stood with them on the strand, and a man hailed us from a boat. He had a child with him, or perhaps it was a dwarf. The boat drew into shore, and the young man put the poor false queen aboard, then stepped in himself. The man in the boat, who had the look of a scholar, thanked us for our trouble and commended himself to the queen. Then the boat put out into the inland sea."

Sergeant Lawlor squinted at Aidris, smiling.

"The false king," she said. "I had the feeling I had seen him once before. He had a look of that tall, yellow-haired tumbler that Grey Company met in a village way to the north of Athron, coming home from the wedding by Wildrode."

Next day, when the snow lay thick, there came word of a large force approaching from the northwest over the plain. The army of Hem Allerdon, Mel'Nir's best and most resourceful commander in the Chameln lands, had left the encampment before Vigrund and set out to meet the Red Hundreds. When they learned that their reinforcements were destroyed, Allerdon's proud warriors moved on over the wintery plain like an army of ghosts. The northern tribes followed, harried the army on the plain and moved into the hills of the center. Zerrah was already recaptured.

The other generals of Mel'Nir had waited confidently by the Danmar for the next encounter with the king's horde. Now shaken by the disaster that had been left for them to discover, some of their numbers were tempted to fly the field, by land or by sea. Yet they would not abandon their countrymen. They moved out to join Allerdon, and their retreat was cut off. The time of pitched battles was over. The forces of Mel'Nir were mauled by the Chameln and turned to seek for winter quarters in the hills of the center.

So it was that a force of the Nureshen and the Oshen who had pursued Allerdon's men arrived at Radroch. Aidris watched them come from her tower and, at last, mounted the new grey colt Berith and rode out to meet Bajan and Jana Am Wetzerik. There was great rejoicing. She saw Nenad Am Charn, Millis, his daughter, mounted upon Tamir, and one Athron knight, the indefatigable Sir Jared Wild of Wildrode, who had determined to see the adventure through to the end.

"But Queen Aidris," he trumpeted, "where is your sweet grey mare, Telavel?"

She bent to stroke Tamir and hid her tears so as not to spoil the pleasure of the meeting.

The winter pressed upon all the armies and upon the Daindru and their personal followers. Radroch and the towns of the plain were garrisoned as far east as Dechar and Winnstrand. Old Zabrandor led out the Morrigar once more and came swiftly to the old walled town of Nevgrod, nearby in the hills, and held it so that the men of Mel'Nir could not take refuge there. The Daindru were brought through to winter in the Old Palace, which rose above the town. This ancient monument had served none but a small garrison of Mel'Nir in the past seven years, and they had quartered their horses in the great hall. It was made fast for winter, cleared of rats and old swallows' nests; and by the time of the winter feast, Sharn Am Zor confessed himself at least half satisfied.

At Nevgrod Aidris learned to sit still and play the queen. Bajan went about and saw to the quartering of the troops; Lingrit came to her with affairs of the kingdom. She had named him her Chancellor and Nenad Am Charn her new Torch Bearer and his son Racha Am Charn the new trading envoy. She had her nobles with whom she dined, her waiting women and the kedran of her escort who knew her tastes, and the hours when she ate and slept. She saw that her court, the court of the Firn, would always be, like Athron, warm, rich, but not glittering like the court of the Zor, which resembled Lien.

Here in the old town, the Daindru held their first audiences: the green branches of suppliants, all those who would beg a favor of the rulers, followed them in the dark streets. Aidris looked at the people of the Chameln lands, at her subjects, the city-dwellers and the poor tenant farmers of the central hills. She felt their love for herself and for Sharn Am Zor, but who or what it was that these poor folk knew or loved she could hardly tell. She was ashamed to stand before them finely dressed, well fed, warmly housed, and hear them cheer for the Daindru. It was not enough to have the common touch, which even Sharn Am Zor so brilliantly displayed; it was not enough to be a symbol, a light for the people of the Chameln lands in their darkness. What was a king or a queen? What was her right to which she had held so jealously? She felt a doubt, an unrest that could never be stilled, that had to do with the harsh lives of her poor subjects and with battle and bloodshed. She felt in herself a great cry that would never be uttered, a questioning of all the forms and uses of the world, echoing up to the halls of the Goddess.

She woke sometimes in the night or in the dark winter morning and saw Bajan asleep by her side. Her love and deep content were tinged with fear. What could divide them? She wanted to wind him in her arms and cling to him, crying out, "I have no one, no friend, no lover except you, in all the world!" Yet she resisted this strong possessive love and told herself that it came from old sorrow, from the loss of her parents, from the loneliness of an exile, of a queen.

She looked into the scrying stone and spoke to the Lady in a new way.

"Are you alone? Are you lonely? Come out . . . declare yourself. We are here, Sharn and I, we are safe. We will come home to Achamar in the spring. Oh come to us there, let us protect you. Is Lien so dear to you?"

But the Lady was as elusive as before. She smiled and said, in that distant voice; "Where is Lien? Where is Achamar?"

On the table in the world of the stone was a spray of whitethorn, the tree of magic and of sacrifice. Aidris found time, during the winter, to work her own magic. A jeweler in Nevgrod polished the large rough stone, the gift of the old Countess Palazan Am Panget, and set it in a silver rim. It was a rare, large carbuncle, deep violet red with a star of light in its depths; she performed her working on it and kept it close to her. She knew it would be her own scrying stone.

Some time after New Year, a messenger came bearing letters from Athron. Gerr of Kerrick came to the queen with a shining face.

"She has borne a son!" he said. "She is well . . . she writes it all herself . . . the child thrives, he is beautiful."

"I long to see them both!" said Aidris.

She missed Sabeth. She thought, fondly, how the Countess of Zerrah would decorate her court and turn heads in the court of the Zor.

"She will come to Zerrah in the spring," said Gerr.

He looked at Aidris with the boyish smile that she remembered from the Wulfental.

"You have rewarded us," he said, "although I had many strange fancies. Aidris . . . Dan Aidris . . . let me say this. I will go on to the end, to Achamar and beyond. I am your 'new man' forever if you will have me."

When he had gone, she paced about upon a small, chill "balcony" of the Old Palace, guarded by a breast-high wall of stone with slits for archers. She thought of her journey into Athron and the years that had followed. If life had its seasons, then the spring of her life had been Athron. But she dismissed this as another strange fancy; her life would be too long. She thought of Prince Ross, ages old, and his bleak memory of seven years exile upon a rock in the ocean.

As she walked about, Yvand came out with her fur cloak, her new sable cloak, Bajan's latest gift, and laid it tenderly about her shoulders. She was indeed entering a new season of her life; she was delivered over to the old wives. The queen was with child.

With the spring she was stifled in the Old Palace; she rode out on Tamir, followed the distant clash of the armies. For the first time she asked Bajan to remain at her side; he rode with her and the king to Grunach and then to Zerrah. She lingered there in the old brown manor house, dazed and fretful, waiting for Sabeth to come, waiting for the Melniros to be driven from the land. The Willowmoon went out in a gale of wind; Allerdon hung on with five hundred of his best soldiers in Ledler Fortress, barring the way to Achamar, but his countrymen treated with the Daindru. An army of the protectorate, stripped of honor and arms, was permitted to take the long way home across the plain to the Nesbath road and the Adderneck, symbol of the humiliation of the Great King. The rumor was abroad that Werris was a fugitive.

Aidris woke from her afternoon nap one mild day near the end of Birchmoon. Yvand, at the bedside, knitting, put a finger to her lips. There beside her on the bed in a nest of pillows was a baby. She bent over it half in a dream, remembering the milky odor, remembering an old feeling of mingled fear and distaste that she had had for babes in arms when she was a small child herself. The plump, fair, red-cheeked stranger opened its eyes, and she saw that they were still an indeterminate cloudy blue. It stared, gave a gaping smile, and began to make soft, cheerful noises.

"Oh *you!*" she said to the trustful creature.

The child's nursemaid curtsied to the queen; it was the young daughter of the Garth midwife. Aidris gathered up the baby unhandily in its wraps and carried it to the window. There on the hillside, among the drifts of spring flowers, was Sabeth, walking with the child Imelda.

"I do not even know Master Kerrick's name," she said to the women.

"Why, the sweet boy is called Huon," said Yvand. "An Athron name. We must begin to think of names, my Queen."

The journey to Ledler in the last ten days of its seige took on the character of a royal progress. As she had foreseen, Sabeth greatly enhanced the court of the Firn, and Sharn paid her gallant attention. Yet, as they drew near, the sight of the massive fortress casting a shadow over the rough green meadows of the hill cotts filled Aidris with dread.

She had no stomach for any of the siege tales, but she remained with Sharn to see Allerdon and his defenders march out. Sickness had brought the siege to an end. The men of Mel'Nir had slaughtered some of their horses for food, released others. Aidris sent to ask for Marshal Brond, but word came back that the envoy was dead, killed during the march eastward over the plain. Allerdon was questioned by Zabrandor and Bajan and given horses for his remaining officers for the long, cruel homeward journey.

The fortress was searched from top to bottom, all of its living quarters and outbuildings and every cranny of the fetid dungeons below ground. No prisoners were found, although Ledler had a reputation as the protector's dungeon for Chameln rebels. No trace was found of Nazran Am Thuven and the Lady Maren, not even a marked grave or the record of their imprisonment. Lingrit came to Aidris where she was resting in a tent in the besieger's camp.

"Werris has destroyed the records," he said. "Even the house servants had gone when Allerdon came in. There is an old graveyard within the wall. I do not doubt that they both lie there."

The way lay open to Achamar. The high road was broad and old, muddy with the spring rains. It wound through a countryside that Aidris found strange as a dream: green yet stony, with grey rock visible on the sides of the hills and, in the valleys, groves of birch. She knew the land and did not know it. Sharn Am Zor, riding at her side, had a good and patient horse at last; but when he cursed or tugged at its rein, she reached out to help, as if he had still been riding Moon, the fractious white pony.

Their royal progress was slow; the folk turned out to meet them by tens and hundreds. Here the Daindru came upon the first of the "changelings," new men indeed—men of Mel'Nir who forswore the protectorate and did homage to the Daindru for their estates. They had all some close connection to the Chameln lands. Some had married women of the Chameln or had married their sons or daughters to neighboring Chameln landowners. Many had gathered their estates long before the protectorate had been established. The changelings trod warily and often brought supporters, Chameln kin or tenants, to persuade the king and the queen to accept their oaths of fealty.

At a last camp in a village, almost within sight of the city walls, Jana Am Wetzerik came to the queen in the main room of the local inn and said, "Here is a changeling who swears he is already your vassal, my queen."

"What, a man of Mel'Nir?"

270

The general smiled and so did Bajan, who had seen the newcomer.

"His wife has tamed him," she said.

She went out into the sunshine, and the big tawny-haired man dismounting from his charger was Hem Rhanar, to whom she had given a small feoff of land by Lake Musna. He went proudly to hold the stirrup of a woman getting down from a Chameln grey. She was still something of a beauty, but now she wore Chameln dress, her boots were muddy, her figure sturdier than it had been. It was Riane.

Aidris took her hands, greeted her with tears. The youngest waiting woman of Queen Hedris brought back a whole chapter of her life in Achamar. The fate of this lady of Lien seemed strange as her own. She looked into Riane's grey eyes and found a hint of resignation but no regret.

"I have borne three sons," said Riane, explaining her life, "and we do very well on my lord's manor."

So Aidris accepted the homage of Hem Rhanar . . . or Haral Am Rhanar, the Lord of Musna Vale, as he was now called. She recalled their last meeting, fateful for all concerned.

"The last time I set eyes upon Baron Werris," she said. "What has become of the protector?"

"Majesty," he said, gazing down at her respectfully, "I never knew or liked the fellow, but I will say this: he was forced to do as he did by the troubled times and by Ghanor, the king. I have heard that he is dead."

A kedran troop had been sent ahead into Achamar to prepare the way for the Daindru. In the morning, the king and the queen, together with their courts, their escorts and their soldiers, set out over the high road. The city walls of wood and stone loomed ahead, curving, receding, then coming nearer, now like a cliff face, now like a forest of trees. Then Sharn Am Zor cried out and pointed, and Aidris laughed with delight. There before them the citizens had opened the Oaken Gate: an event of such moment that it was supposed to take place only once in a hundred years. The Oaken Gate had last been opened to let in Zendra Am Zor and Ochim Am Firn, the warrior queen and king who had put down the rebellious northern tribes. Now the mighty oaken sections of the wall that formed the "gate" had been cast down again into a hollowed place in the road.

The dust was still rising from the gate's fall as they rode over the ancient logs and entered Achamar.

The city spread out before them like a tapestry; the trees were in full leaf for the spring; the two palaces rose up like wonders of the world. They followed the ring road, and the citizens cheered them round about. Aidris, more contained than she had expected, looked into their faces. Had they suffered? Had the poor always bound their feet with rags, had the merchants always been so fat? What did they see looking at the queen? Were there any who truly recalled that child who rode out in the mornings at Nazran's side, who crossed the city yard by yard with her mother with the honored merchants smoothing the way in the snow? Might not a pretender have done as well, the poor false queen out of Balufir, Hazard's light o' love? They passed the south hall, and she saw that there had been fires lit in the yard. On the sharp gables of the gatehouse there were two severed heads. Revenge had been taken upon the garrison of Mel'Nir. She would not look, turned away sickened, and urged Tamir forward. Sharn Am Zor paid not much heed to the trophies.

The procession came to the Palace of the Zor in the east, and the Daindru parted formally. Bajan rode at her side along the ring road until they returned almost to their starting point at the Oaken Gate, and there arose the Palace of the Firn, large as her dreams and filled with life, green branches springing from every cornice and balcony. The chorus of wonder from the Athron folk in her train reached her ears at last. There had not been many suppliants along the way; she half knew, in the way that things were known to her these days, by hints and whispers, that petitioners were hustled out of the way at her approach because her escort knew that the queen did not care to be pressed. Now, as they came up to the central gate of the palace, two suppliants sprang up in her path, an old man and a child. Before Gefion could pounce, Aidris cried out to the escort:

"Let them come to me!"

She waited, in a dream, as they walked towards her hand in hand. They both wore ragged clothes of greyish homespun and leather sandals. The old man . . . and he looked truly old . . . had a straggling beard, unkempt yellow-grey locks; he might have been a shaman from the northern tribes. Yet it was Jalmar Raiz.

She leaned down and took the green branch from Pinga, the greddle, and he smiled at her, saying, "See the truth, Dan Aidris!"

"What will you have, old man?"

She fixed her eyes on him.

"You have sent for me to be a healer in Achamar," he replied. "I have come to serve you."

"What shall I call you?" she asked.

"Some call me Jaraz," he replied, humble and unsmiling. "This is my elder son, Pinga. I had another son, but he has sailed to the lands below the world."

"I accept your service," she said. "Find a lodging in the city and wait till I send for you."

The suppliants bowed and stood aside, and she rode into the palace yard.

"Will you have him then?" murmured Bajan. "After all that he has done?"

"I did send for this healer," she said, smiling. "He has come ten years late. I will have him."

There were no secrets between them. Bajan had a gleam in his eye of pure jealousy—half-real, half-feigned—for those he called "Venn's admirers": Raff Raiz and Terril of Varda. She knew too that in the north there was a child of five years, Bajan's daughter, given into the care of the Nureshen by a woman of the Ingari. Exile was long. Now they had come home together. In her love for him she found, at that moment, the true feeling of comfort and elation for such a homecoming.

So they went in, and she remembered the turmoil of allotting rooms for courtiers and guests. She admitted herself tired and sat taking the sun in a room that had been part of her father's suite on the west side, for he had given the best and warmest chambers to his queen. Lingrit came to her with a strange look.

"A room, an inner room on the courtyard, was purified," he said. "Will you hear the reason from me or from a servant who was here with the protector?"

"Tell me . . ."

So she heard at last of Werris, the end of Werris, that handsome dark man, the courtier, the usurper, the self-styled protector. He had taken his own life with poison and with a knife. She cried out as the tale continued, thinking of the small dark room they had chosen. For Werris had not been alone; Micha

Am Firn had died at his side. It was a love death. The poor widow had given her heart to the usurper. Aidris felt wonder and guilt and a vile relief at the tale. No mercy could have been given to Werris., Micha Am Firn had loved without hope. In past times her own life might have been forfeit. The queen had been spared; she would not have to be cruel. Now these two lay hastily interred, unblessed, in the palace grounds, by the royal graveyard of the Firn.

Suddenly she was very tired indeed. She could only stare out into the grounds of the palace and hear the women in the room behind her setting things to rights. The child stirred in her womb. She looked out and saw a few birch trees where once she and Nazran had practised shooting with her toy bow. There was a sound like the sea beyond the whispered arrangements of the women. The people of Achamar were rejoicing for the return of the Daindru. She began to count, as she had done for Sabeth and for Telavel ... Birchmoon, Elmmoon, Oakmoon, Applemoon. . . .

The Queen of the Firn came to her labor late in the Thornmoon, the moon of sacrifice, and after three days and three nights, she bore a prince. The midwife, Gezi, Chieftainess of the Nureshen, helped draw the child forth and showed it to the witnesses, Lingrit Am Thuven and Lord Zabrandor, who attended by custom for the House of the Zor. Yet she feared for the life of the queen and called her son, Danu Bajan, and the Queen's friend, the Countess of Zerrah, and at last the healer, Jaraz of Lien. He practised his healing art and, some said, his magic upon the queen.

Aidris saw the eyes of Jalmar Raiz fixed upon her, then a mist gathered, her pain lessened. She came to herself feeling cold and found that she was walking across an endless plain. The ground under her feet was thick with frost; she was crossing the frost fields. She saw, not far off, a tall mounted figure made all of light and knew that this was the White Warrior, come to take her to the halls of the Goddess. She saw as she came closer still that he led another horse, and it was Telavel, her true companion in exile.

She longed to go with them, but she stood gazing up at the

White Warrior and said, "I cannot go with you. It is not yet time!"

As she spoke, she began to hear voices, a groundswell of distant voices, all the folk of the Chameln land who called back the Queen of the Firn, and nearer, she heard Bajan's voice and Sabeth's voice, calling her by name. She heard the thin cry of a child.

"So be it," said the White Warrior, his voice as soft and cold as the crackle of frost under her boot soles, "So be it, Aidris Am Firn. Go in peace. We will be waiting."

Then she was rushing upwards towards the light. She saw Jalmar Raiz, still standing at the foot of her bed, and felt the constraining cloth in which she had been wound. There was still a sensation of cold; her lower body had been wrapped in ice-cold linen to stop the bleeding. She saw Bajan, his mother, Gezi Am Nuresh, and Sabeth, holding the child in her arms. Sabeth wept and tried to smile through her weeping.

"Hush," said Aidris. "I have come back . . ."

Bajan knelt beside the bed. Sabeth knelt too, and showed her the child. It was small and red-faced and sturdy, with clenched fists waving and black hair, a child of the Firn, a prince. She looked at the child and at the faces of those around her wistfully, coldly, as if she took leave of them. For now she knew that her foreboding was true: she would live to be very old, to be the Old Queen; she would outlive them all save only the newborn child. Her childhood, her exile would be half forgotten in the course of a long life, returning as pictures or legends, just as her long life itself passed in a moment upon the eternal plain.

THE DARWATH TRILOGY
Barbara Hambly

Book 1
The Time of the Dark

For several nights Gil had found herself dreaming of an impossible city where alien horrors swarmed from underground lairs of darkness. She had dreamed also of the wizard Ingold Inglorion. Then the same wizard crossed the Void to seek sanctuary for the last Prince of Dar and revealed himself to a young drifter, Rudy. But one of the monstrous, evil Dark followed in his wake and in attempting to help Ingold, Gil and Rudy were drawn back into the nightmare world of the Dark. There they had to remain – unless they could solve the mystery of the Dark. Then, before they could realise their fate, the Dark struck!

Book 2
The Walls of Air

In the shelter of the great Keep of Renwath eight thousand people shelter from the Dark. The only hope for the beseiged is to seek help from the hidden city of Quo. Ingold and Rudy set out to cross two thousand miles of desert. Beyond it they have to penetrate the walls of illusion that separate Quo from the world.

Book 3
The Armies of Daylight

The survivors of the once-great Realm of Darwath shelter, squabble and struggle for power. Meanwhile the monstrous Dark threaten their great Keep. Is there a reason for the re-awakening of the Dark? The final volume of *The Darwath Trilogy* builds to a shattering and unexpected climax.

THE LAST WARRIOR QUEEN
Mary Mackey

From the City of the Dove came Enkimdu. He brought with him tales of a city where people traced their lineage through their mothers and grandmothers and where women were free to choose and take their own lovers without shame or censor. It was a city with two Goddesses: Lanla, the Good and Hut, Mother of the Night.

For Inanna, born into a fierce nomadic society, a member of the Black Headed People, he represented hope and love. For she had been forced to witness the savage execution of her beloved sister for adultery – an execution carried out by their brother Pulal.

Inanna, forced to make her own escape, headed west for the city. There she met Seb, Enkimdu's half-brother; his mother, a philosopher queen with a dream of peace, and one High Priestess, Rheti, a servant of Hut, who tempted her with the prospect of revenge. But the price of revenge is high and tragic. Inanna, trained as a warrior and obsessed by her hatred launched her army against her brother.

Available in Unicorn

The Darwath Trilogy *Barbara Hambly*

Book One: The Time of the Dark	£2.50	☐
Book Two: The Walls of Air	£2.50	☐
Book Three: The Armies of Daylight	£2.50	☐

Asgard *Nigel Frith*	£2.95	☐
Beyond Lands of Never *Maxim Jakubowski*	£2.50	☐
The Castle of Dark *Tanith Lee*	£2.95	☐
The Children of the Wind (Seven Citadels: 2) *Geraldine Harris*	£2.50	☐
The Dead Kingdom (Seven Citadels: 3) *Geraldine Harris*	£2.50	☐
Divine Endurance *Gwyneth Jones*	£2.95	☐
The Fishers of Darksea *Roger Eldridge*	£2.95	☐
Krishna *Nigel Frith*	£2.95	☐
The Last Warrior Queen *Mary Mackey*	£2.95	☐
The Lord of the Rings (one volume) *J. R. R. Tolkien*	£6.95	☐
Monkey *Arthur D. Waley (Transl)*	£2.95	☐
Prince of the Godborn (Seven Citadels: 1)	£2.50	☐
The Silmarillion *J. R. R. Tolkien*	£2.95	☐
The Seventh Gate (Seven Citadels: 4) *Geraldine Harris*	£2.95	☐
Unfinished Tales *J. R. R. Tolkien*	£2.95	☐
The Warrior Who Carried Life *Geoff Ryman*	£2.95	☐

All these books are available at your local bookshop or newsagent, or can be ordered direct by post. Just tick the titles you want and fill in the form below.

Name...

Address ....

....

....

Write to Unwin Cash Sales, PO Box 11, Falmouth, Cornwall TR10 9EN.

Please enclose remittance to the value of the cover price plus:

UK: 55p for the first book plus 22p for the second book, thereafter 14p for each additional book ordered to a maximum charge of £1.75.

BFPO and EIRE: 55p for the first book plus 22p for the second book and 14p for the next 7 books and thereafter 8p per book.

OVERSEAS: £1.00 for the first book plus 25p per copy for each additional book.

Unwin Paperbacks reserve the right to show new retail prices on covers, which may differ from those previously advertised in the text or elsewhere. Postage rates are also subject to revision.